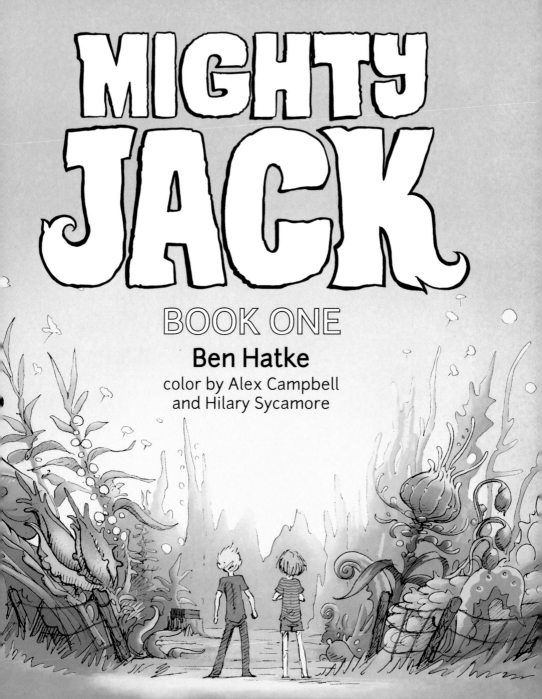

MIGHTY JACK

BOOK ONE

Ben Hatke

color by Alex Campbell
and Hilary Sycamore

First Second
New York

This one's for my mom,
who taught me about the
magic of libraries

I started working on this story in 2006, so it's been a long road and there are plenty of people to thank.

First and foremost, great thanks and love go to my wife, Anna, who patiently listened to this story develop, and who believed in my voice. My gratitude also goes out to my friends who listened to me eagerly tell them early versions of this tale: Bill Powell, Andy O'Neill, Ryan Corrigan, Jaime Gorman, Regina Schmiedicke, Anna Formaggio, and Nick Marmalejo. To Sara Ricci, who listened to me tell this story in my terrible Italian and many other good people.

To the village of Gravagna Montale, where everyone was patient while I once again declined invitations to hike and instead drew all the pages of this book.

Huge thanks to my daughters, Angelica, Zita, Julia, Ronia, and Ida who all, individually and as a pack, keep me excited about my work. To Hilary Sycamore and Alex Campbell, my colorists for this book. This was my first time working with colorists for a whole book and you made it a pleasure.

And, of course, to the team at First Second: Mark, Gina, Danielle, and Joyana. And to Calista, editor and friend, who lets me ramble on at her about Marvel movies before we get to the good stuff. Big thanks to my agent, Judy Hansen, who works so tirelessly on my behalf. And special thanks to Kat Kopit, my very first editor, who is once again lending her sharp eyes to my stories. I'm ridiculously lucky to be surrounded by y'all.

"Pullin' weeds and pickin' stones,
Man is made of dreams and bones..."

—David Mallett,
from *The Garden Song*

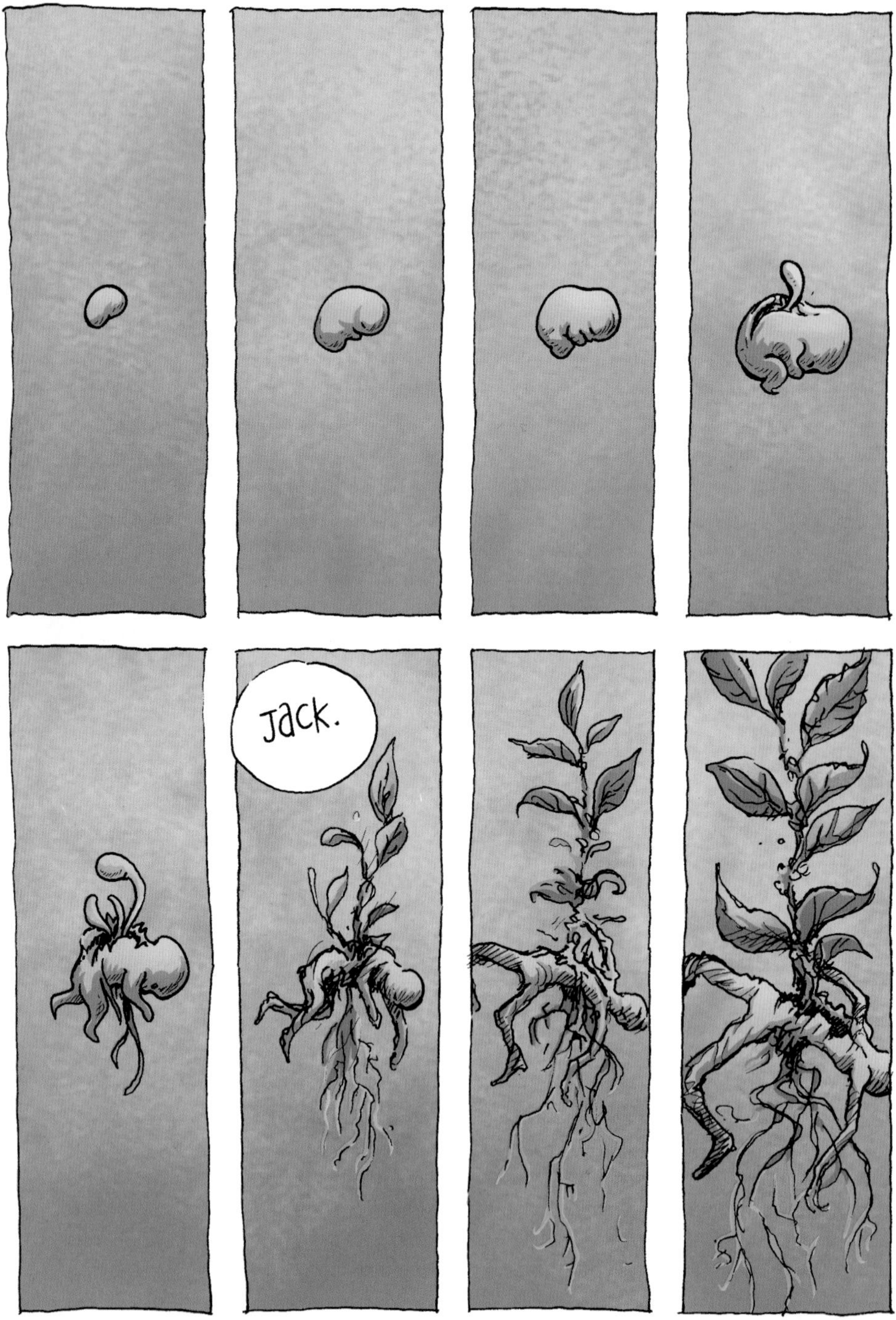
JACK.

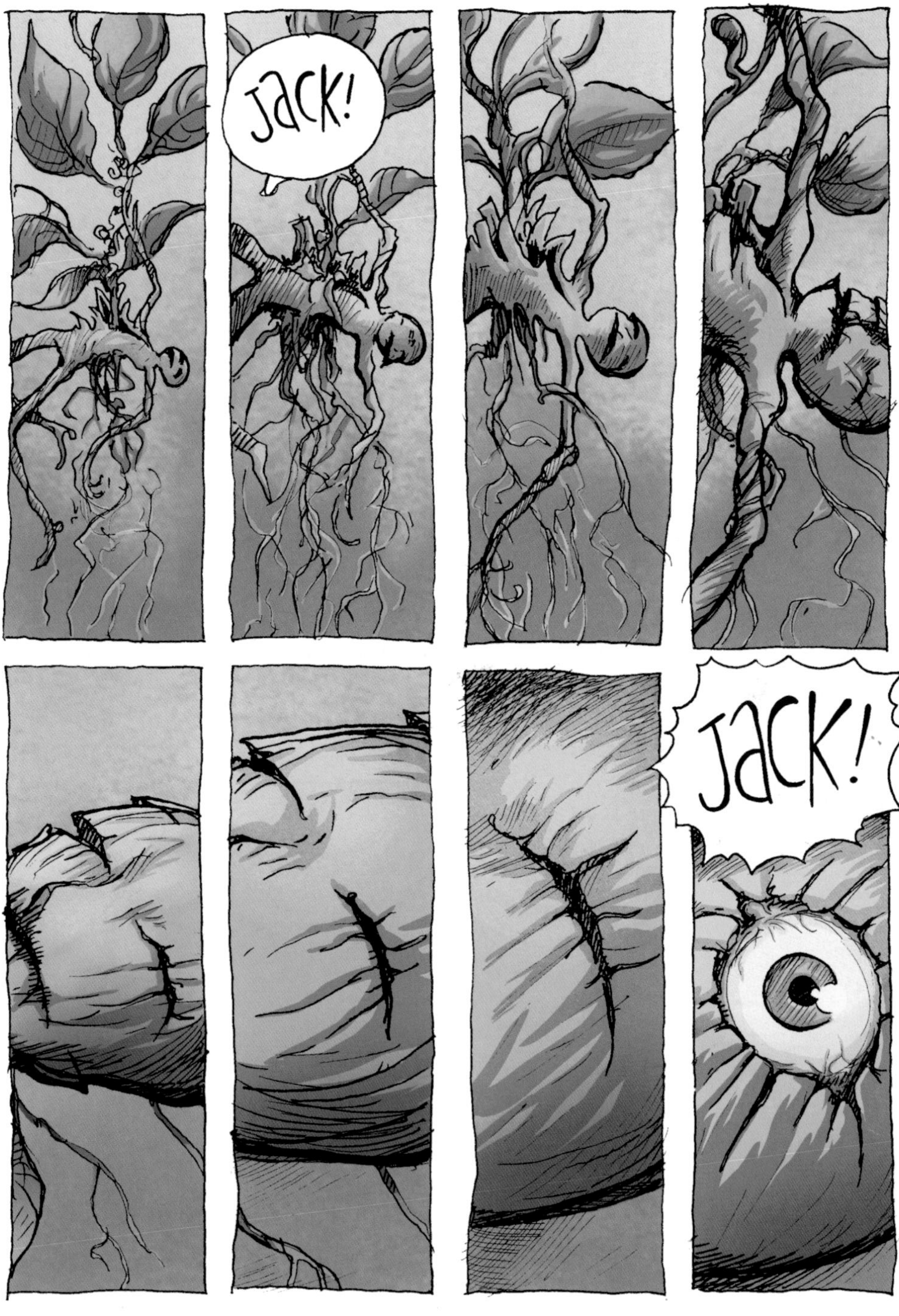
JACK!
JACK!

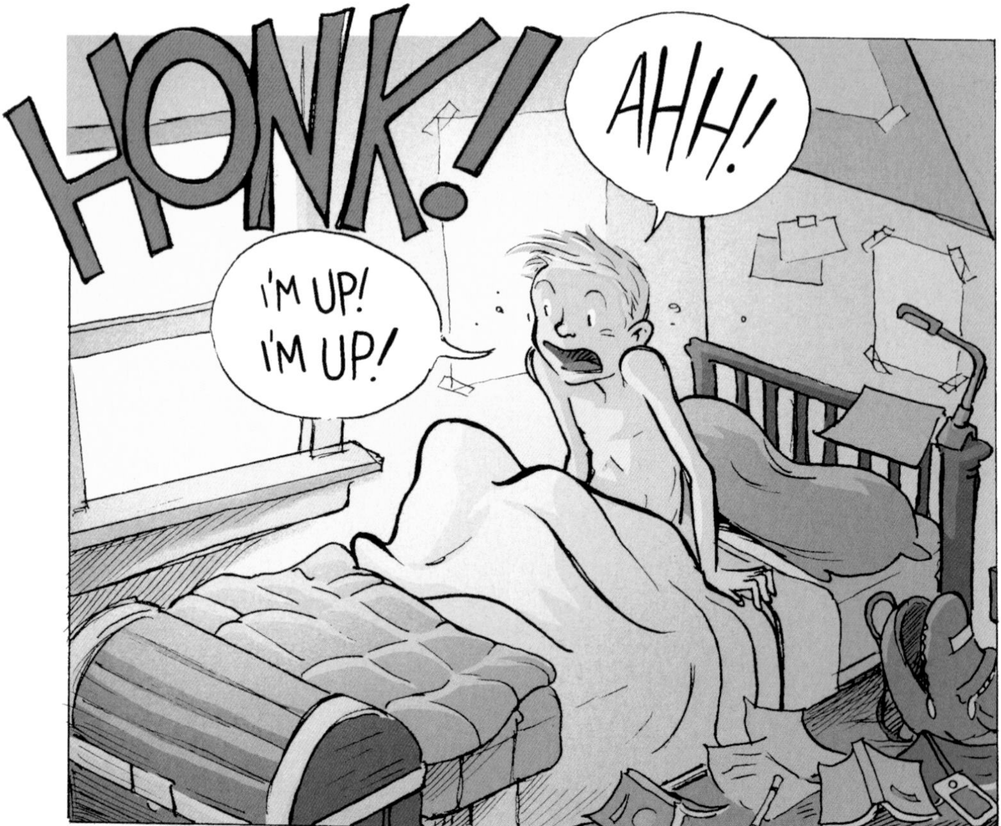
HONK!
AHH!
I'M UP! I'M UP!

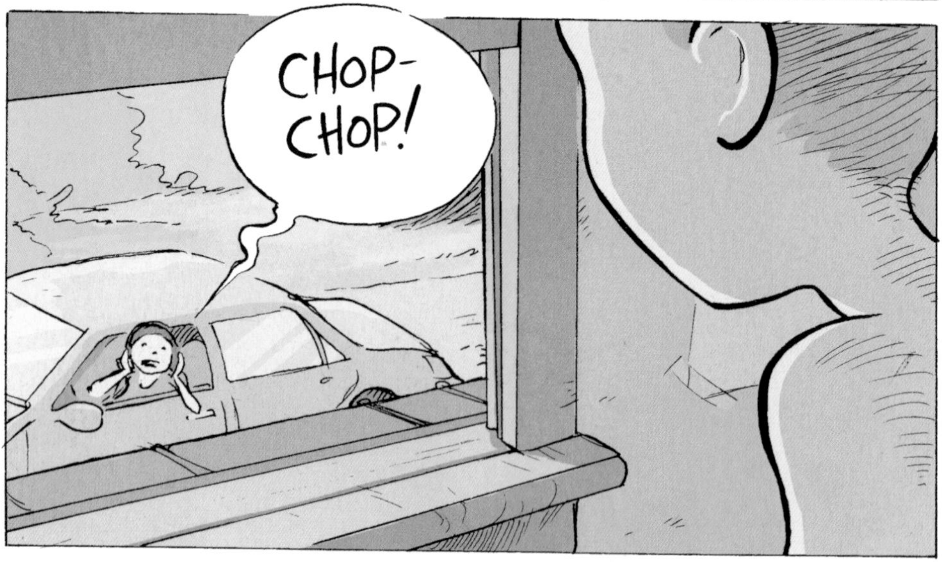
CHOP-CHOP!

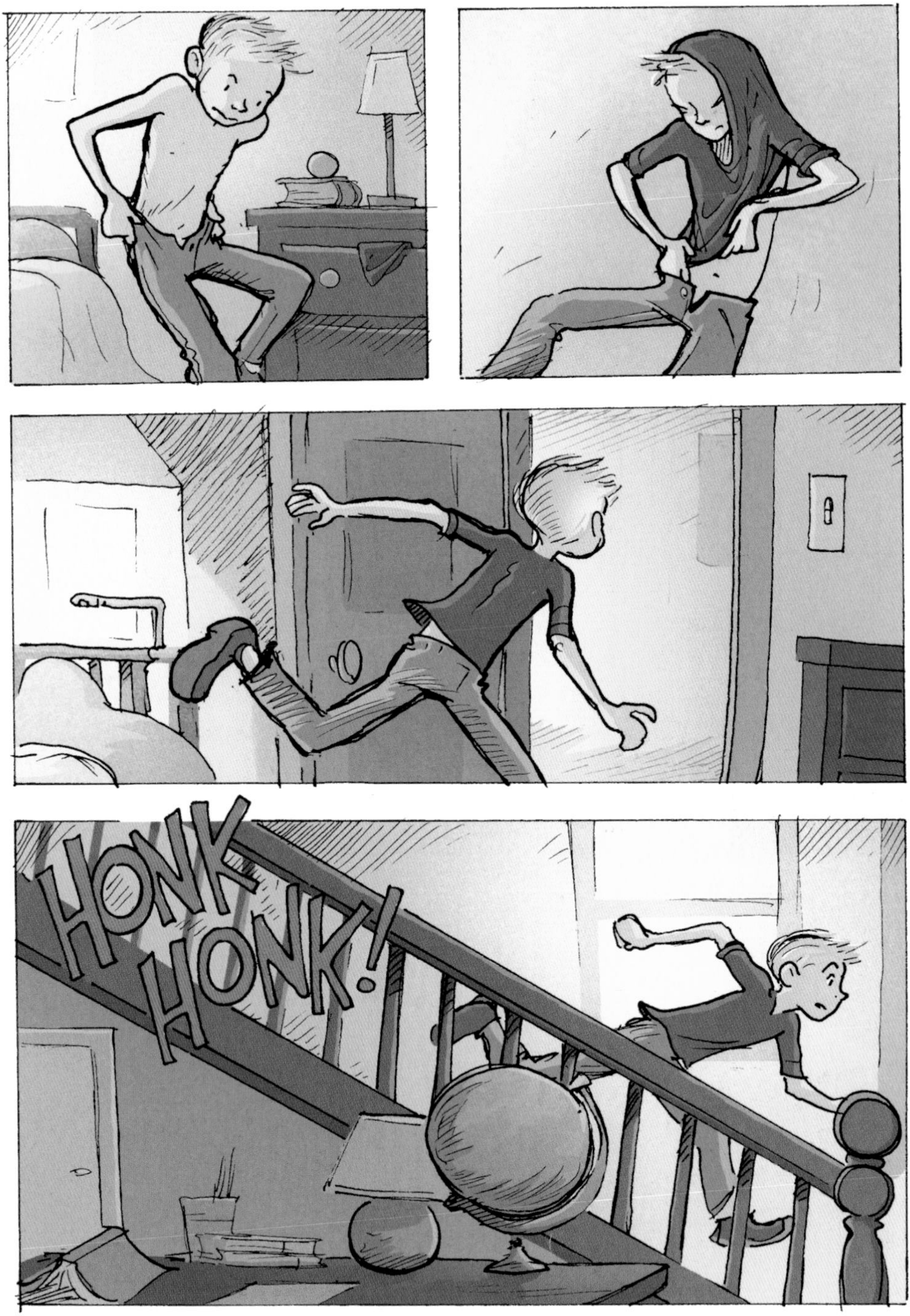
HONK HONK!

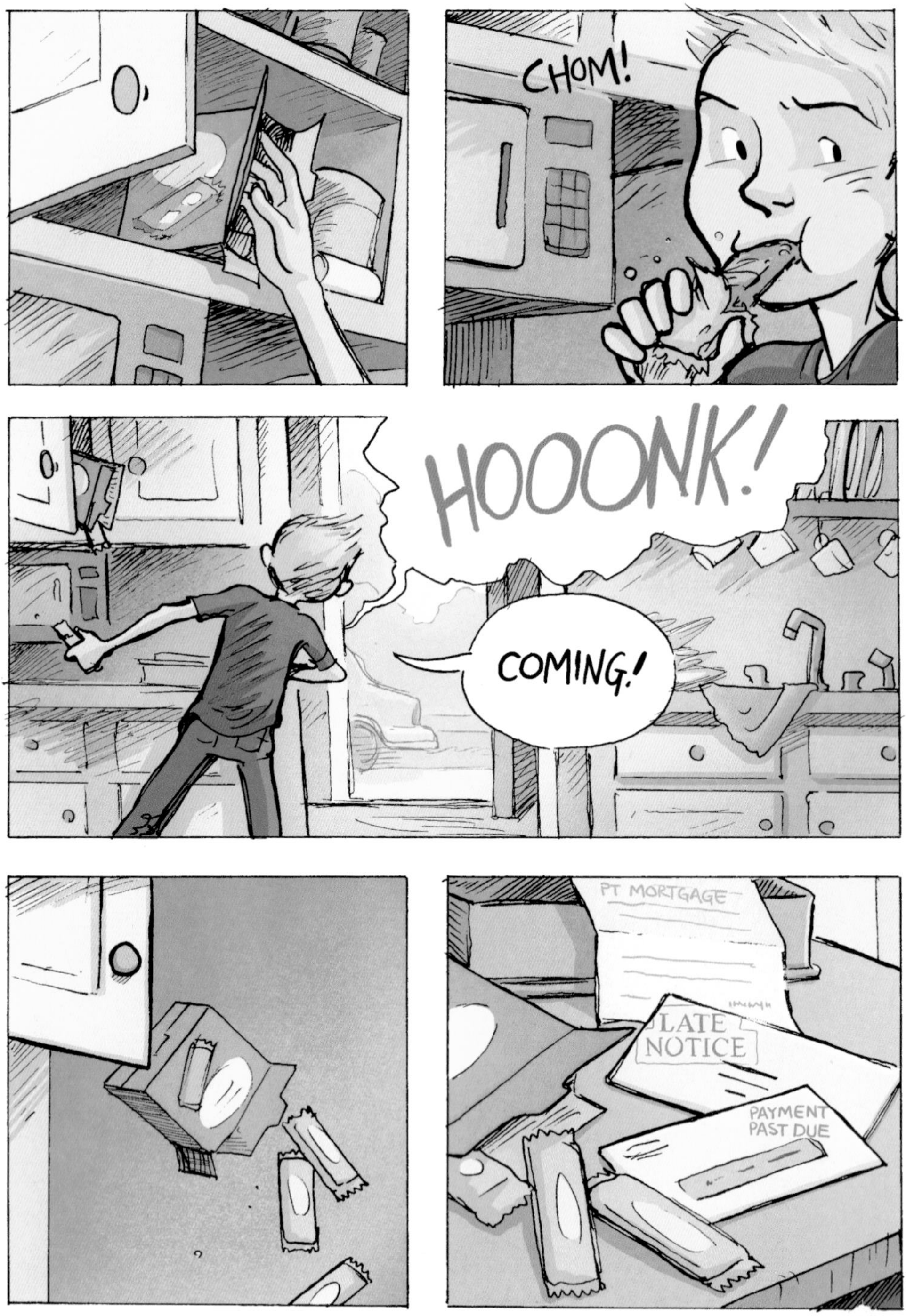
CHOM!
HOOOONK!
COMING!
PT MORTGAGE
LATE NOTICE
PAYMENT PAST DUE

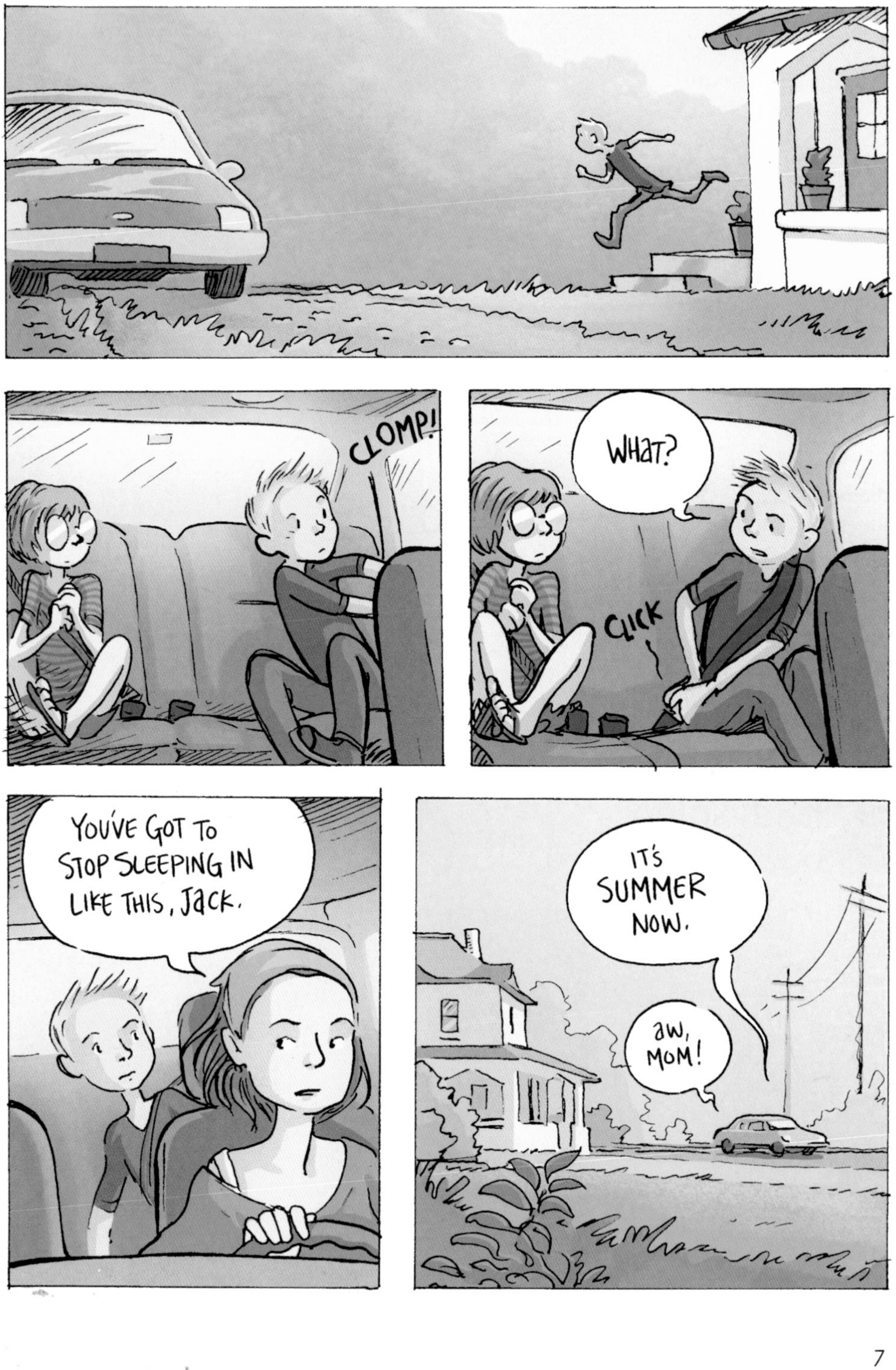
CLOMP!
WHAT?
CLICK
YOU'VE GOT TO STOP SLEEPING IN LIKE THIS, JACK.
IT'S SUMMER NOW.
AW, MOM!

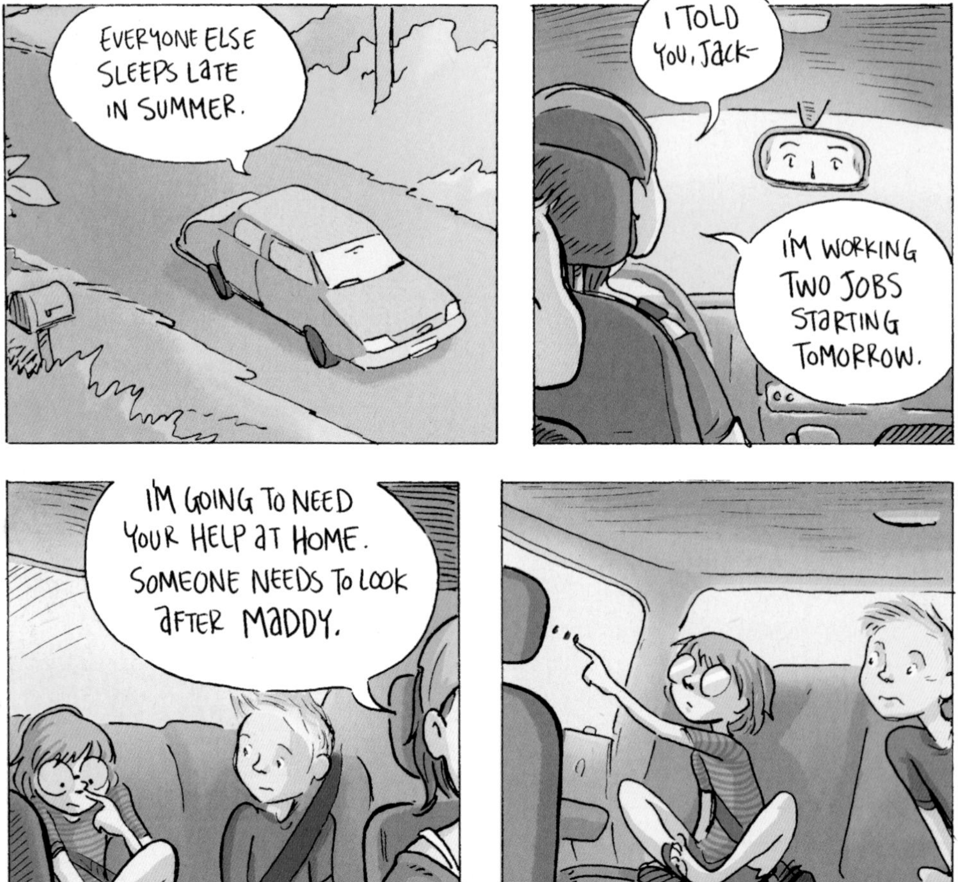
EVERYONE ELSE SLEEPS LATE IN SUMMER.
I TOLD YOU, JACK–
I'M WORKING TWO JOBS STARTING TOMORROW.
I'M GOING TO NEED YOUR HELP AT HOME. SOMEONE NEEDS TO LOOK AFTER MADDY.
RGH.

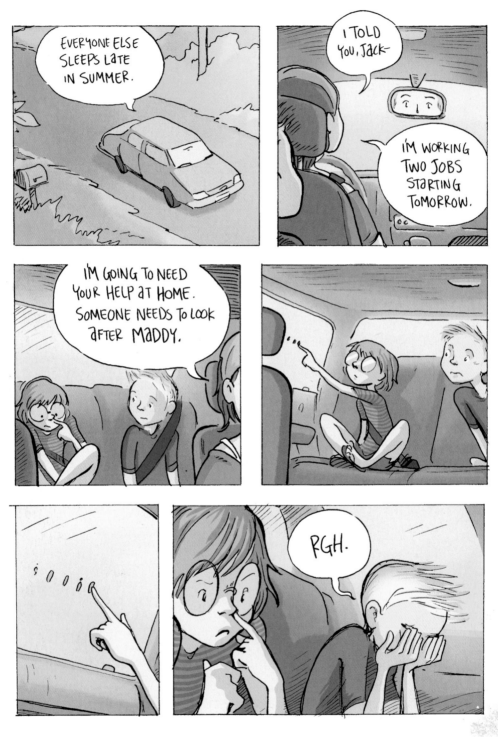

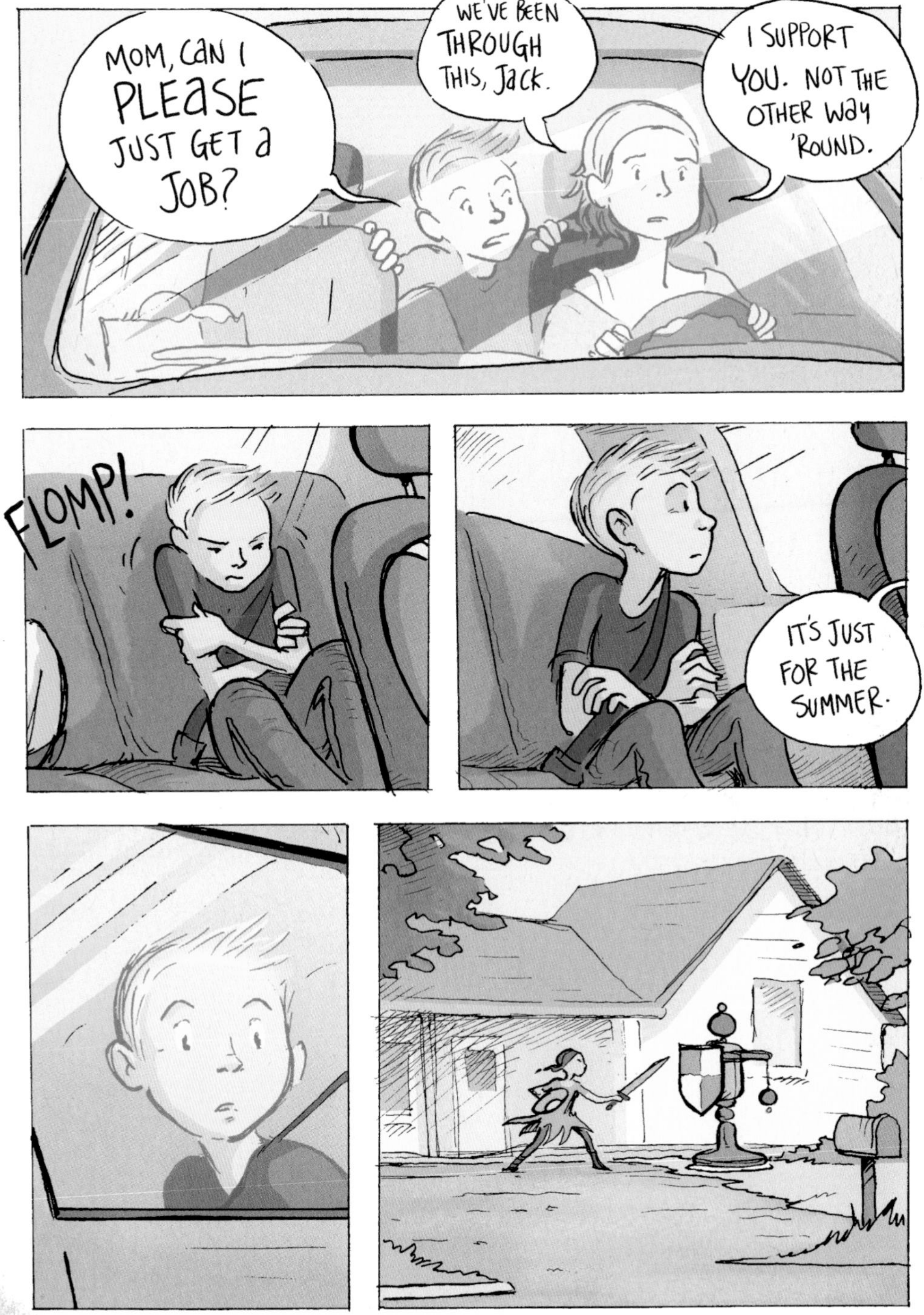
MOM, CAN I PLEASE JUST GET A JOB?
WE'VE BEEN THROUGH THIS, JACK.
I SUPPORT YOU. NOT THE OTHER WAY 'ROUND.
FLOMP!
IT'S JUST FOR THE SUMMER.

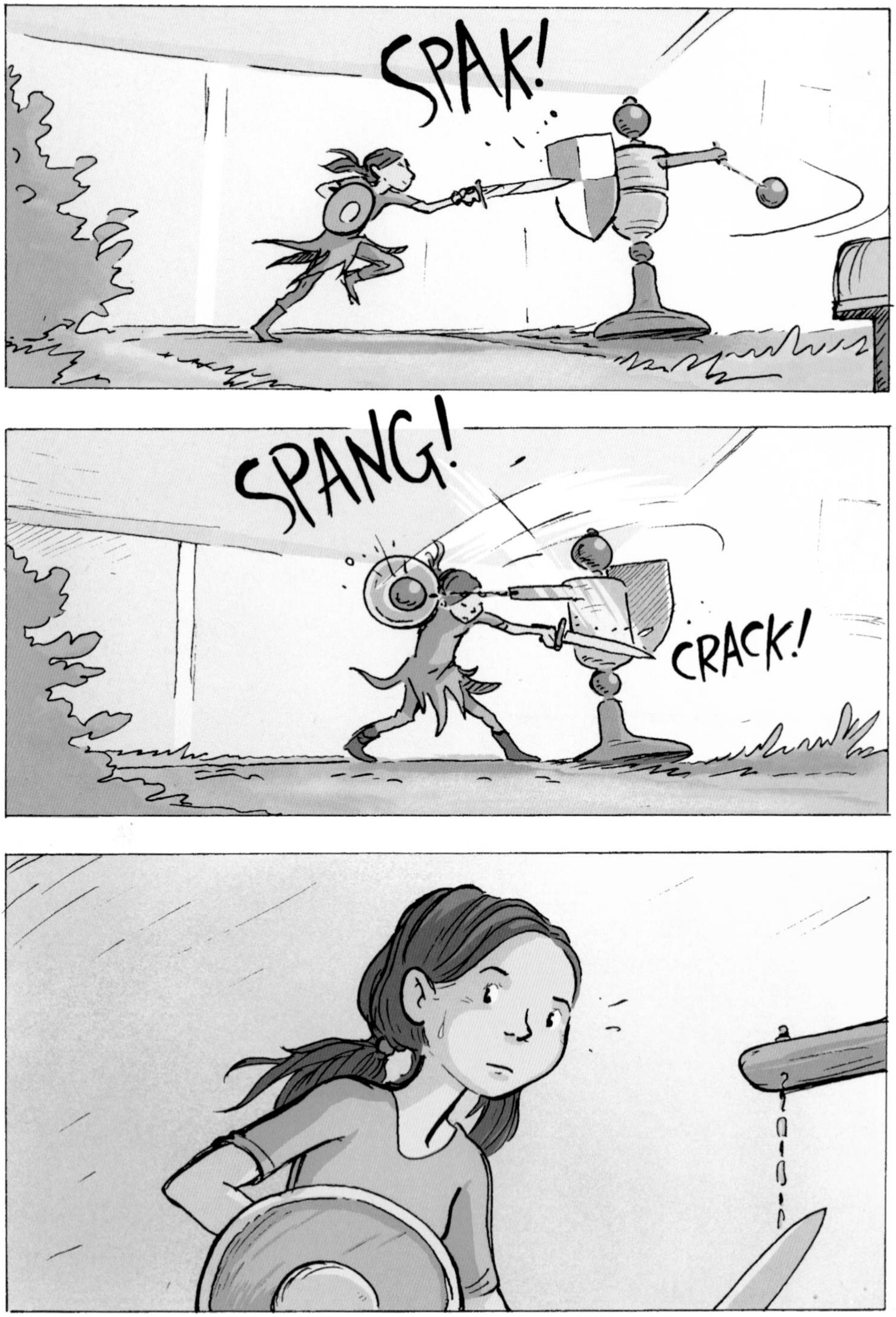
SPAK!
SPANG!
CRACK!

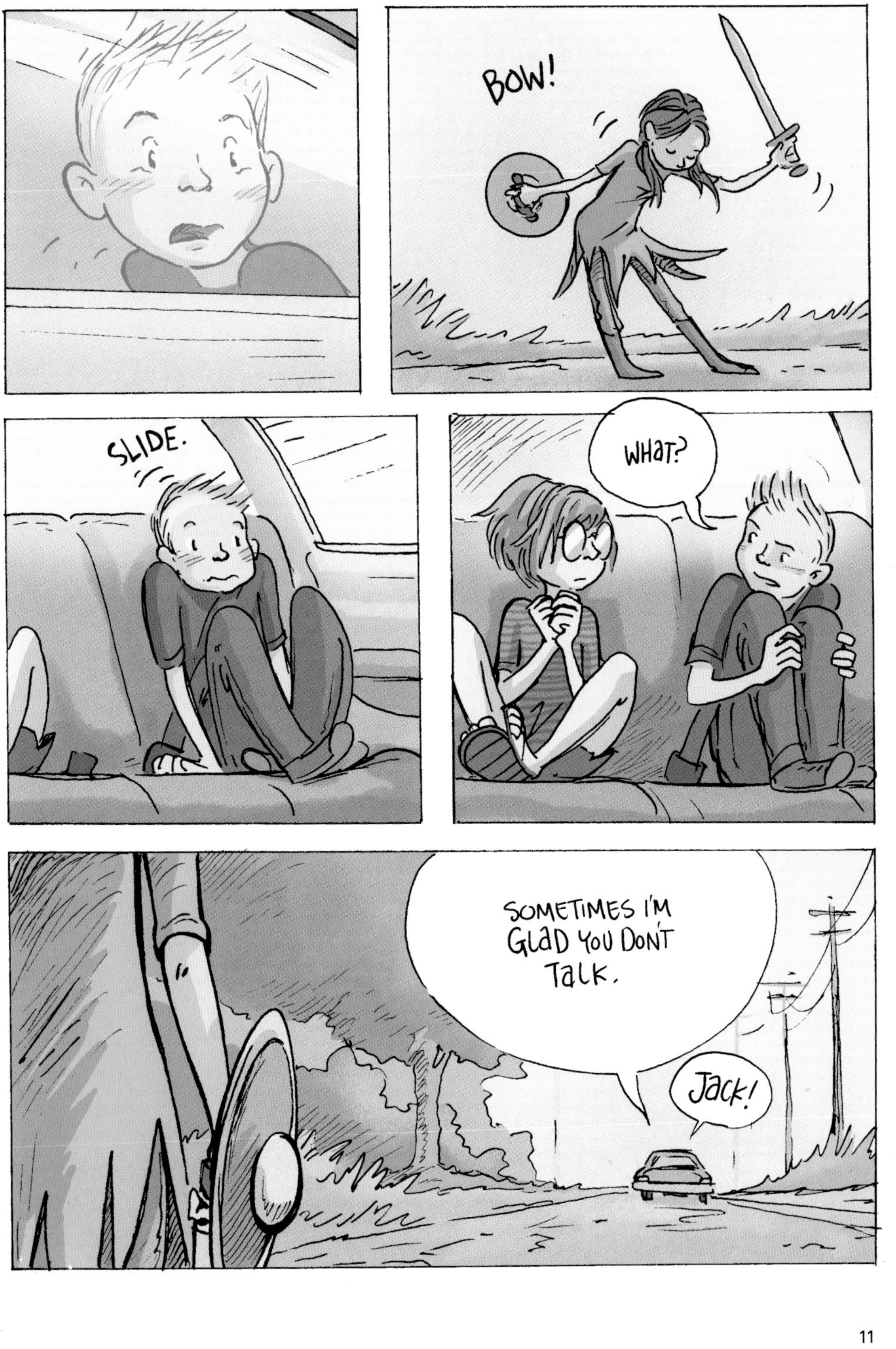
BOW!
SLIDE.
WHAT?
SOMETIMES I'M GLAD YOU DON'T TALK.
JACK!

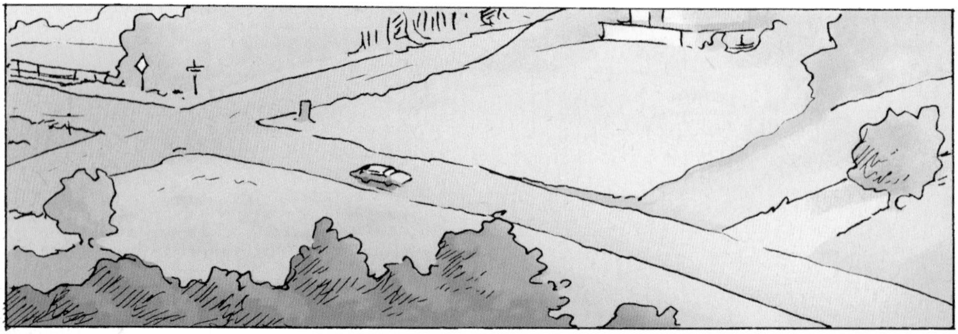

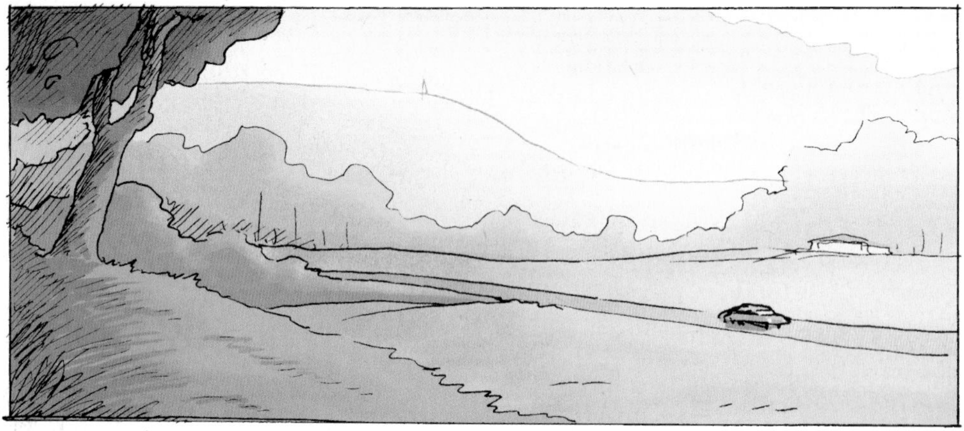

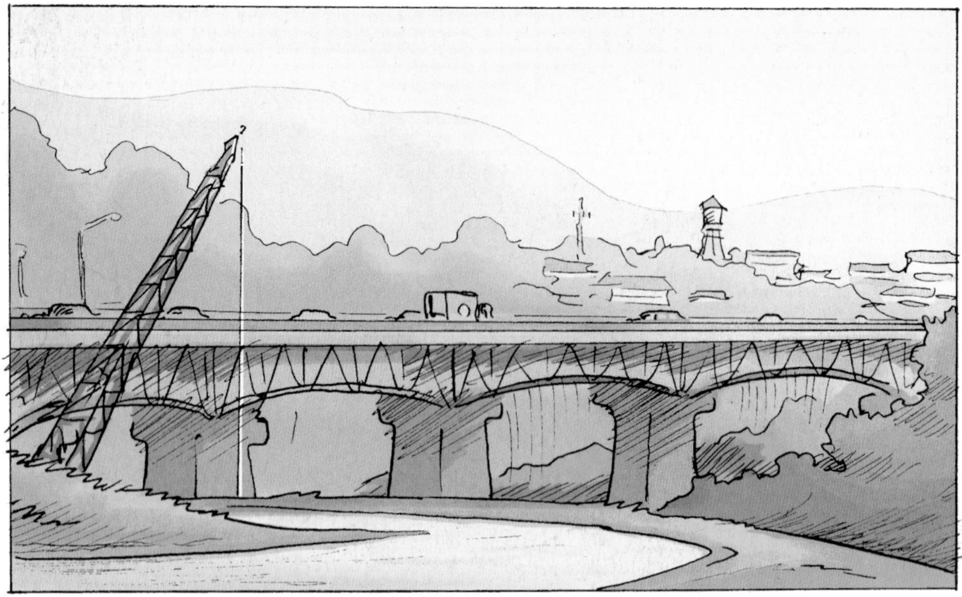

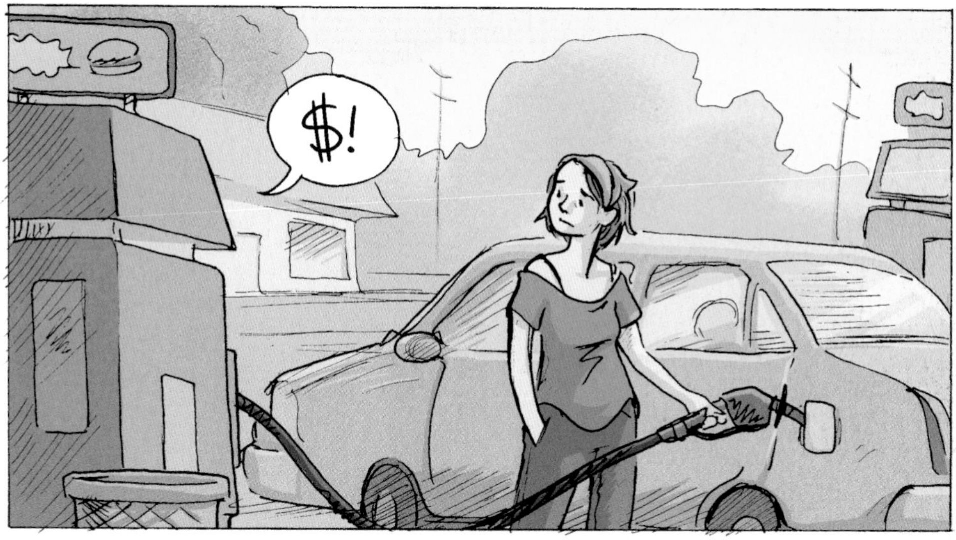
$!

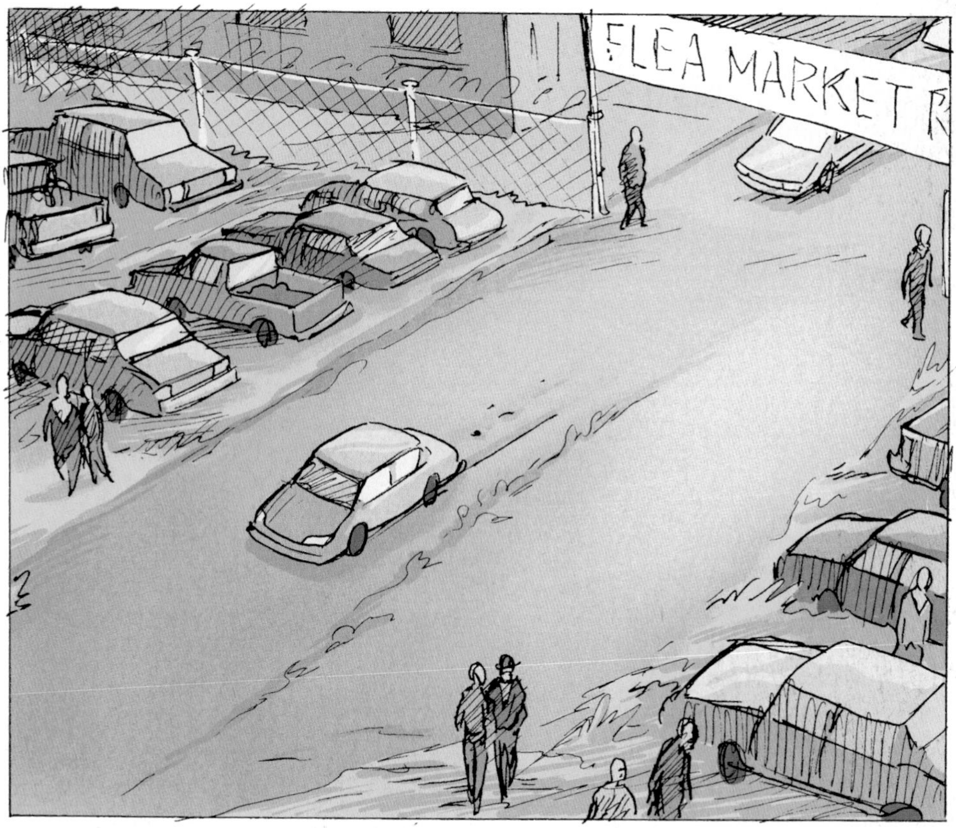
FLEA MARKET

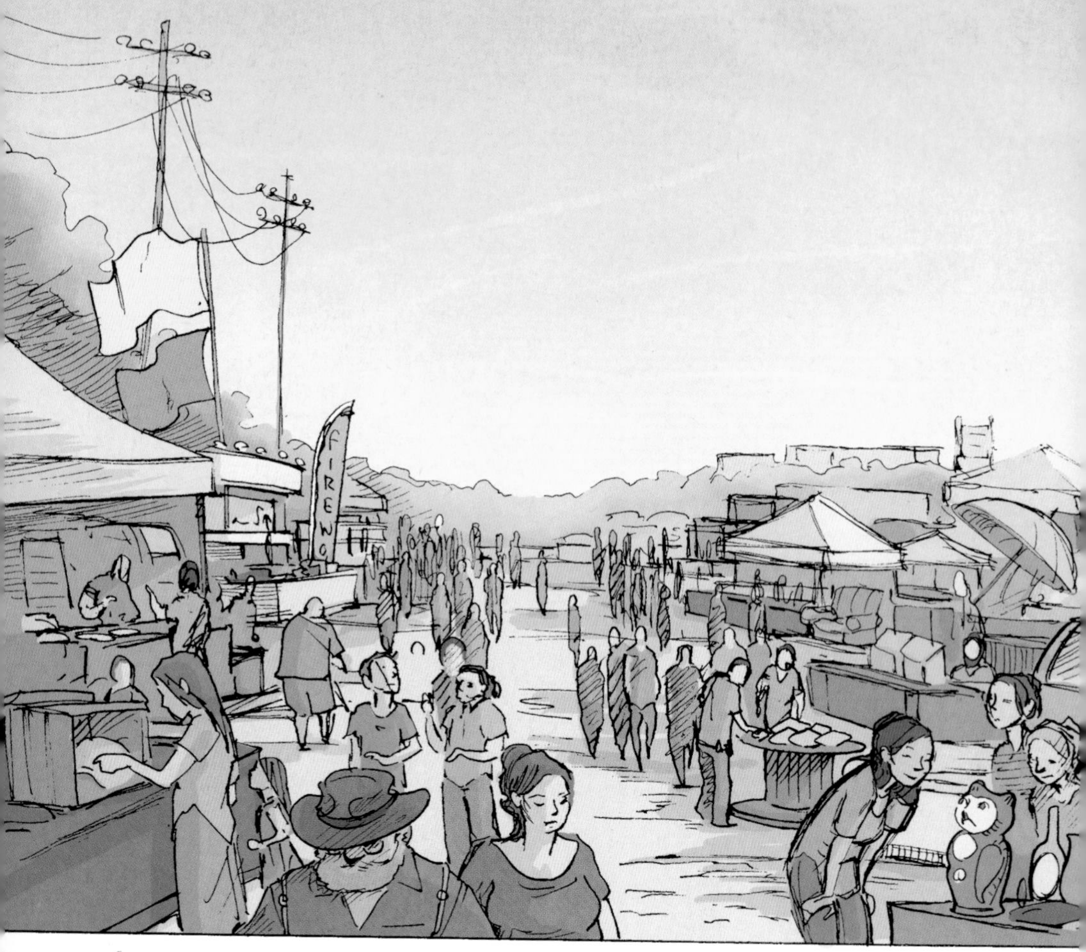
FIREWO

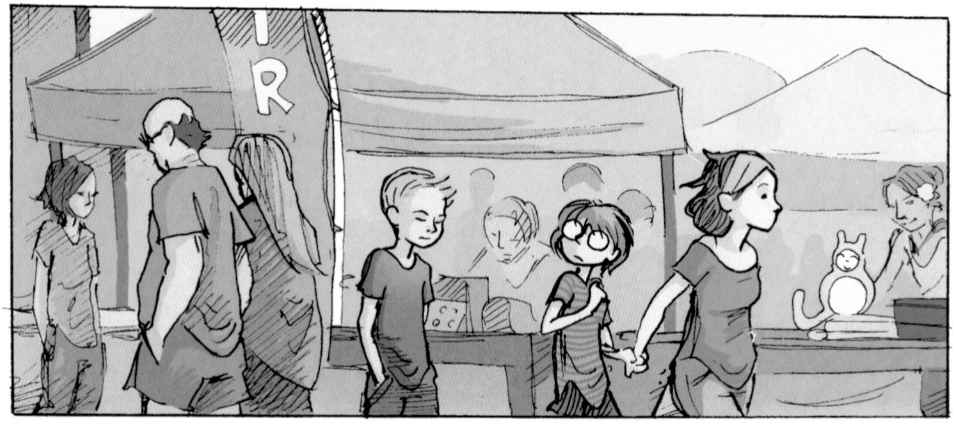

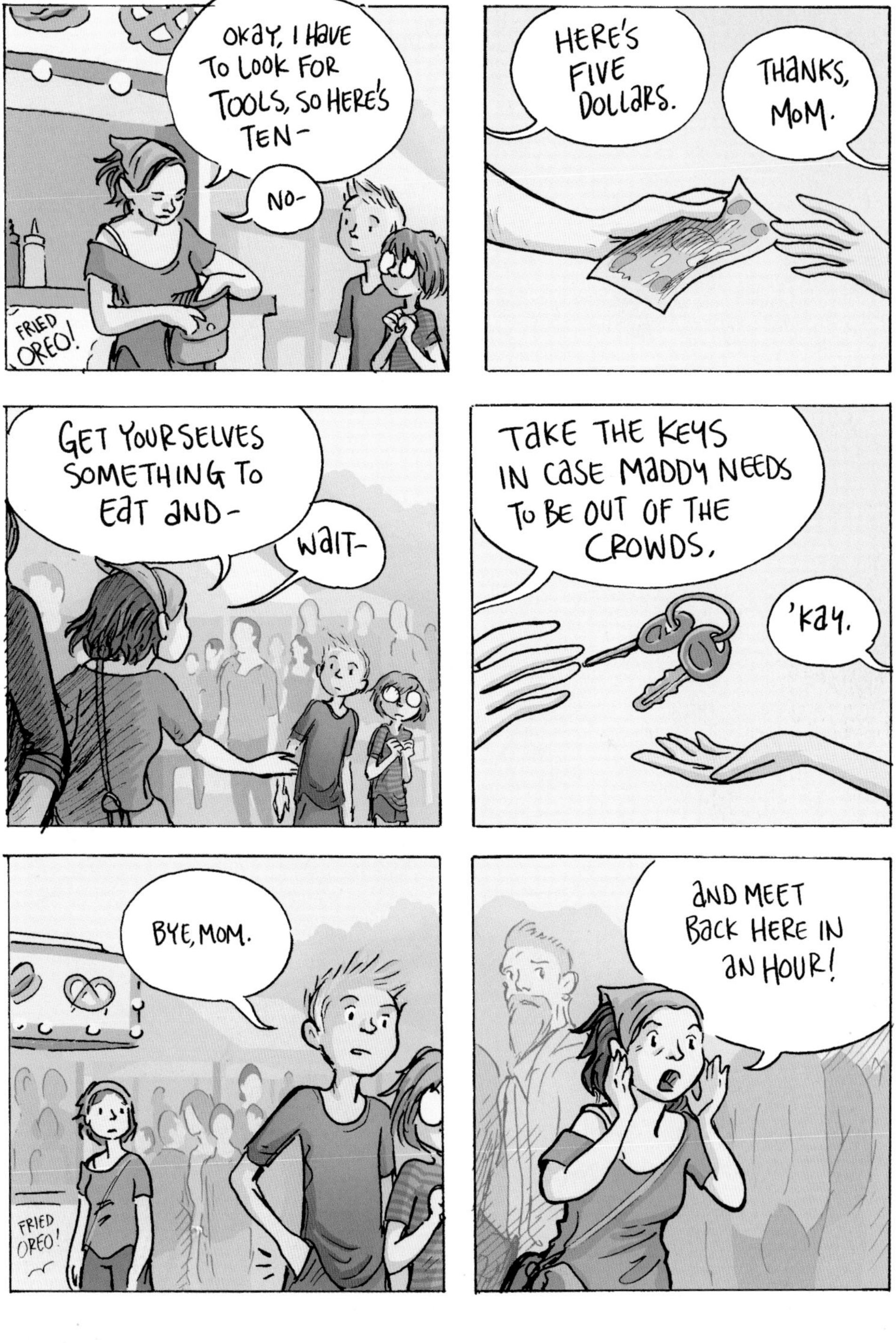
OKAY, I HAVE TO LOOK FOR TOOLS, SO HERE'S TEN-
NO-
FRIED OREO!
HERE'S FIVE DOLLARS.
THANKS, MOM.
GET YOURSELVES SOMETHING TO EAT AND-
WAIT-
TAKE THE KEYS IN CASE MADDY NEEDS TO BE OUT OF THE CROWDS.
'KAY.
BYE, MOM.
FRIED OREO!
AND MEET BACK HERE IN AN HOUR!

MUNCH

'STALS

RAWK!

25% OFF!

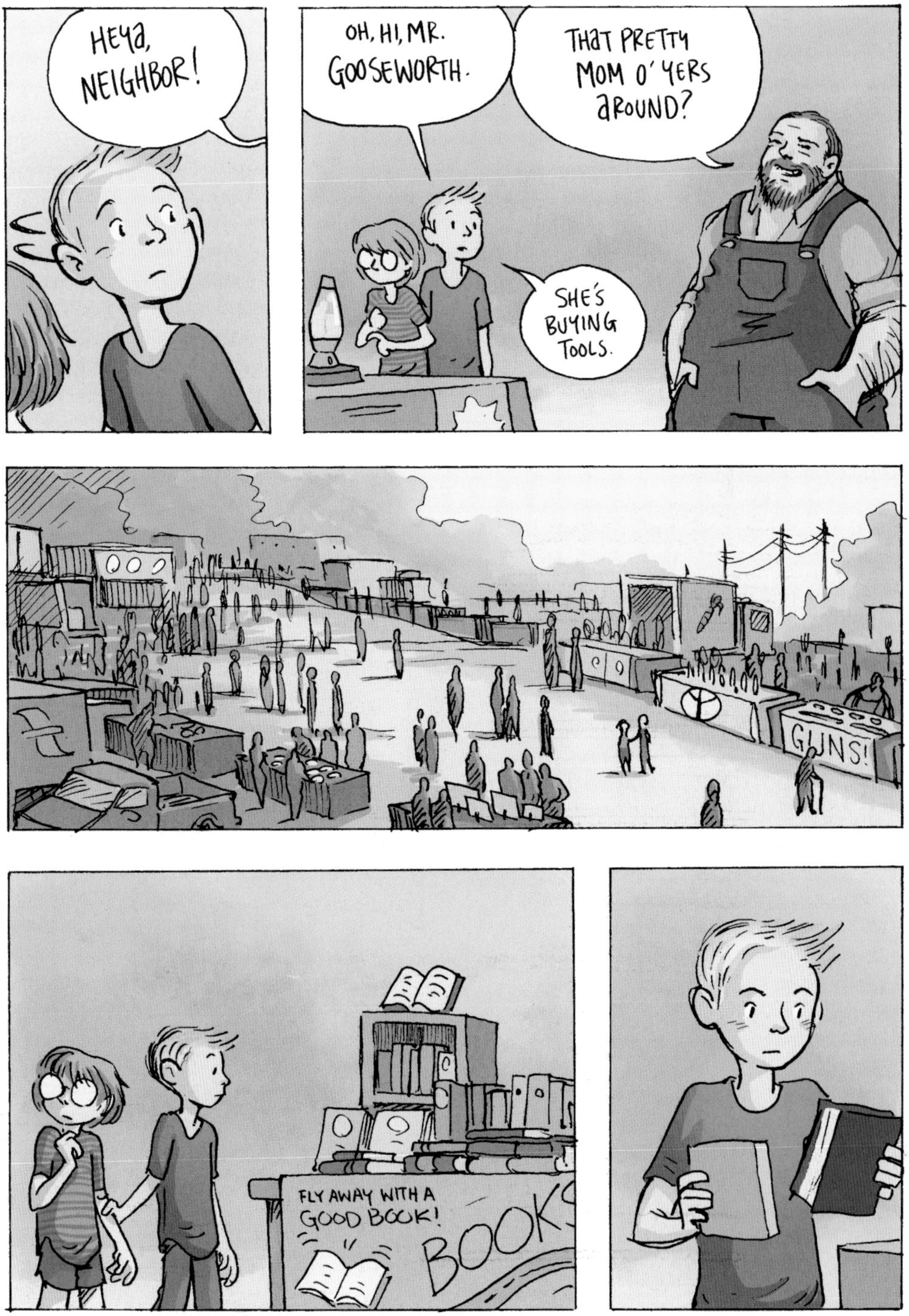
HEYA, NEIGHBOR!
OH, HI, MR. GOOSEWORTH.
THAT PRETTY MOM O' YERS AROUND?
SHE'S BUYING TOOLS.
GUNS!
FLY AWAY WITH A GOOD BOOK!
BOOKS

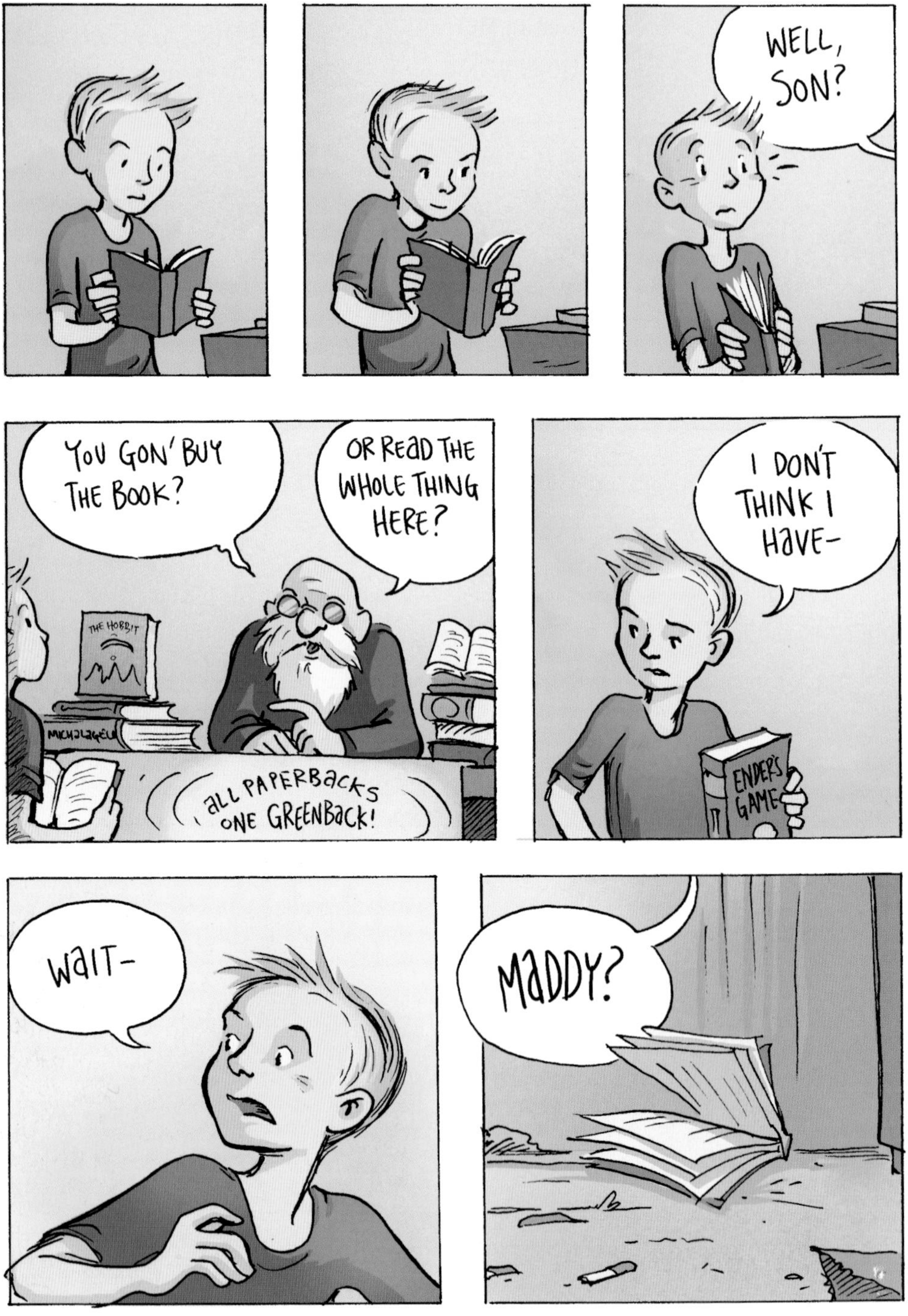
WELL, SON?
YOU GON' BUY THE BOOK?
OR READ THE WHOLE THING HERE?
THE HOBBIT
MICHALAGELU
ALL PAPERBACKS ONE GREENBACK!
I DON'T THINK I HAVE-
ENDER'S GAME
WAIT-
MADDY?

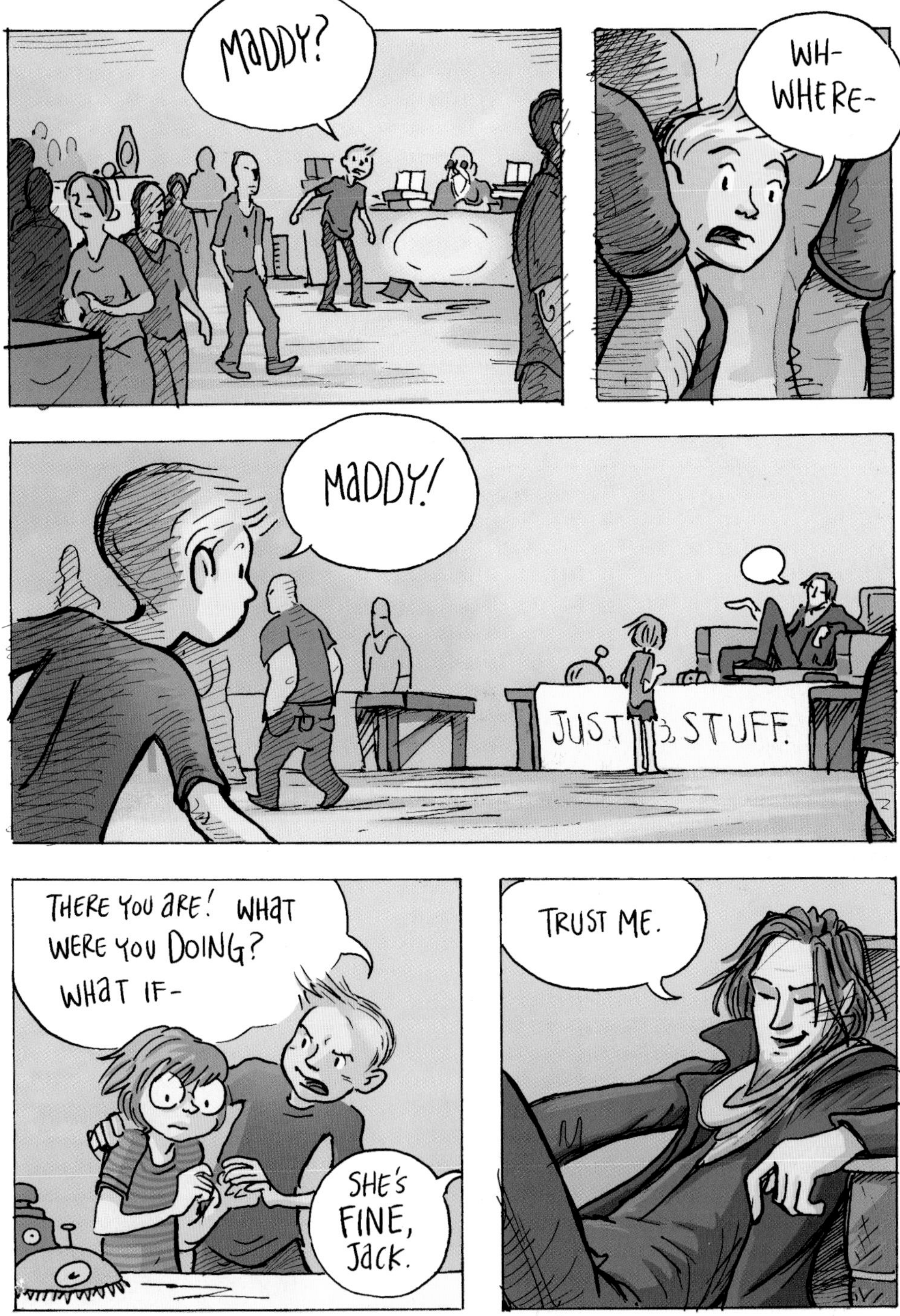

MaDDY?
WH-
WHERE-
MaDDY!
JUST STUFF.
THERE YOU aRE! WHaT WERE YOU DOING? WHaT IF-
SHE'S FINE, JaCK.
TRUST ME.

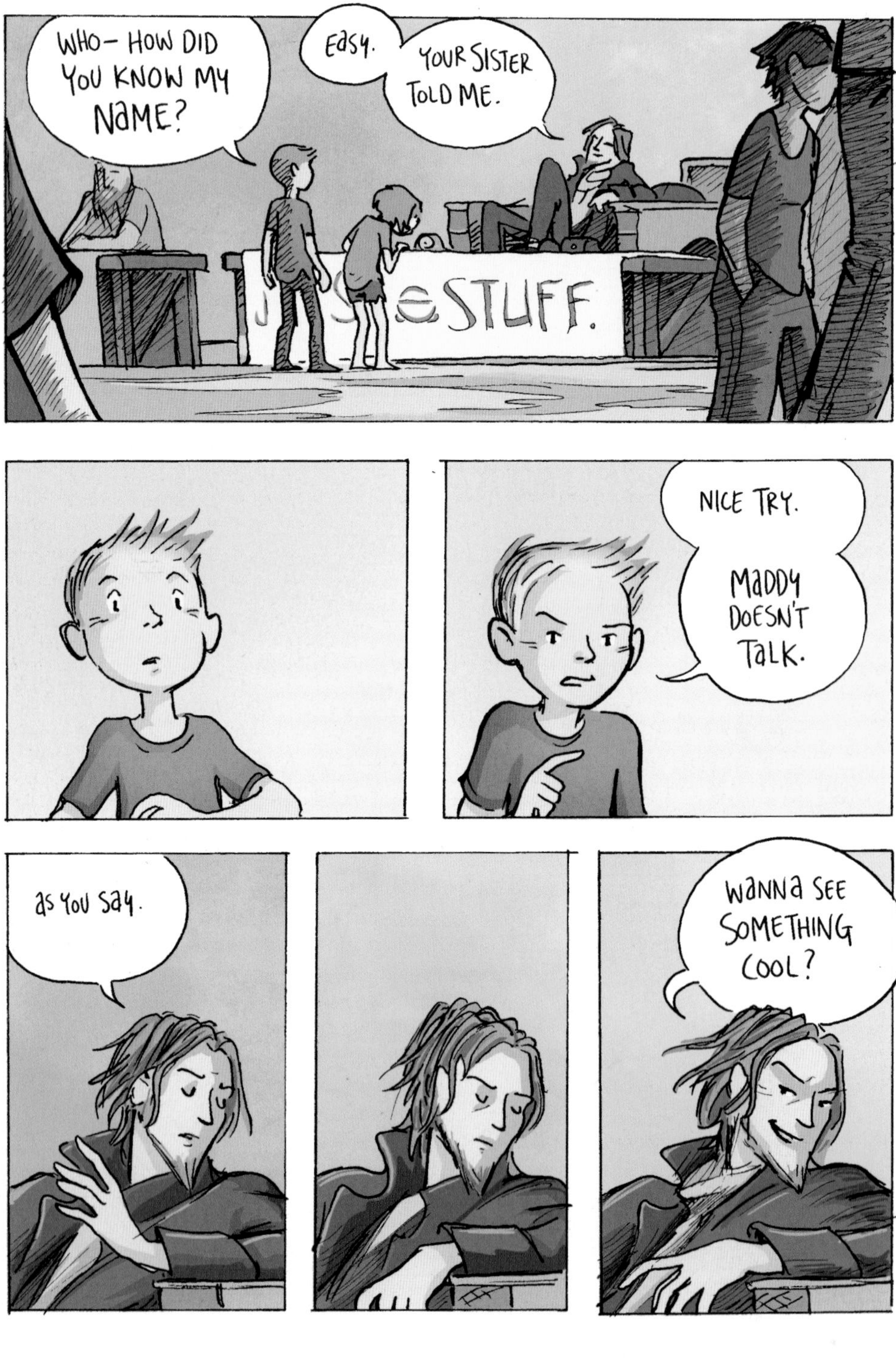
WHO- HOW DID YOU KNOW MY NAME?
Easy.
YOUR SISTER TOLD ME.
STUFF.
NICE TRY.
MADDY DOESN'T TALK.
as you say.
WANNA SEE SOMETHING COOL?

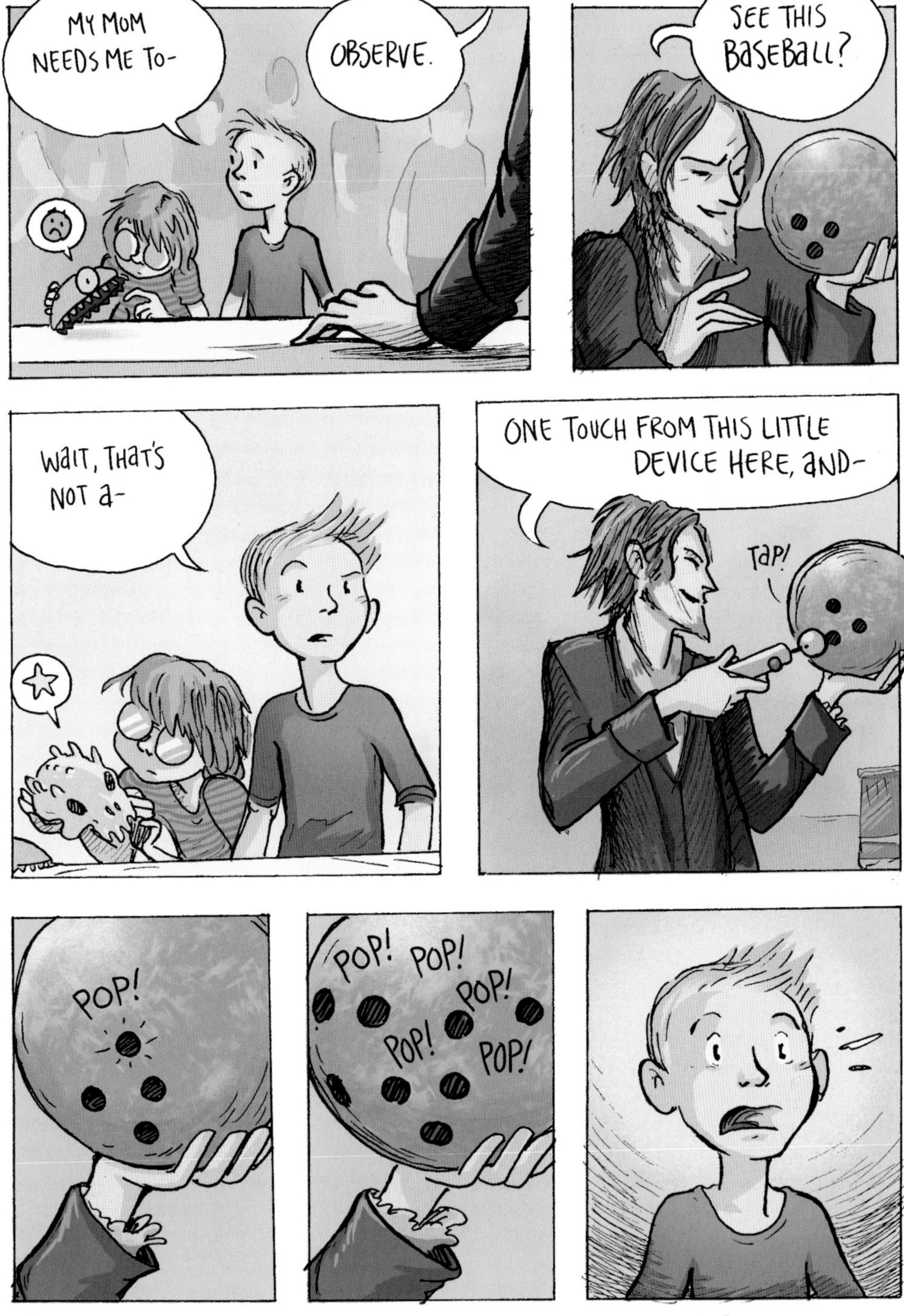
MY MOM NEEDS ME TO-
OBSERVE.
SEE THIS BASEBALL?
WAIT, THAT'S NOT A-
ONE TOUCH FROM THIS LITTLE DEVICE HERE, AND-
TAP!
POP!
POP! POP! POP! POP! POP!

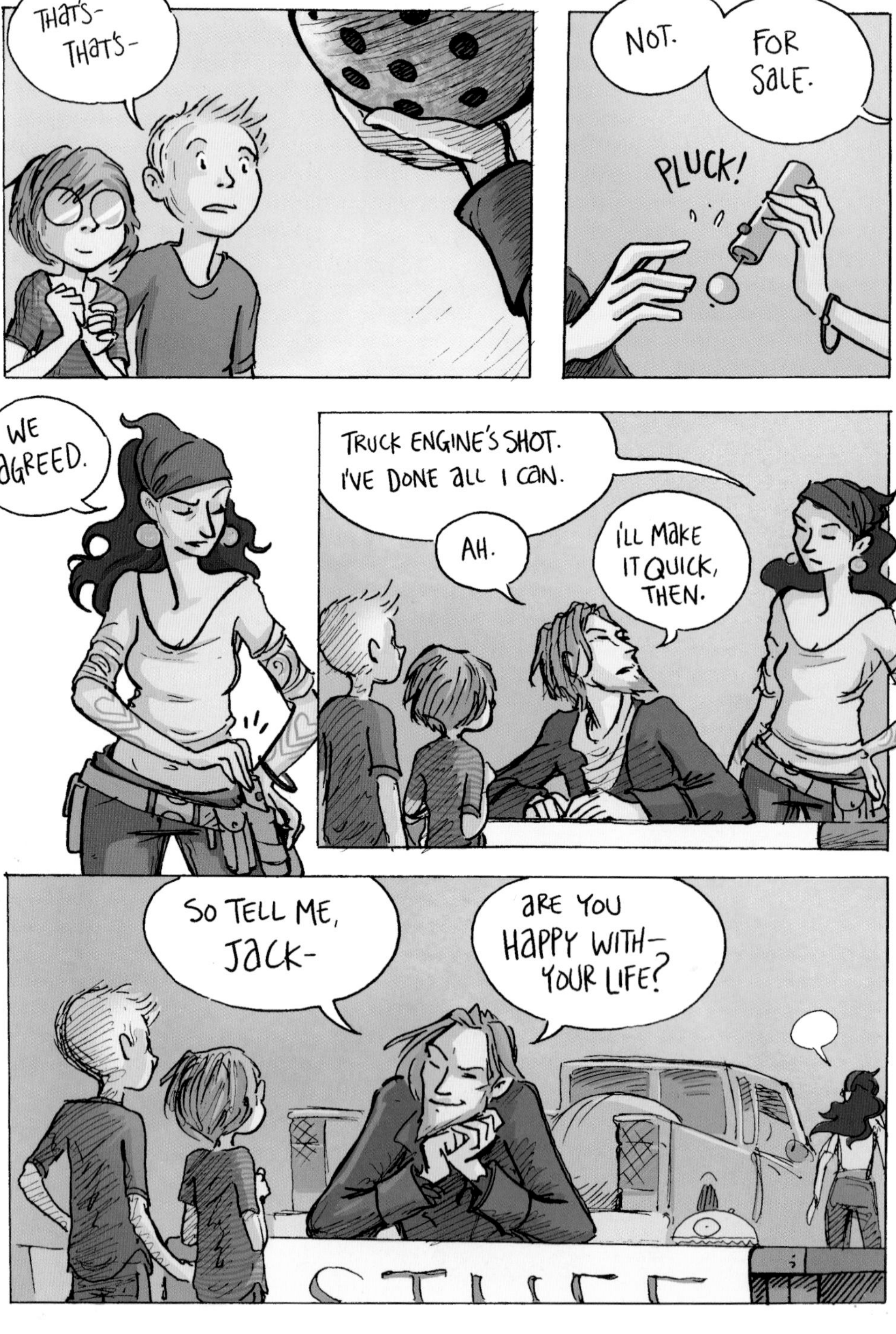
THAT'S-
THAT'S-
NOT.
FOR SALE.
PLUCK!
WE AGREED.
TRUCK ENGINE'S SHOT. I'VE DONE ALL I CAN.
AH.
I'LL MAKE IT QUICK, THEN.
SO TELL ME, JACK-
ARE YOU HAPPY WITH- YOUR LIFE?

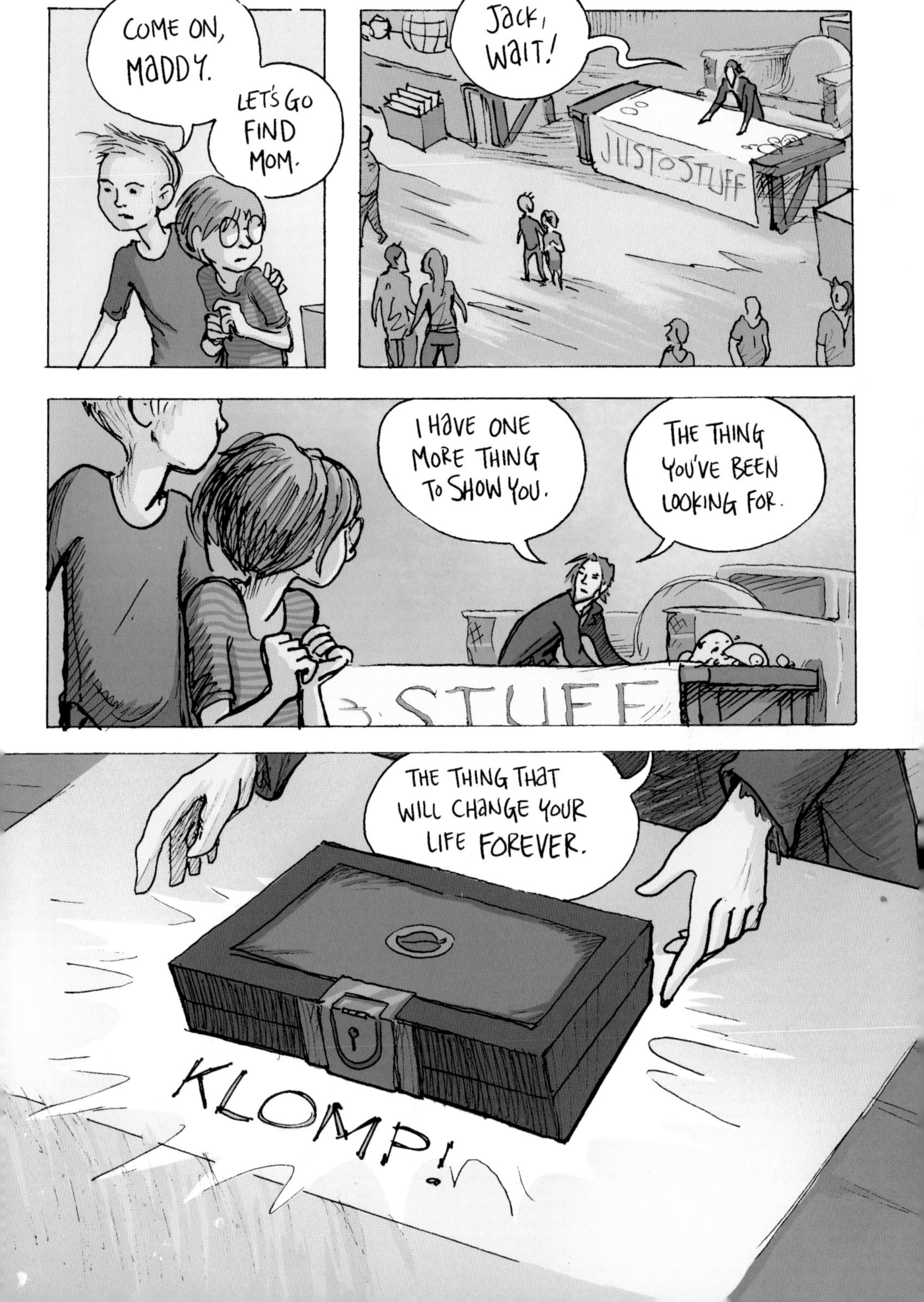
COME ON, MADDY.
LET'S GO FIND MOM.
Jack, WAIT!
JUST STUFF
I HAVE ONE MORE THING TO SHOW YOU.
THE THING YOU'VE BEEN LOOKING FOR.
STUFF
THE THING THAT WILL CHANGE YOUR LIFE FOREVER.
KLOMP!

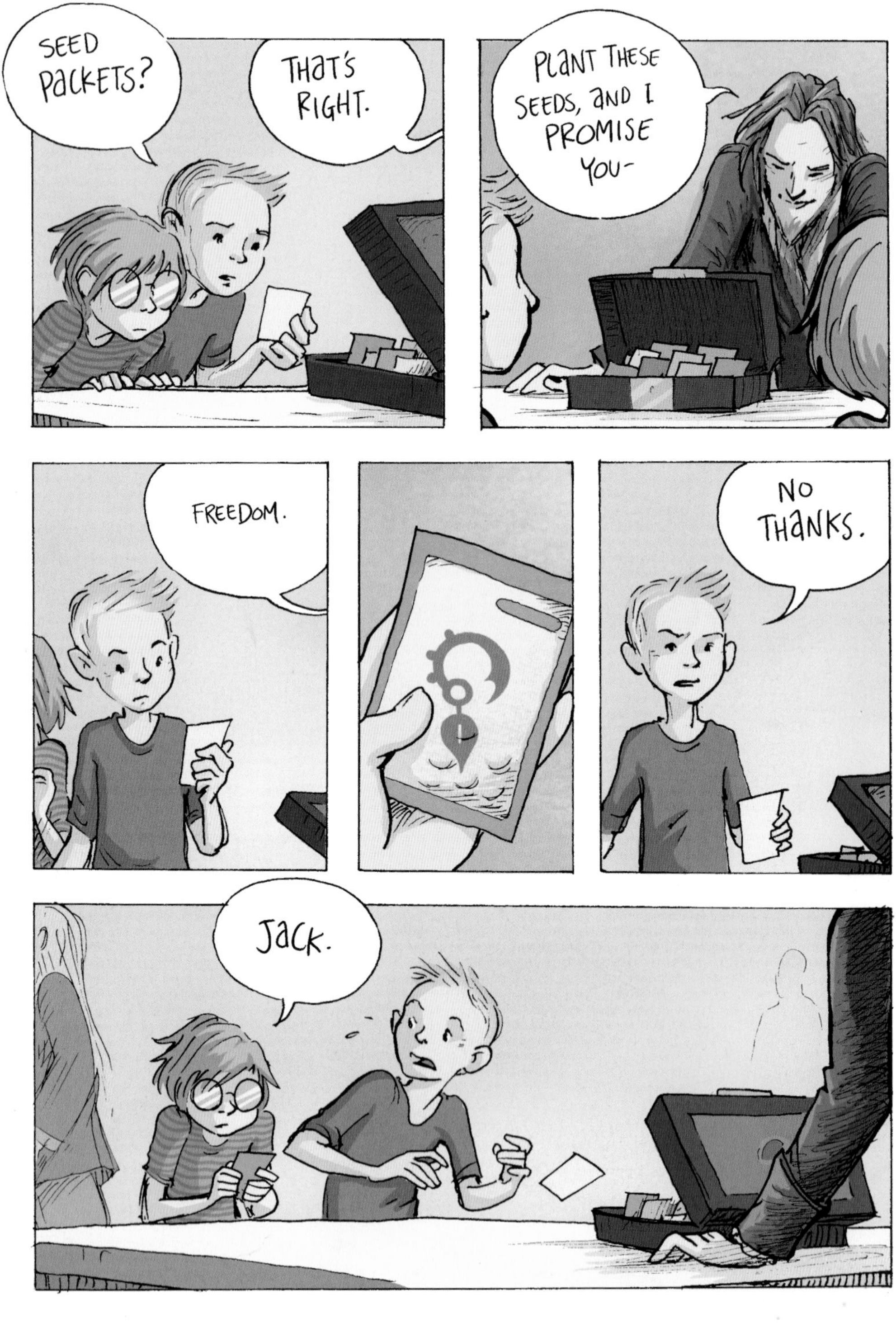
SEED PACKETS?
THAT'S RIGHT.
PLANT THESE SEEDS, AND I PROMISE YOU-
FREEDOM.
NO THANKS.
JACK.

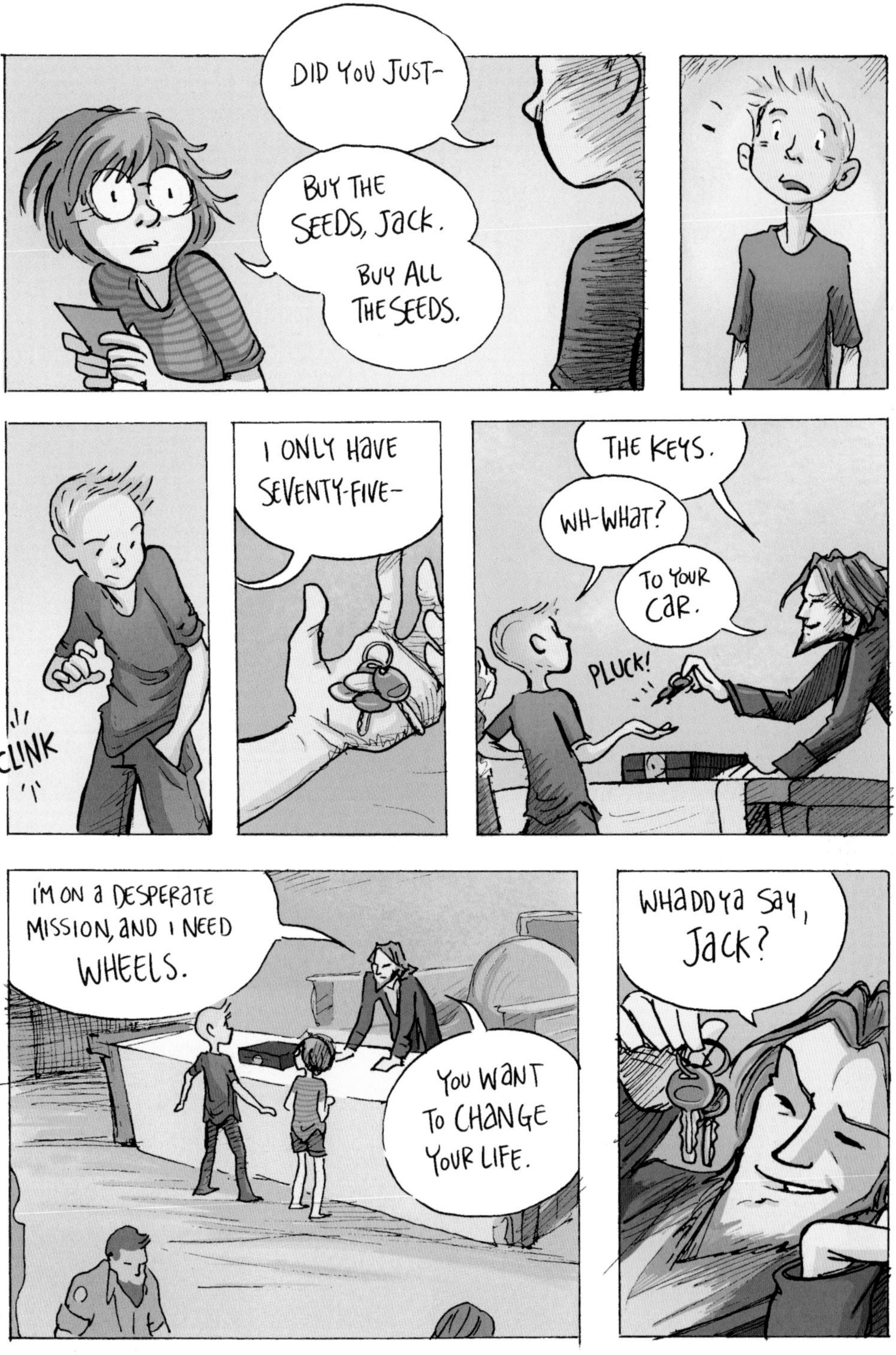
DID YOU JUST-
BUY THE SEEDS, JACK.
BUY ALL THE SEEDS.
CLINK
I ONLY HAVE SEVENTY-FIVE-
THE KEYS.
WH-WHAT?
TO YOUR CAR.
PLUCK!
I'M ON A DESPERATE MISSION, AND I NEED WHEELS.
YOU WANT TO CHANGE YOUR LIFE.
WHADDYA SAY, JACK?

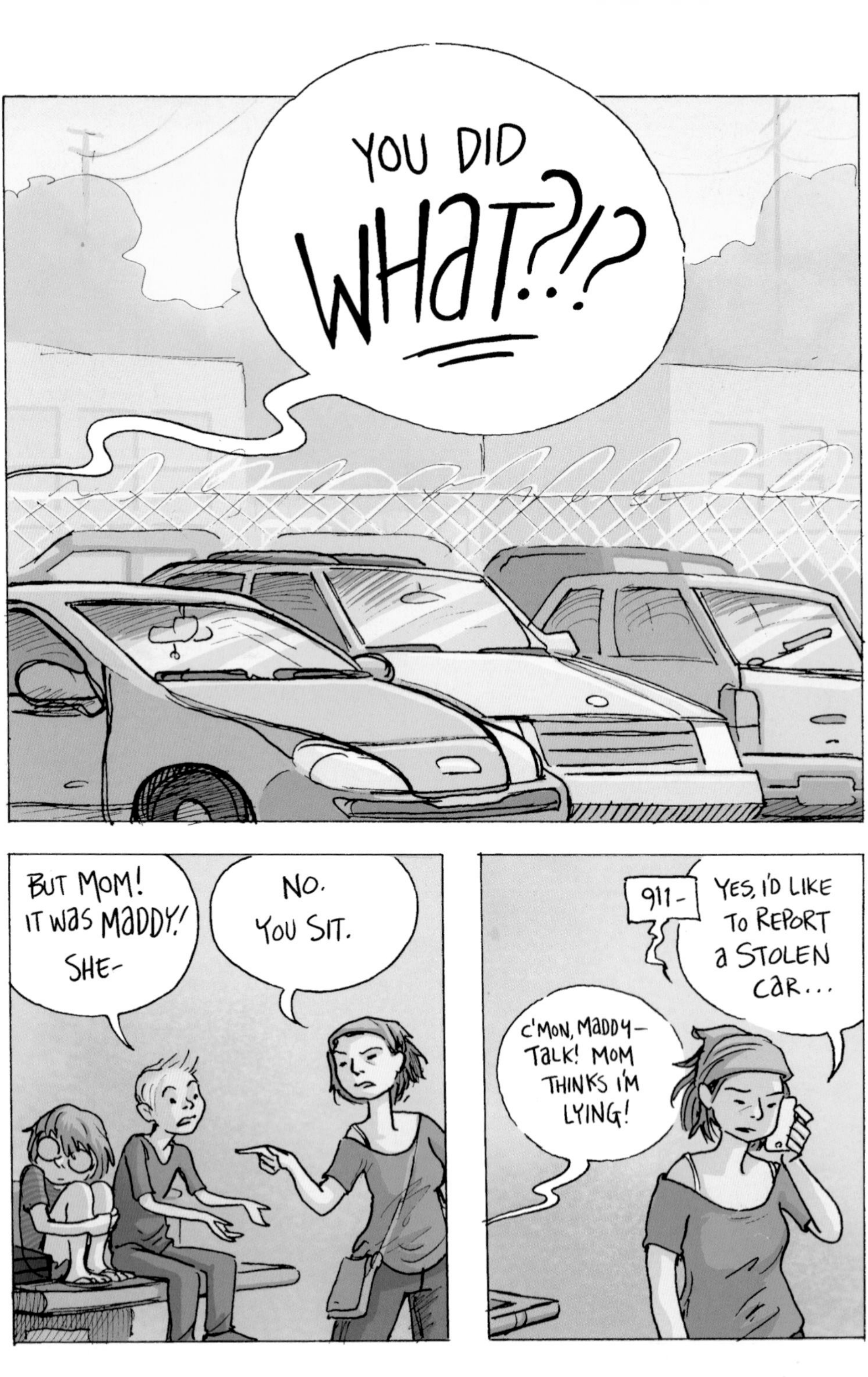
YOU DID WHAT?!?
BUT MOM! IT WAS MADDY! SHE-
NO. YOU SIT.
911-
YES, I'D LIKE TO REPORT A STOLEN CAR...
C'MON, MADDY- TALK! MOM THINKS I'M LYING!

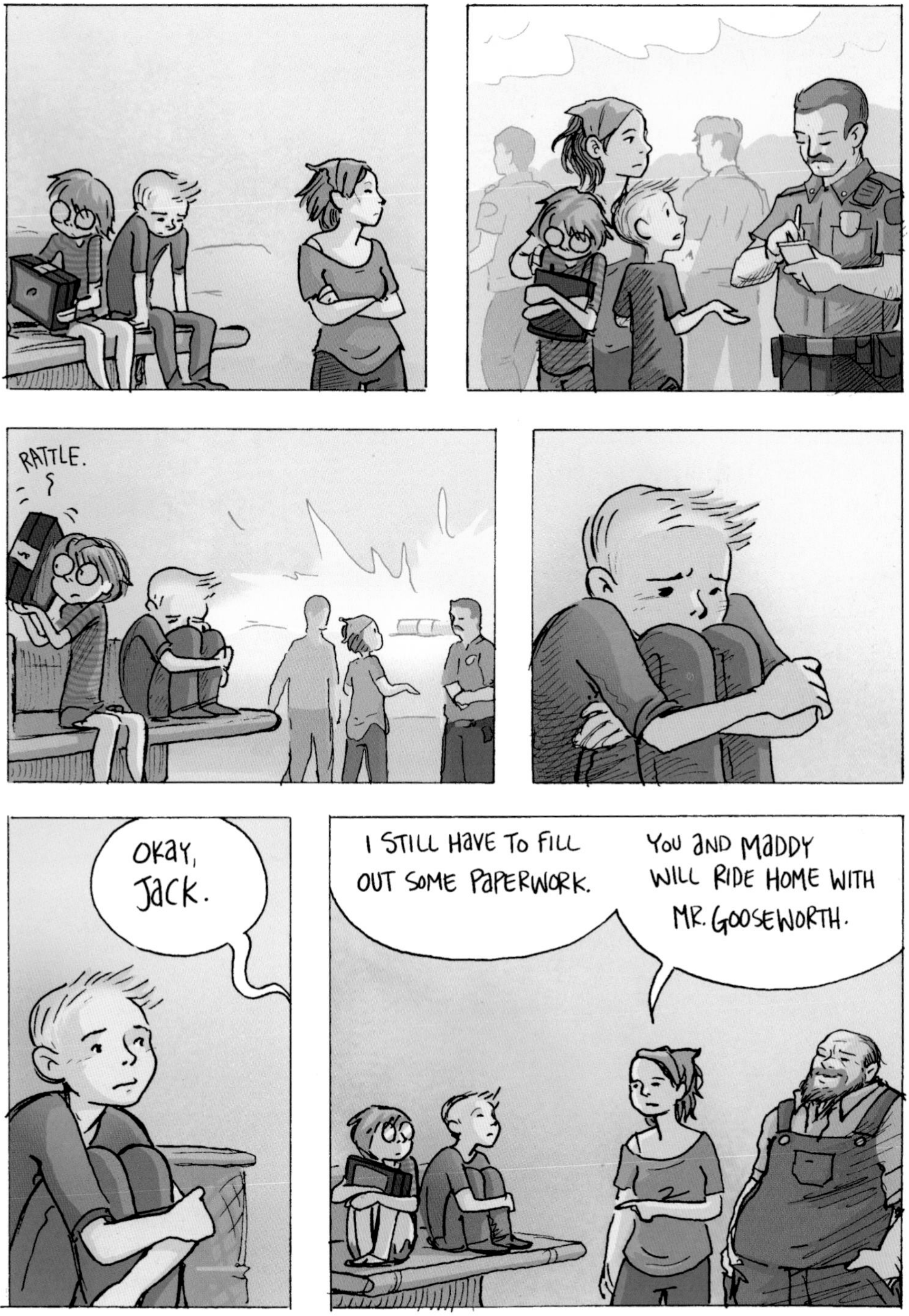
RATTLE.
Okay, Jack.
I STILL HAVE TO FILL OUT SOME PAPERWORK.
YOU AND MADDY WILL RIDE HOME WITH MR. GOOSEWORTH.

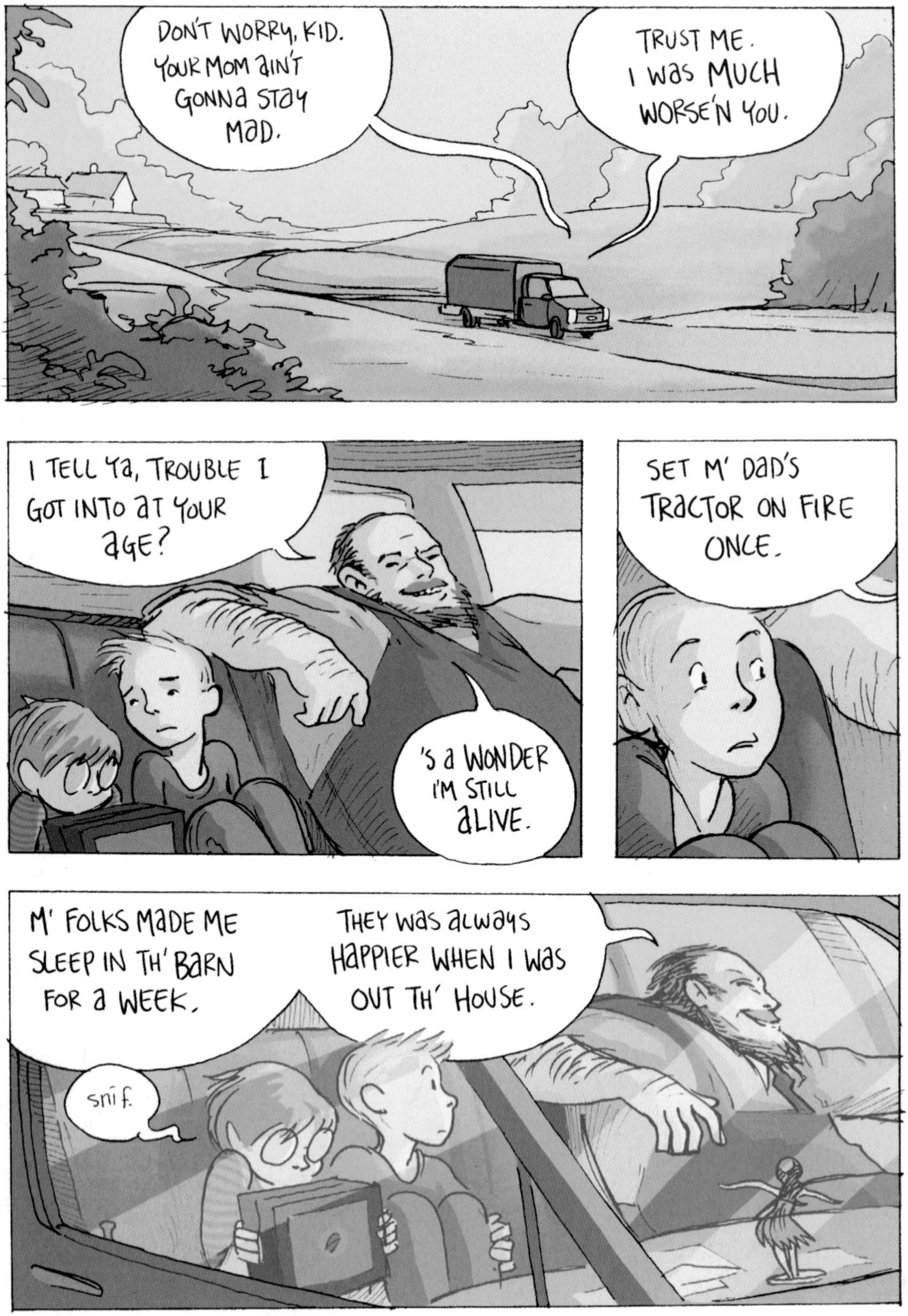
DON'T WORRY, KID. YOUR MOM AIN'T GONNA STAY MAD.
TRUST ME. I WAS MUCH WORSE'N YOU.
I TELL YA, TROUBLE I GOT INTO AT YOUR AGE?
'S A WONDER I'M STILL ALIVE.
SET M' DAD'S TRACTOR ON FIRE ONCE.
M' FOLKS MADE ME SLEEP IN TH' BARN FOR A WEEK.
THEY WAS ALWAYS HAPPIER WHEN I WAS OUT TH' HOUSE.
snif.

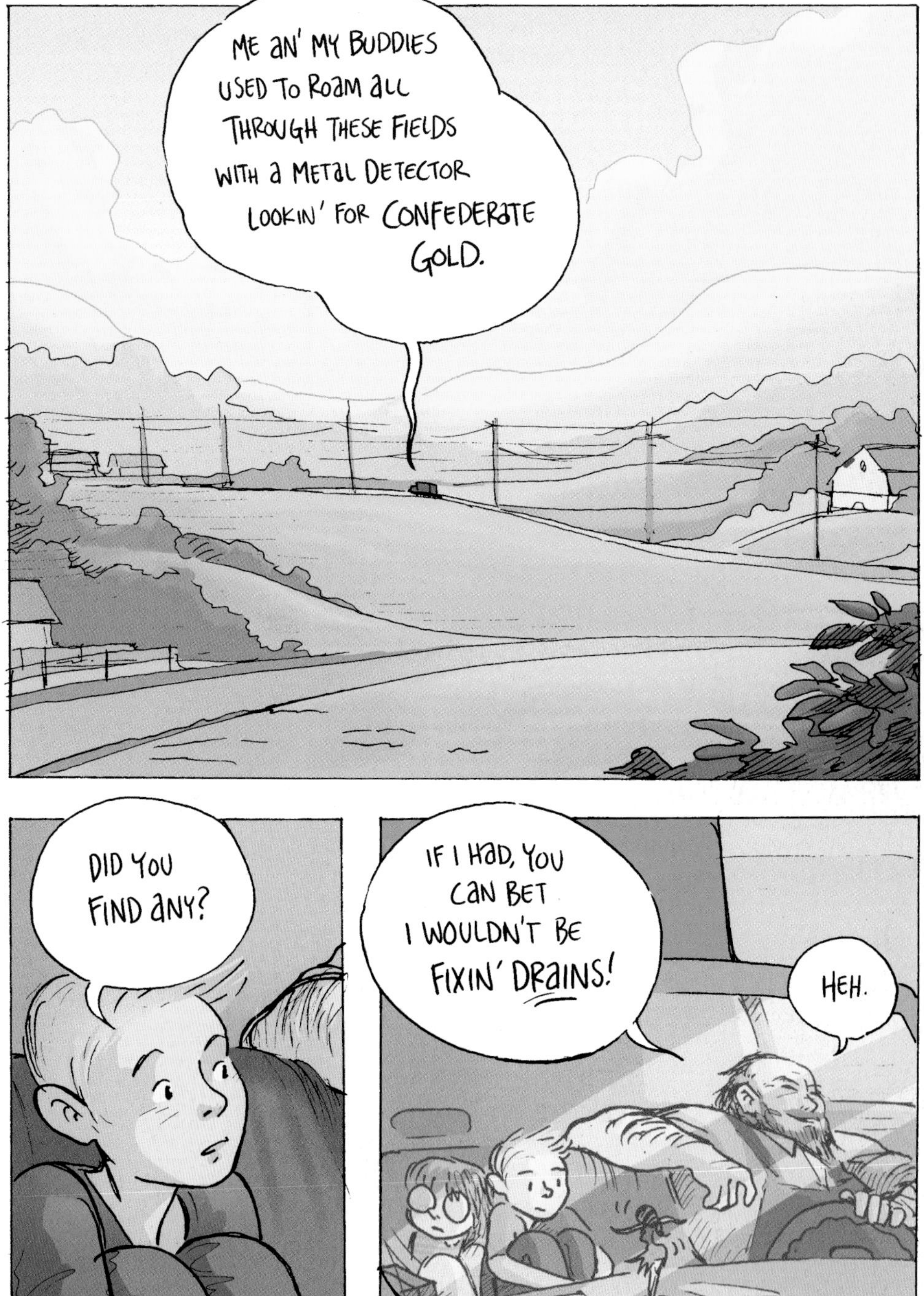
ME AN' MY BUDDIES USED TO ROAM ALL THROUGH THESE FIELDS WITH A METAL DETECTOR LOOKIN' FOR CONFEDERATE GOLD.
DID YOU FIND ANY?
IF I HAD, YOU CAN BET I WOULDN'T BE FIXIN' DRAINS!
HEH.

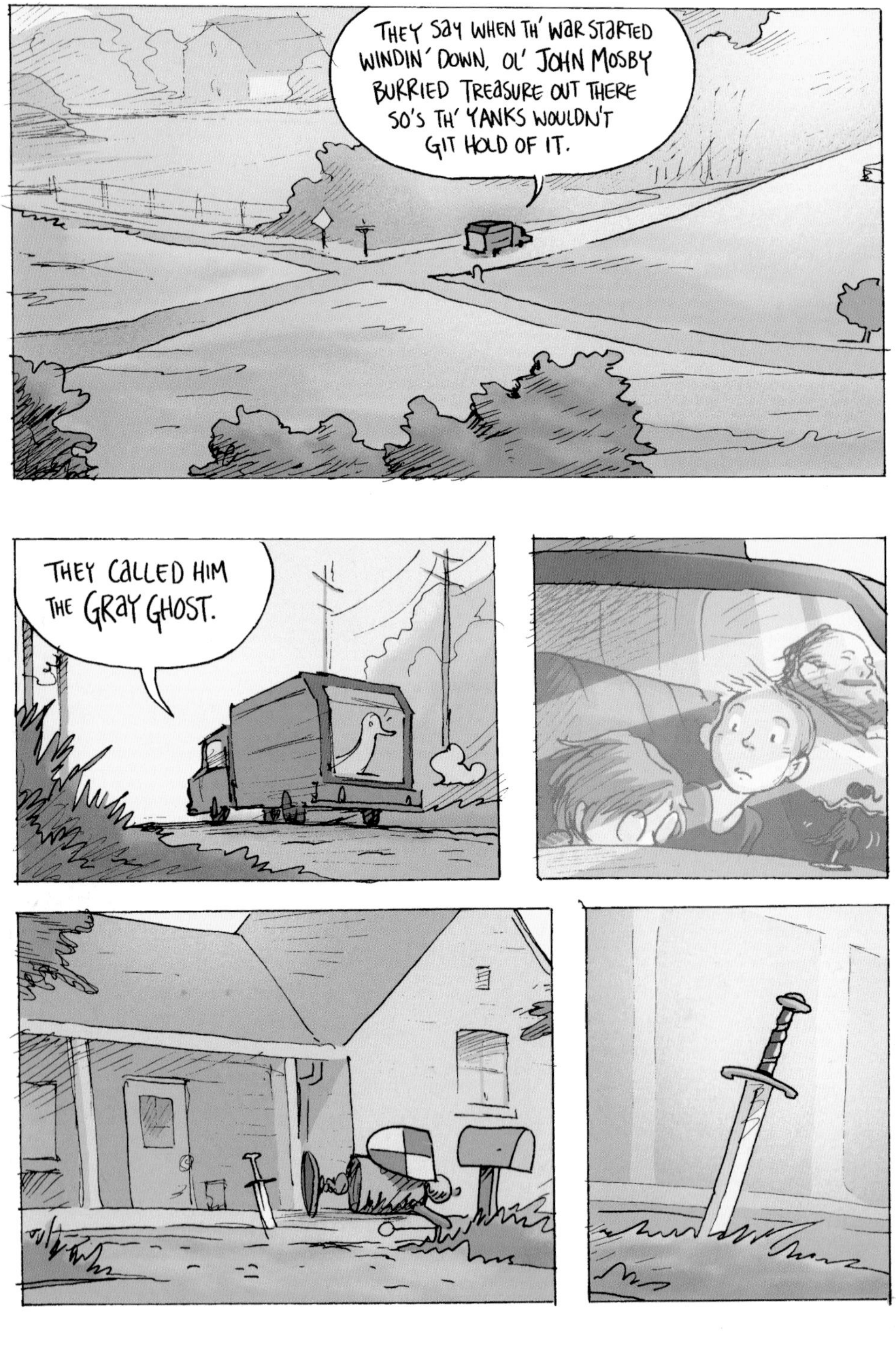
THEY SAY WHEN TH' WAR STARTED WINDIN' DOWN, OL' JOHN MOSBY BURRIED TREASURE OUT THERE SO'S TH' YANKS WOULDN'T GIT HOLD OF IT.
THEY CALLED HIM THE GRAY GHOST.

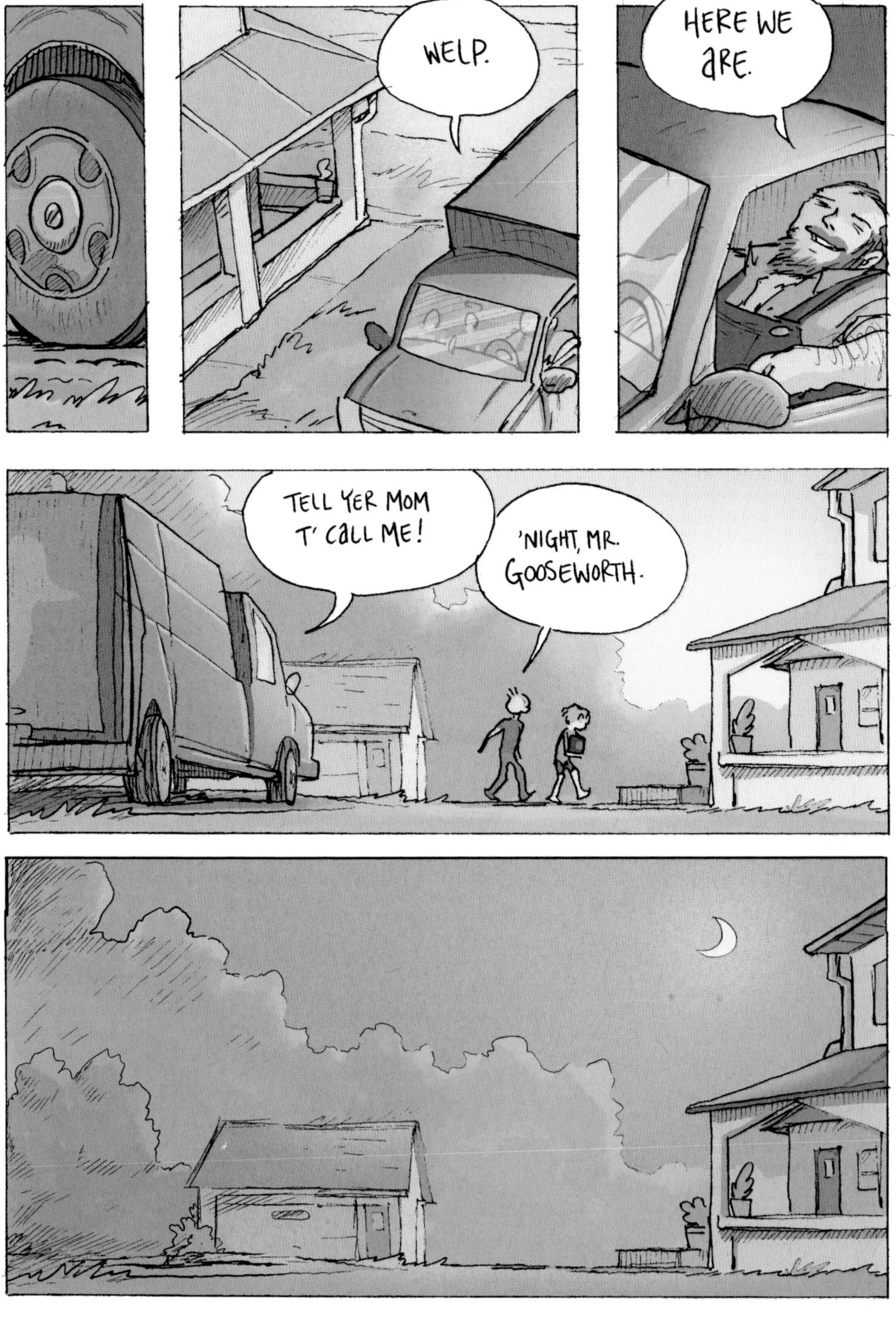
WELP.
HERE WE ARE.
TELL YER MOM T' CALL ME!
'NIGHT, MR. GOOSEWORTH.

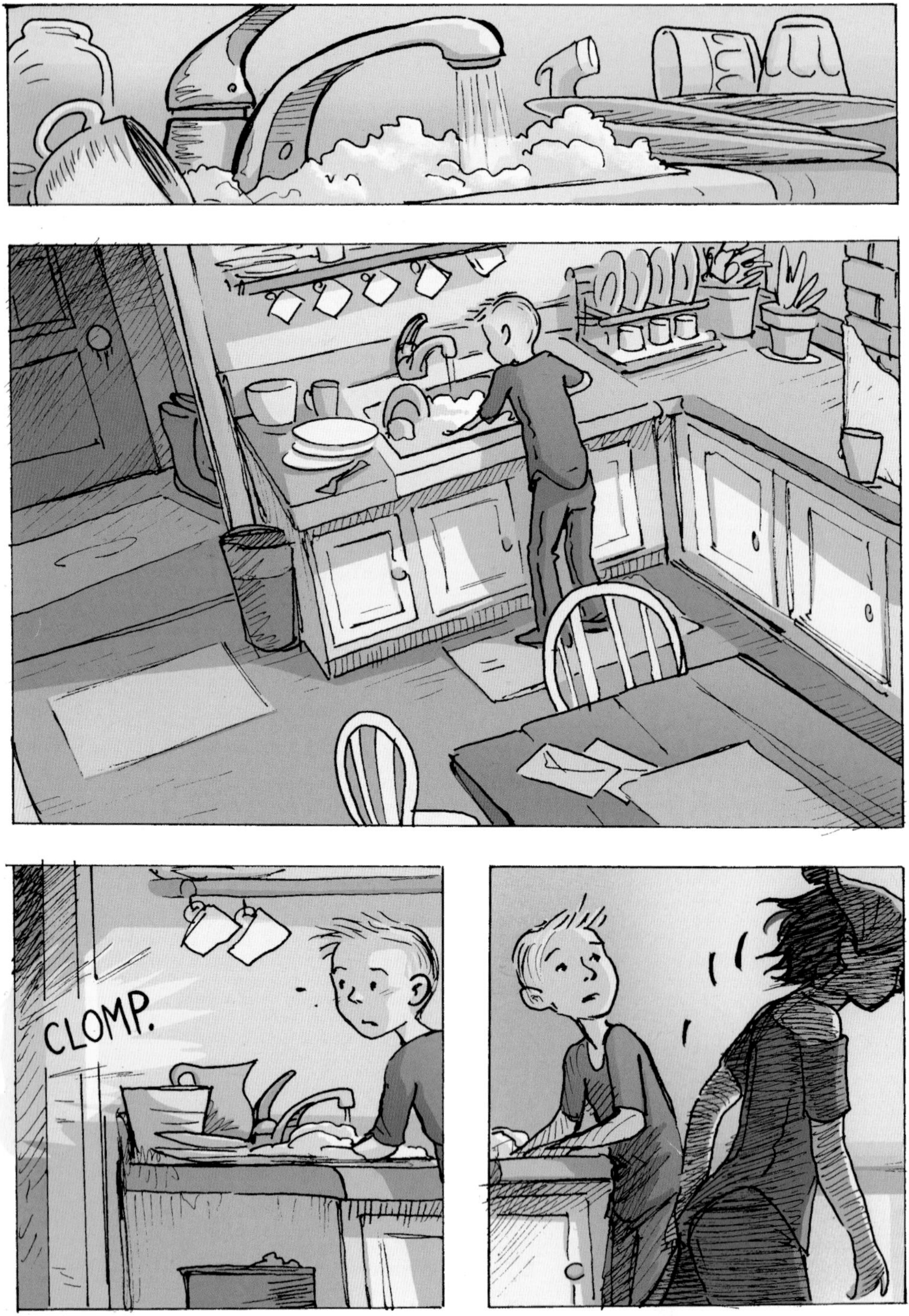
CLOMP.

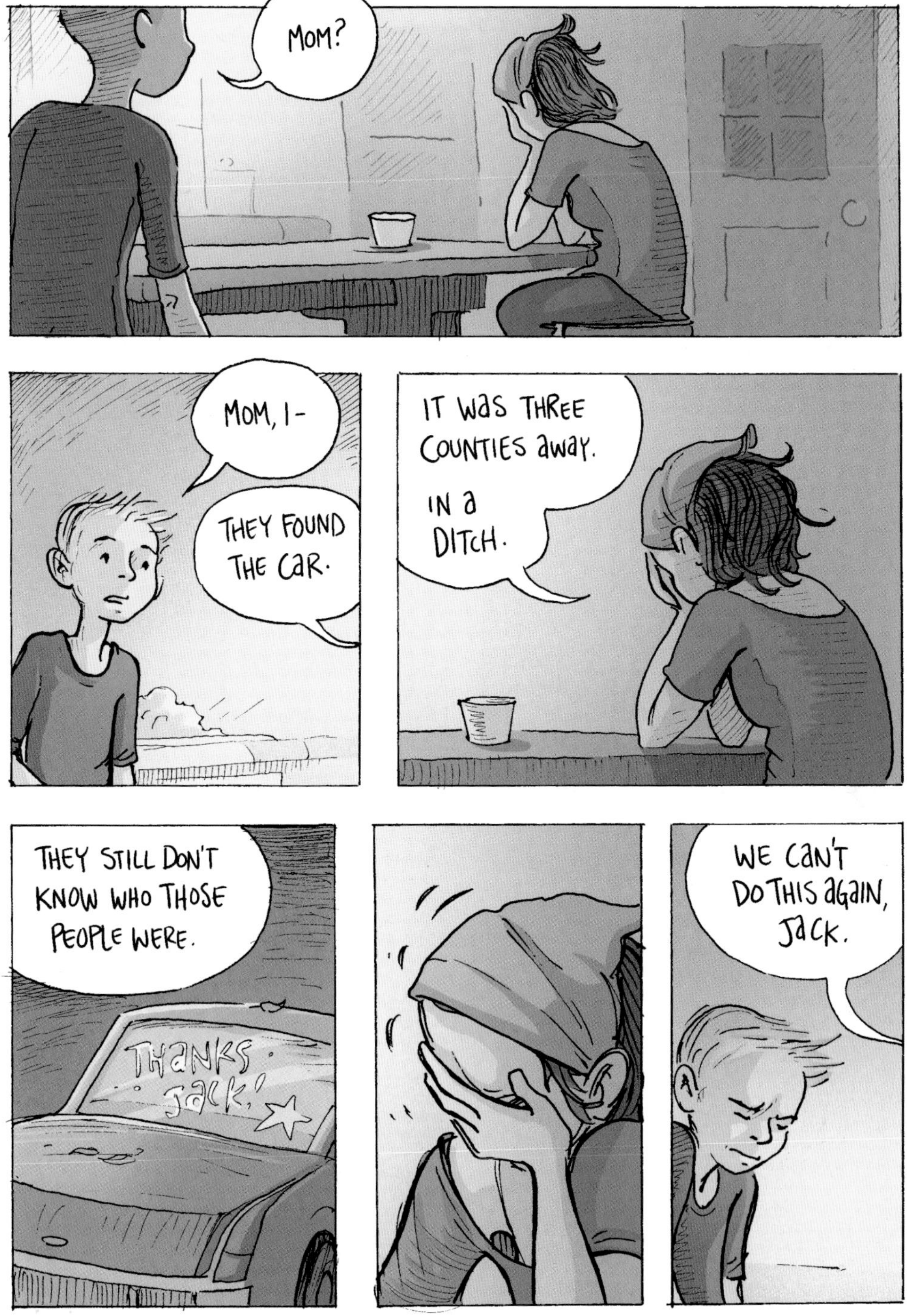
MOM?
MOM, I-
THEY FOUND THE CAR.
IT WAS THREE COUNTIES AWAY.
IN A DITCH.
THEY STILL DON'T KNOW WHO THOSE PEOPLE WERE.
THANKS JACK!
WE CAN'T DO THIS AGAIN, JACK.

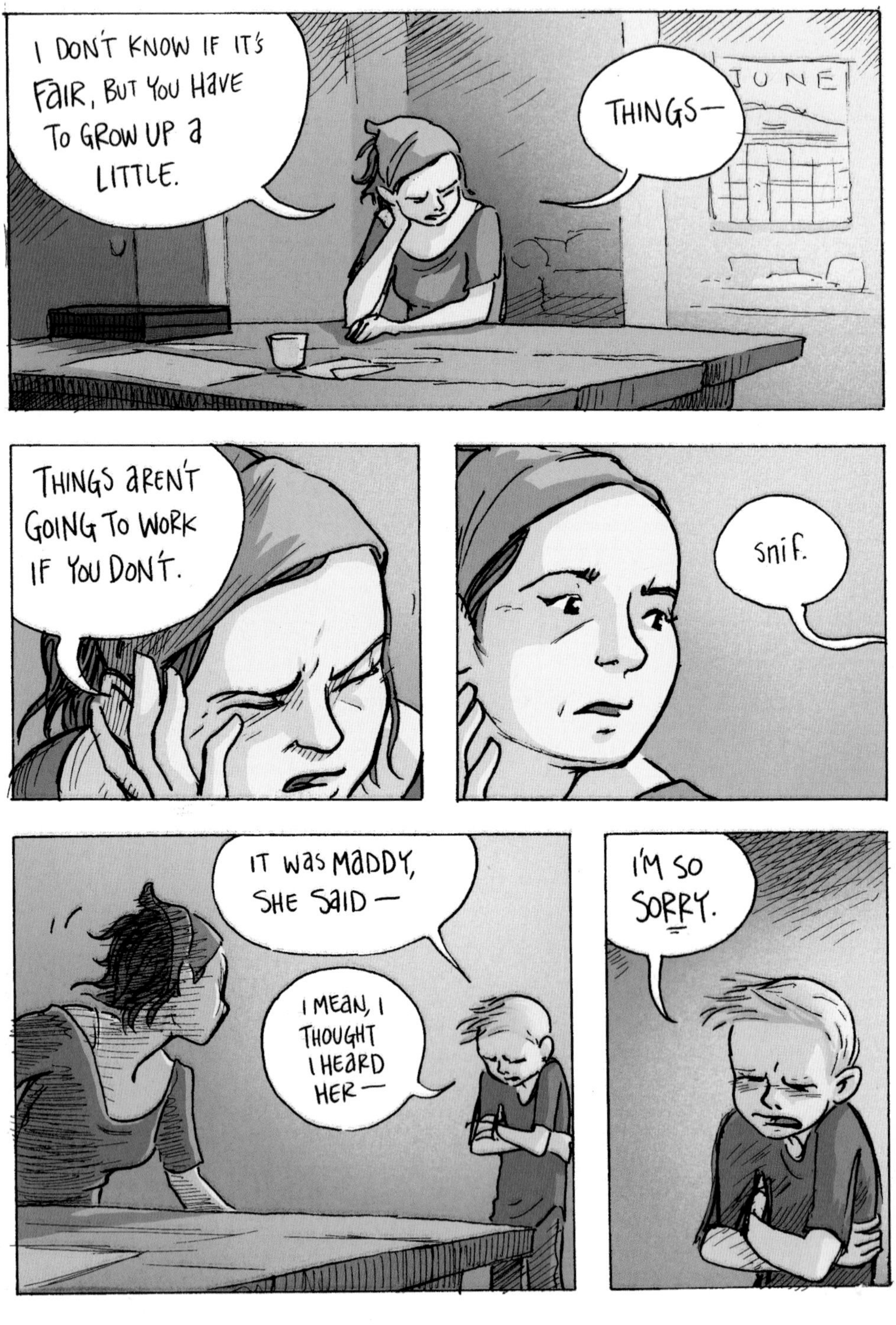
I DON'T KNOW IF IT'S FAIR, BUT YOU HAVE TO GROW UP A LITTLE.
THINGS—
JUNE
THINGS AREN'T GOING TO WORK IF YOU DON'T.
SNIF.
IT WAS MADDY, SHE SAID—
I MEAN, I THOUGHT I HEARD HER—
I'M SO SORRY.

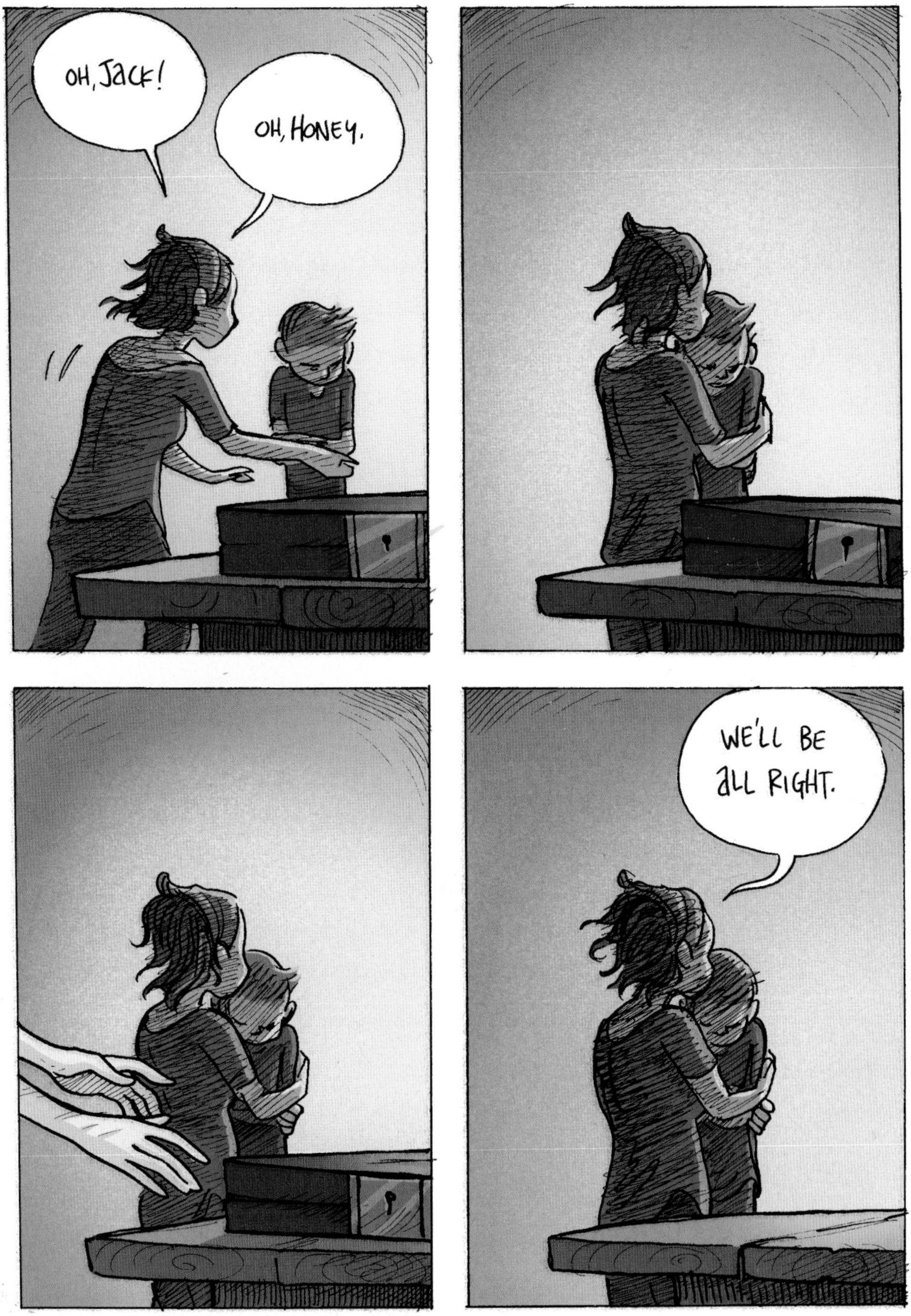
OH, JACK!
OH, HONEY.
WE'LL BE ALL RIGHT.

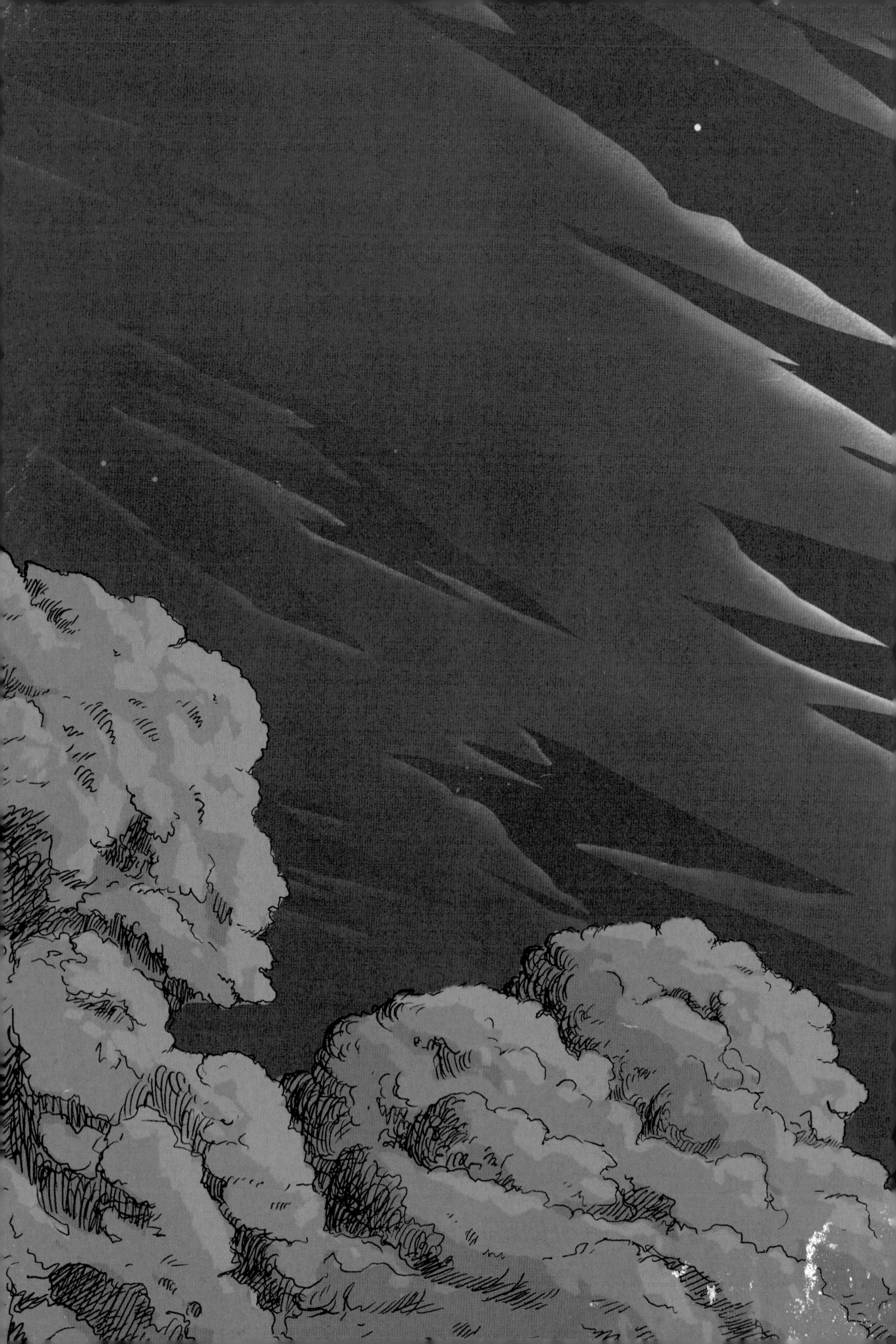

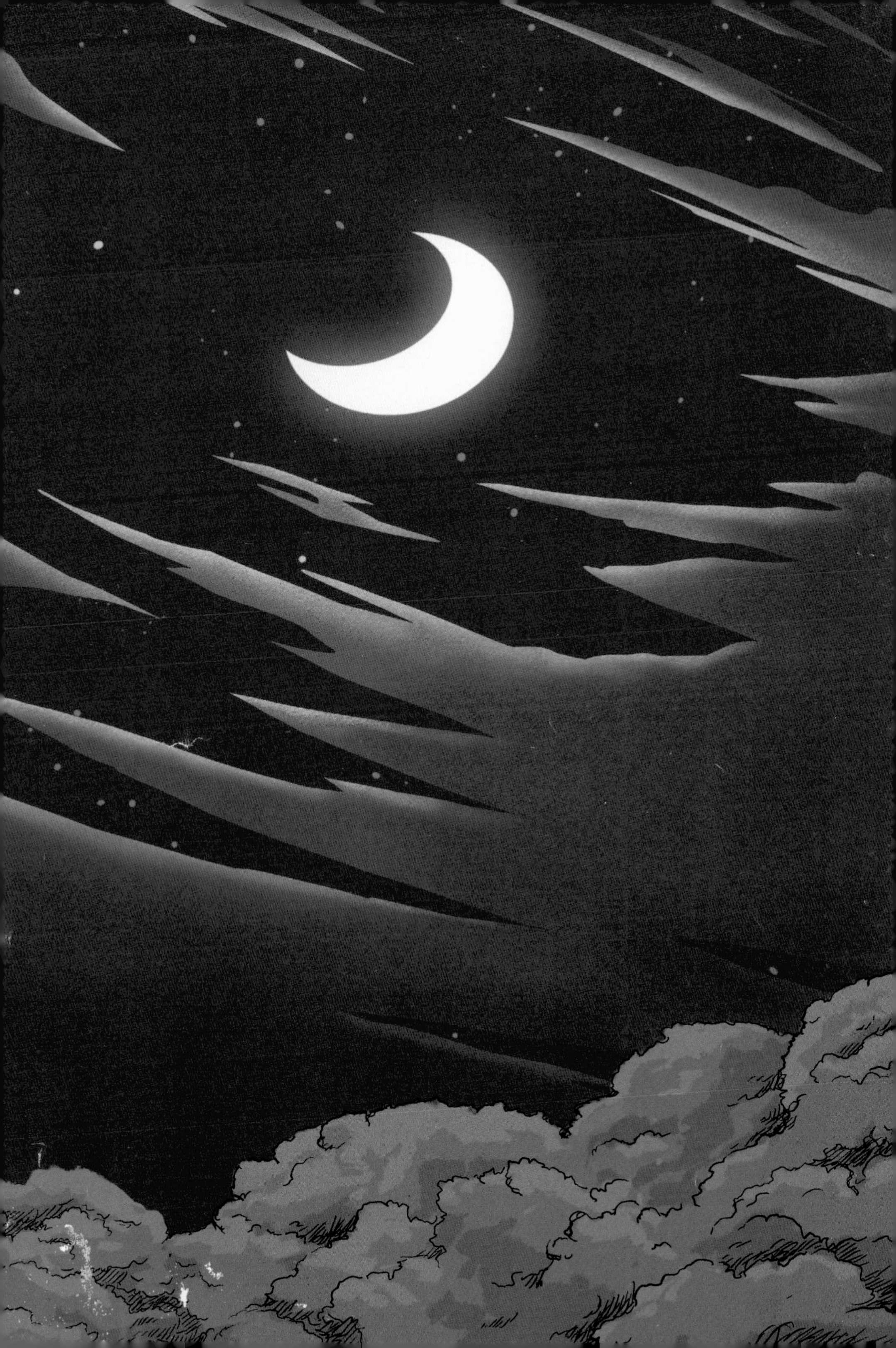

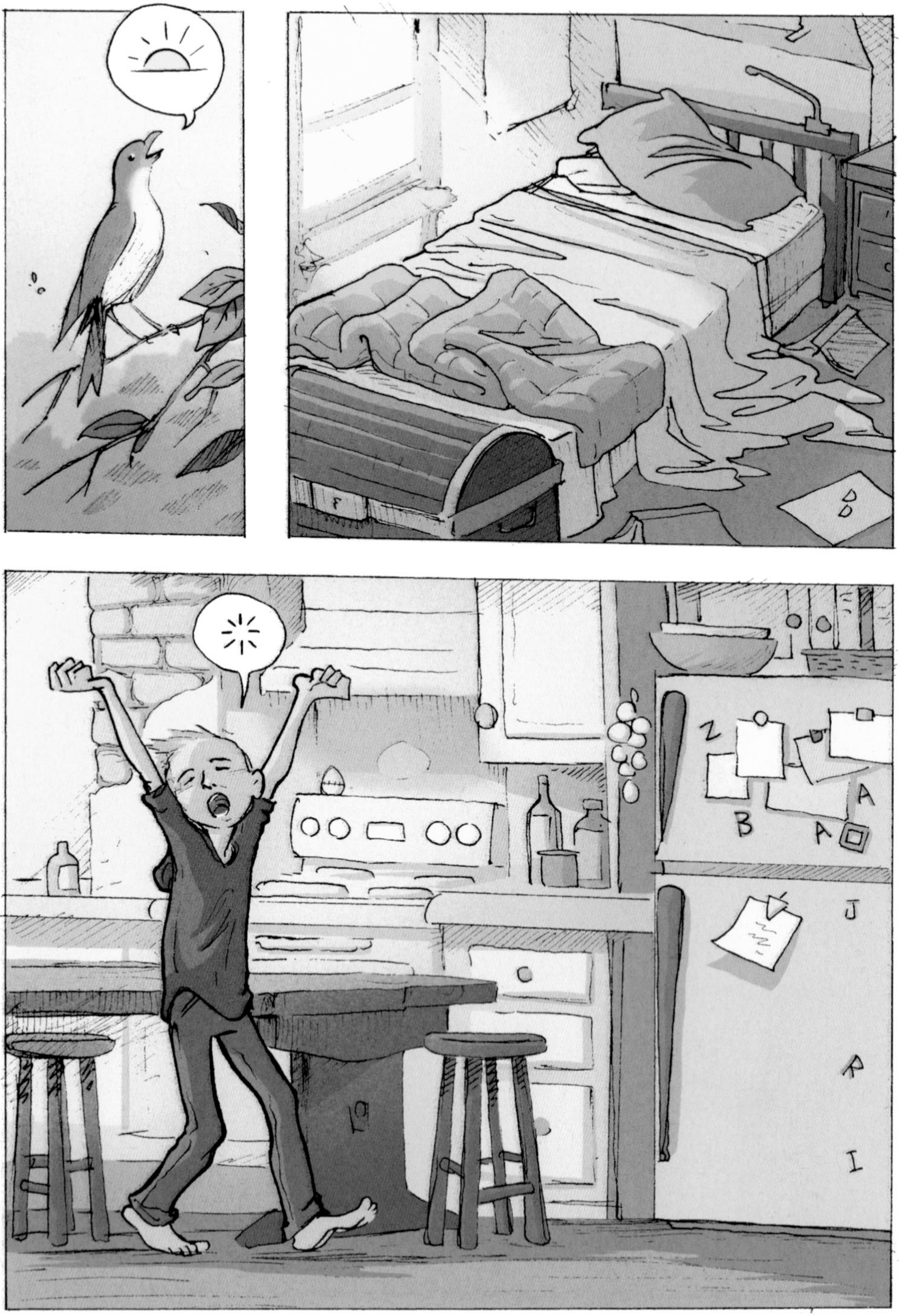

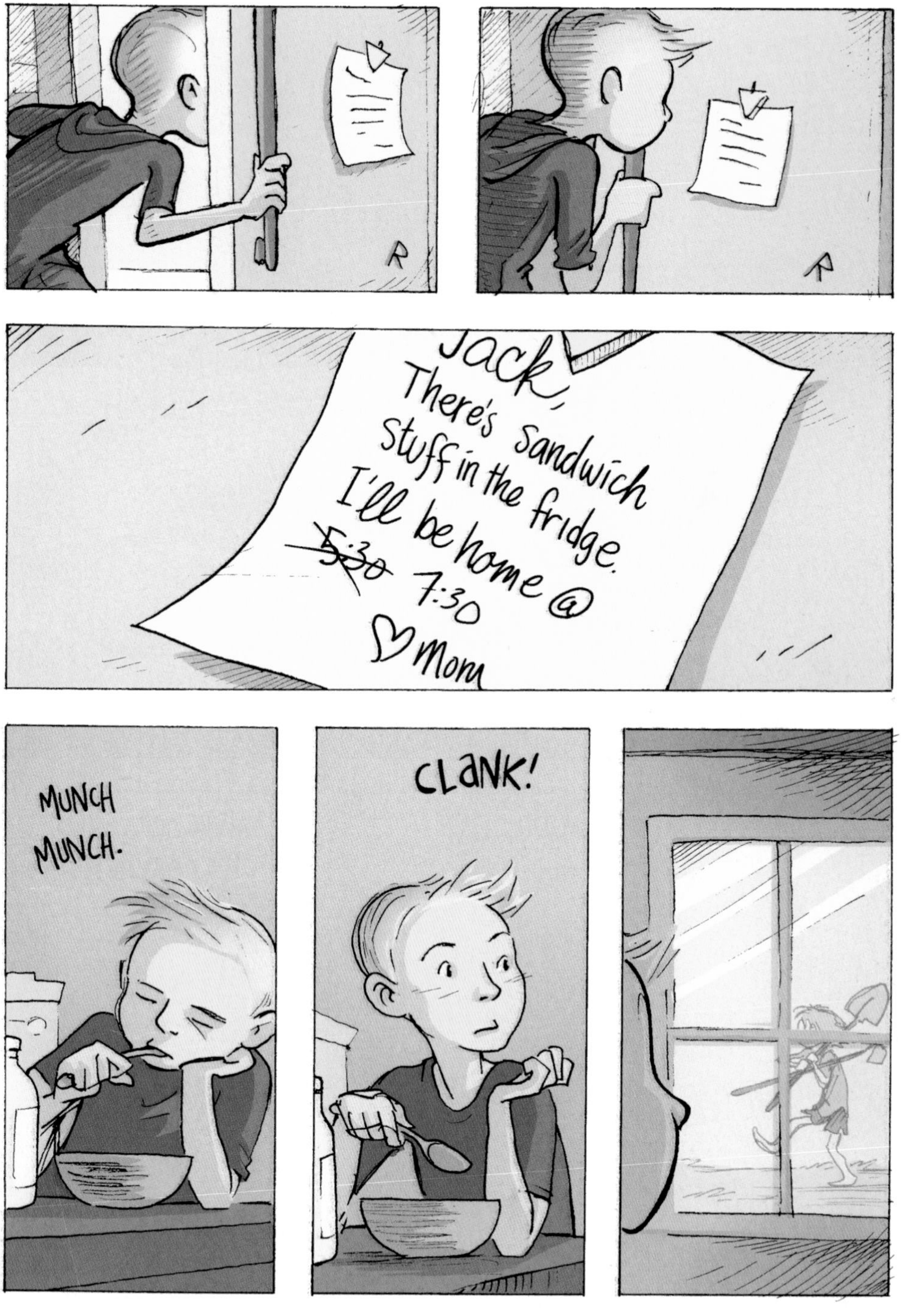
R
R
Jack,
There's sandwich
stuff in the fridge.
I'll be home @
5:30 7:30
♡ Mom
MUNCH
MUNCH.
CLANK!

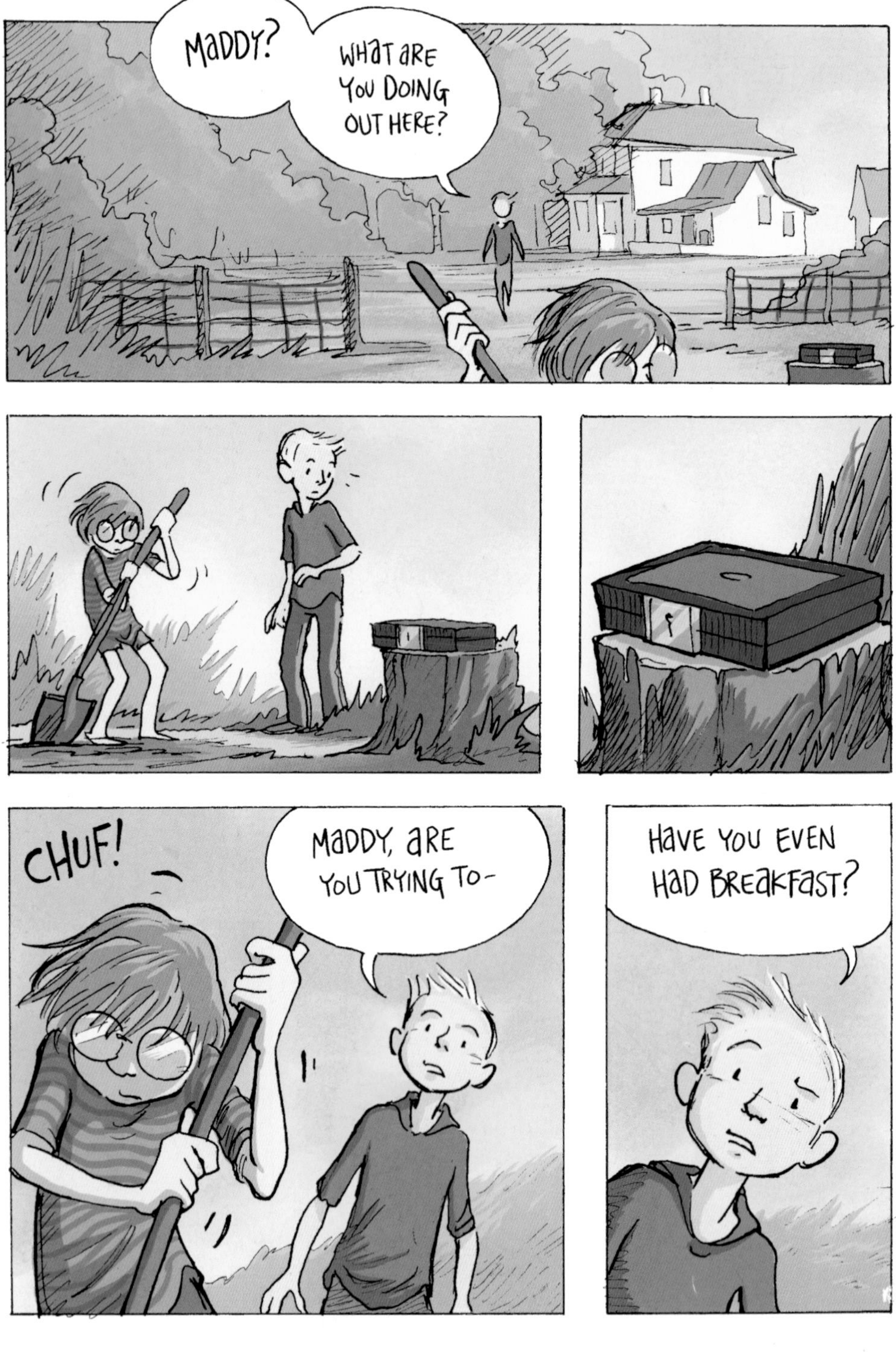
MADDY?
WHAT ARE YOU DOING OUT HERE?
CHUF!
MADDY, ARE YOU TRYING TO-
HAVE YOU EVEN HAD BREAKFAST?

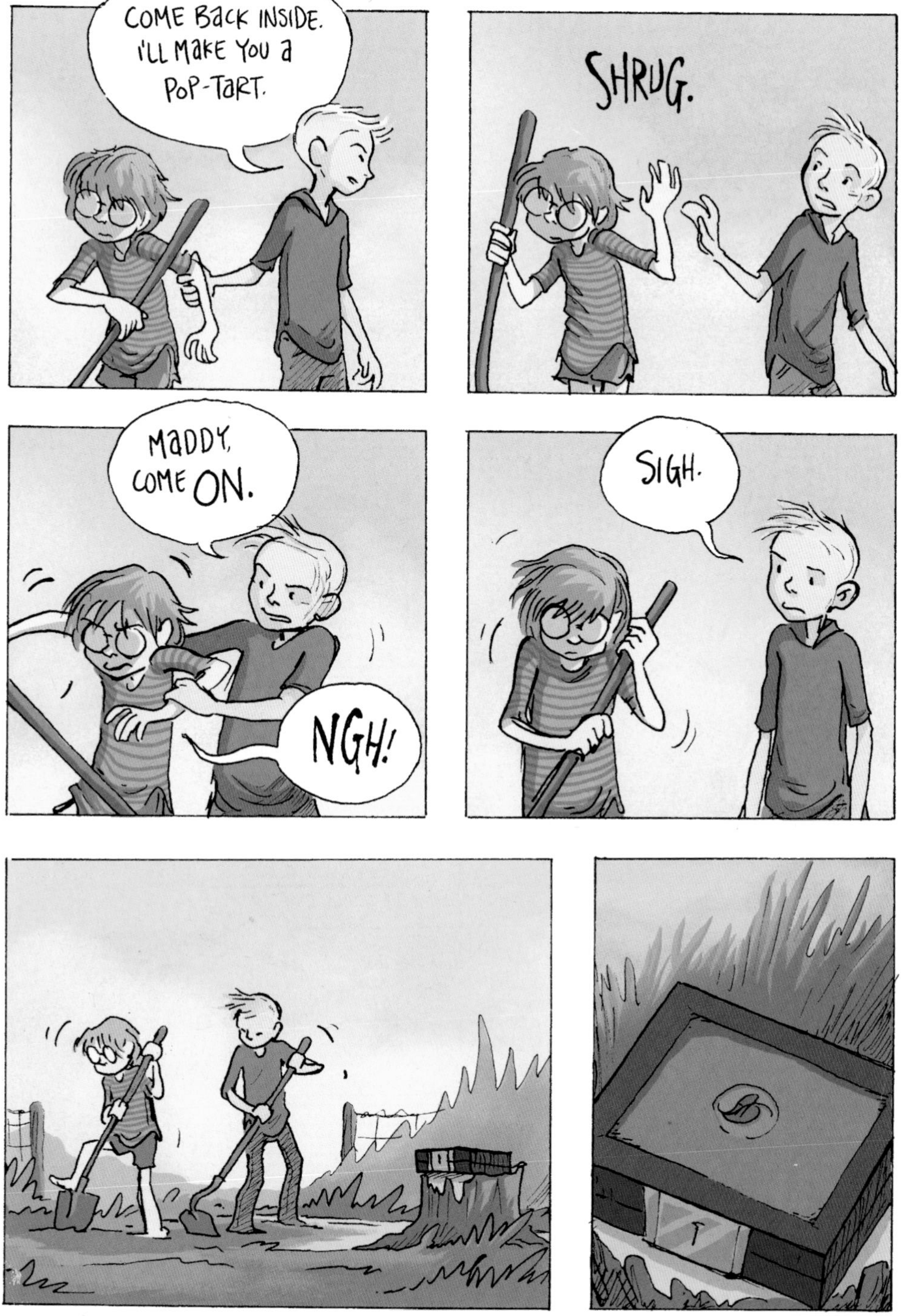
COME BACK INSIDE. I'LL MAKE YOU A POP-TART.
SHRUG.
MADDY, COME ON.
NGH!
SIGH.

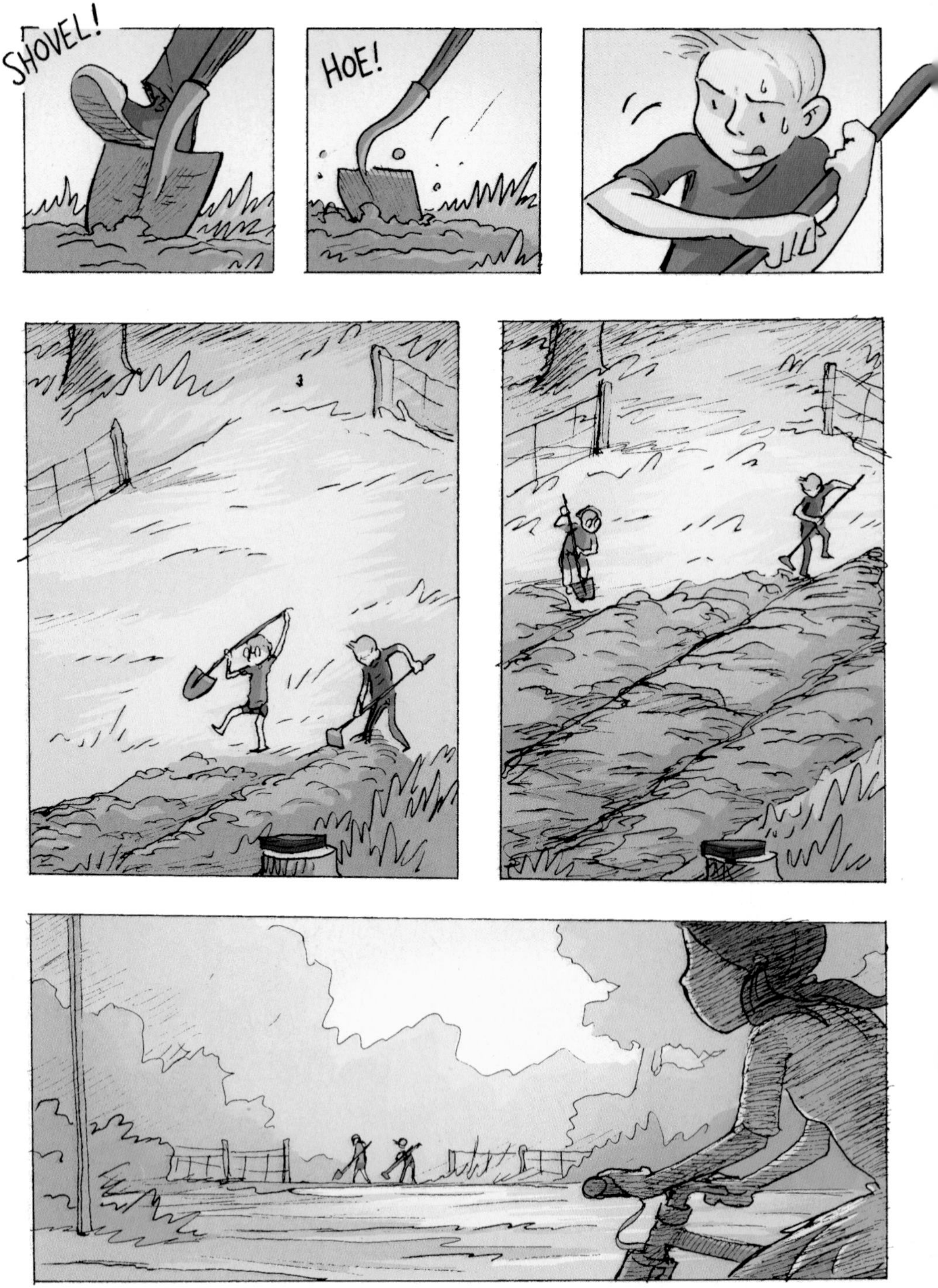
SHOVEL!
HOE!

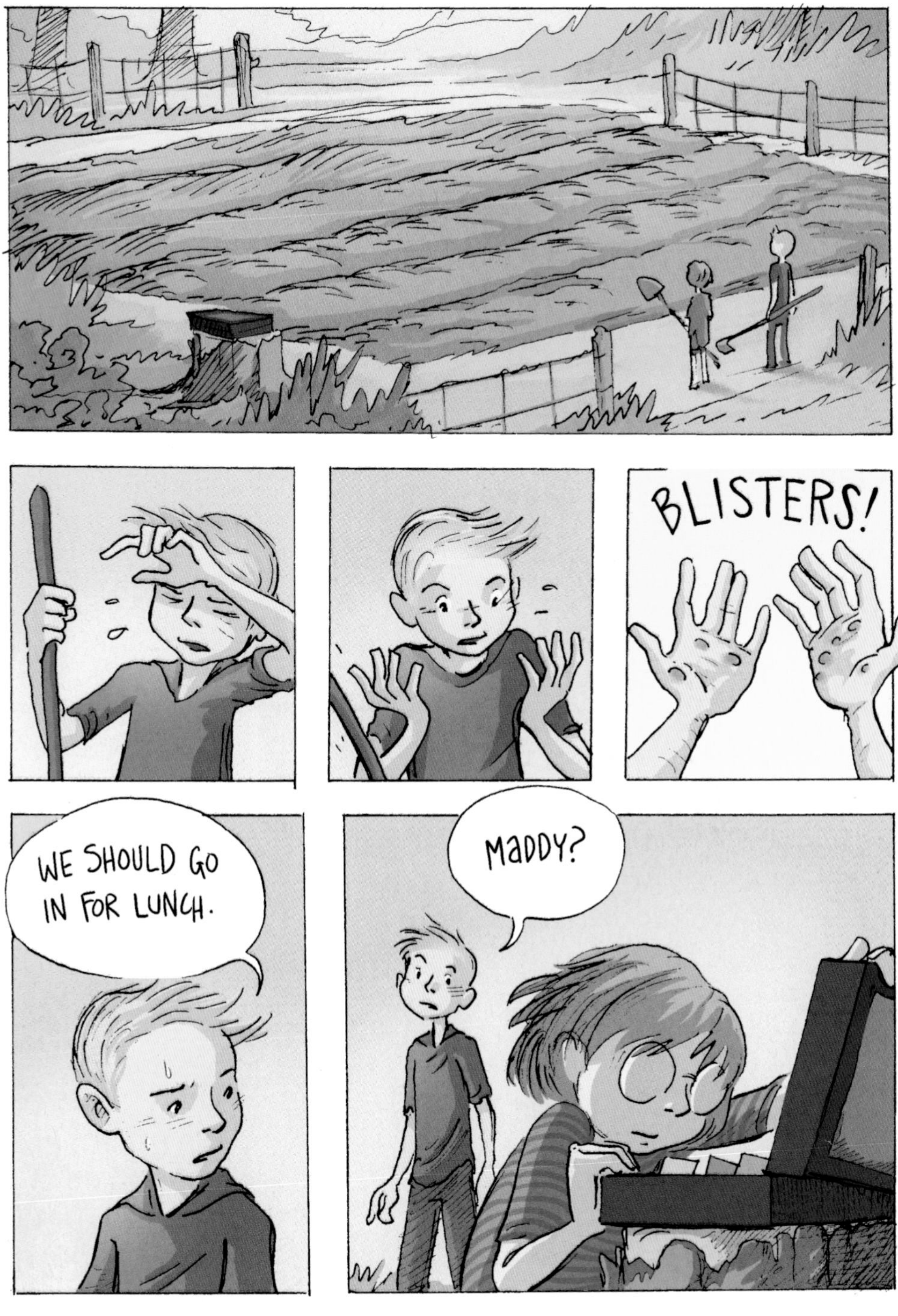
BLISTERS!
WE SHOULD GO IN FOR LUNCH.
MADDY?

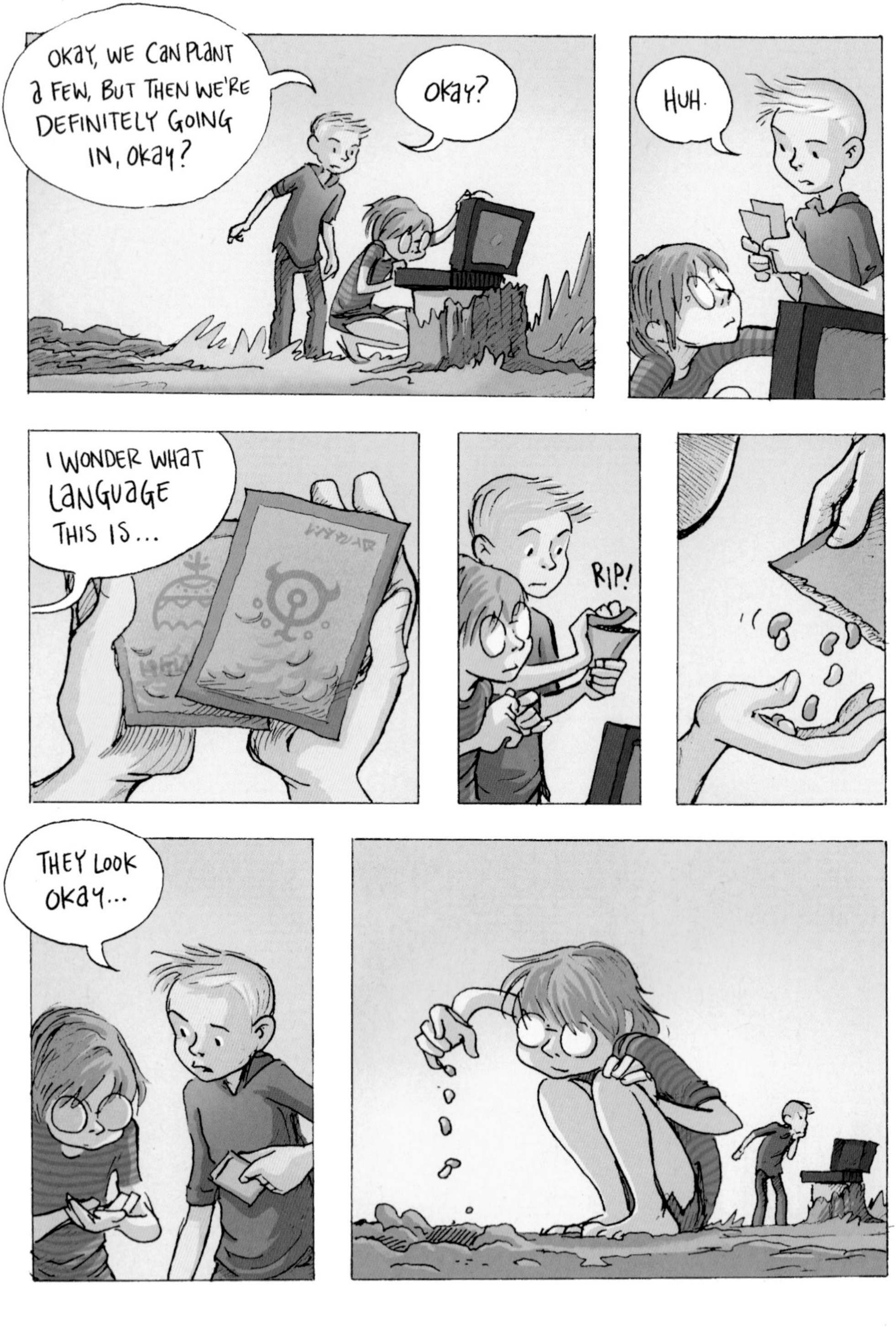
OKAY, WE CAN PLANT A FEW, BUT THEN WE'RE DEFINITELY GOING IN, OKAY?
OKAY?
HUH.
I WONDER WHAT LANGUAGE THIS IS...
RIP!
THEY LOOK OKAY...

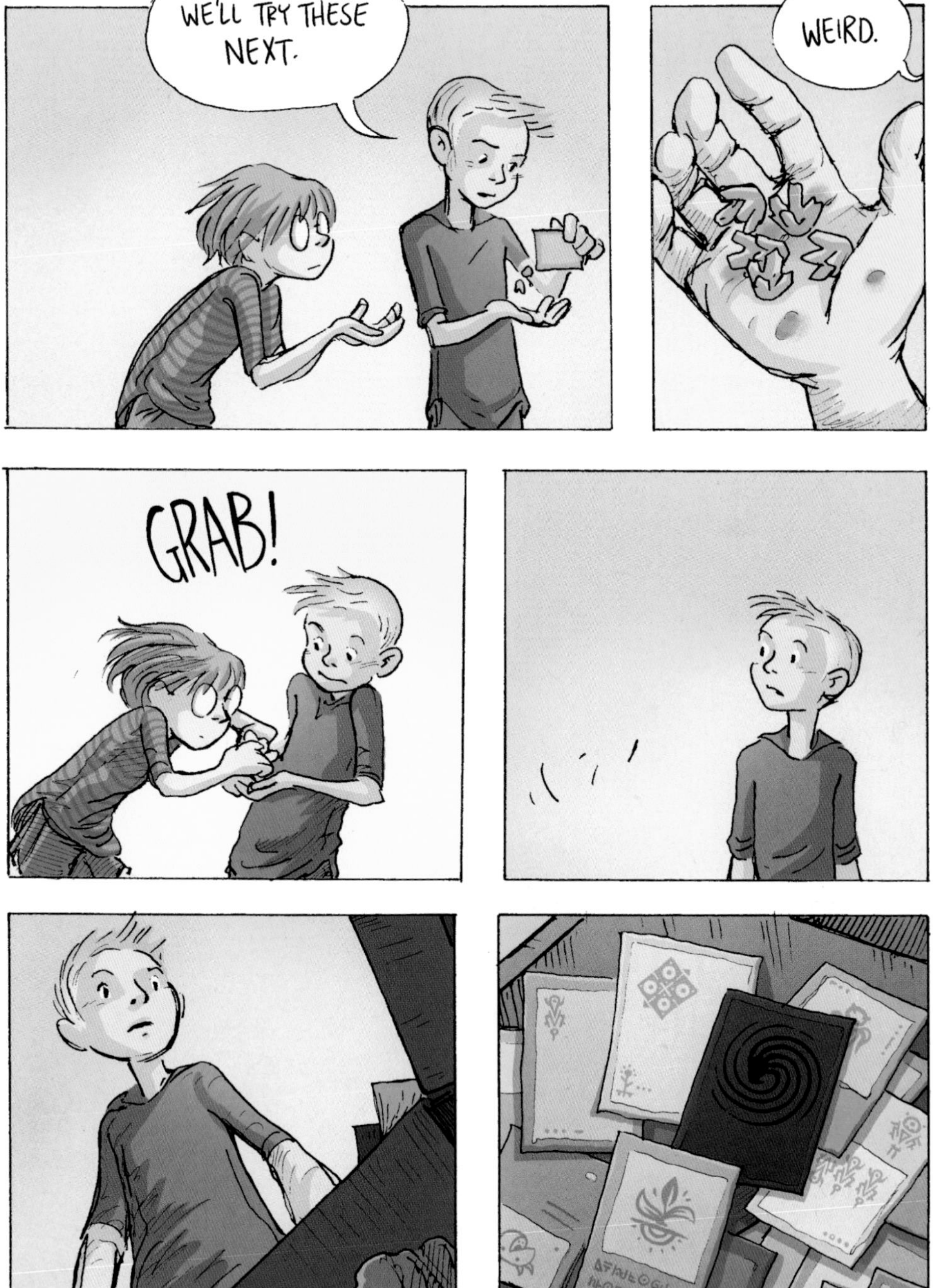
WE'LL TRY THESE NEXT.
WEIRD.
GRAB!

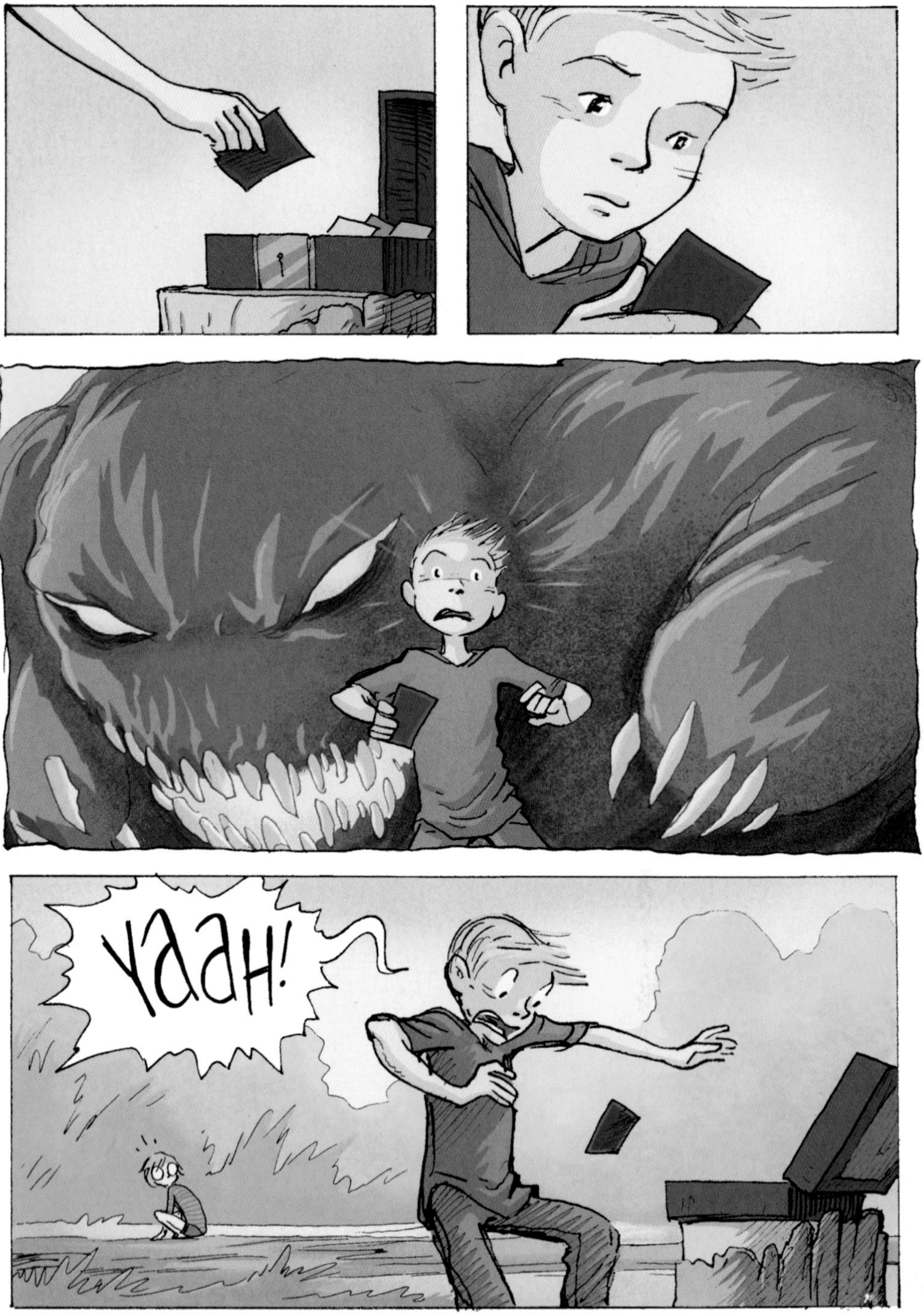
YAAH!

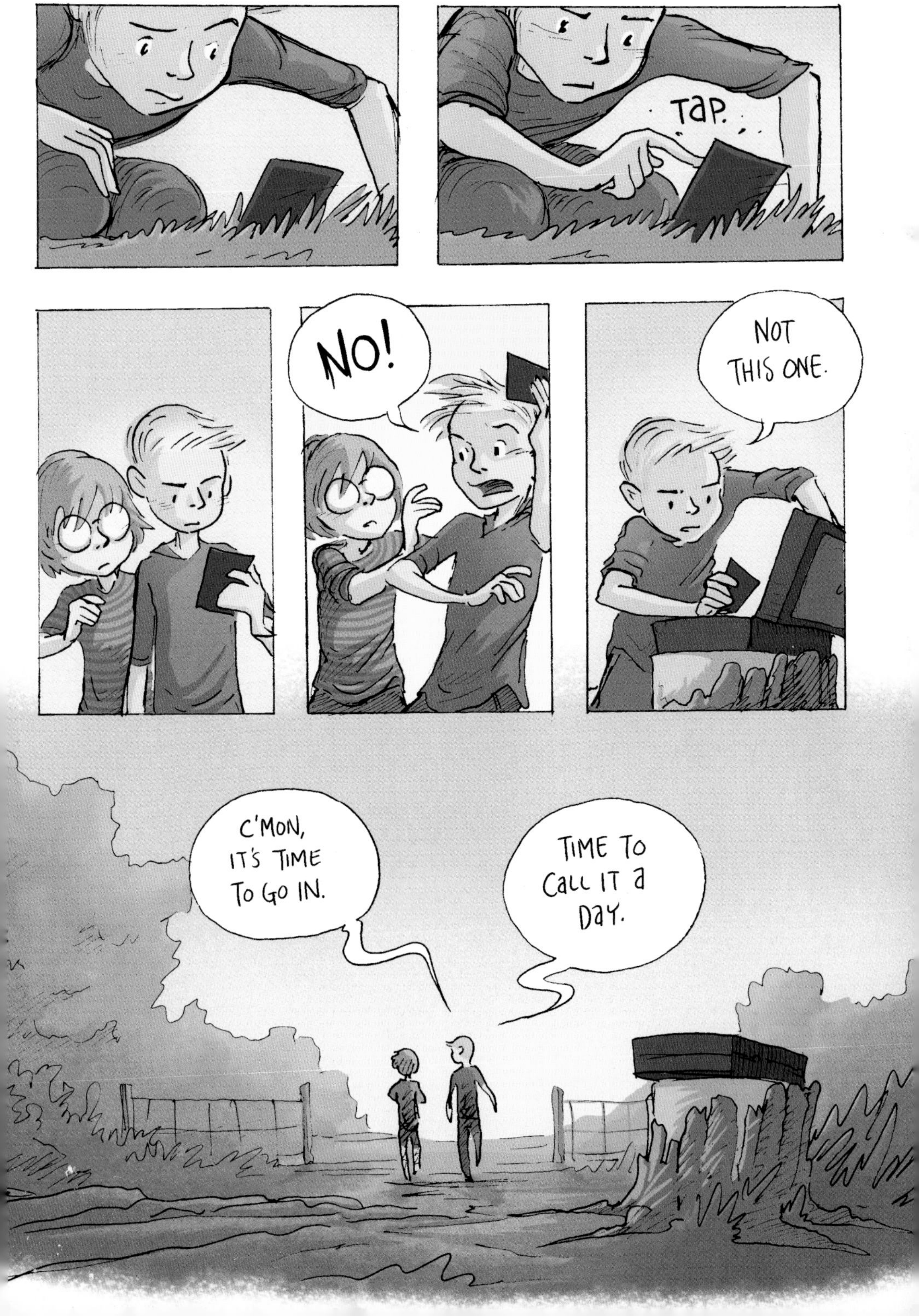
TAP.
NO!
NOT THIS ONE.
C'MON, IT'S TIME TO GO IN.
TIME TO CALL IT A DAY.

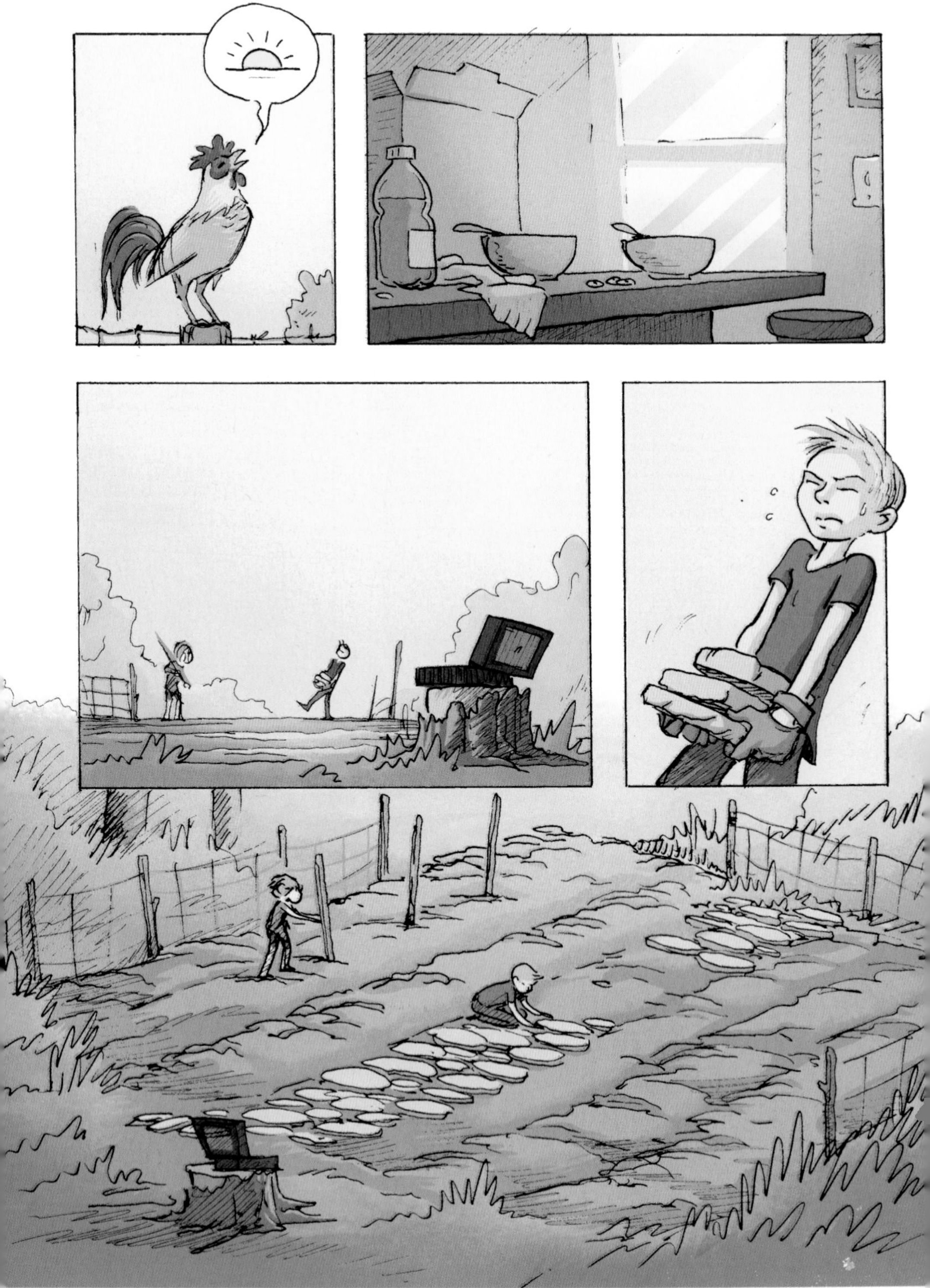

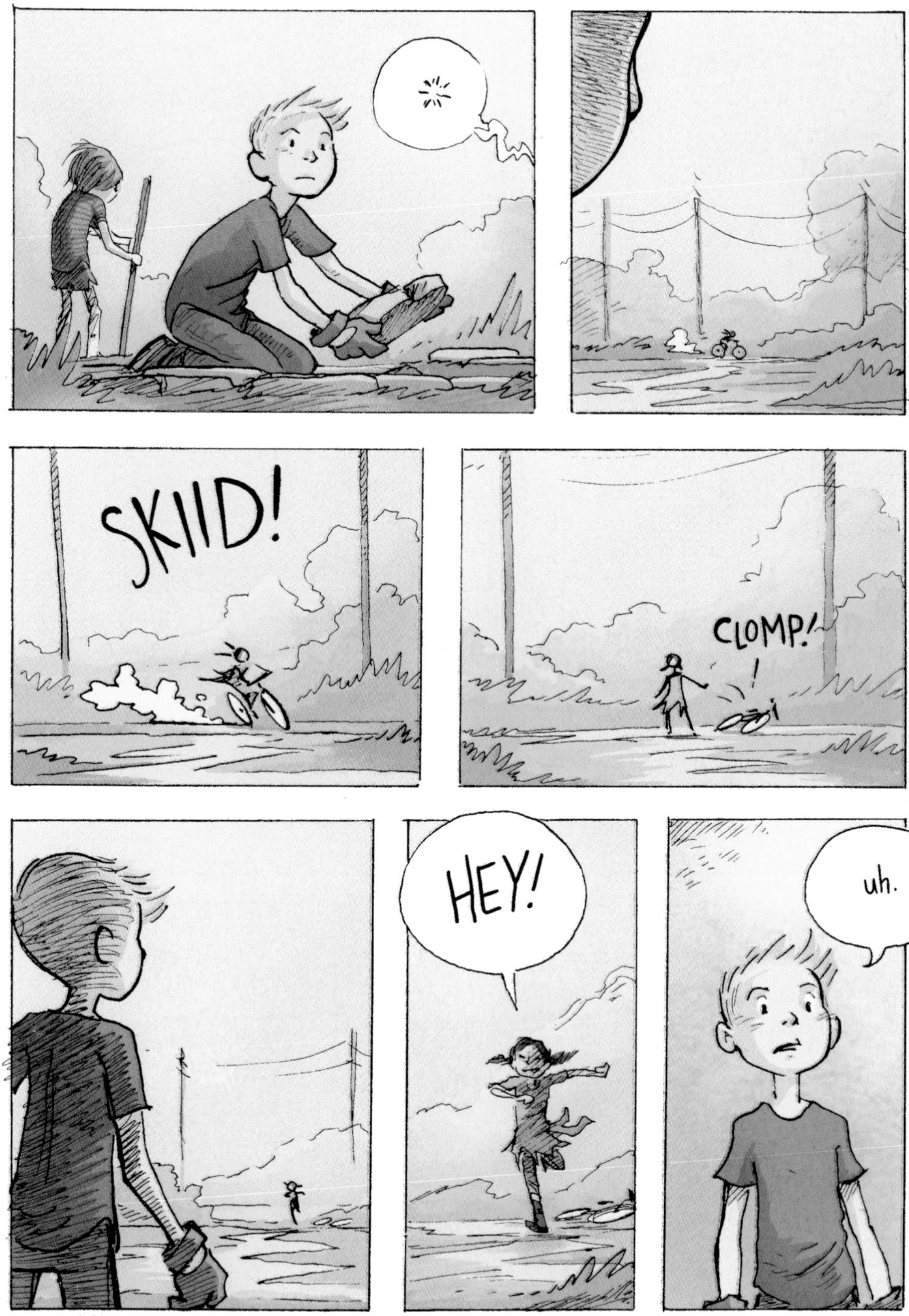
SKIID!
CLOMP!
HEY!
uh.

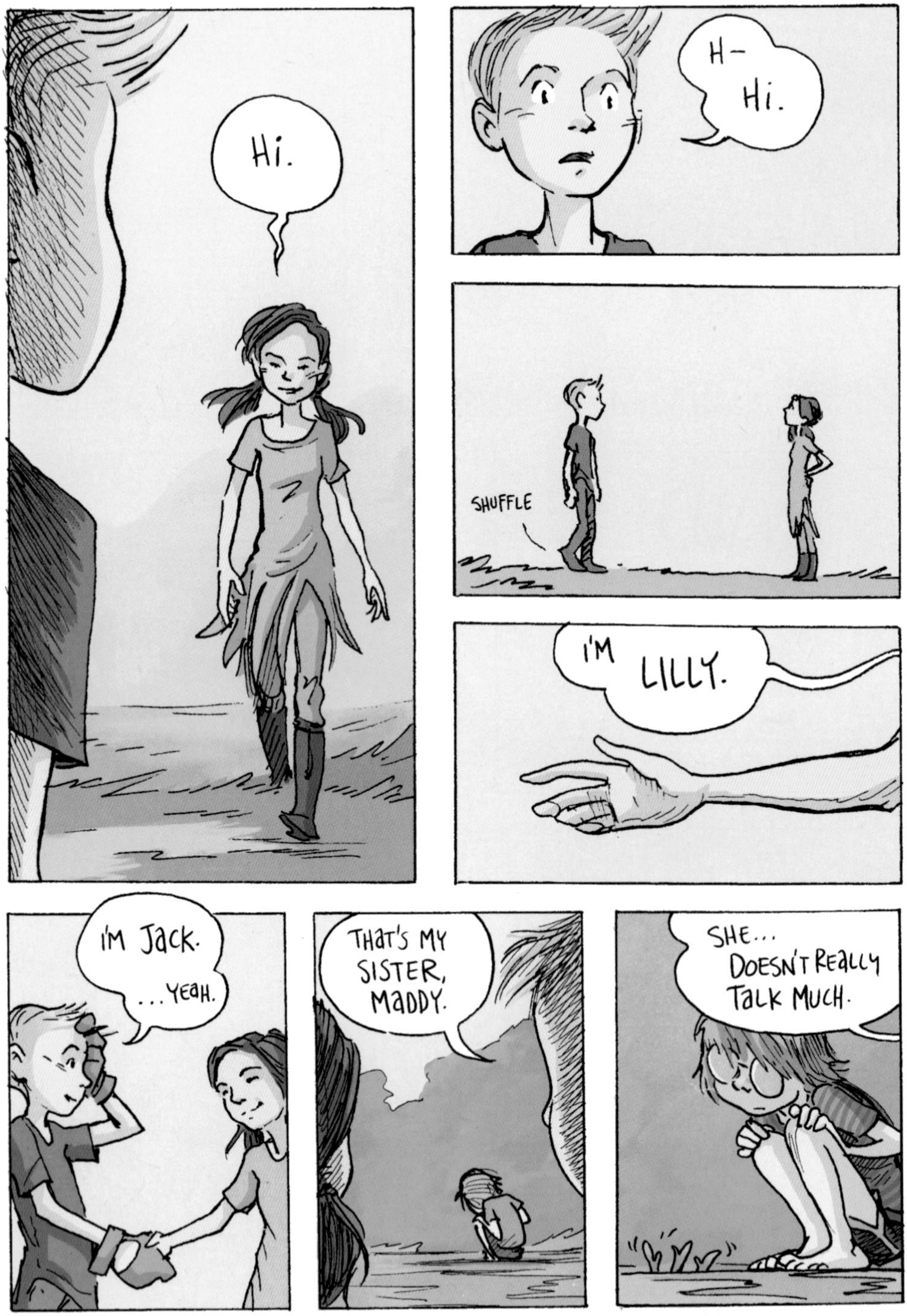
Hi.
H–
Hi.
SHUFFLE
I'M
LILLY.
I'M JACK.
...YEAH.
THAT'S MY
SISTER,
MADDY.
SHE...
DOESN'T REALLY
TALK MUCH.

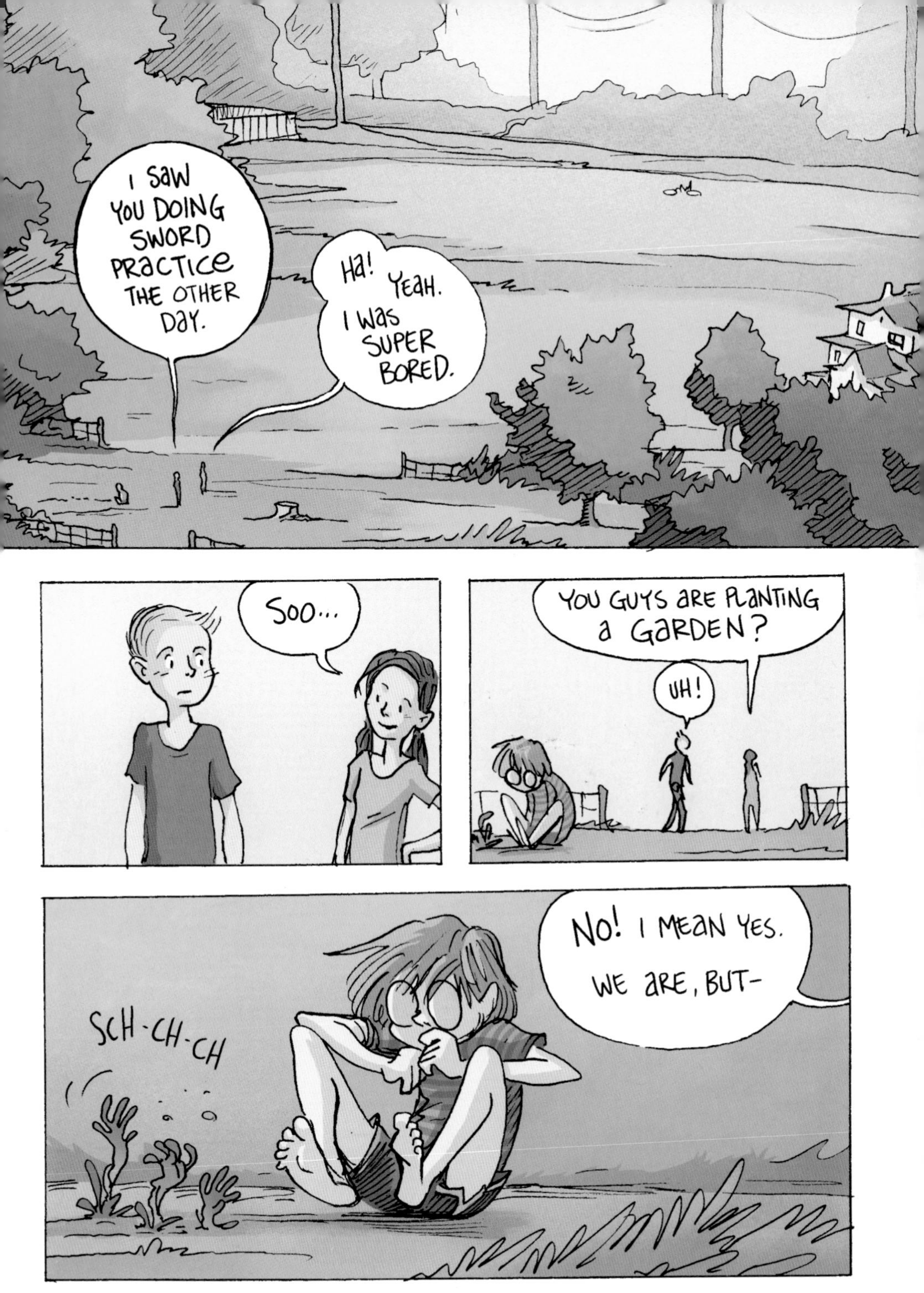

I SAW YOU DOING SWORD PRACTICE THE OTHER DAY.
HA! YEAH. I WAS SUPER BORED.
SOO...
YOU GUYS ARE PLANTING A GARDEN?
UH!
NO! I MEAN YES. WE ARE, BUT-
SCH-CH-CH

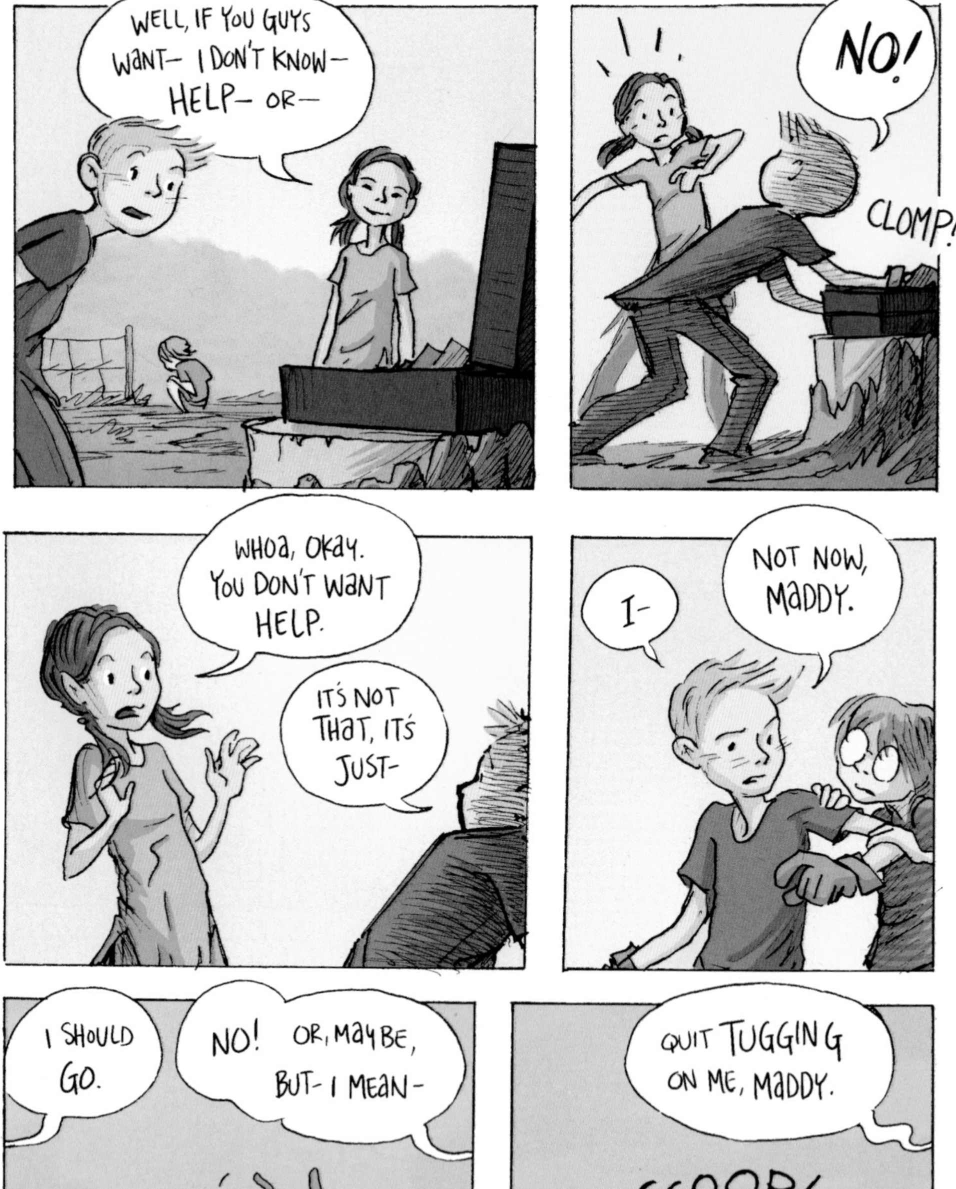
WELL, IF YOU GUYS WANT— I DON'T KNOW— HELP— OR—
NO!
CLOMP!
WHOA, OKAY. YOU DON'T WANT HELP.
IT'S NOT THAT, IT'S JUST-
I-
NOT NOW, MADDY.
I SHOULD GO.
NO! OR, MAYBE, BUT- I MEAN-
QUIT TUGGING ON ME, MADDY.
SCOOP!

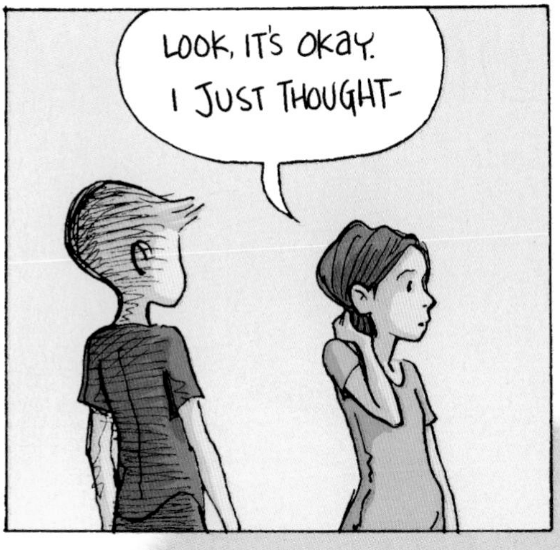
LOOK, IT'S OKAY. I JUST THOUGHT-

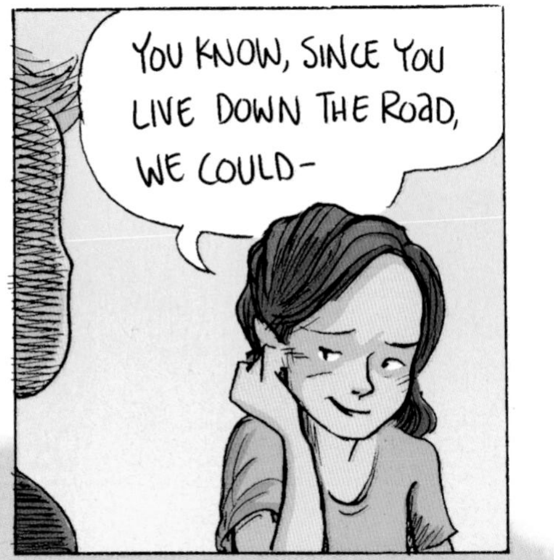
YOU KNOW, SINCE YOU LIVE DOWN THE ROAD, WE COULD-

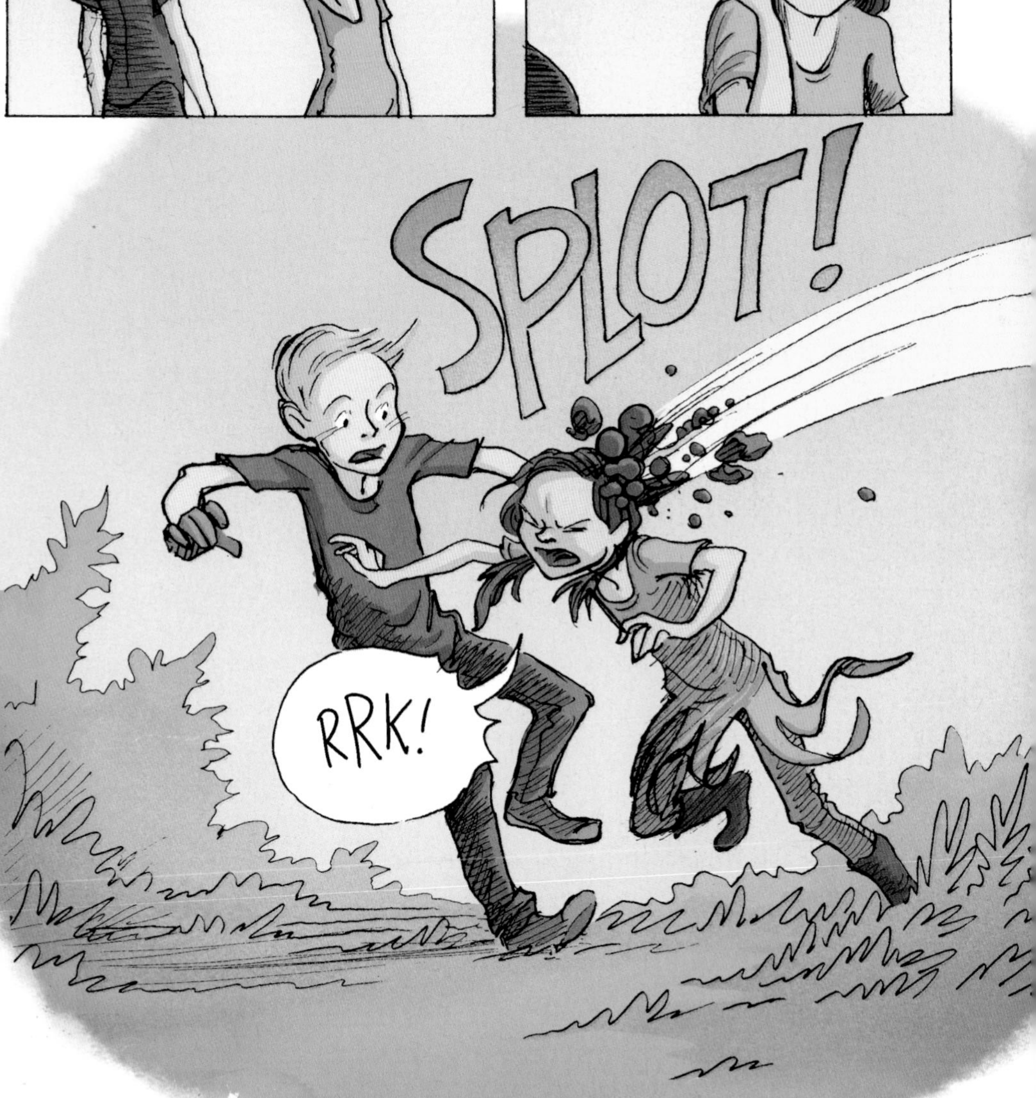
SPLOT!
RRK!

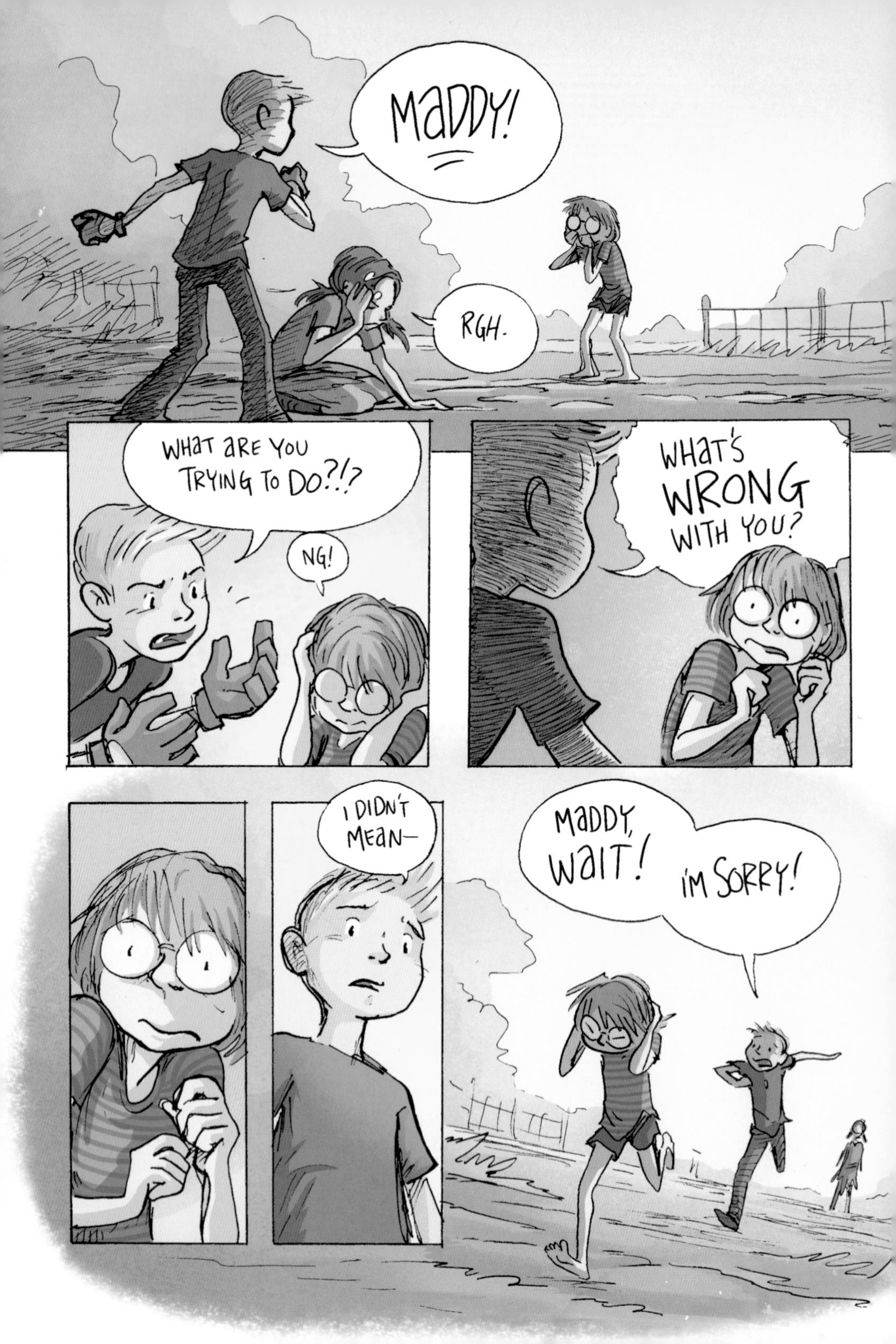
MADDY!
RGH.
WHAT ARE YOU TRYING TO DO?!?
NG!
WHAT'S WRONG WITH YOU?
I DIDN'T MEAN—
MADDY, WAIT!
I'M SORRY!

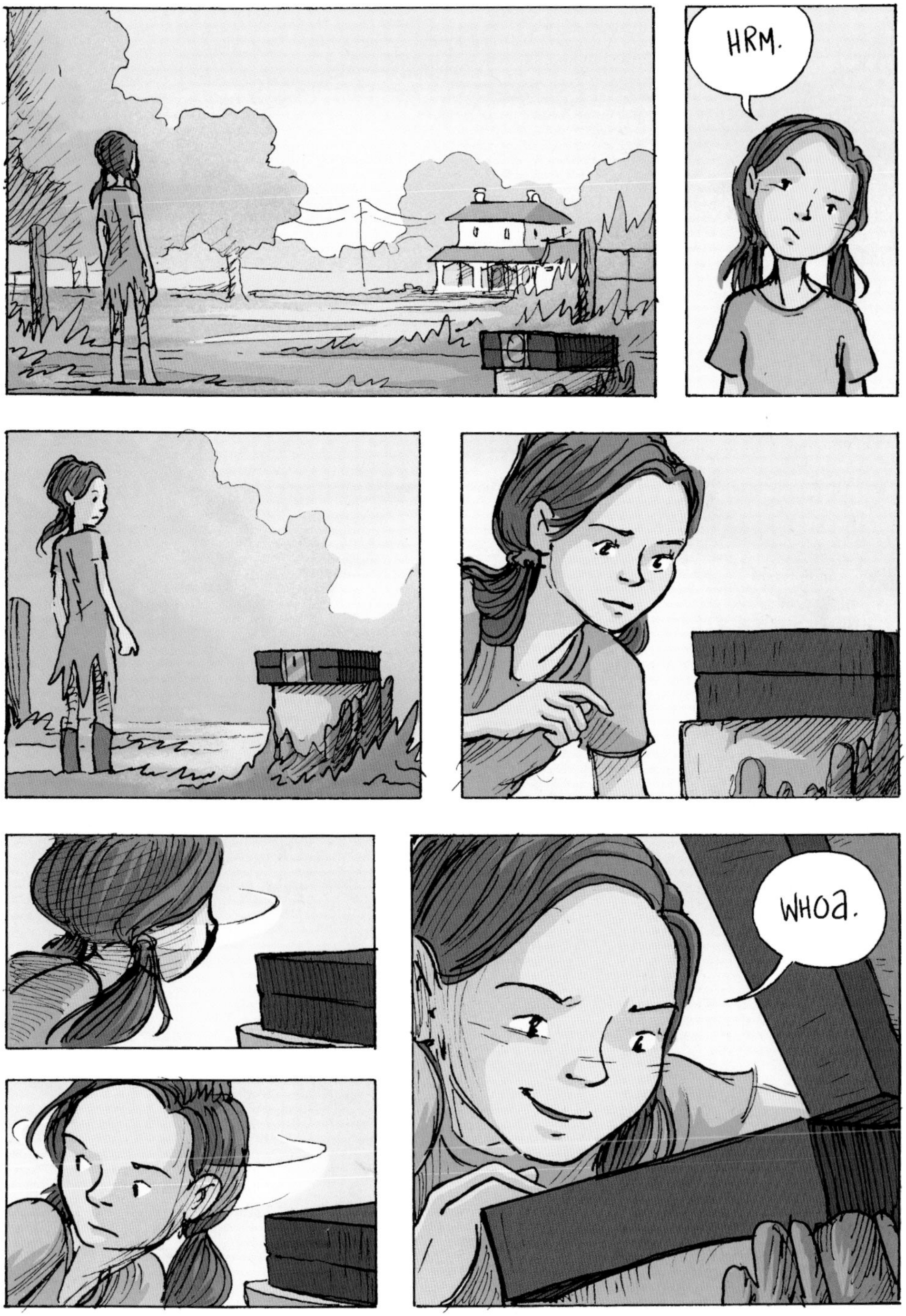
HRM.
WHOA.

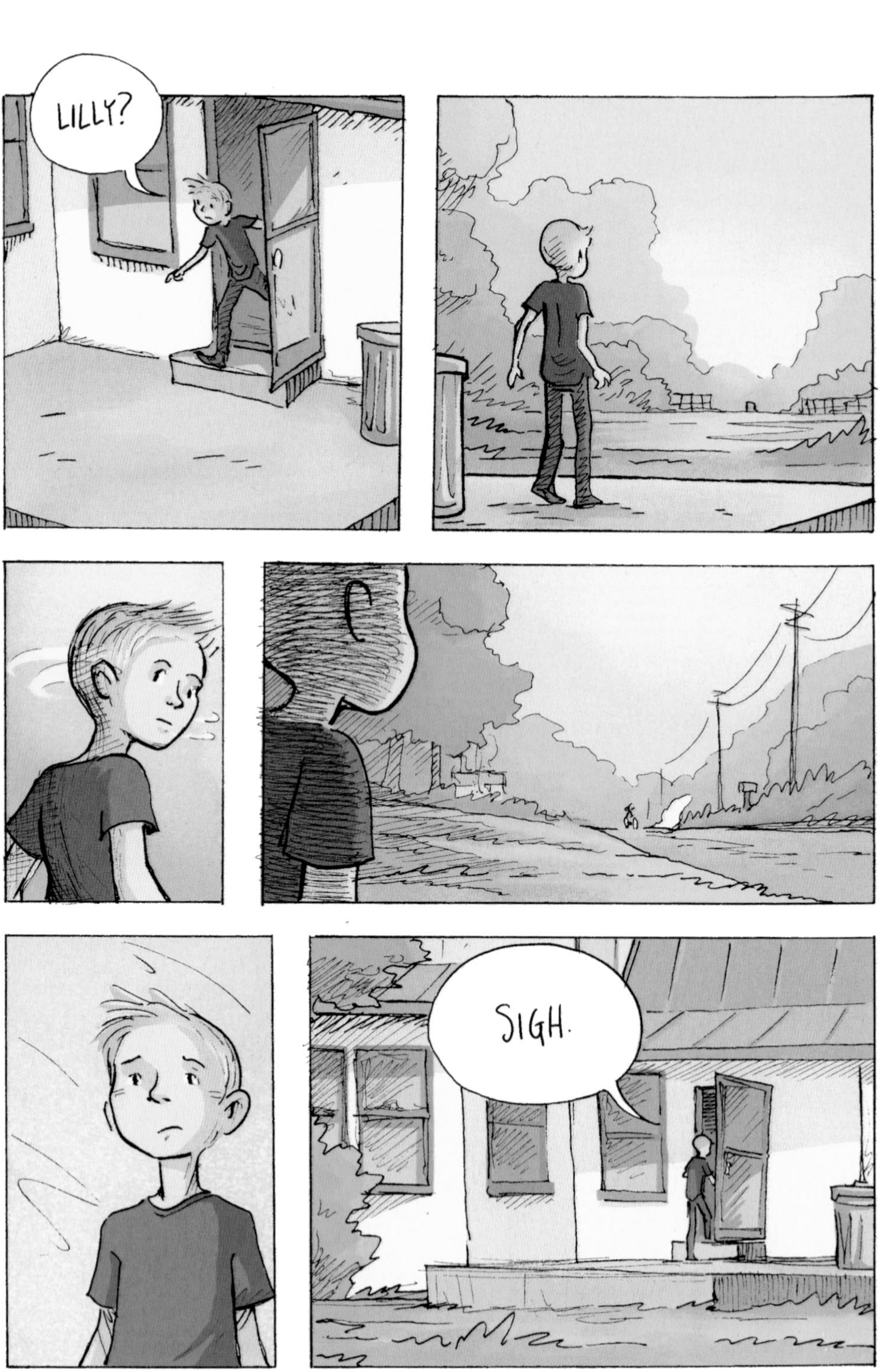
LILLY?
SIGH.

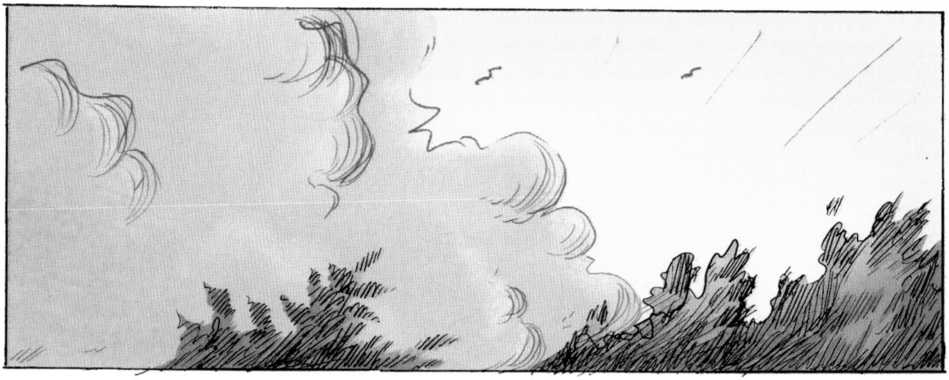

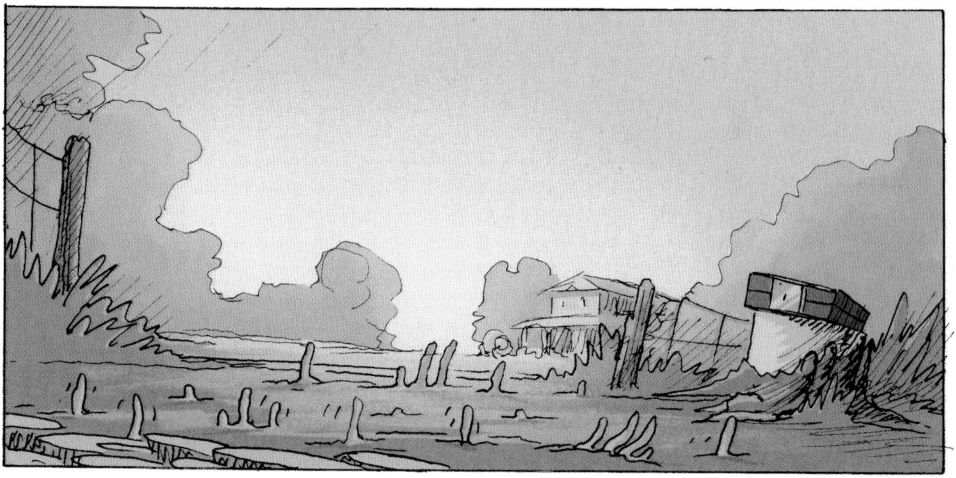

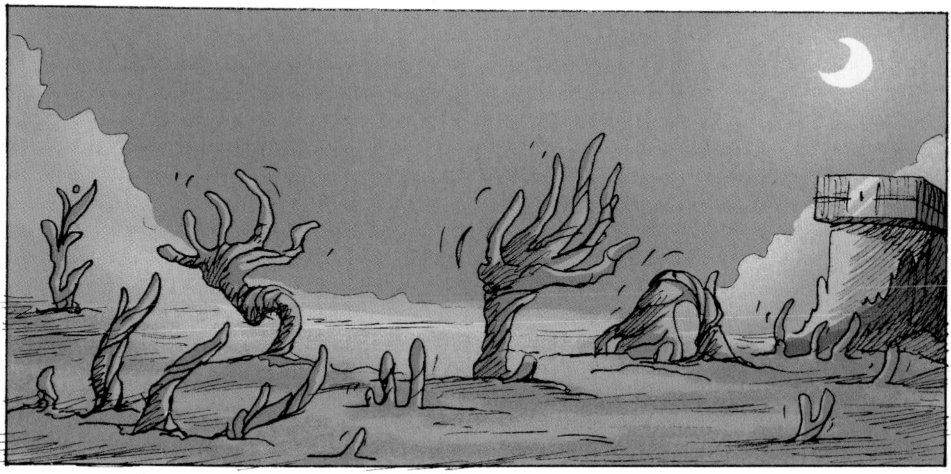

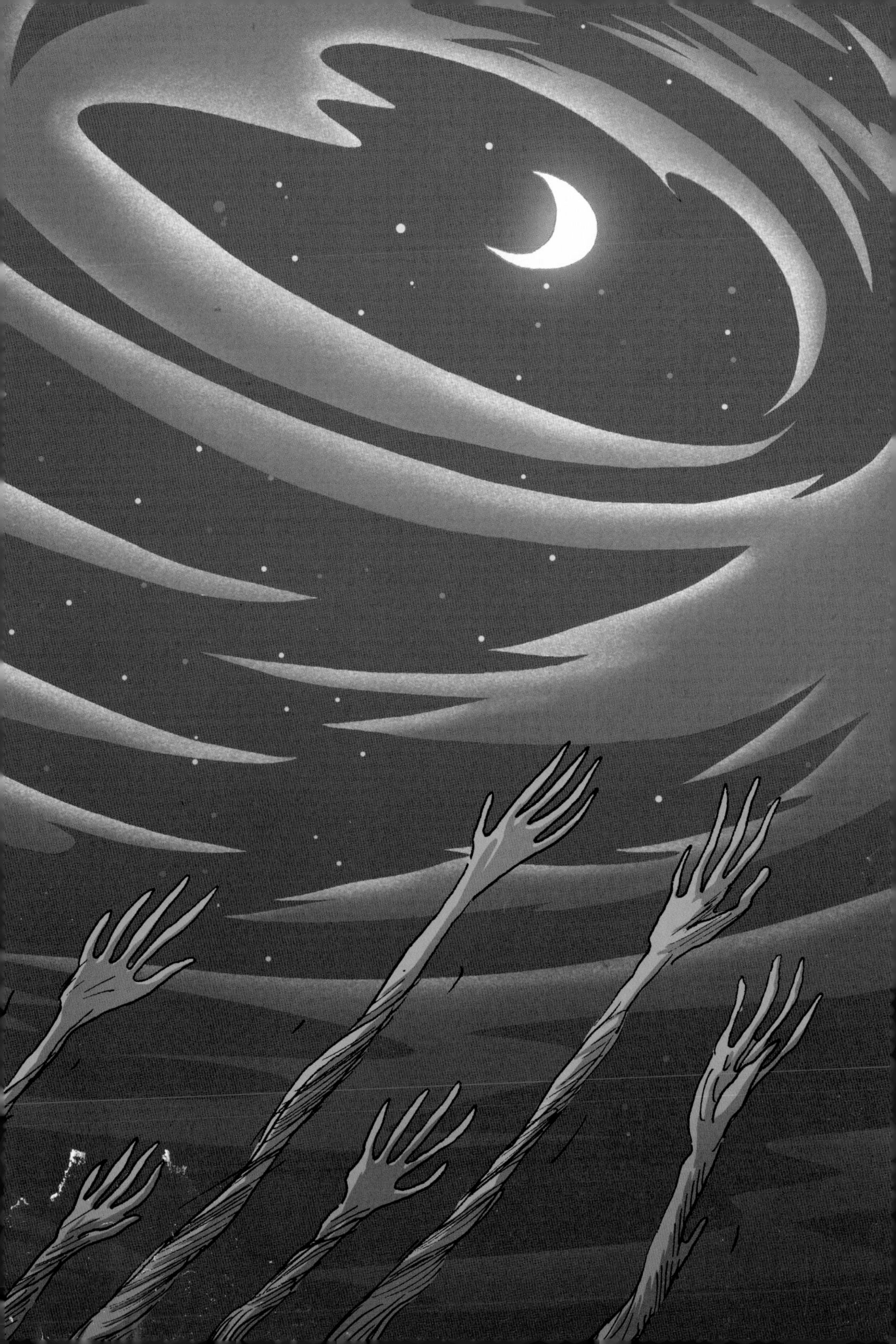

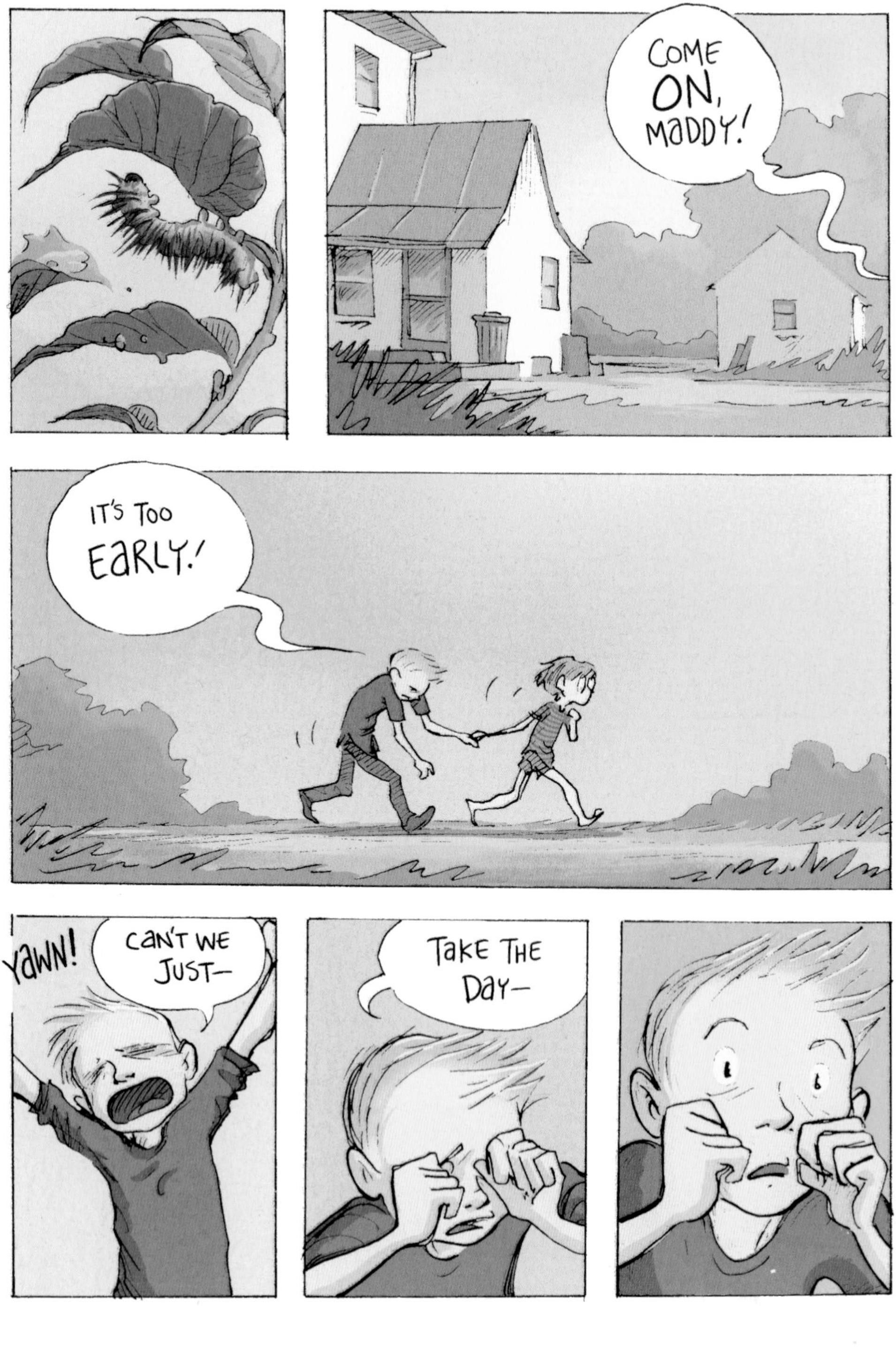
COME ON, MADDY!
IT'S TOO EARLY!
YAWN!
CAN'T WE JUST—
TAKE THE DAY—

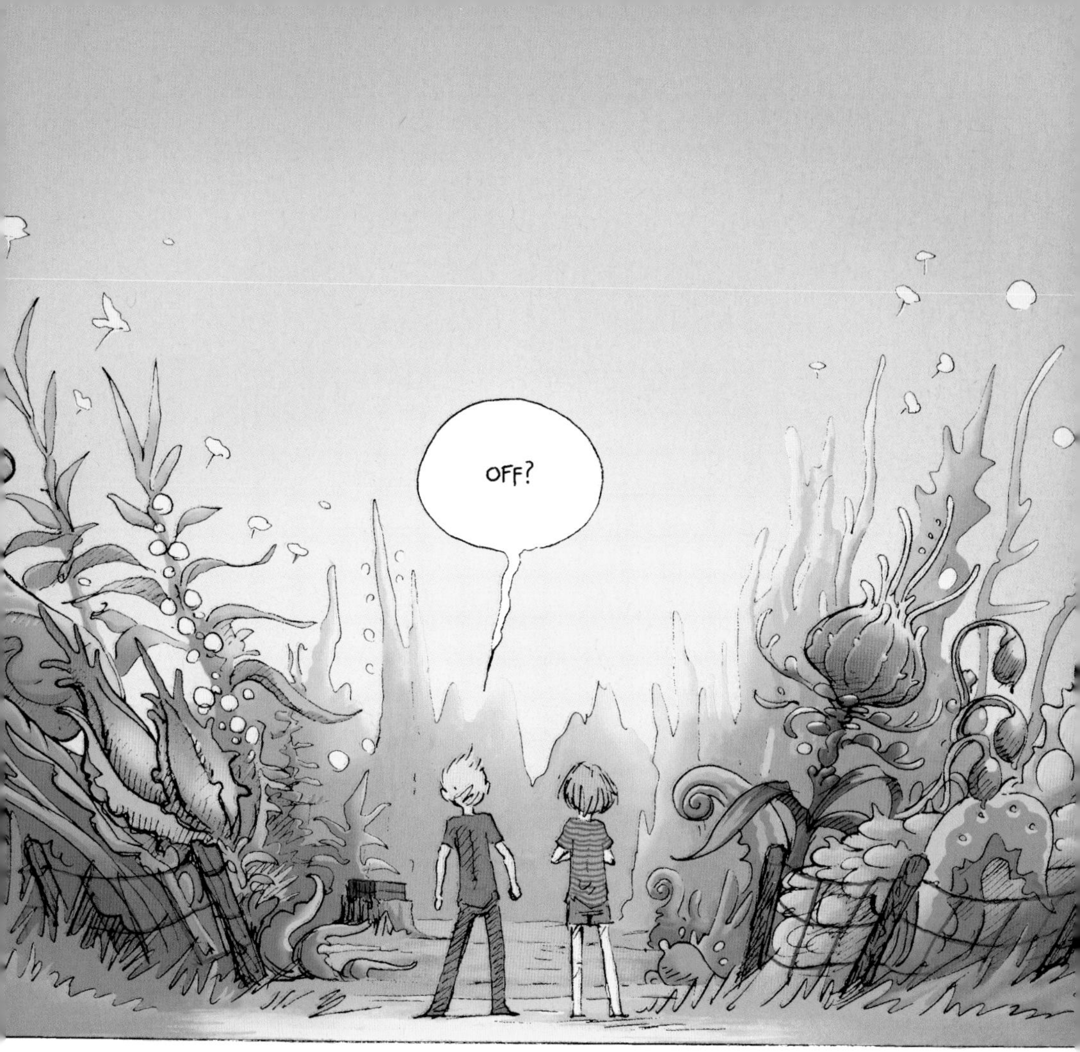
OFF?

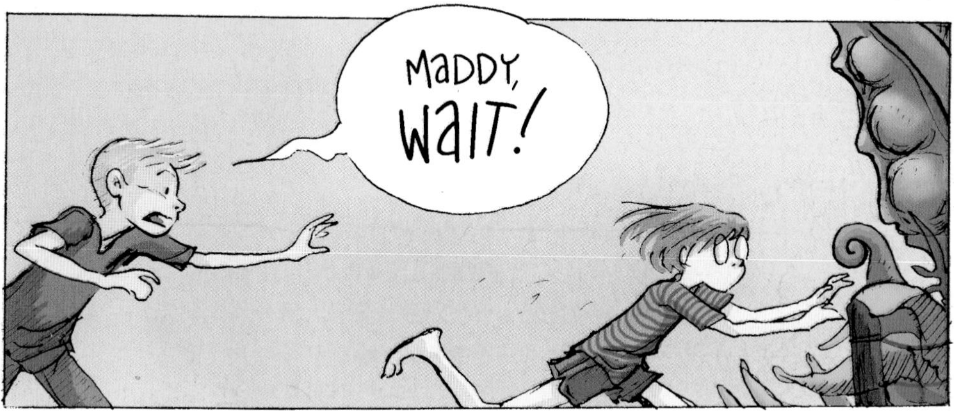
MADDY, WAIT!

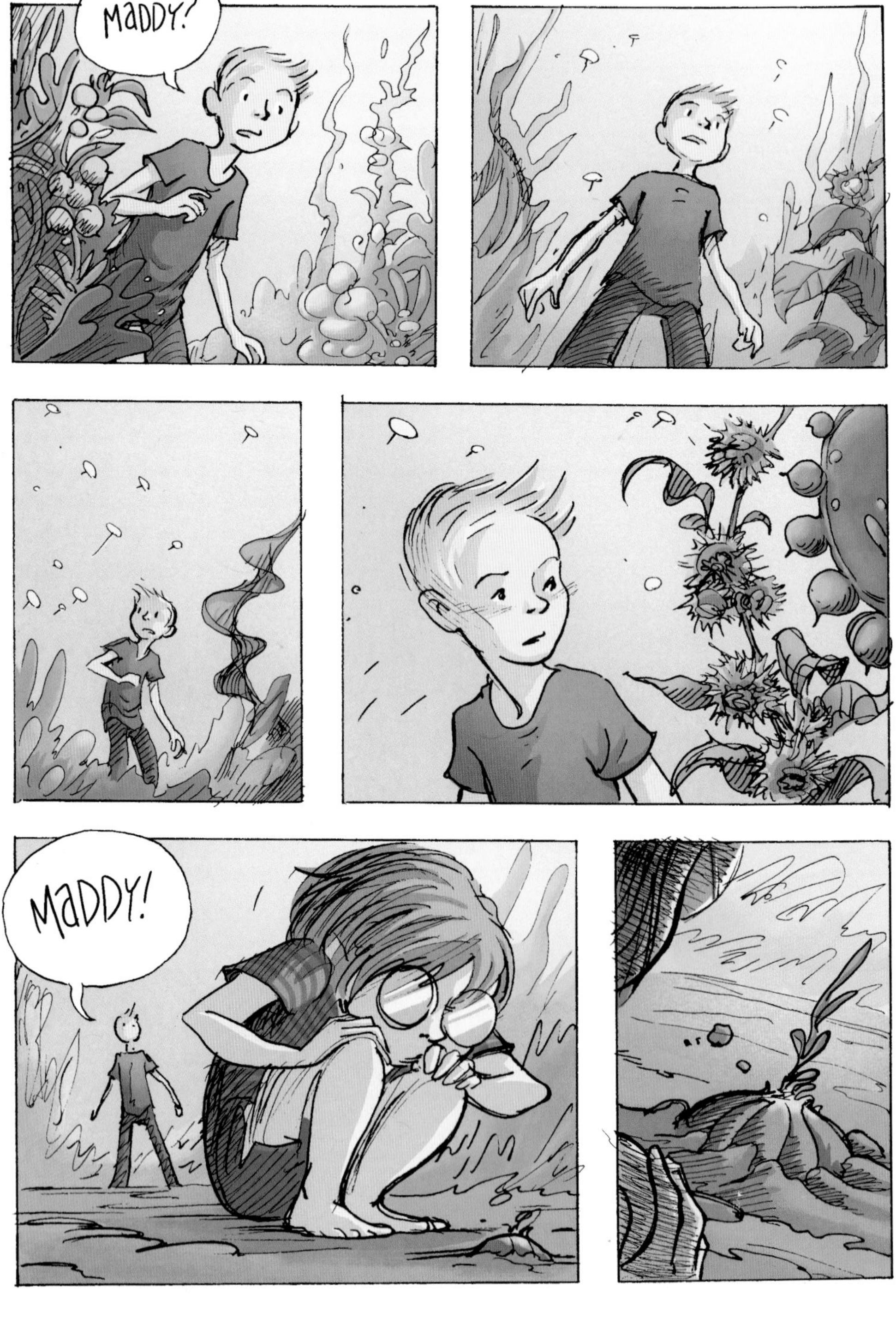
MADDY?
MADDY!

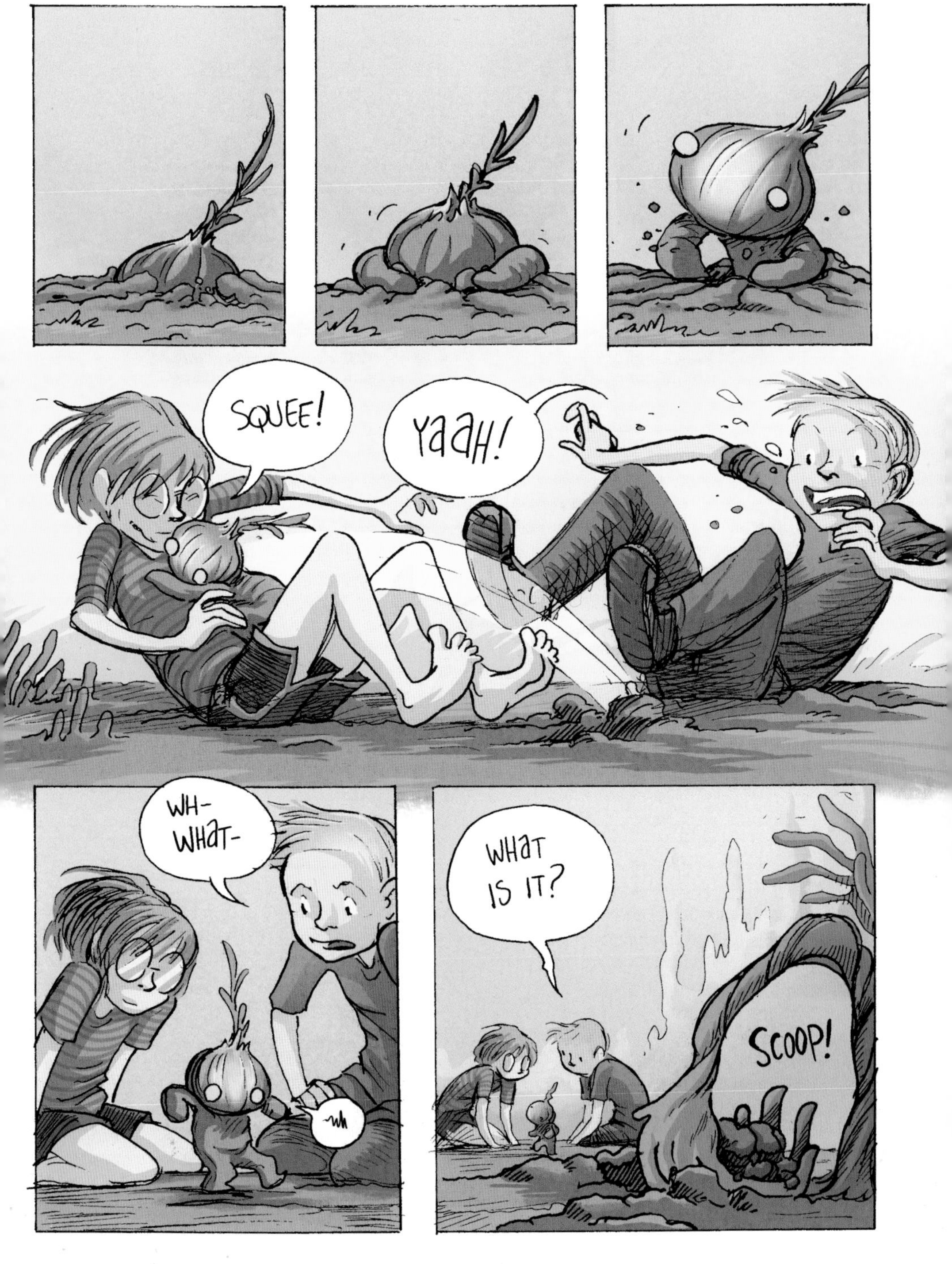
SQUEE!
YAAH!
WH-
WHAT-
~wh
WHAT
IS IT?
SCOOP!

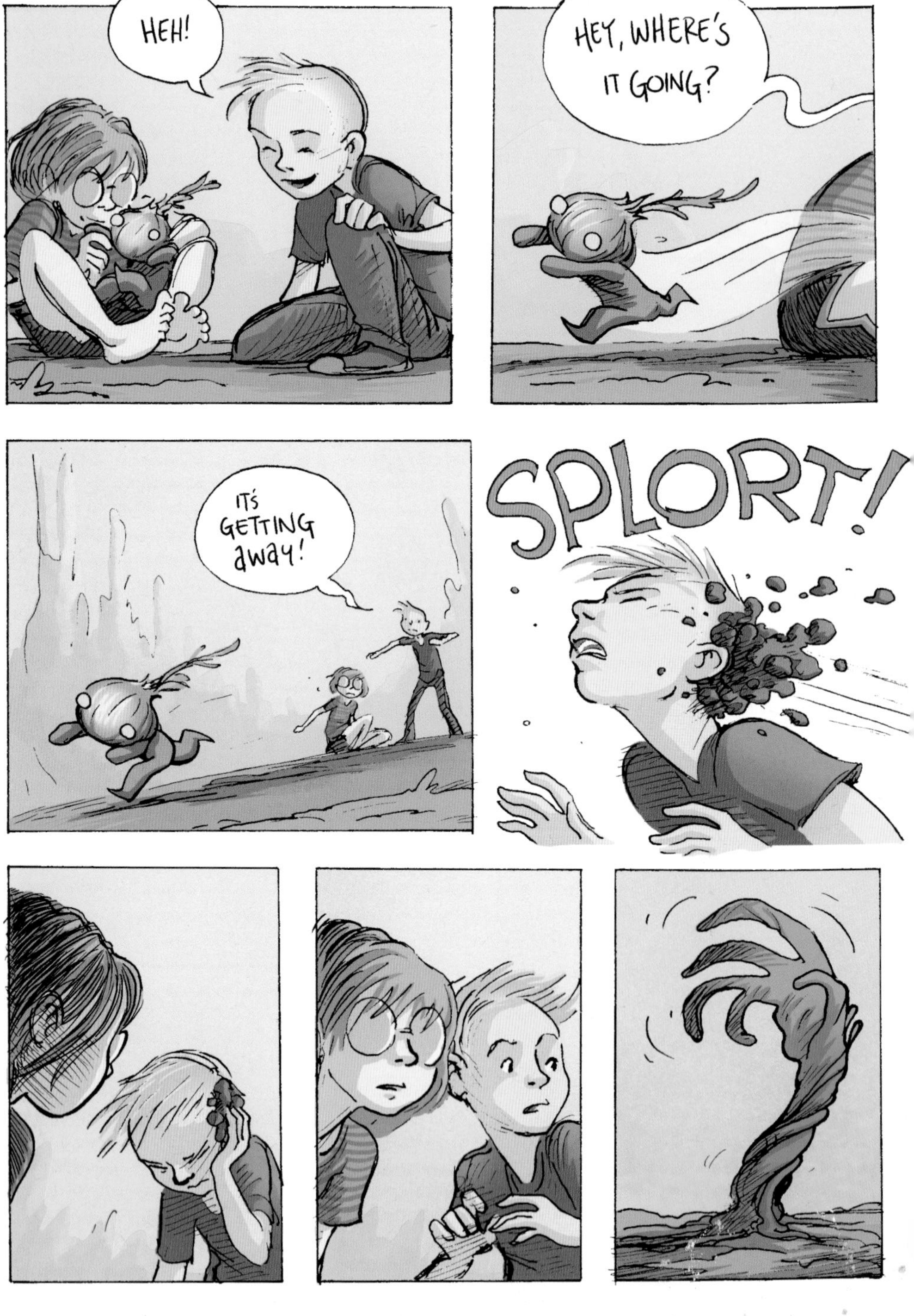
HEH!
HEY, WHERE'S IT GOING?
IT'S GETTING away!
SPLORT!

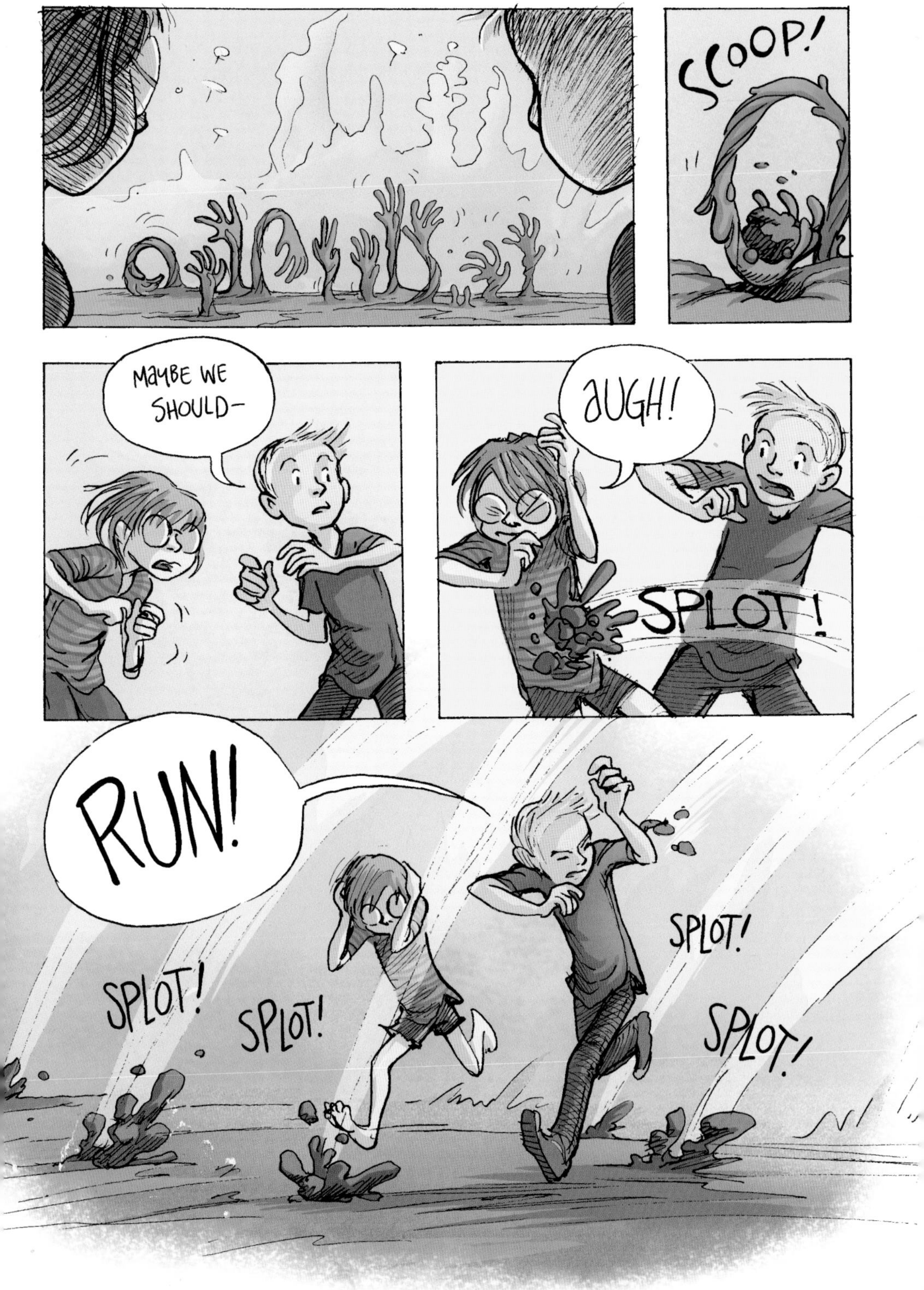
SCOOP!
MAYBE WE SHOULD-
AUGH!
SPLOT!
RUN!
SPLOT!
SPLOT!
SPLOT!
SPLOT!

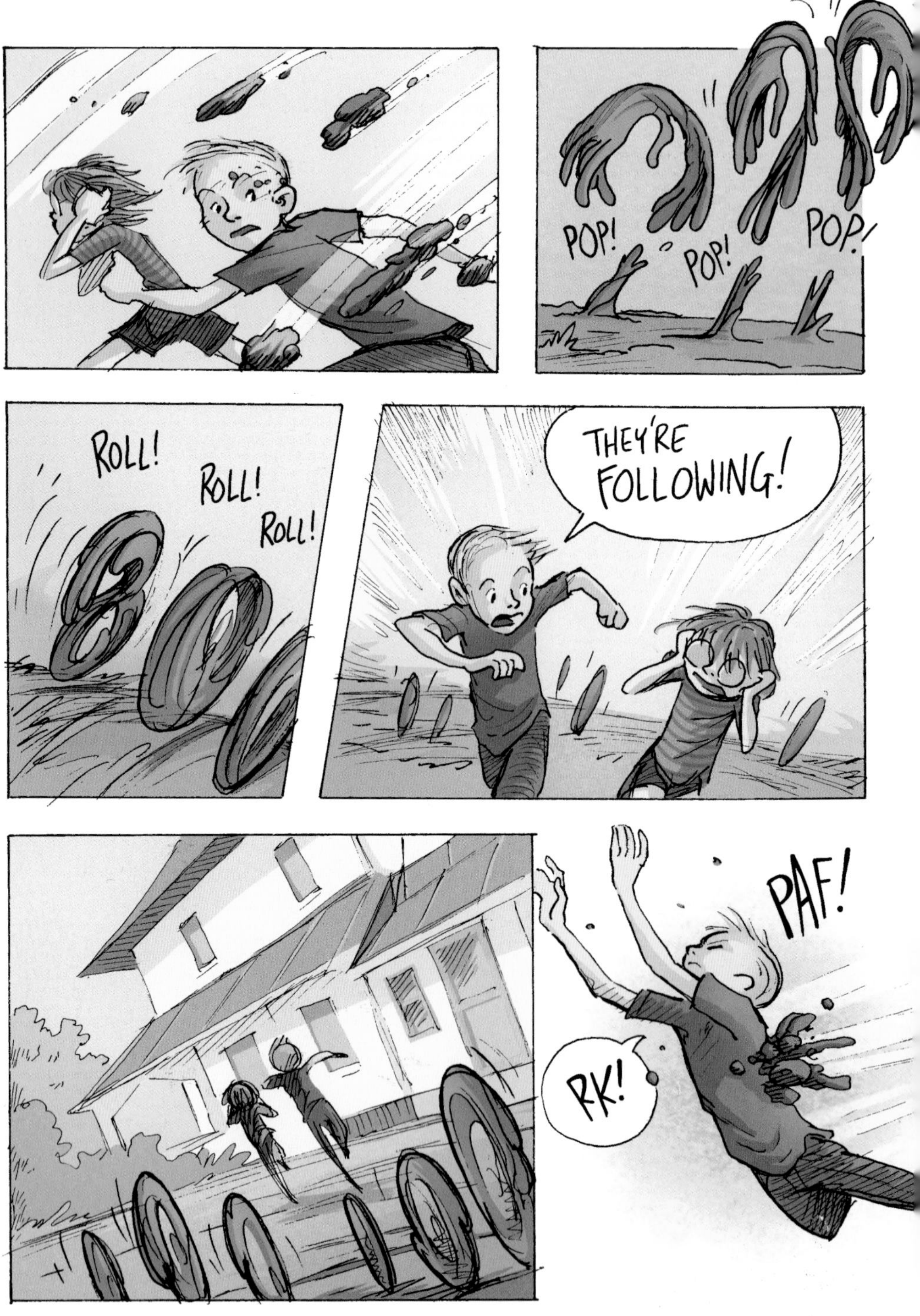
POP!
POP!
POP!
ROLL!
ROLL!
ROLL!
THEY'RE FOLLOWING!
PAF!
RK!

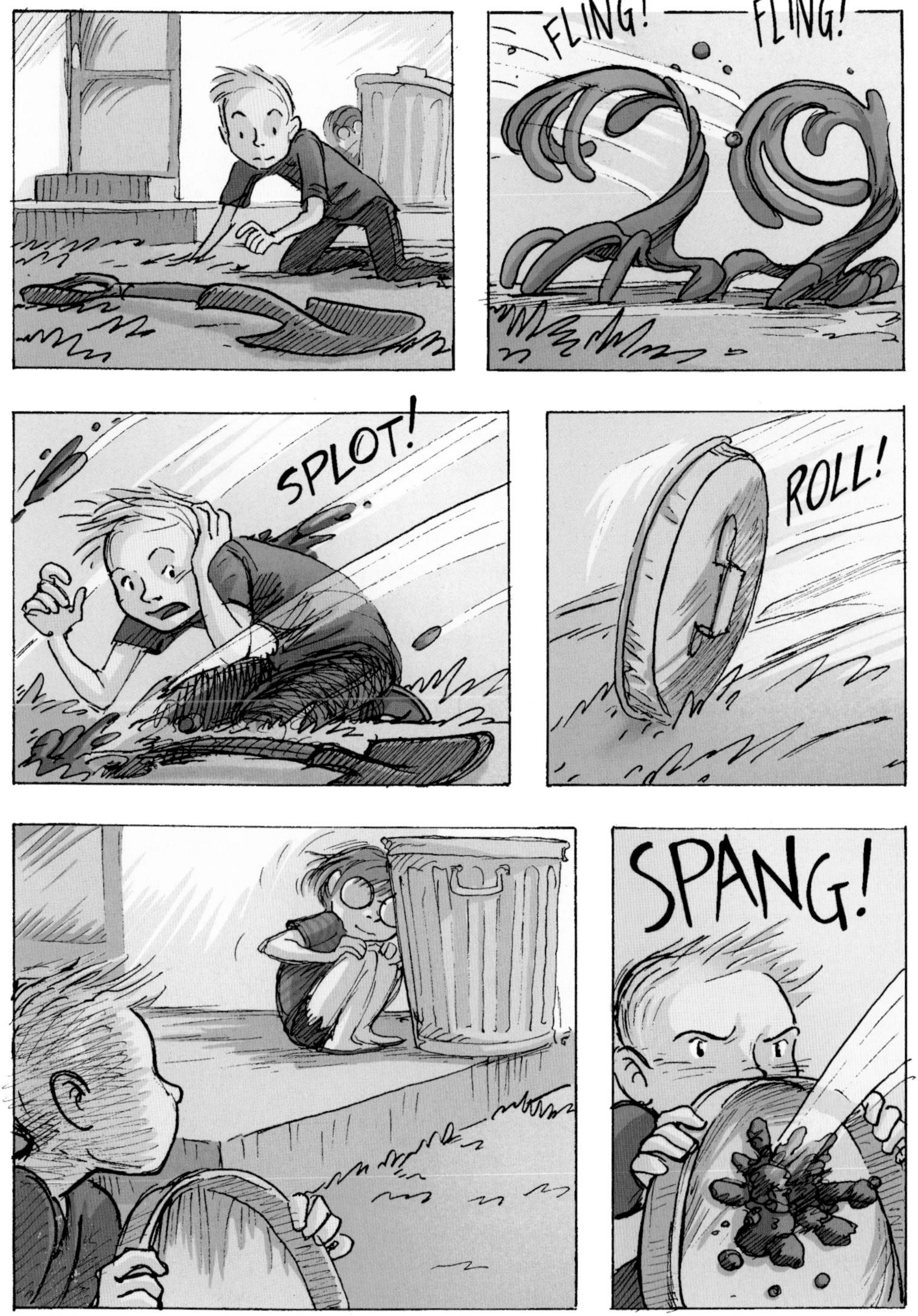
FLING!
FLING!
SPLOT!
ROLL!
SPANG!

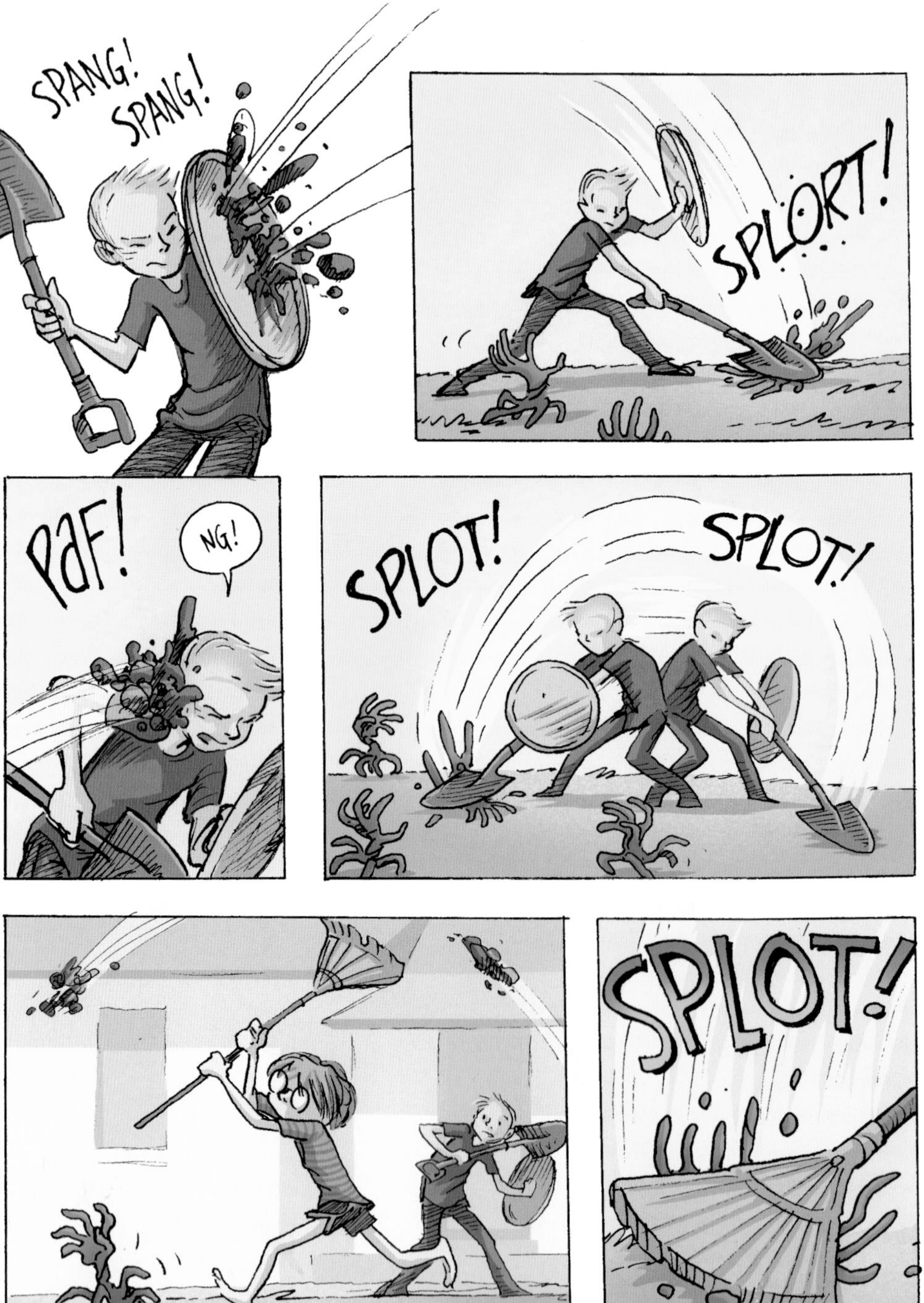
SPANG!
SPANG!
SPLORT!
PAF!
NG!
SPLOT!
SPLOT!
SPLOT!

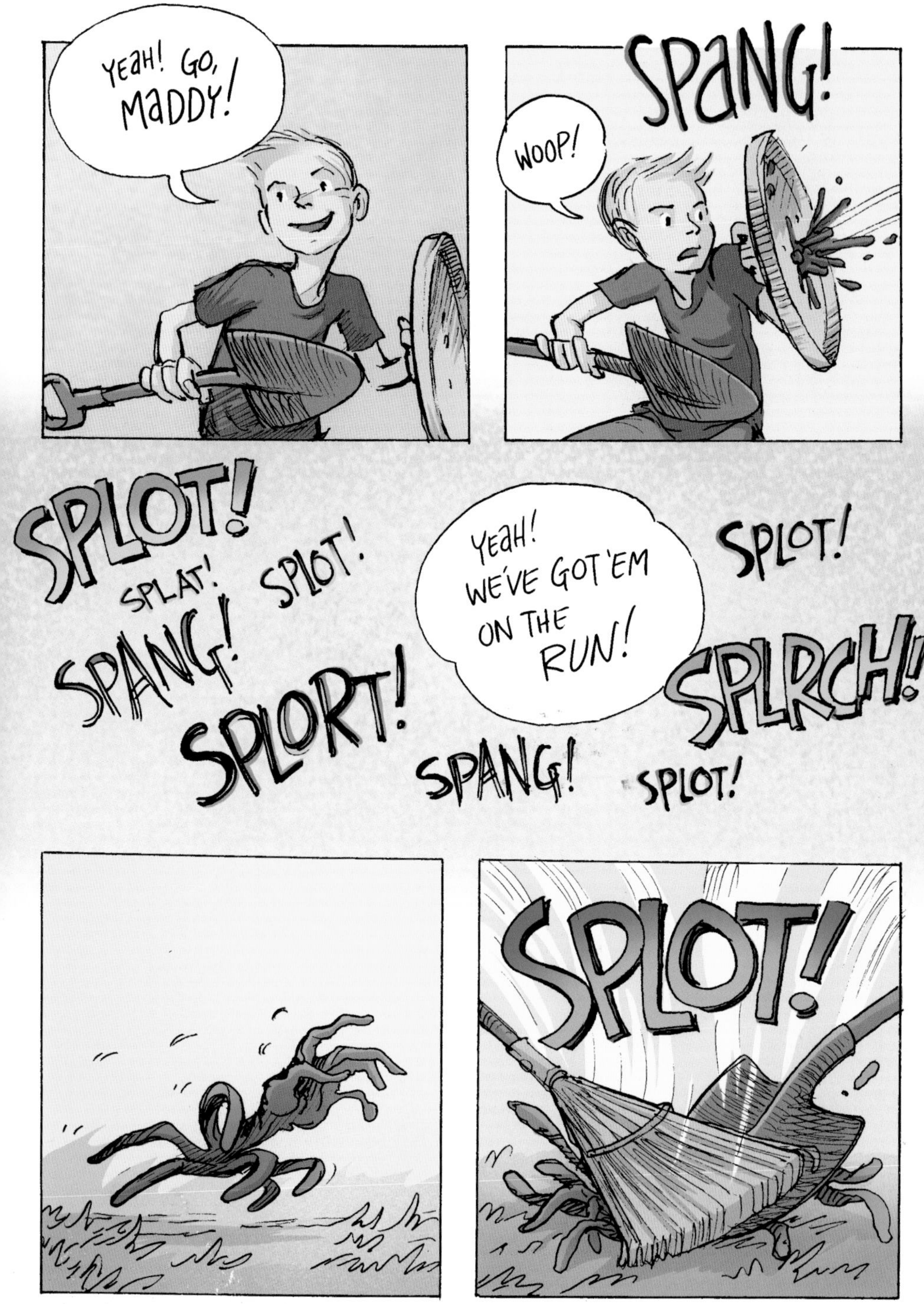
YEAH! GO, MADDY!
SPANG!
WOOP!
SPLOT!
SPLAT!
SPLOT!
SPANG!
SPLORT!
YEAH! WE'VE GOT 'EM ON THE RUN!
SPLOT!
SPLRCH!
SPANG!
SPLOT!
SPLOT!

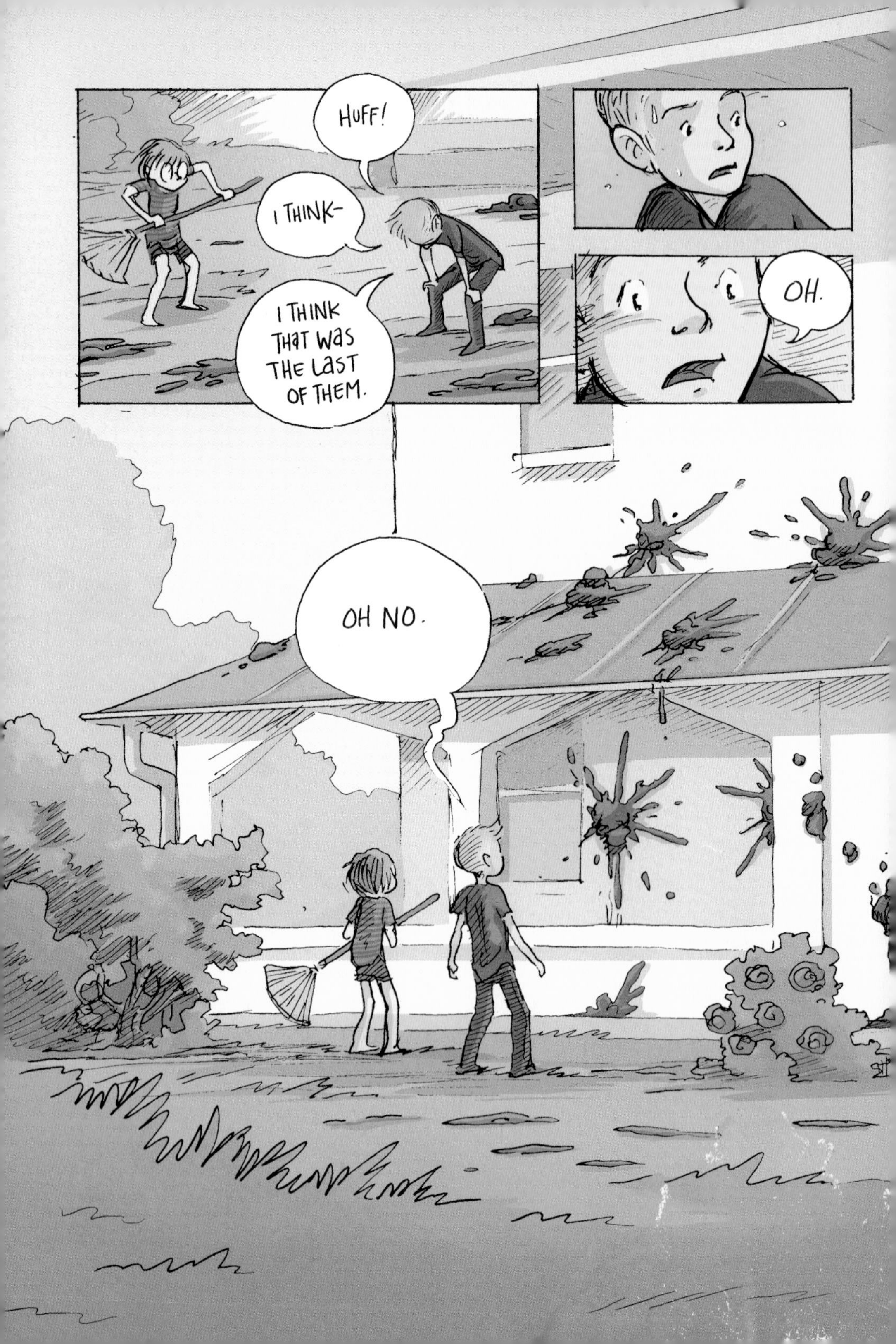
HUFF!
I THINK-
I THINK THAT WAS THE LAST OF THEM.
OH.
OH NO.

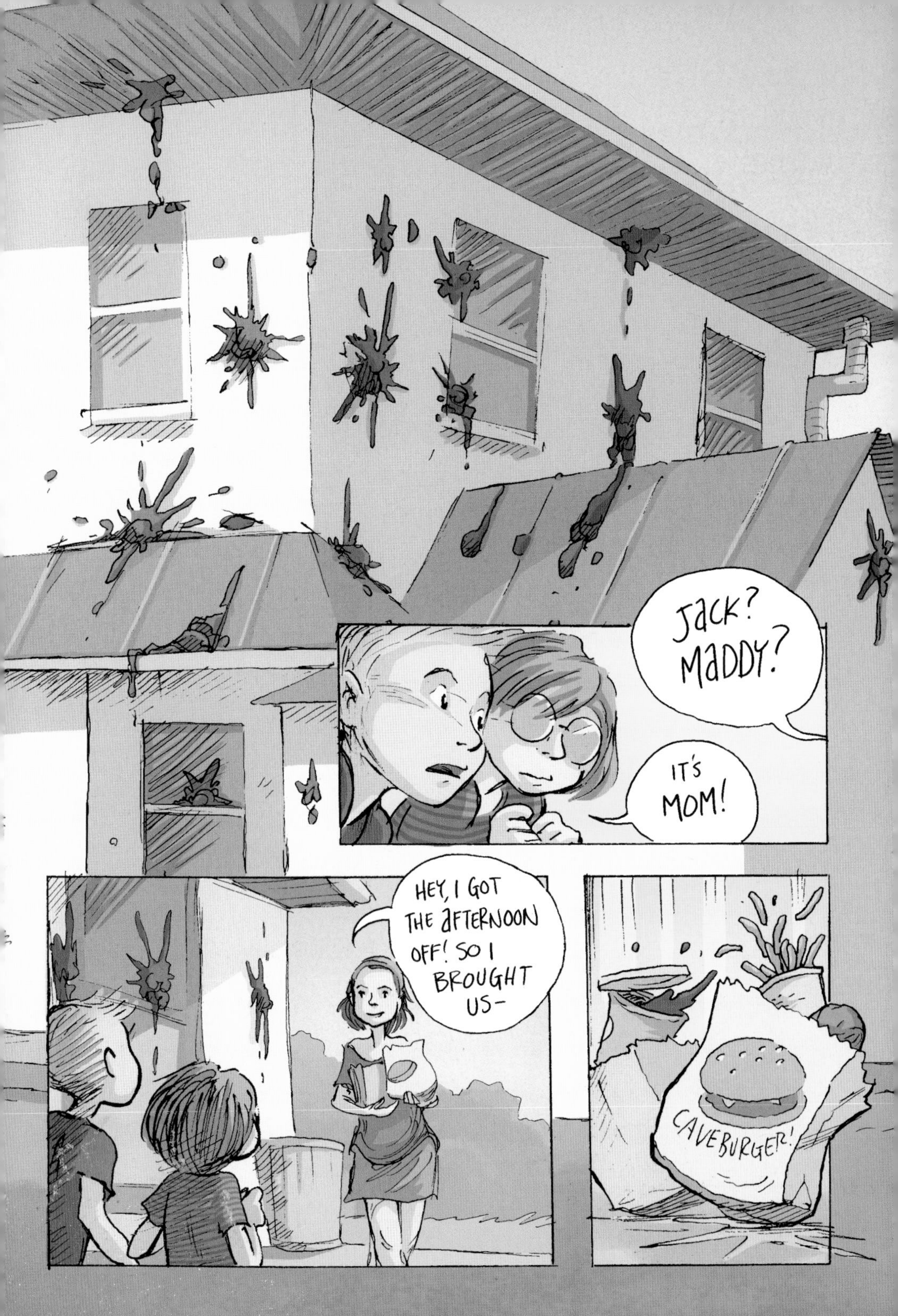
JACK? MADDY?
IT'S MOM!
HEY, I GOT THE AFTERNOON OFF! SO I BROUGHT US-
CAVEBURGER!

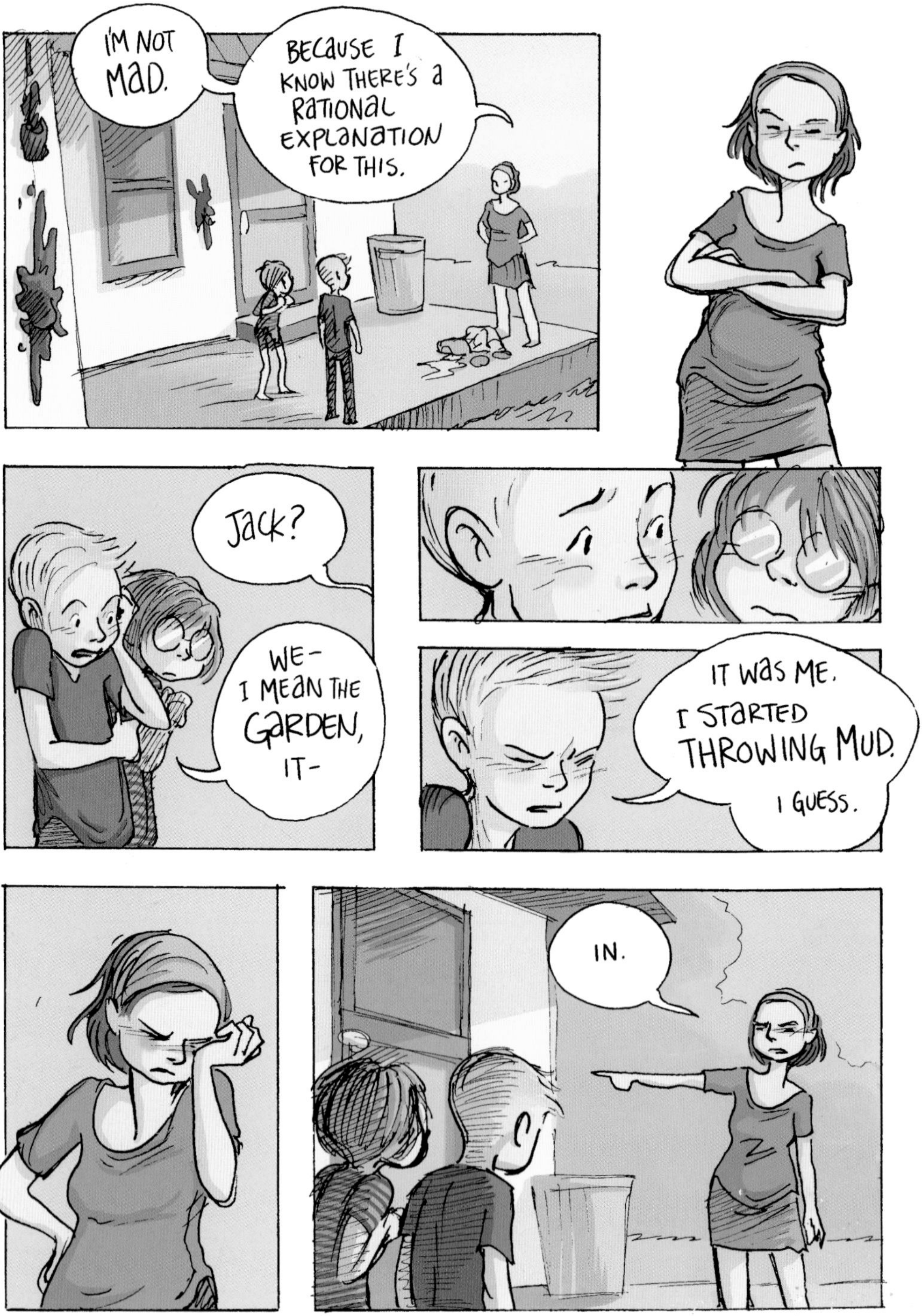
I'M NOT MAD.
BECAUSE I KNOW THERE'S A RATIONAL EXPLANATION FOR THIS.
JACK?
WE- I MEAN THE GARDEN, IT-
IT WAS ME. I STARTED THROWING MUD. I GUESS.
IN.

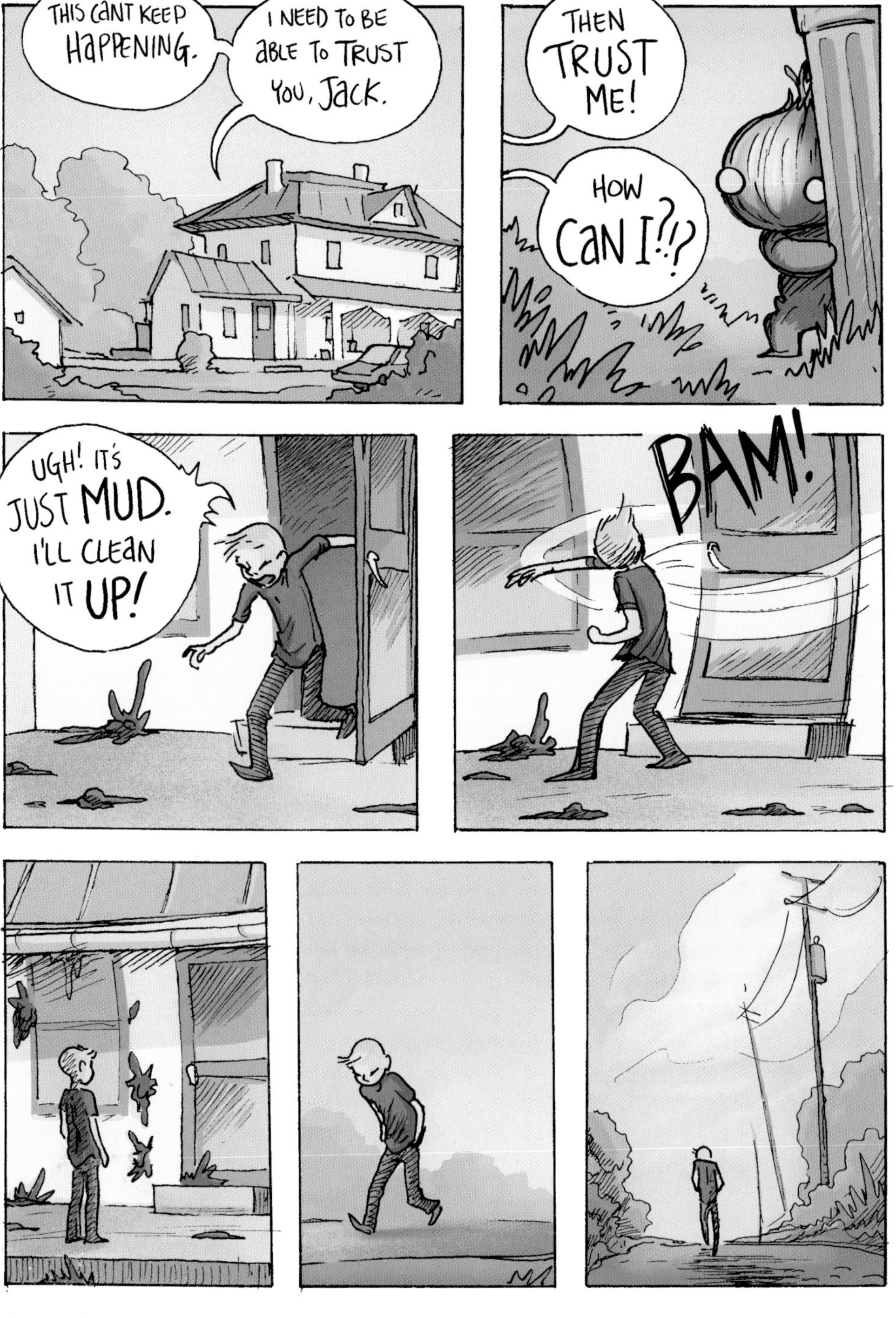
THIS CAN'T KEEP HAPPENING.
I NEED TO BE ABLE TO TRUST YOU, JACK.
THEN TRUST ME!
HOW CAN I?!?
UGH! IT'S JUST MUD. I'LL CLEAN IT UP!
BAM!

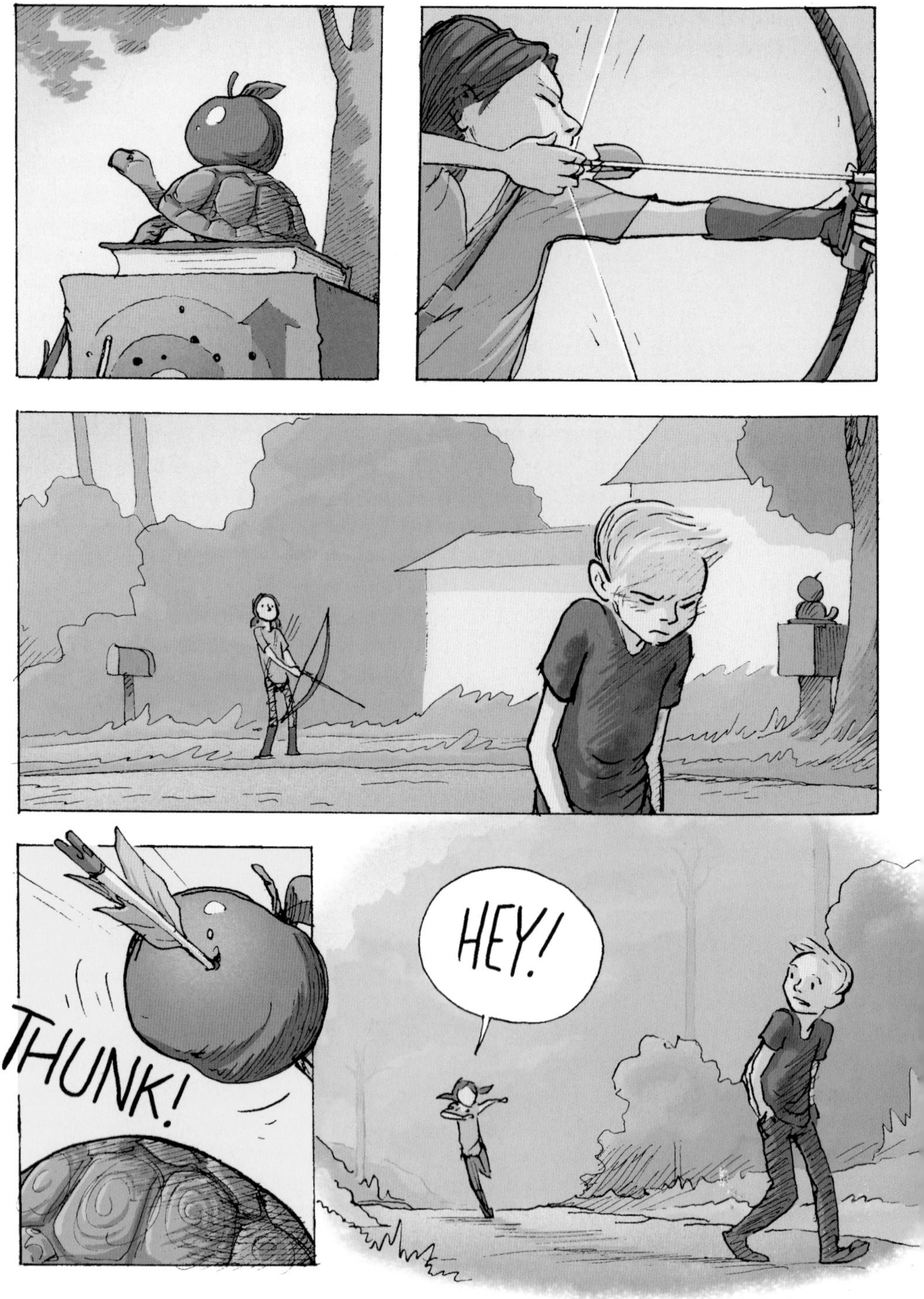
THUNK!
HEY!

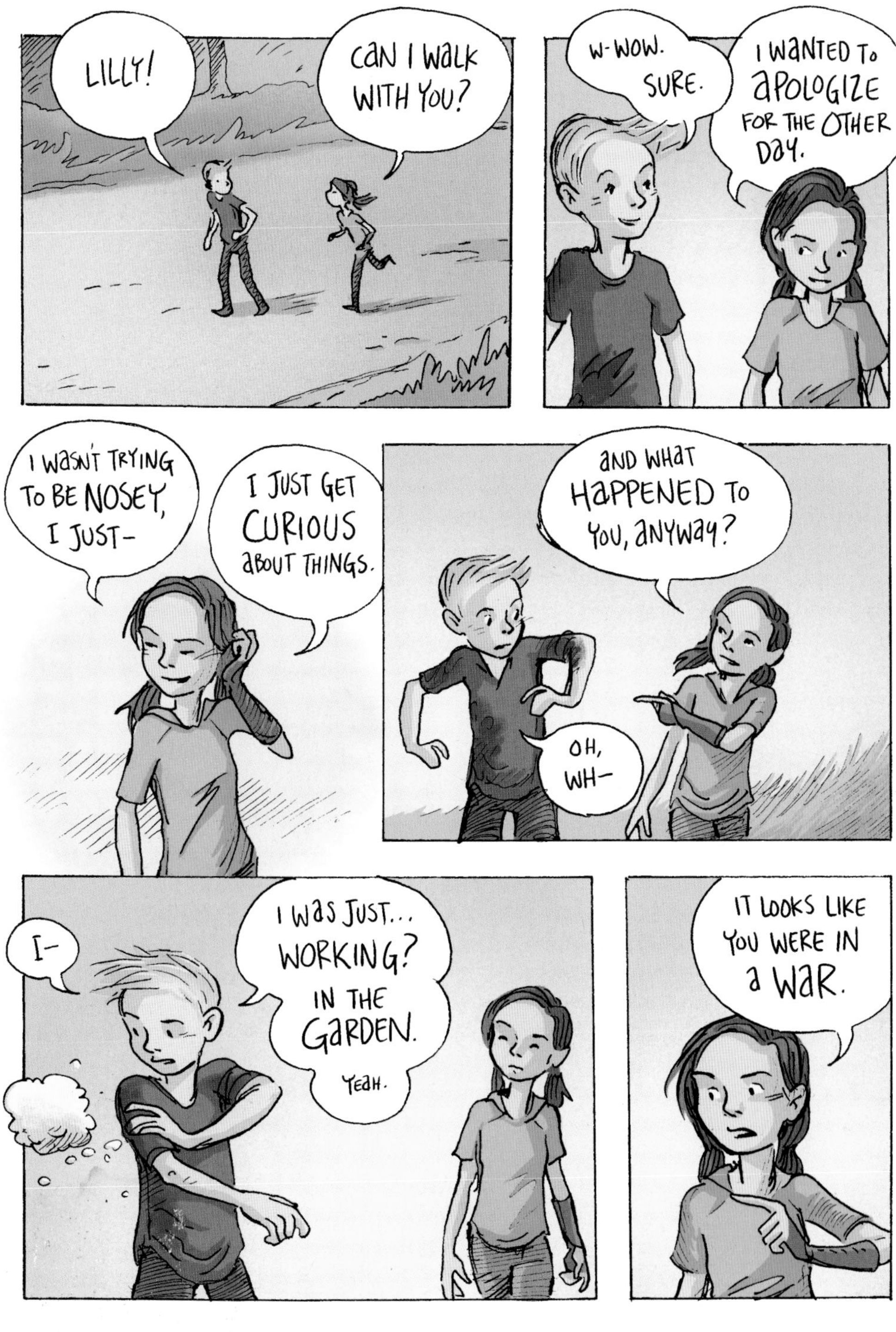
LILLY!
CAN I WALK WITH YOU?
W-WOW. SURE.
I WANTED TO APOLOGIZE FOR THE OTHER DAY.
I WASN'T TRYING TO BE NOSEY, I JUST-
I JUST GET CURIOUS ABOUT THINGS.
AND WHAT HAPPENED TO YOU, ANYWAY?
OH, WH-
I-
I WAS JUST... WORKING? IN THE GARDEN.
YEAH.
IT LOOKS LIKE YOU WERE IN A WAR.

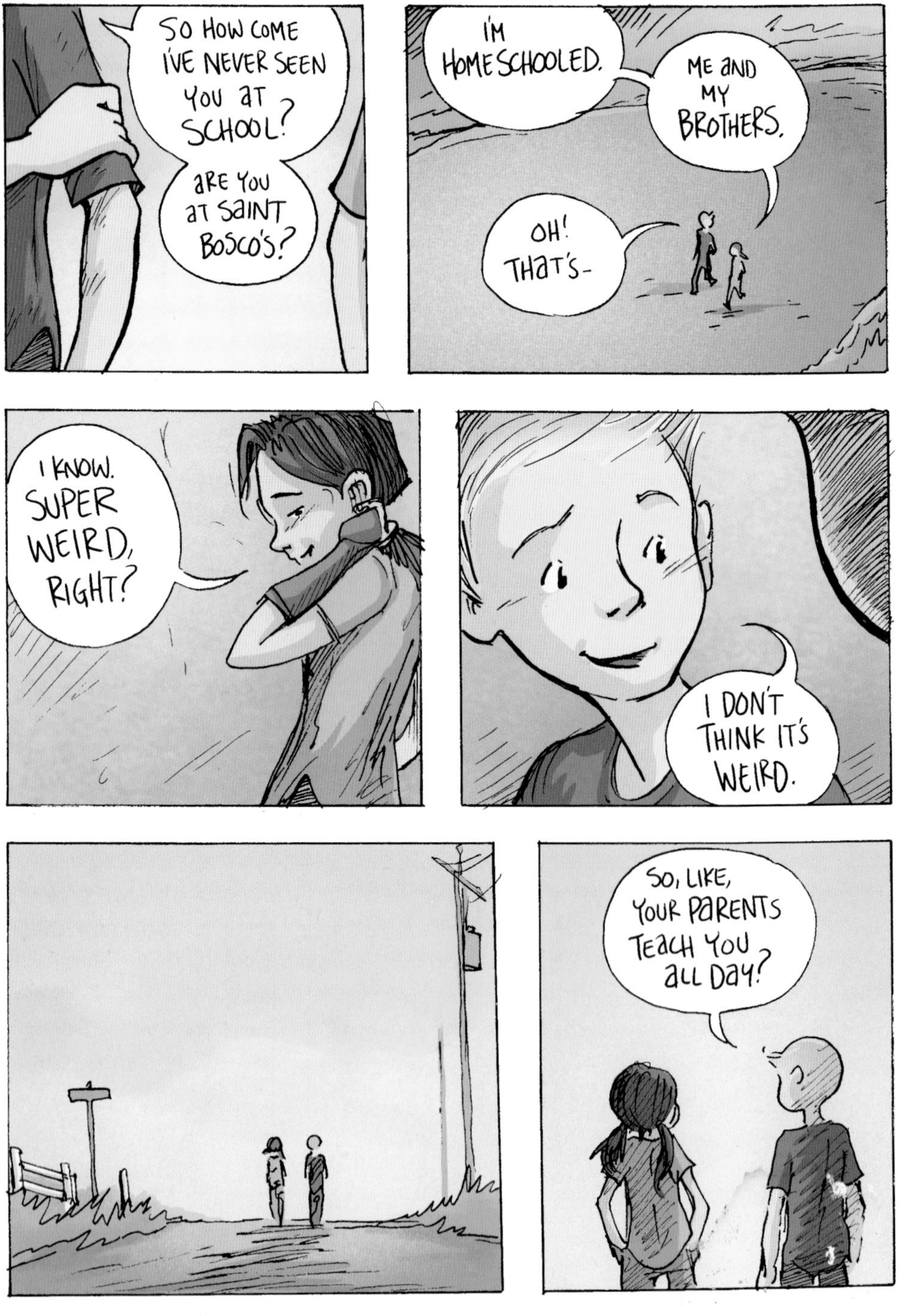
SO HOW COME I'VE NEVER SEEN YOU AT SCHOOL?
ARE YOU AT SAINT BOSCO'S?
I'M HOMESCHOOLED.
ME AND MY BROTHERS.
OH! THAT'S–
I KNOW. SUPER WEIRD, RIGHT?
I DON'T THINK IT'S WEIRD.
SO, LIKE, YOUR PARENTS TEACH YOU ALL DAY?

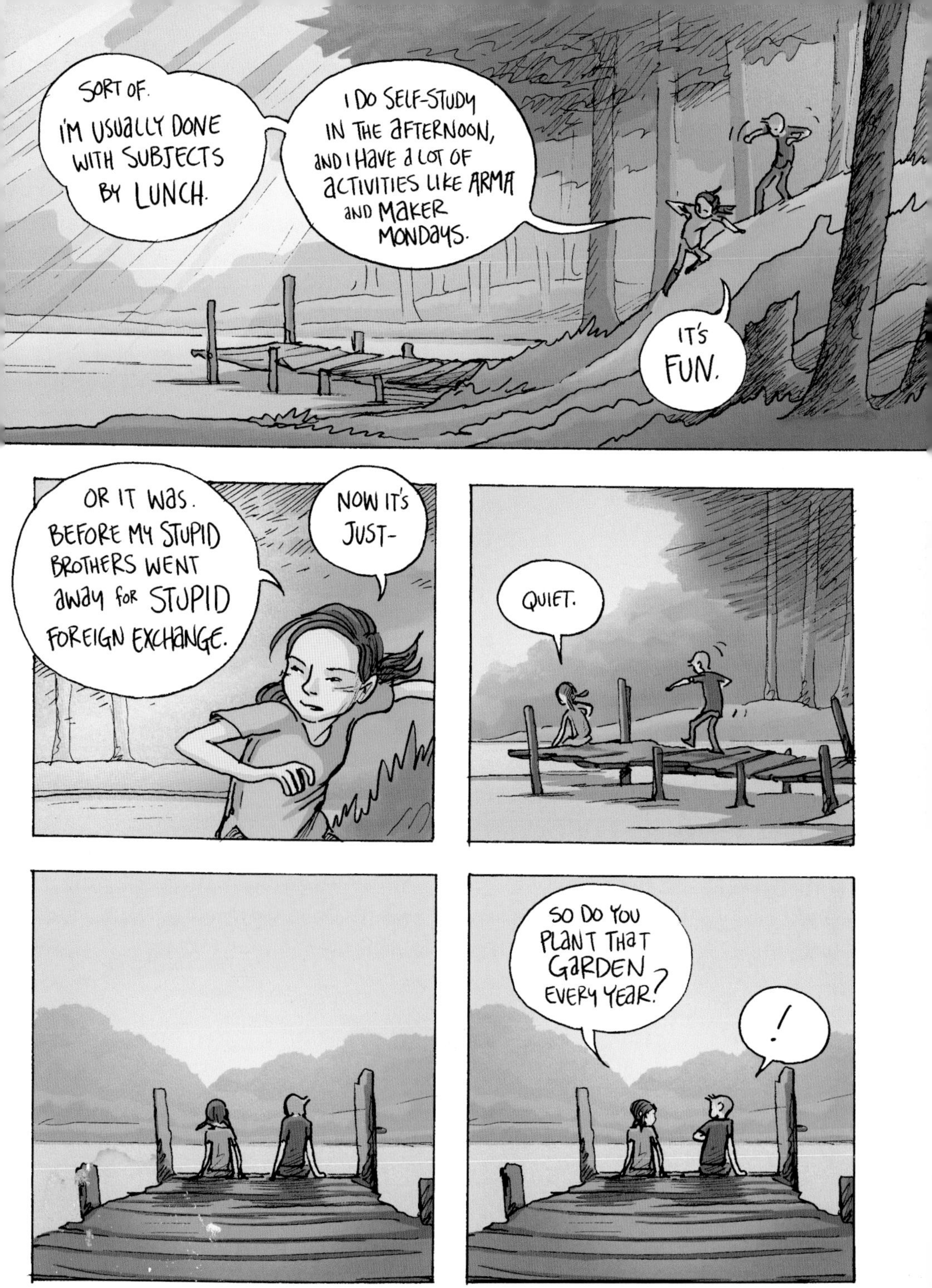
SORT OF.
I'M USUALLY DONE WITH SUBJECTS BY LUNCH.
I DO SELF-STUDY IN THE AFTERNOON, AND I HAVE A LOT OF ACTIVITIES LIKE ARMA AND MAKER MONDAYS.
IT'S FUN.
OR IT WAS. BEFORE MY STUPID BROTHERS WENT AWAY FOR STUPID FOREIGN EXCHANGE.
NOW IT'S JUST-
QUIET.
SO DO YOU PLANT THAT GARDEN EVERY YEAR?
!

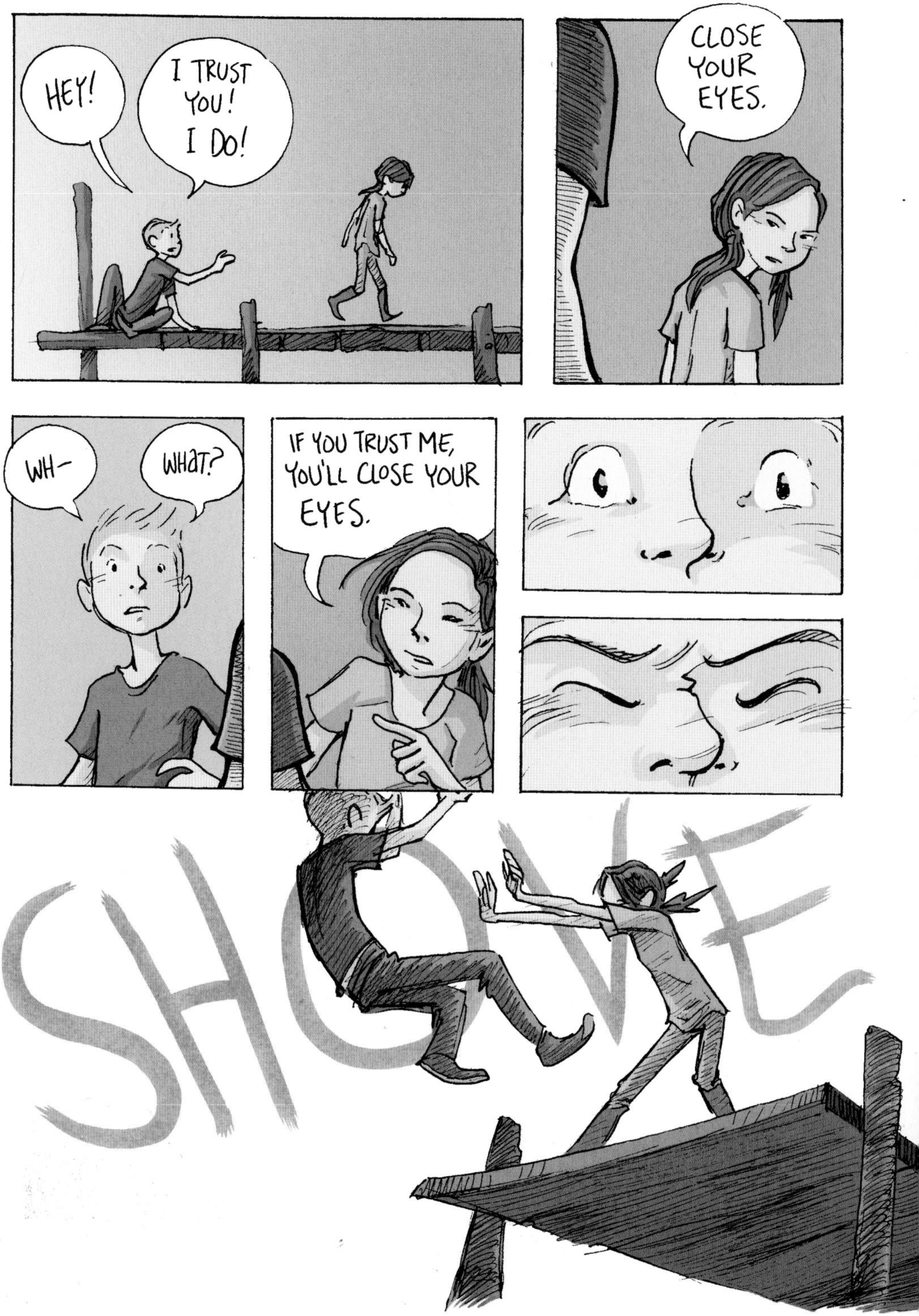
HEY!
I TRUST YOU! I DO!
CLOSE YOUR EYES.
WH-
WHAT?
IF YOU TRUST ME, YOU'LL CLOSE YOUR EYES.
SHOVE

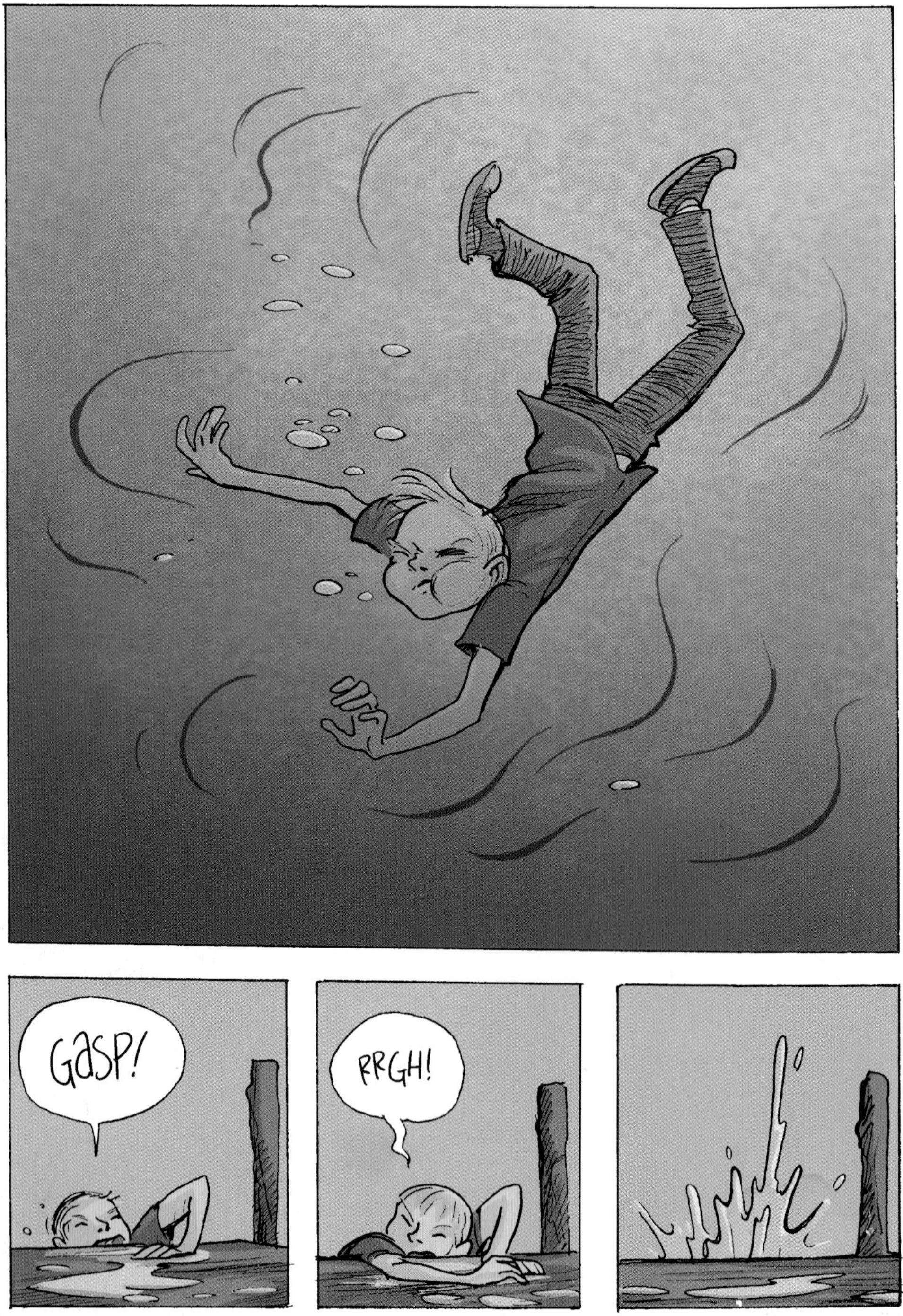
GASP!
RRGH!

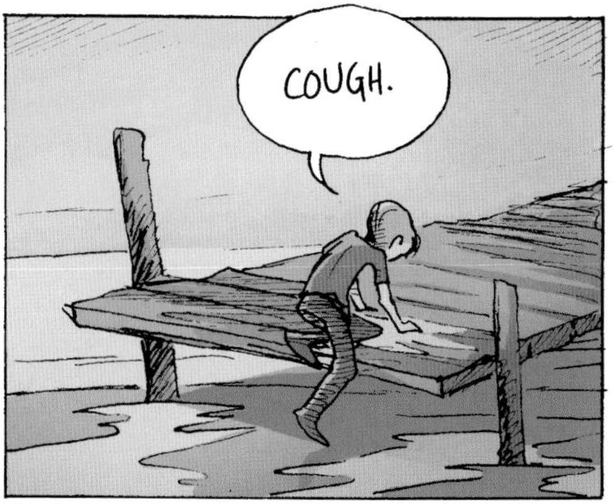
COUGH.

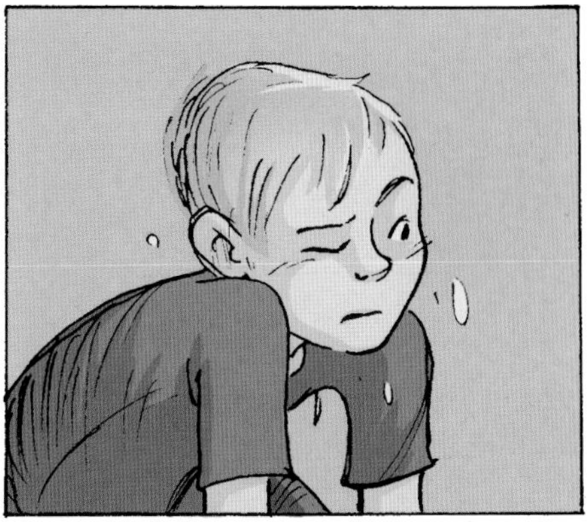

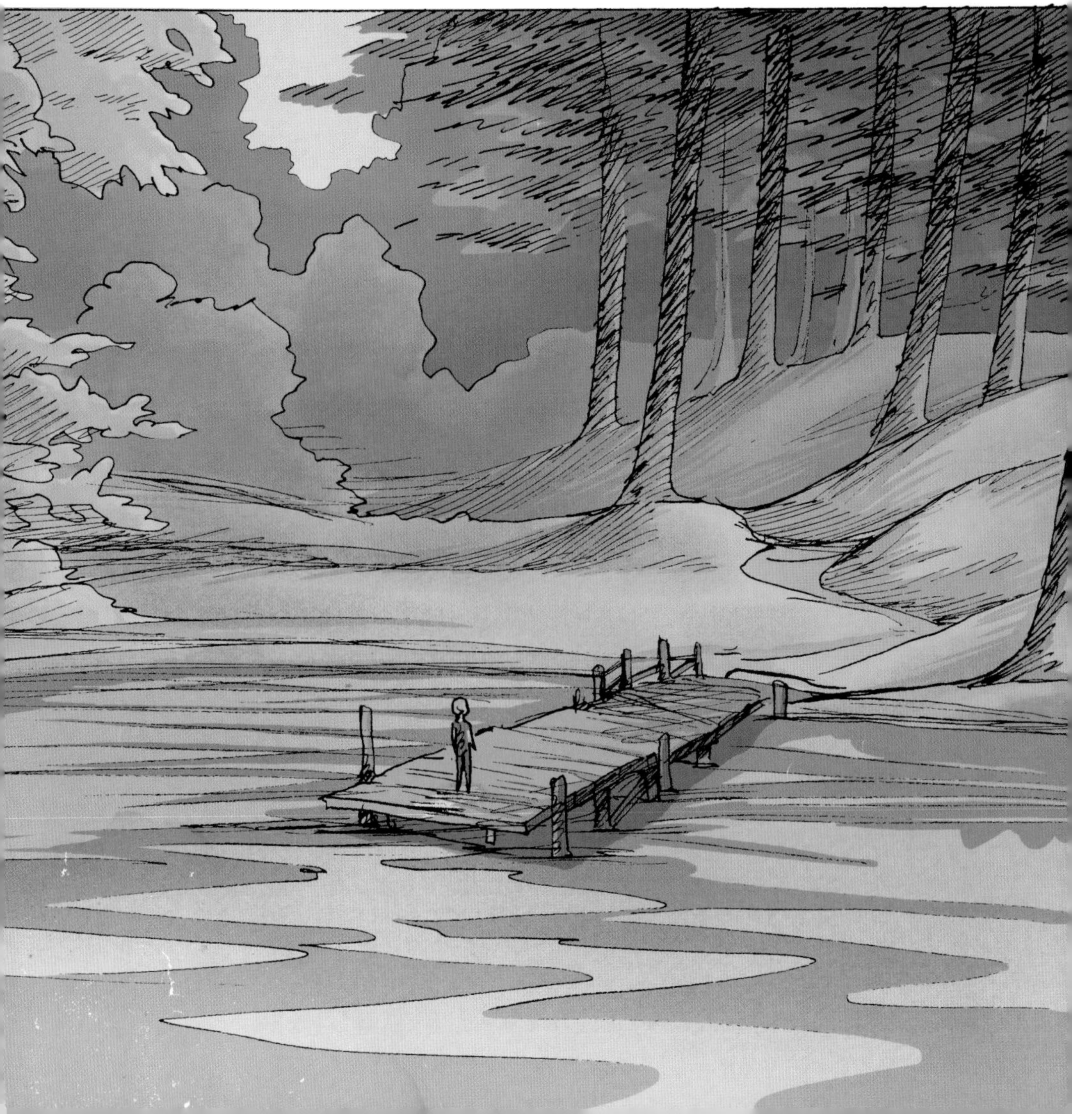

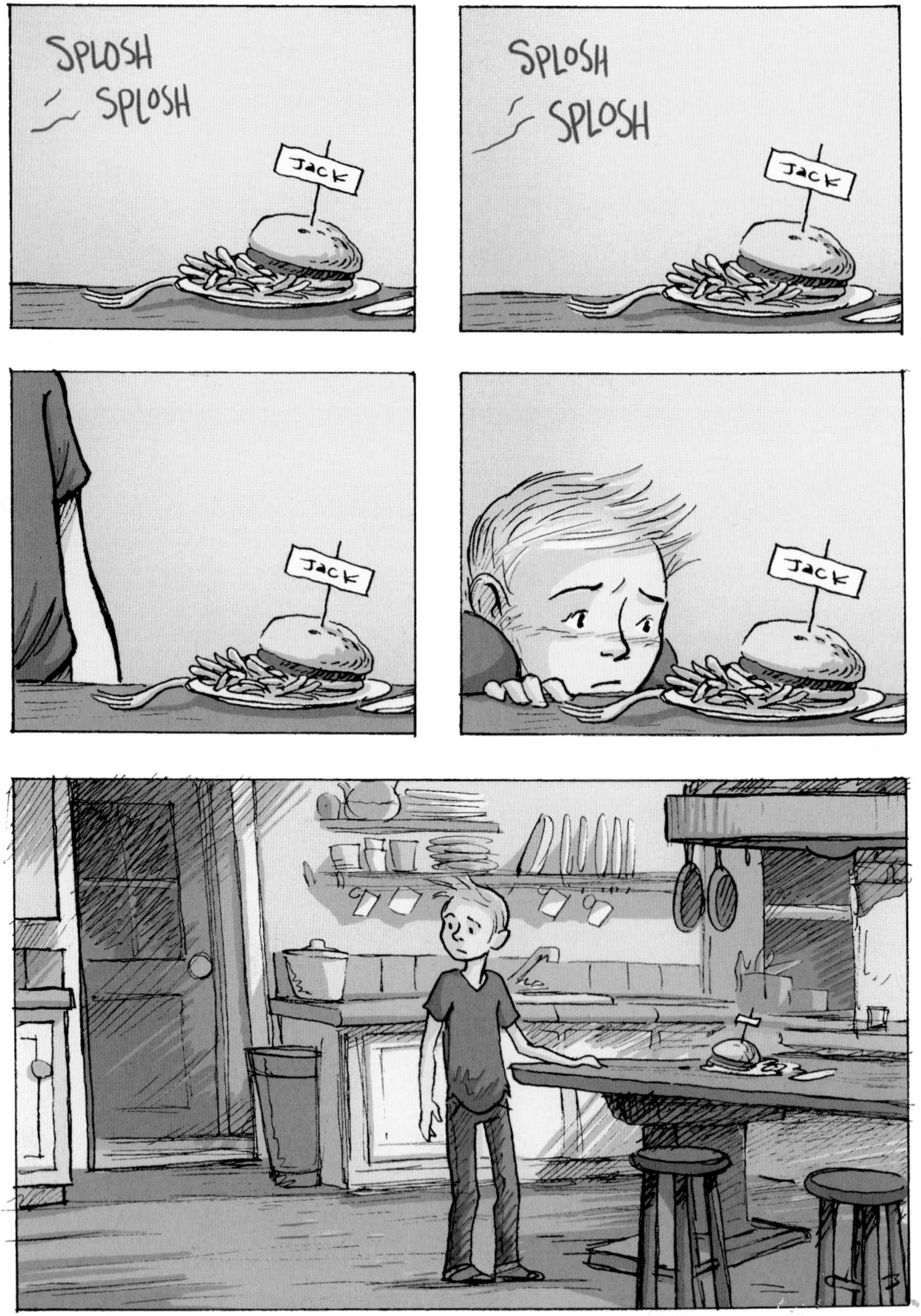
SPLOSH
SPLOSH
JACK
SPLOSH
SPLOSH
JACK
JACK
JACK

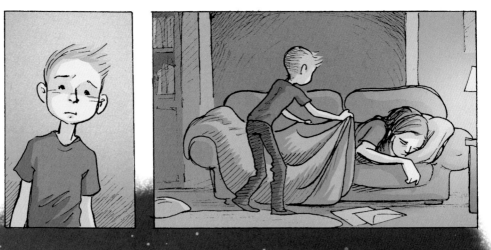

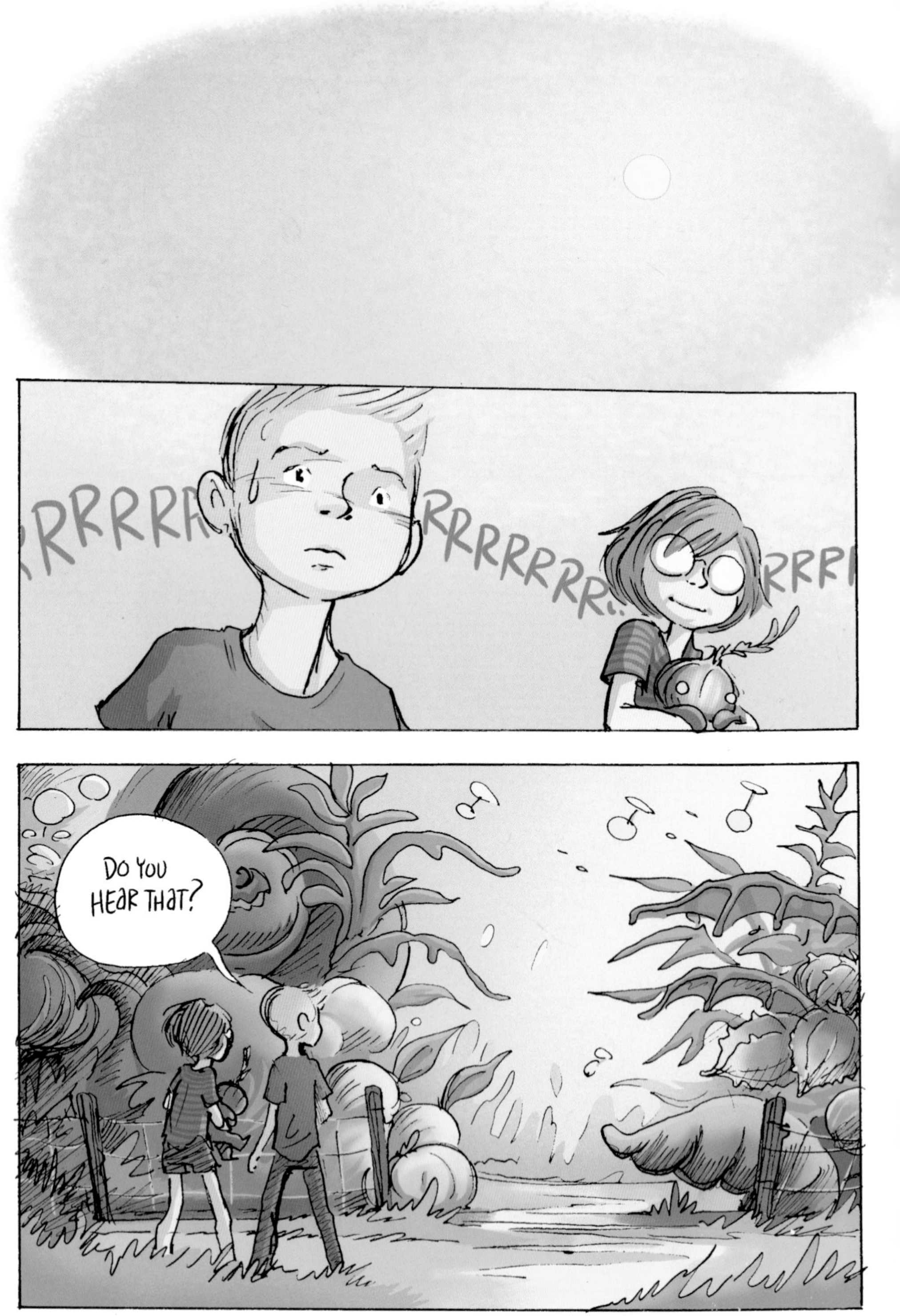
RRRRR
RRRRRRR..
RRRR
DO YOU HEAR THAT?

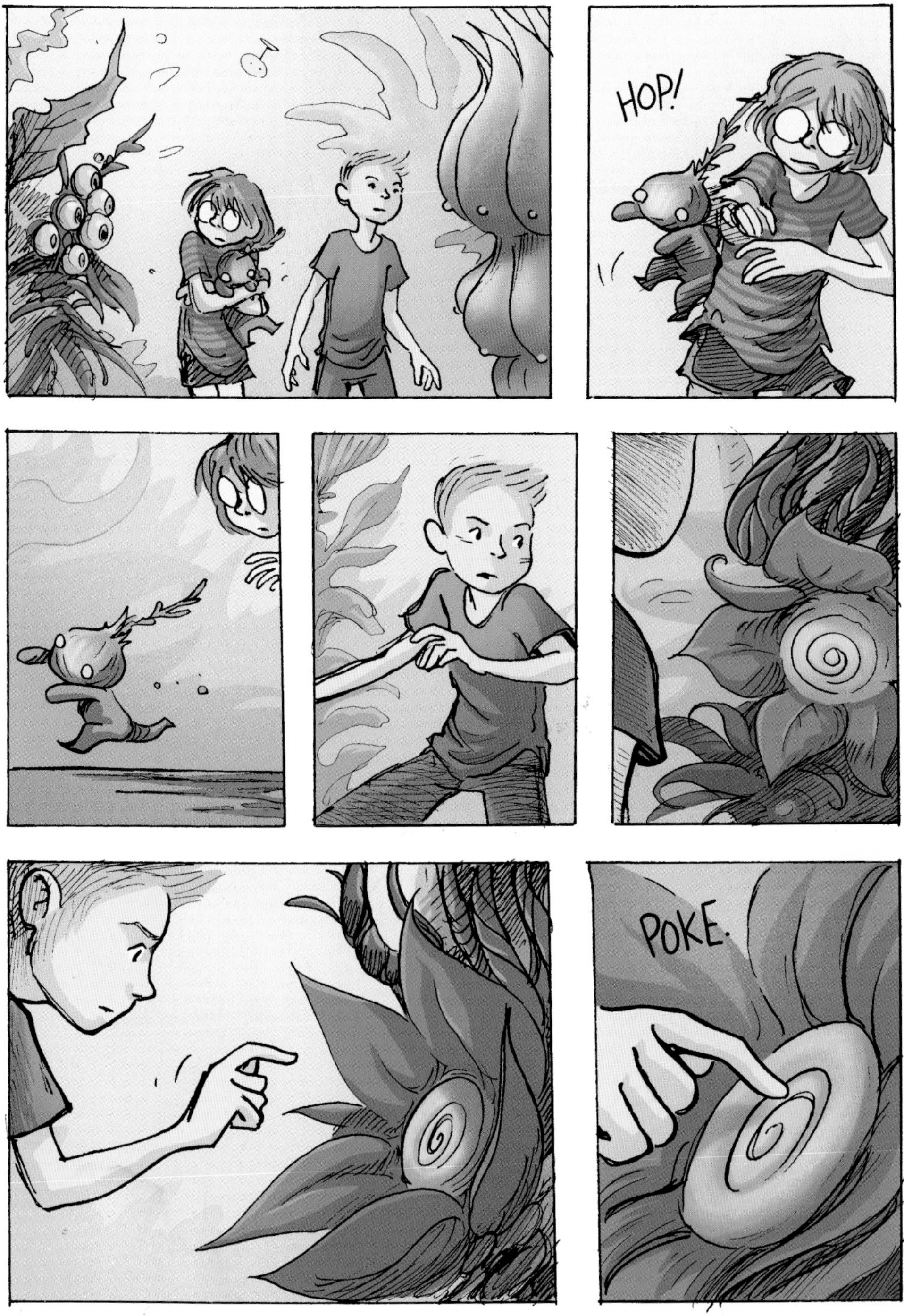
HOP!
POKE.

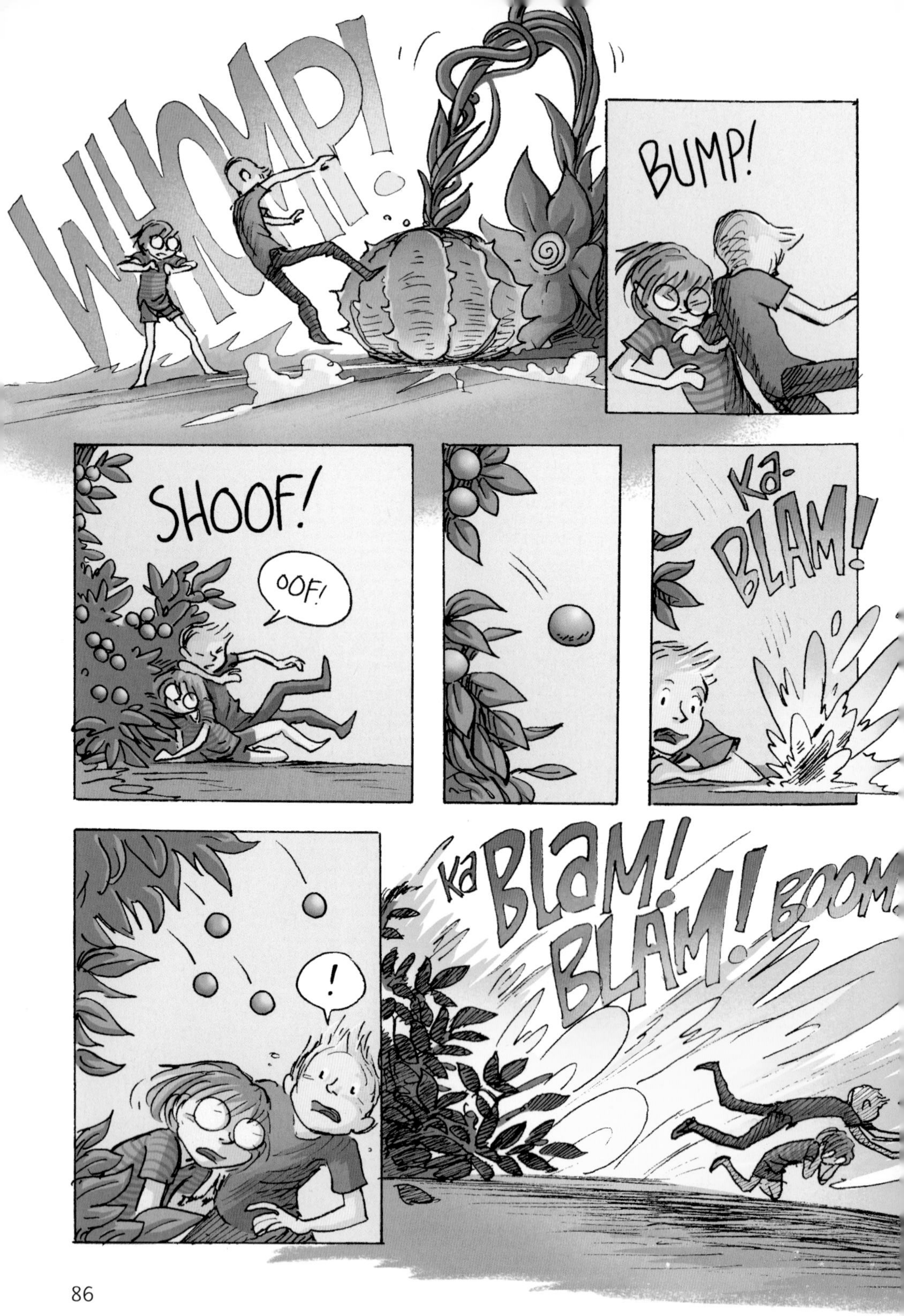
WHOMP!
BUMP!
SHOOF!
OOF!
KA-BLAM!
!
KA BLAM!
BLAM!
BOOM

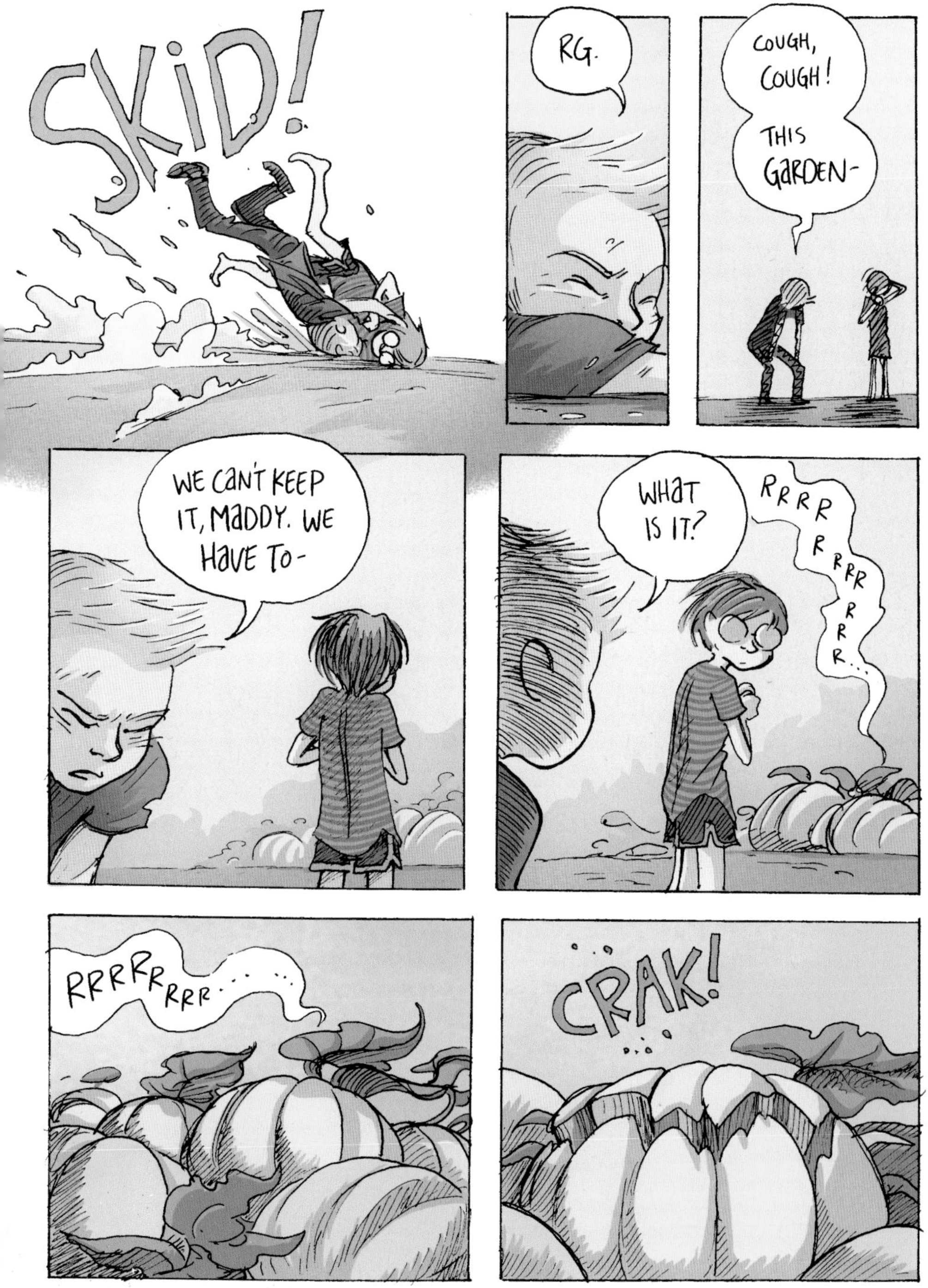
SKID!
RG.
COUGH, COUGH!
THIS GARDEN-
WE CAN'T KEEP IT, MADDY. WE HAVE TO-
WHAT IS IT?
RRRR RRRR RRR...
RRRRRRRR.....
CRAK!

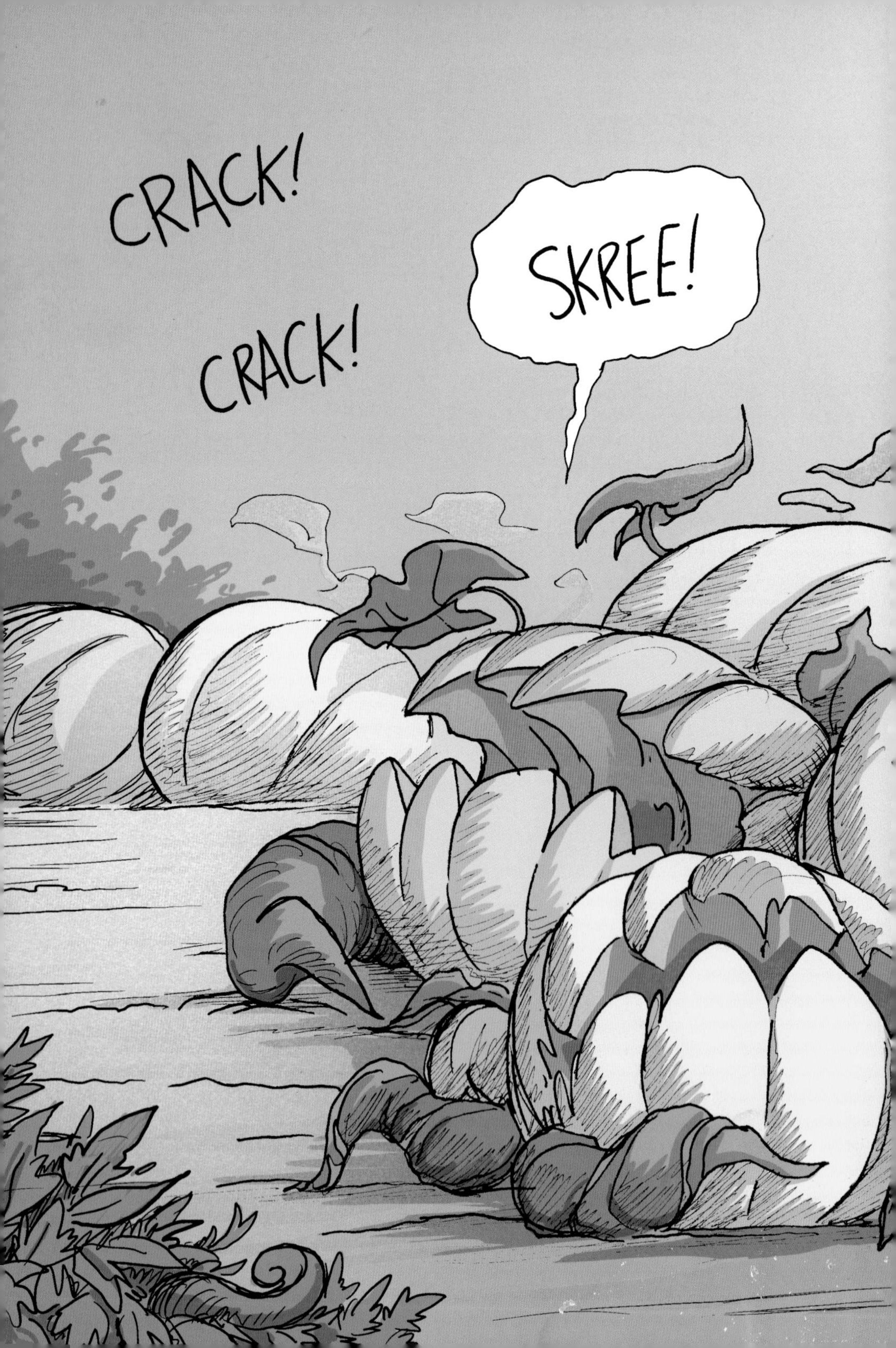
CRACK!
CRACK!
SKREE!

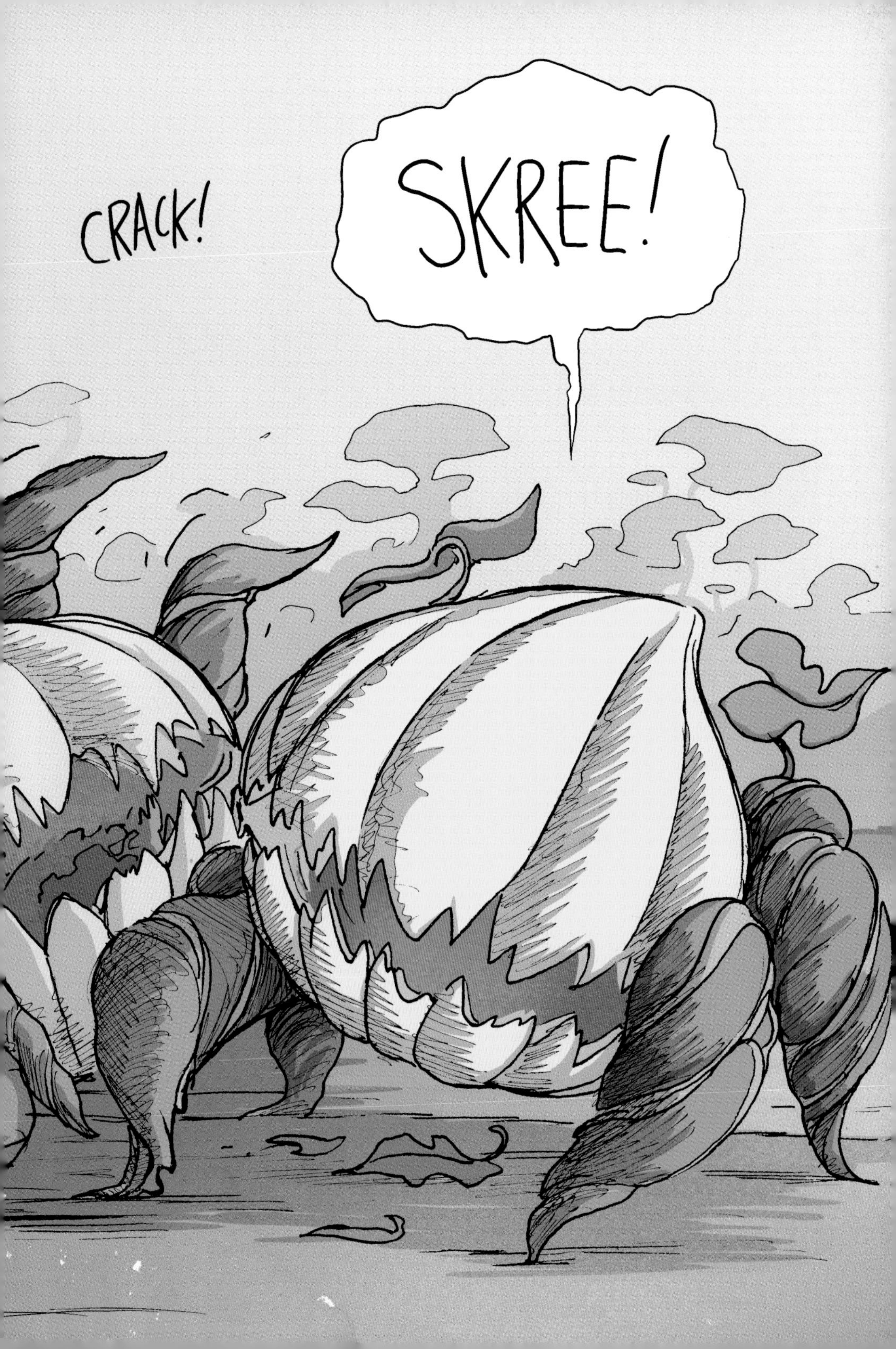
CRACK!
SKREE!

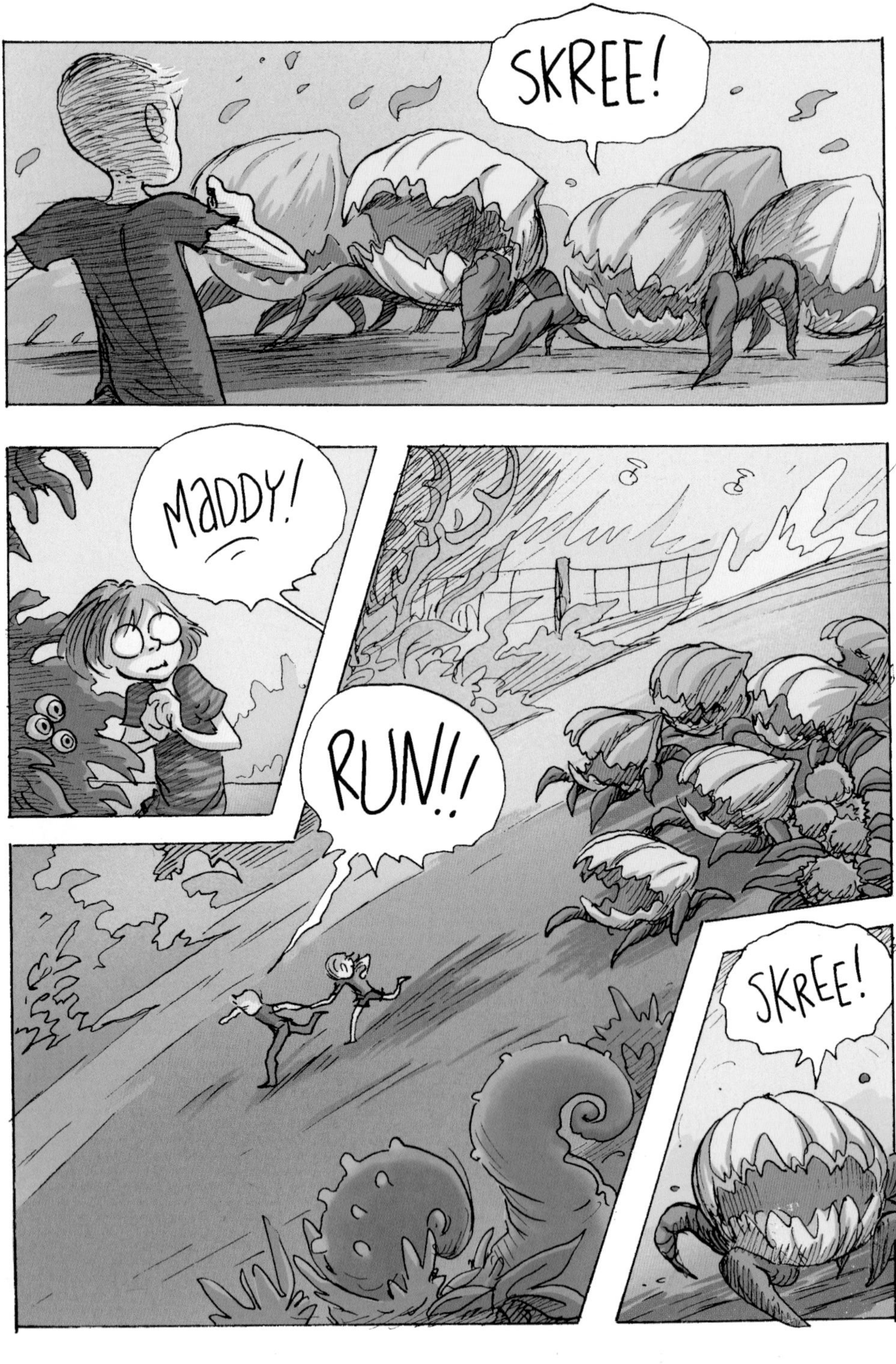
SKREE!
MADDY!
RUN!!
SKREE!

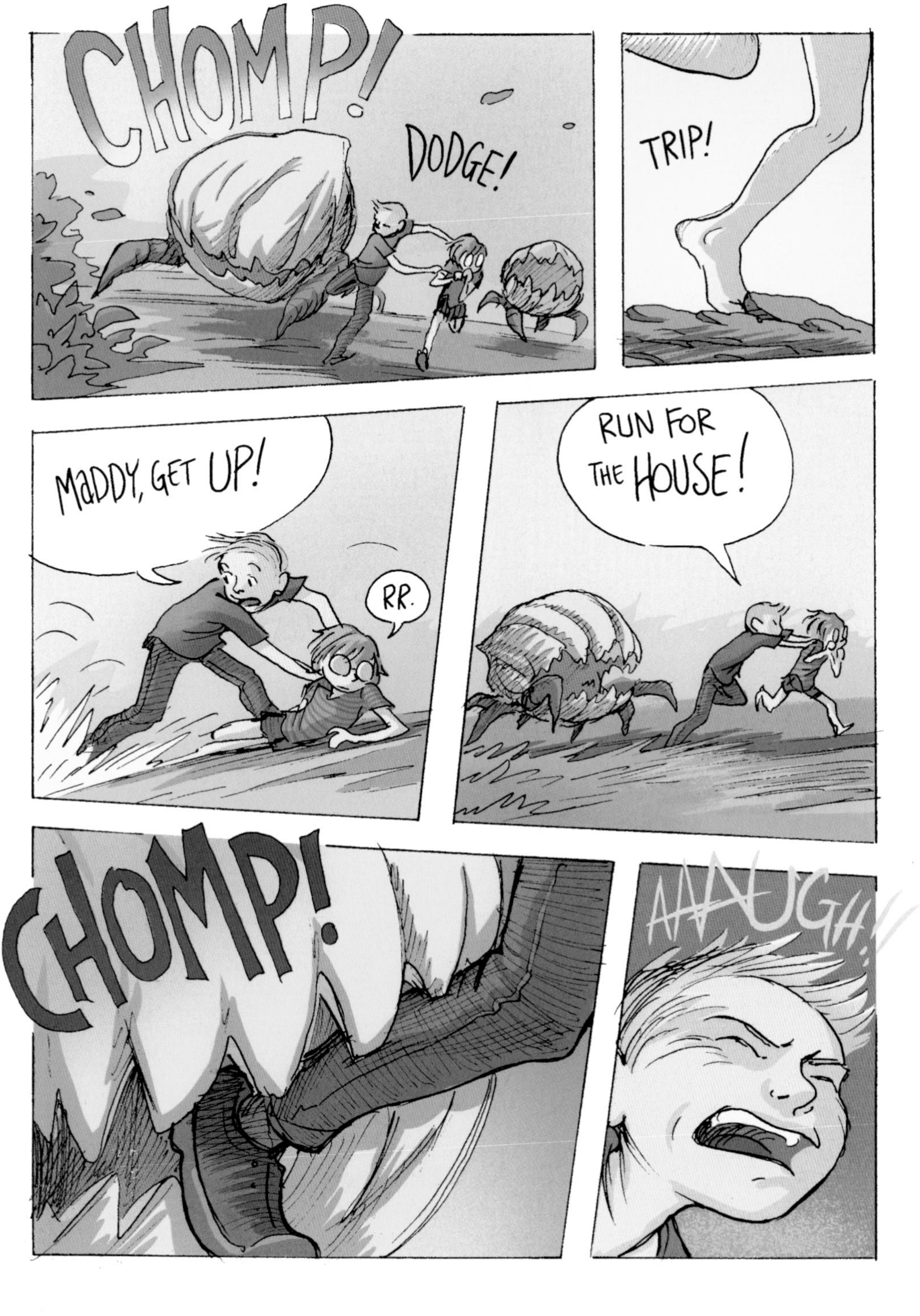
CHOMP!
DODGE!
TRIP!
MADDY, GET UP!
RR.
RUN FOR THE HOUSE!
CHOMP!
AAAUGH!

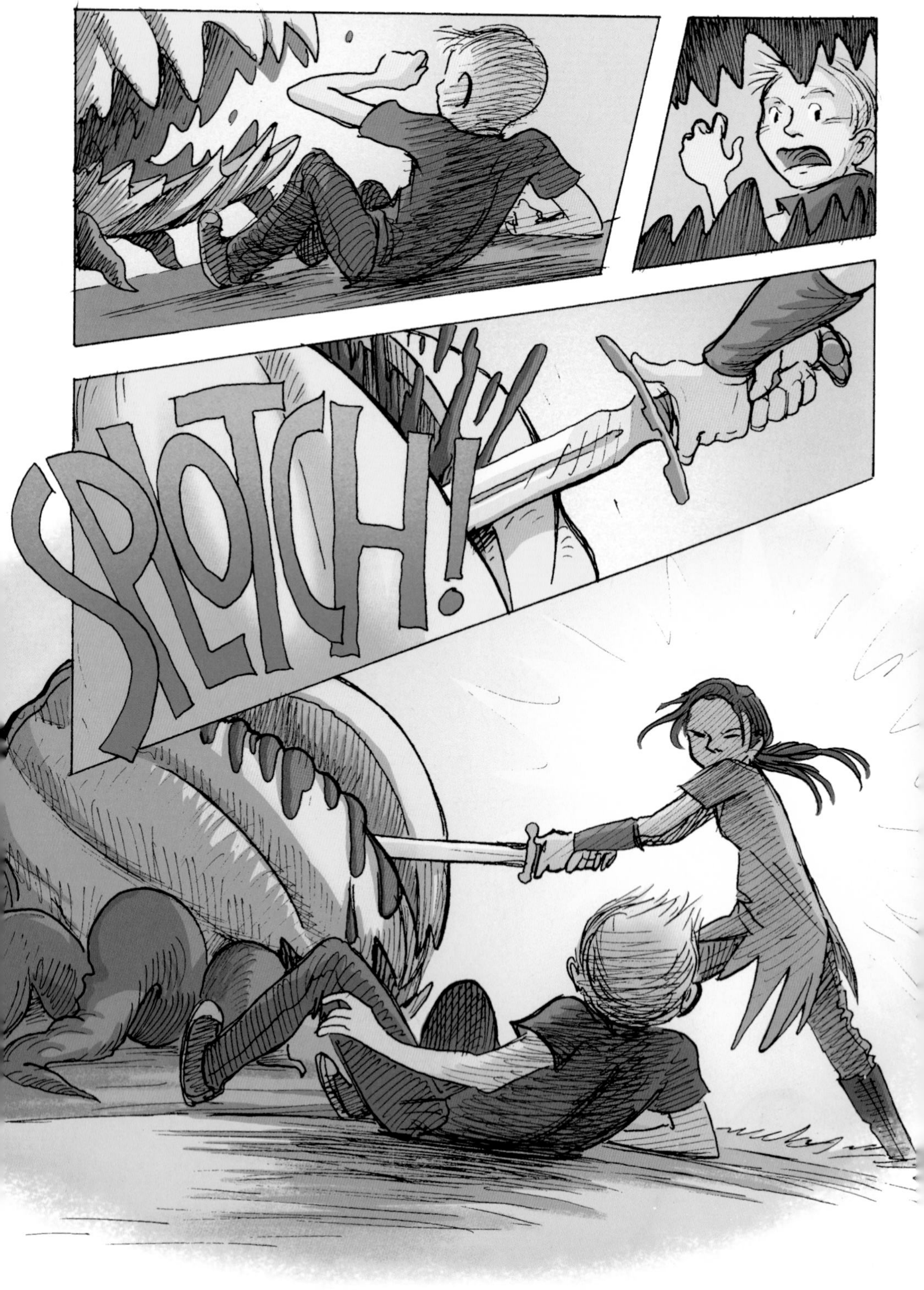
SPLOTCH!

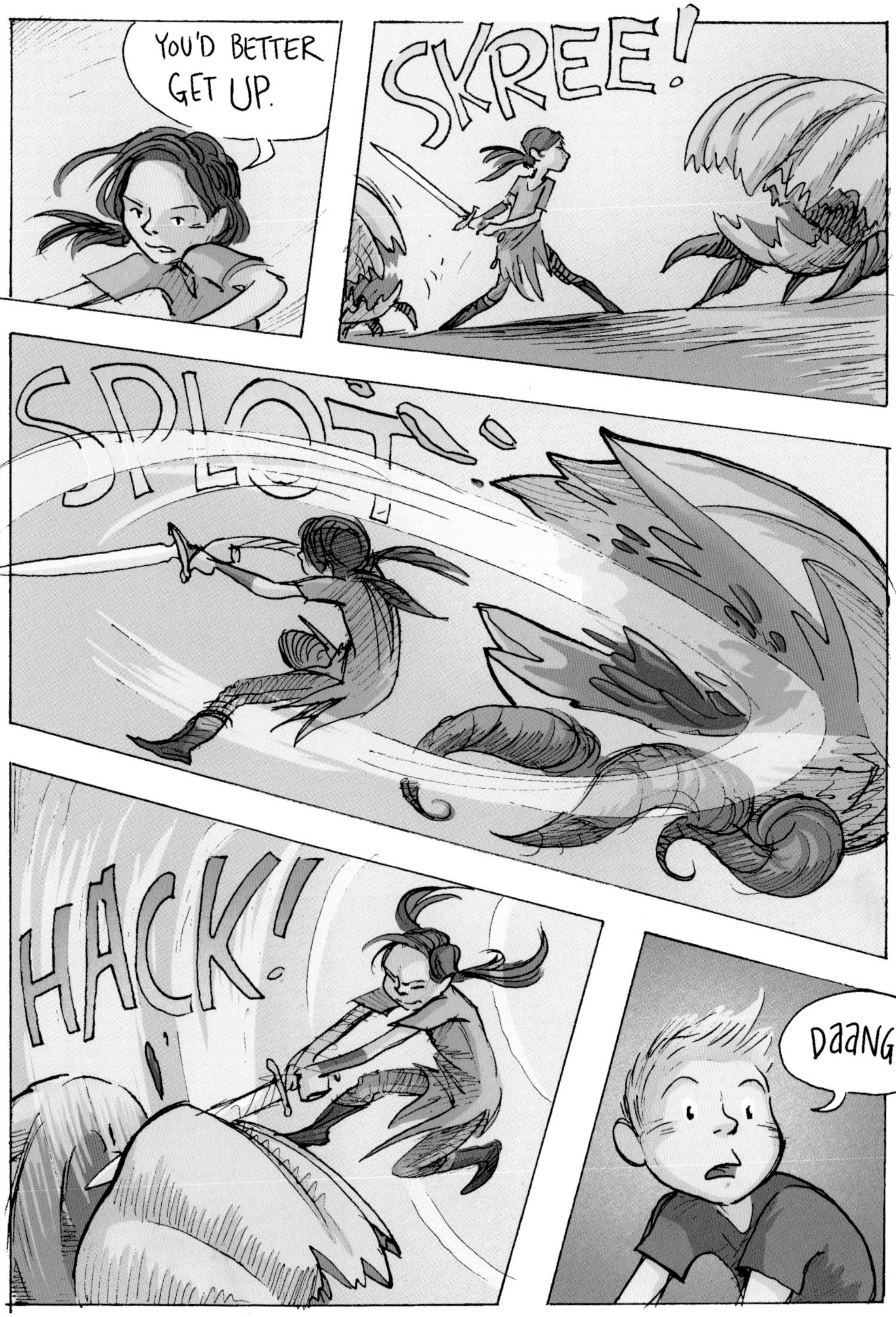
YOU'D BETTER GET UP.
SKREE!
SPLOT!
HACK!
DaaNG.

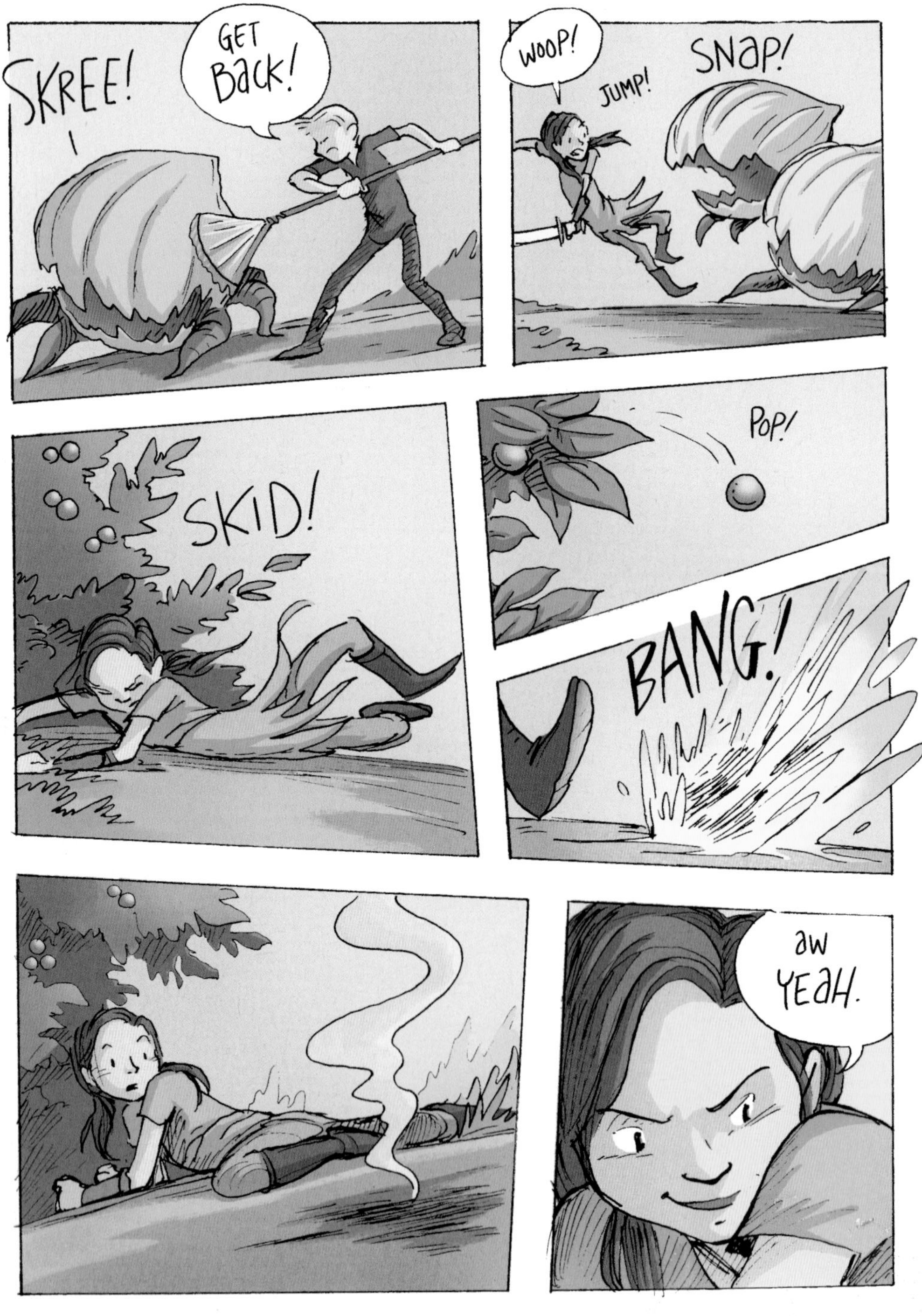
SKREE!
GET BACK!
WOOP!
JUMP!
SNAP!
SKID!
POP!
BANG!
aw YEAH.

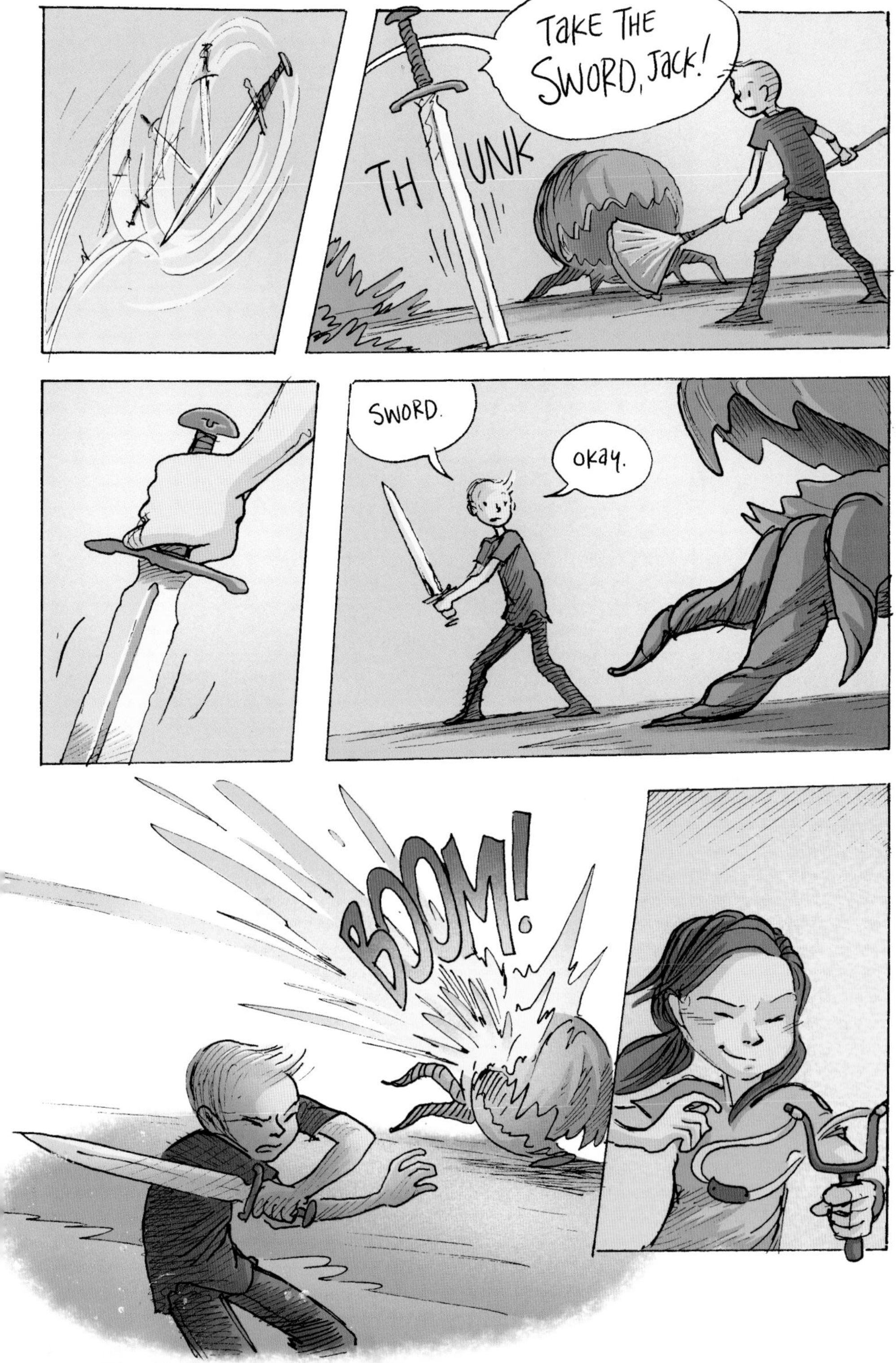
TAKE THE SWORD, Jack!
TH UNK
SWORD.
okay.
BOOM!

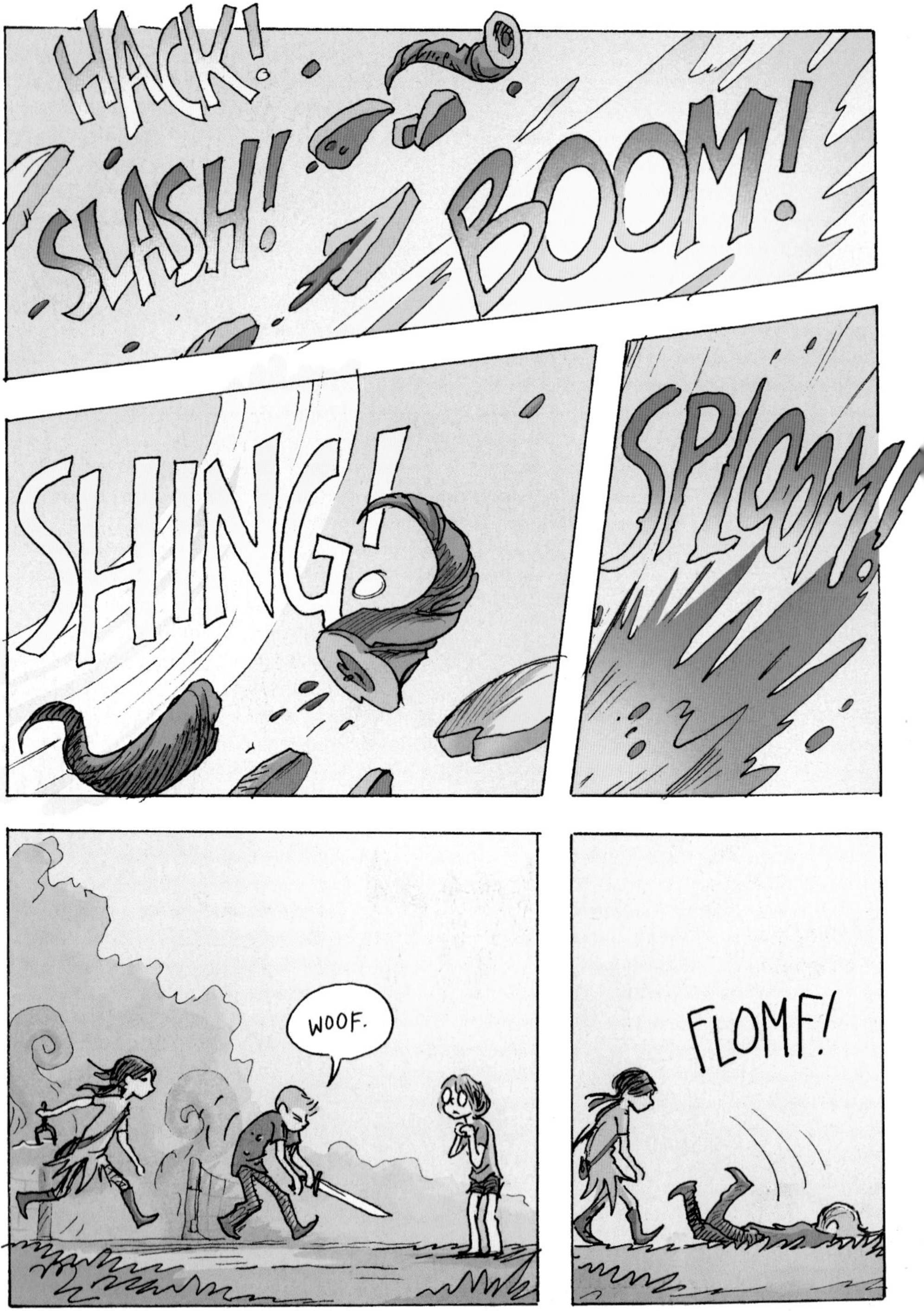
HACK!
SLASH!
BOOM!
SHING!
SPLOOM!
WOOF.
FLOMF!

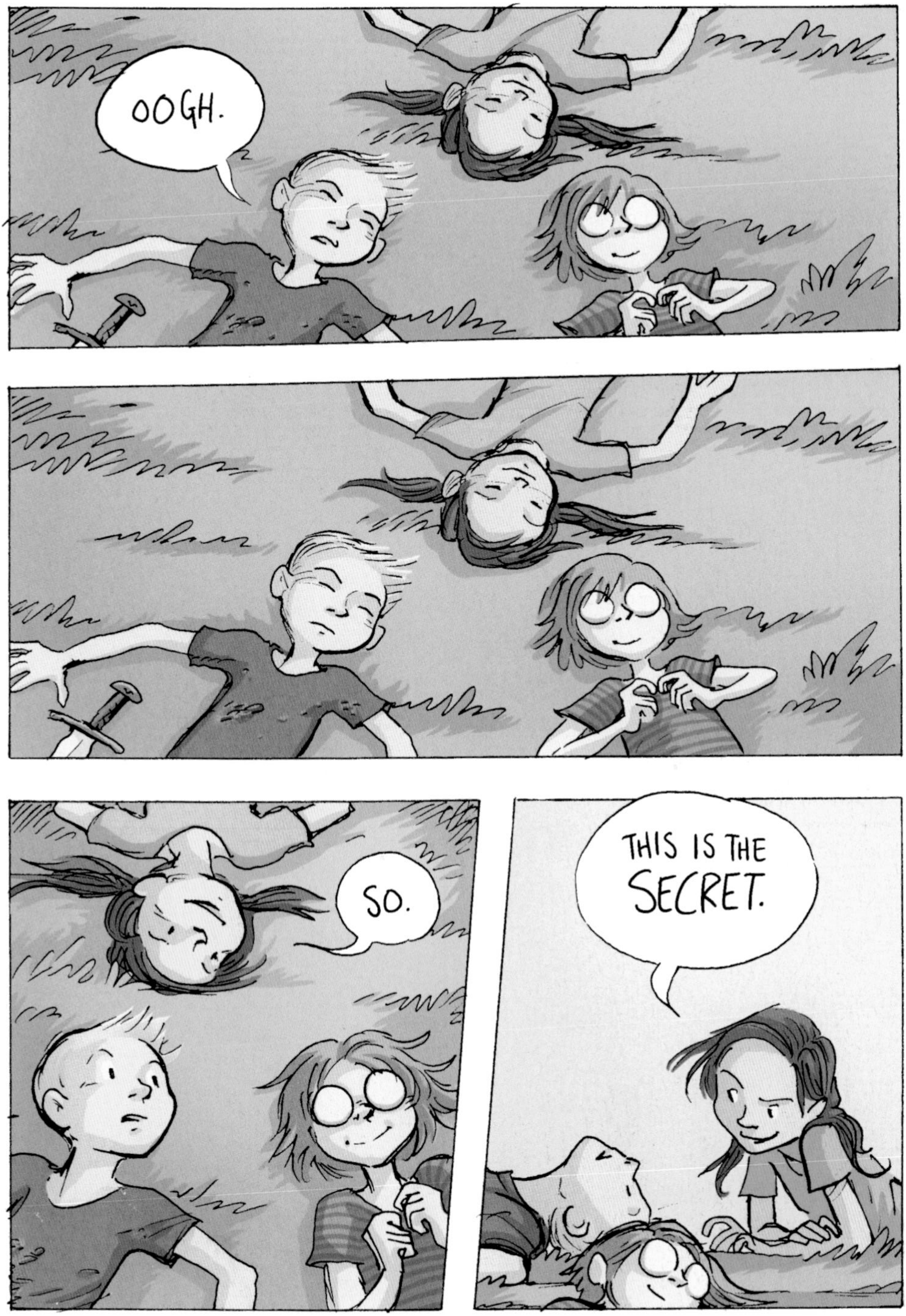
OOGH.
SO.
THIS IS THE SECRET.

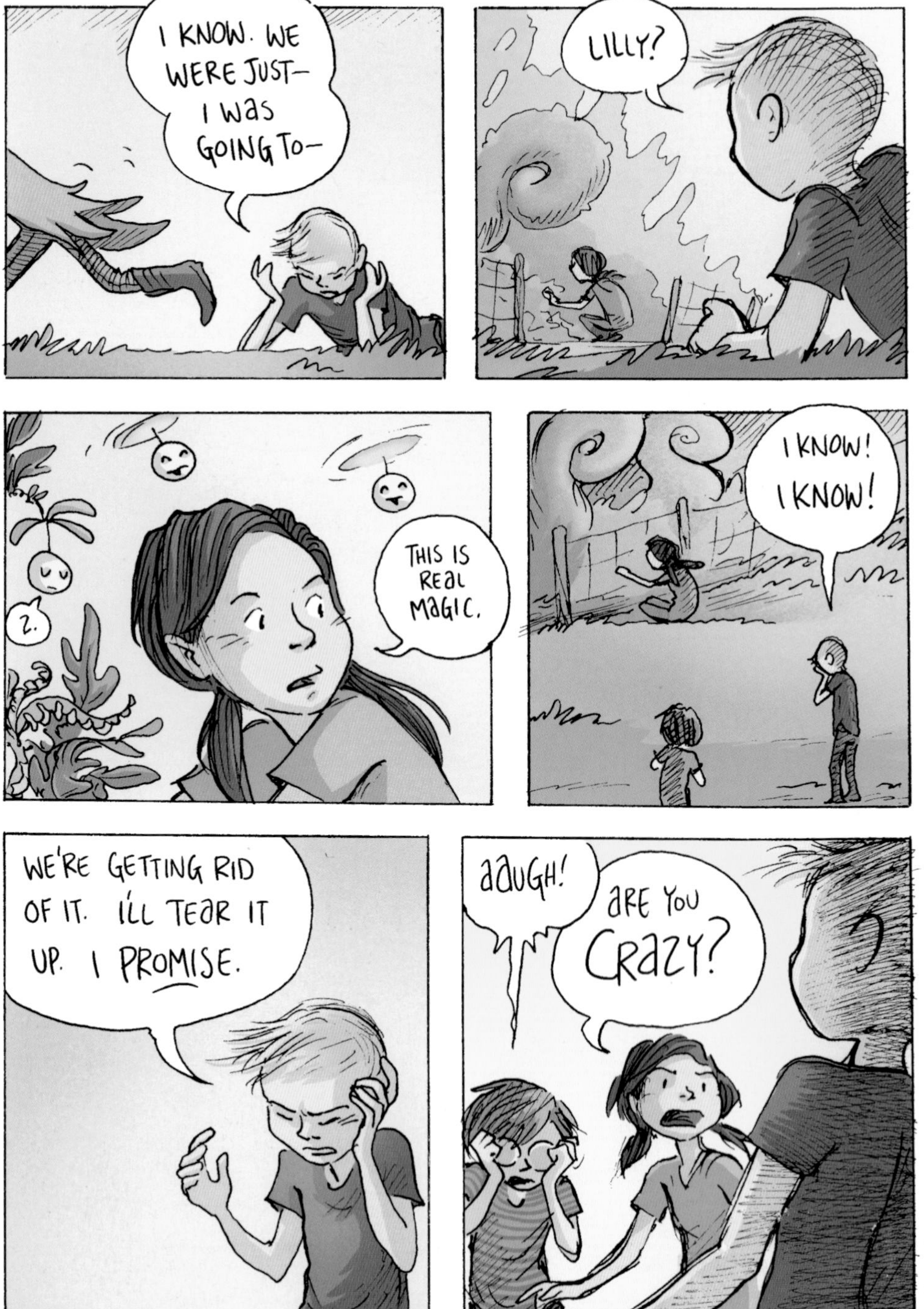
I KNOW. WE WERE JUST— I WAS GOING TO—
LILLY?
THIS IS REAL MAGIC.
?
I KNOW! I KNOW!
WE'RE GETTING RID OF IT. I'LL TEAR IT UP. I PROMISE.
AAUGH!
ARE YOU CRAZY?

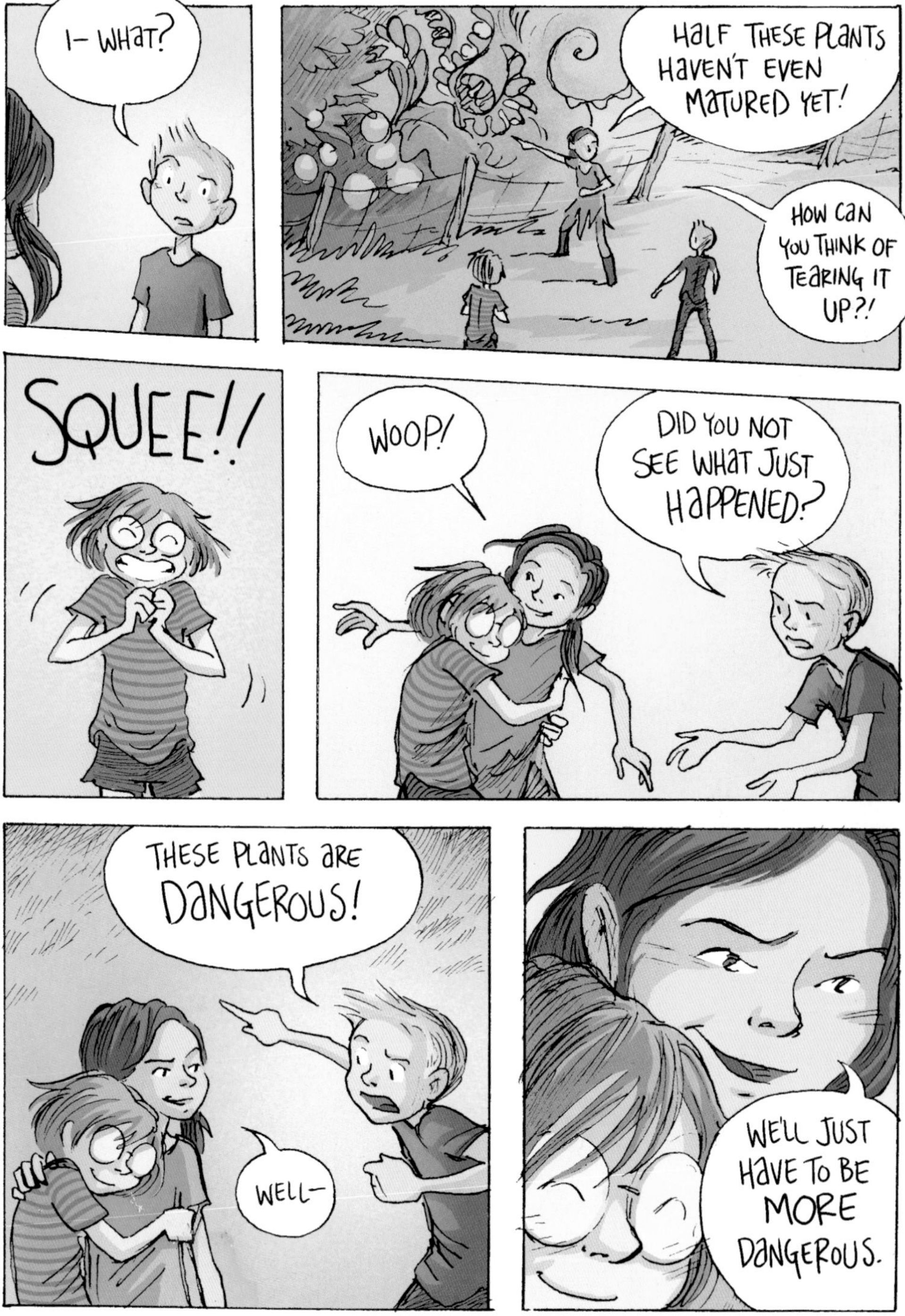
I- WHAT?
HALF THESE PLANTS HAVEN'T EVEN MATURED YET!
HOW CAN YOU THINK OF TEARING IT UP?!
SQUEE!!
WOOP!
DID YOU NOT SEE WHAT JUST HAPPENED?
THESE PLANTS ARE DANGEROUS!
WELL-
WE'LL JUST HAVE TO BE MORE DANGEROUS.

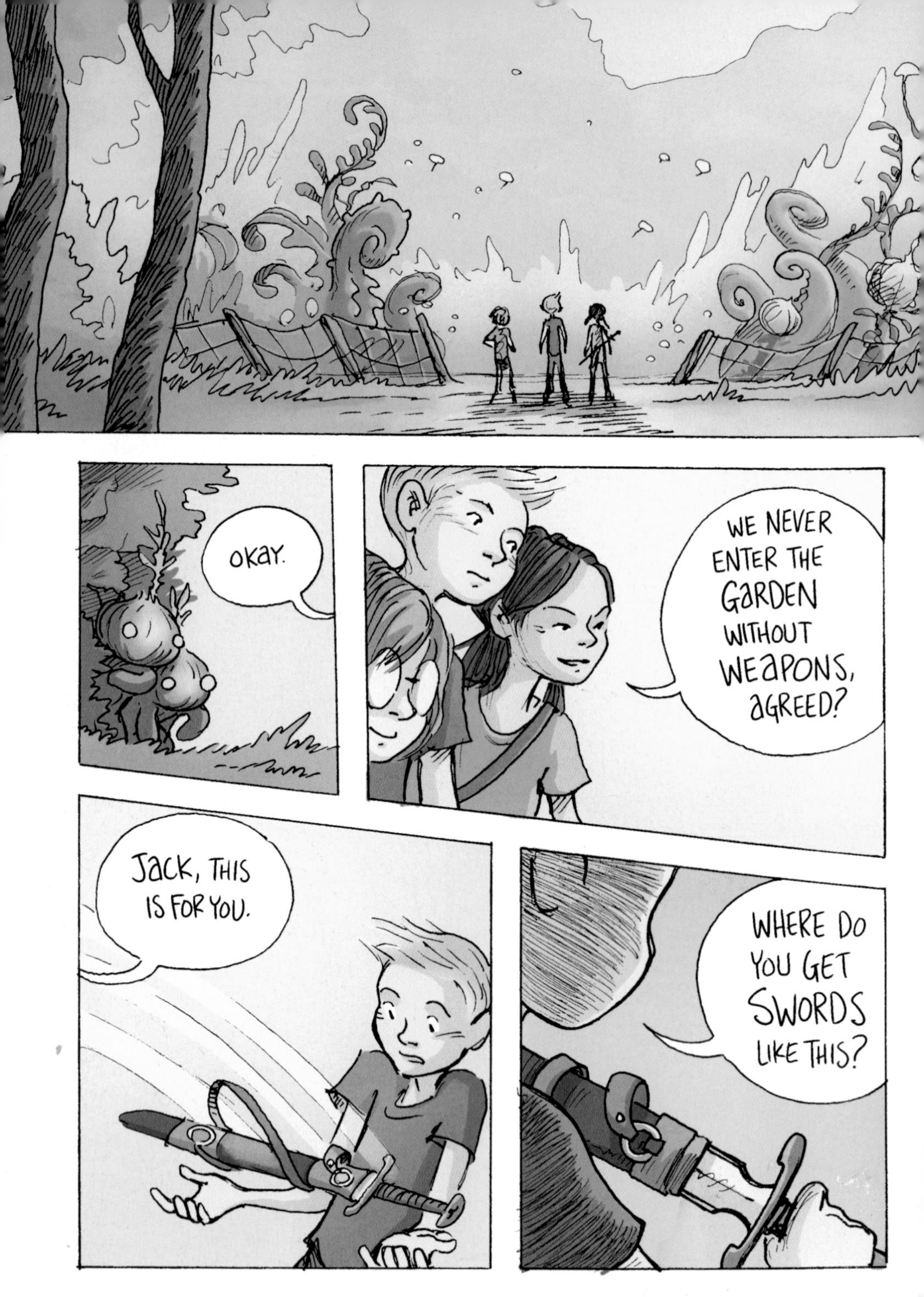
OKAY.
WE NEVER ENTER THE GARDEN WITHOUT WEAPONS, AGREED?
JACK, THIS IS FOR YOU.
WHERE DO YOU GET SWORDS LIKE THIS?

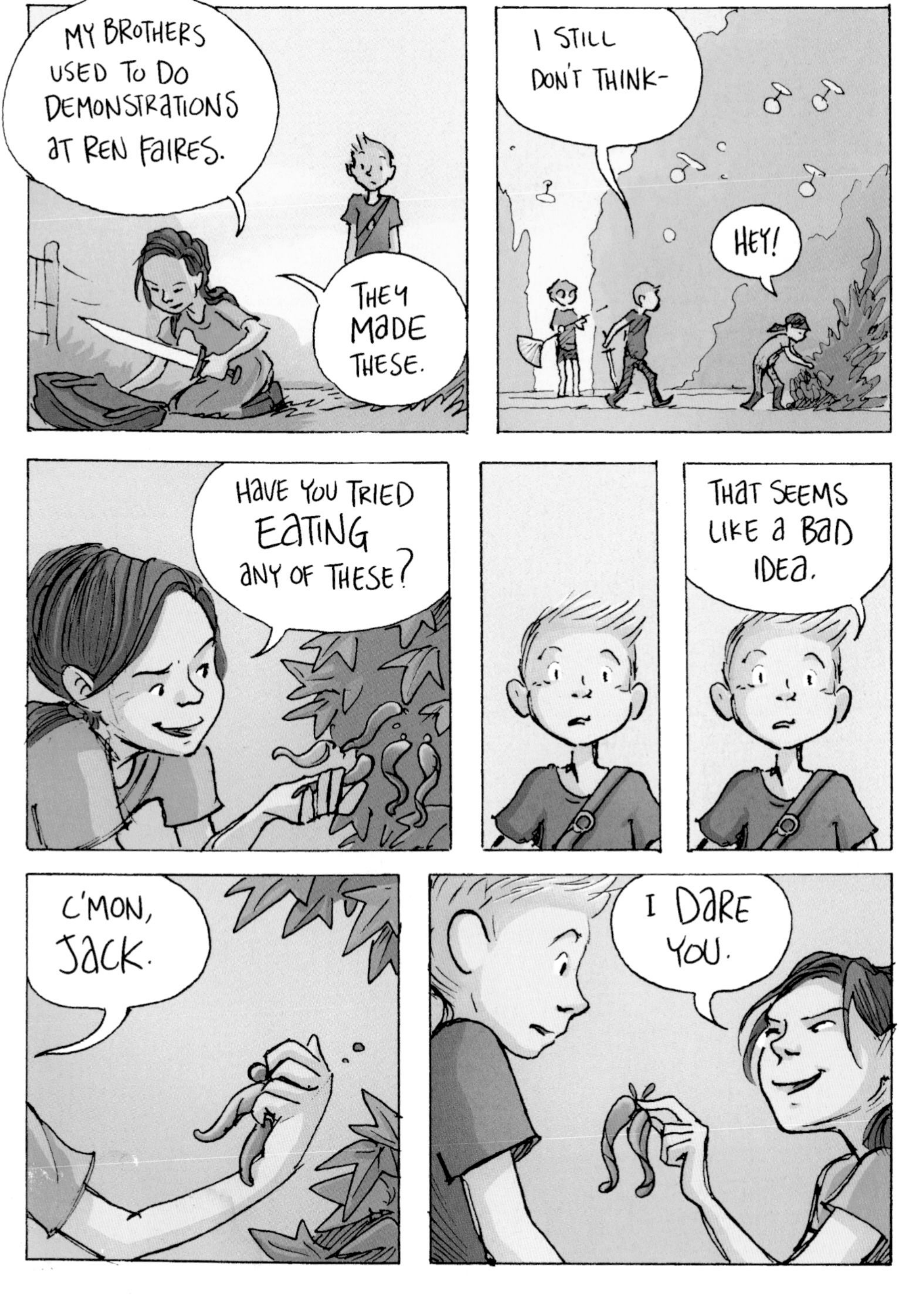

MY BROTHERS USED TO DO DEMONSTRATIONS AT REN FAIRES.
THEY MADE THESE.
I STILL DON'T THINK-
HEY!
HAVE YOU TRIED EATING ANY OF THESE?
THAT SEEMS LIKE A BAD IDEA.
C'MON, JACK.
I DARE YOU.

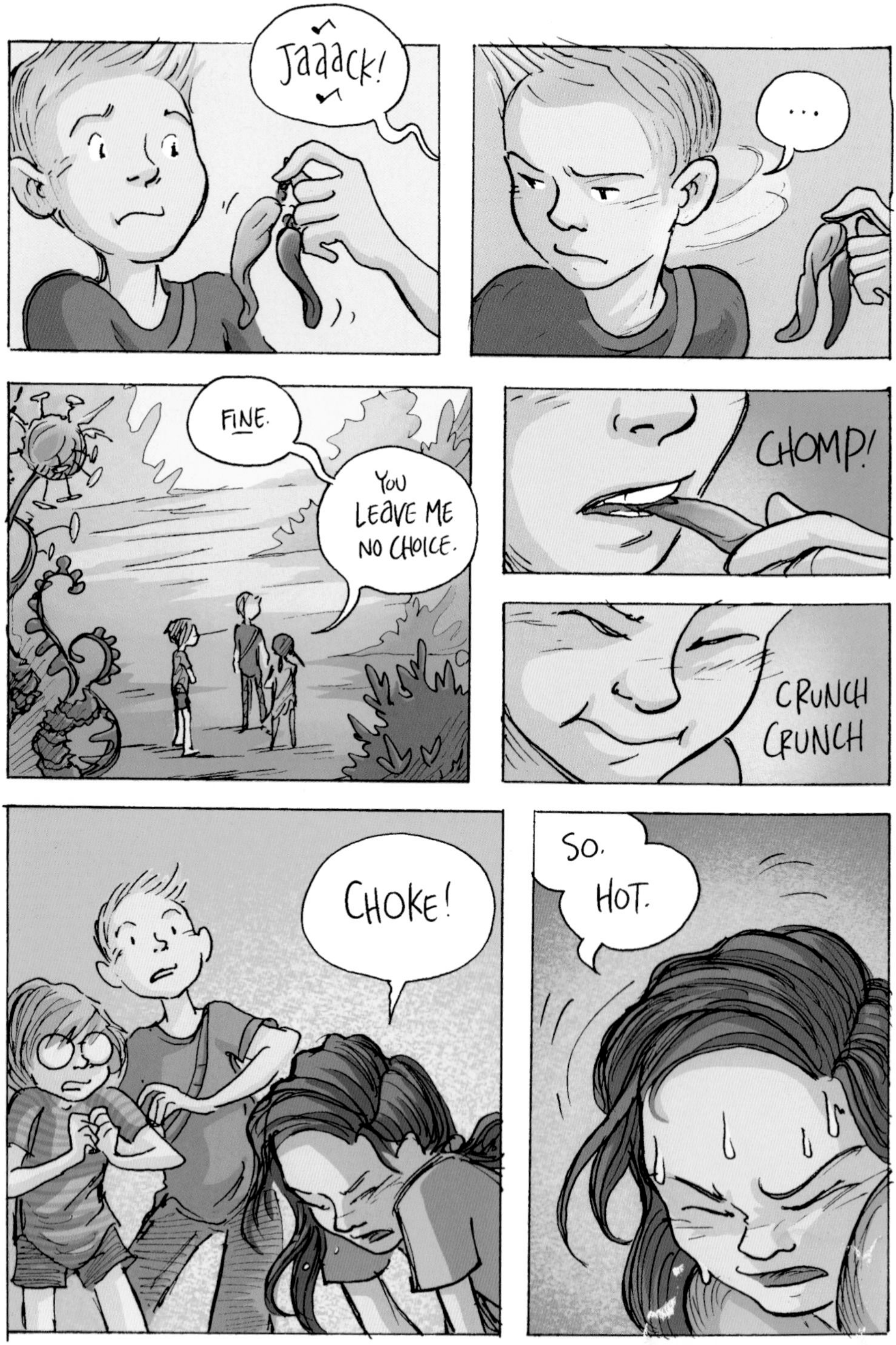
Jaaack!
...
FINE.
YOU LEAVE ME NO CHOICE.
CHOMP!
CRUNCH CRUNCH
CHOKE!
SO. HOT.

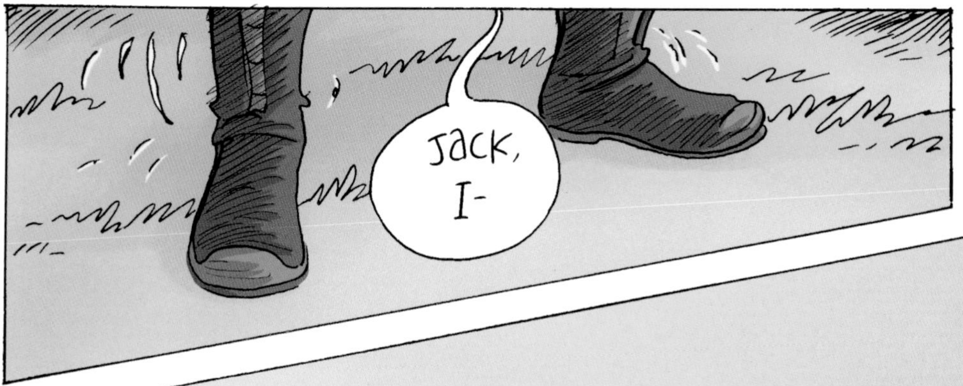

Jack, I-

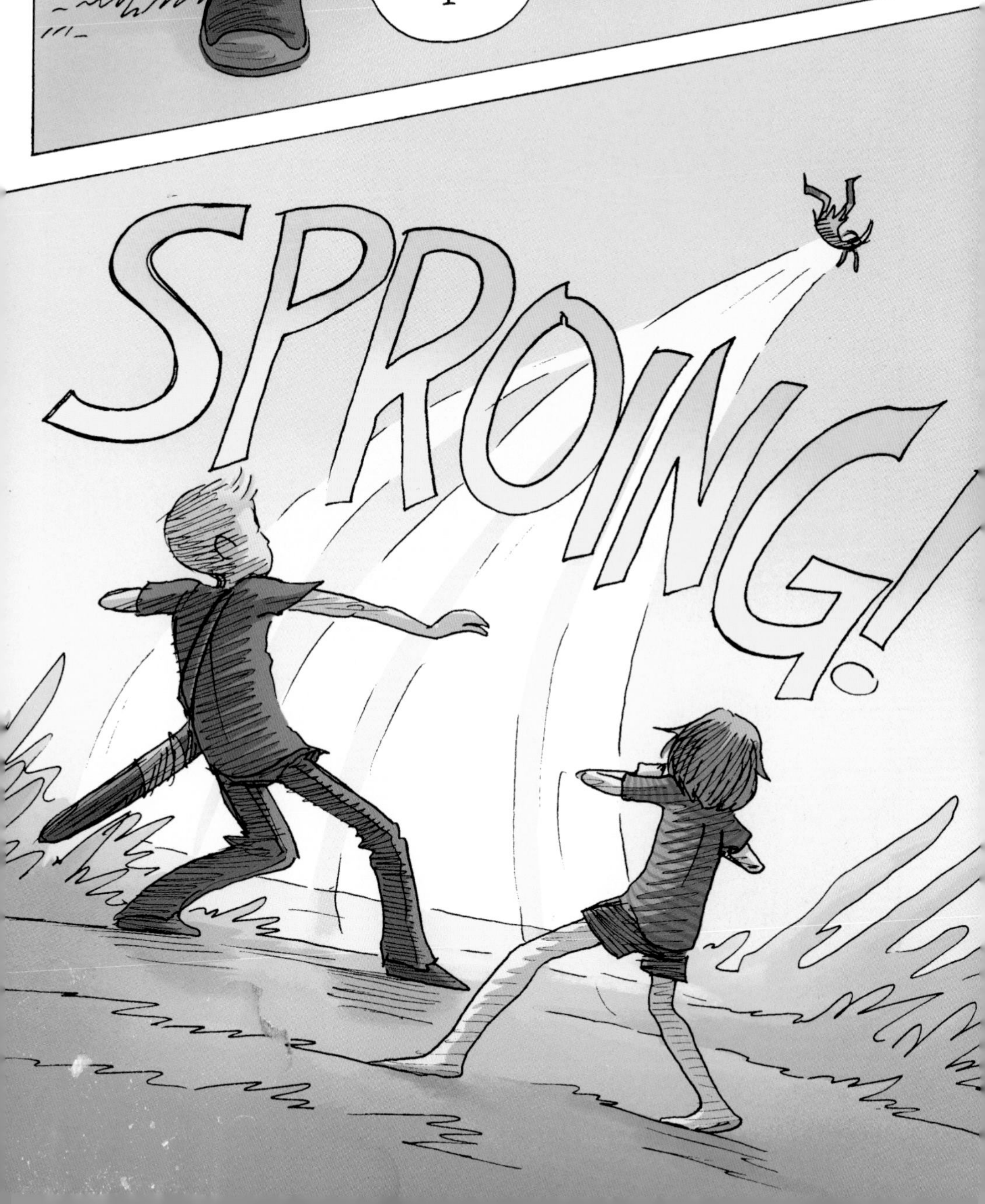

SPRONG!

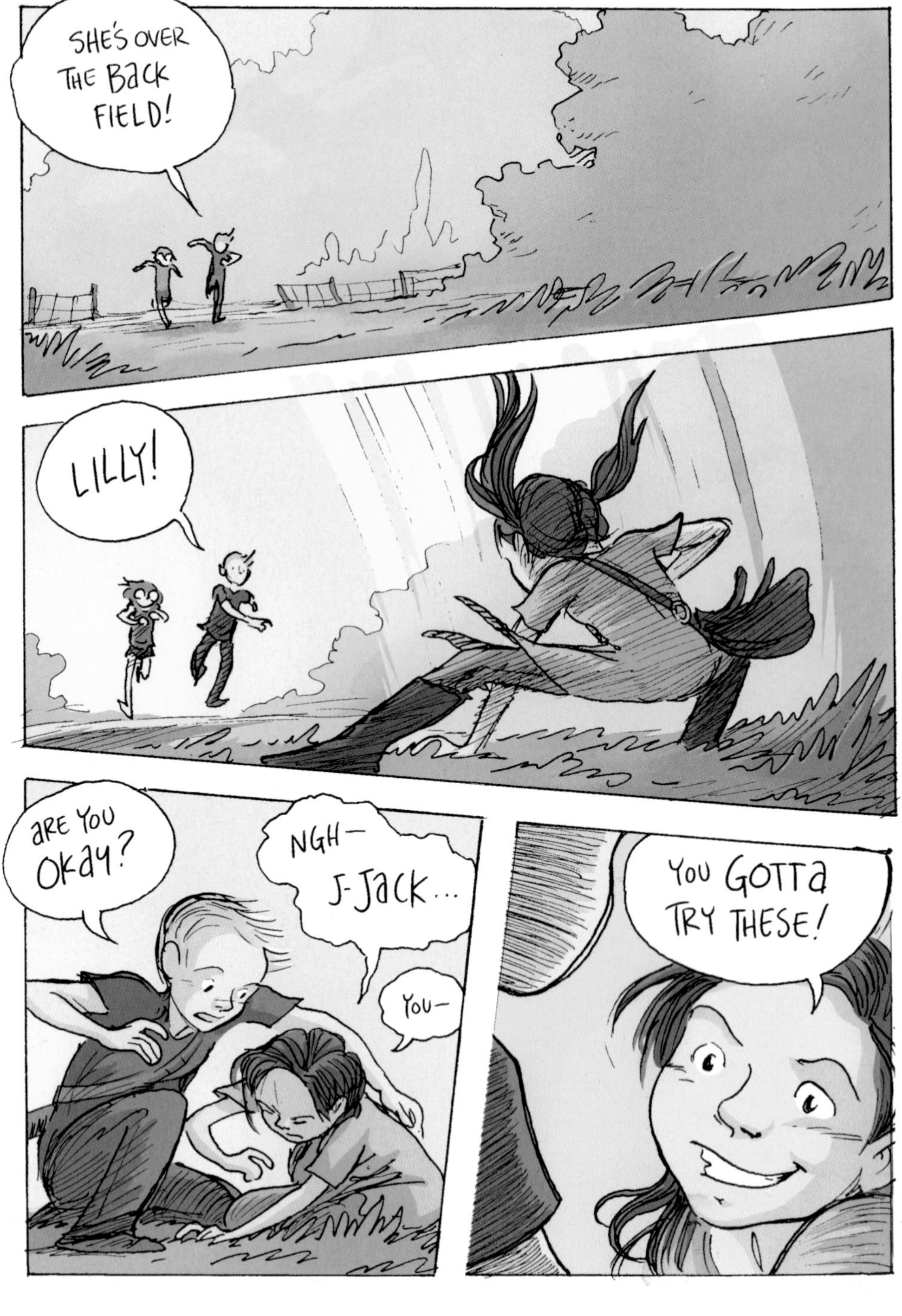
SHE'S OVER THE BACK FIELD!
LILLY!
ARE YOU OKAY?
NGH— J-JACK...
YOU—
YOU GOTTA TRY THESE!

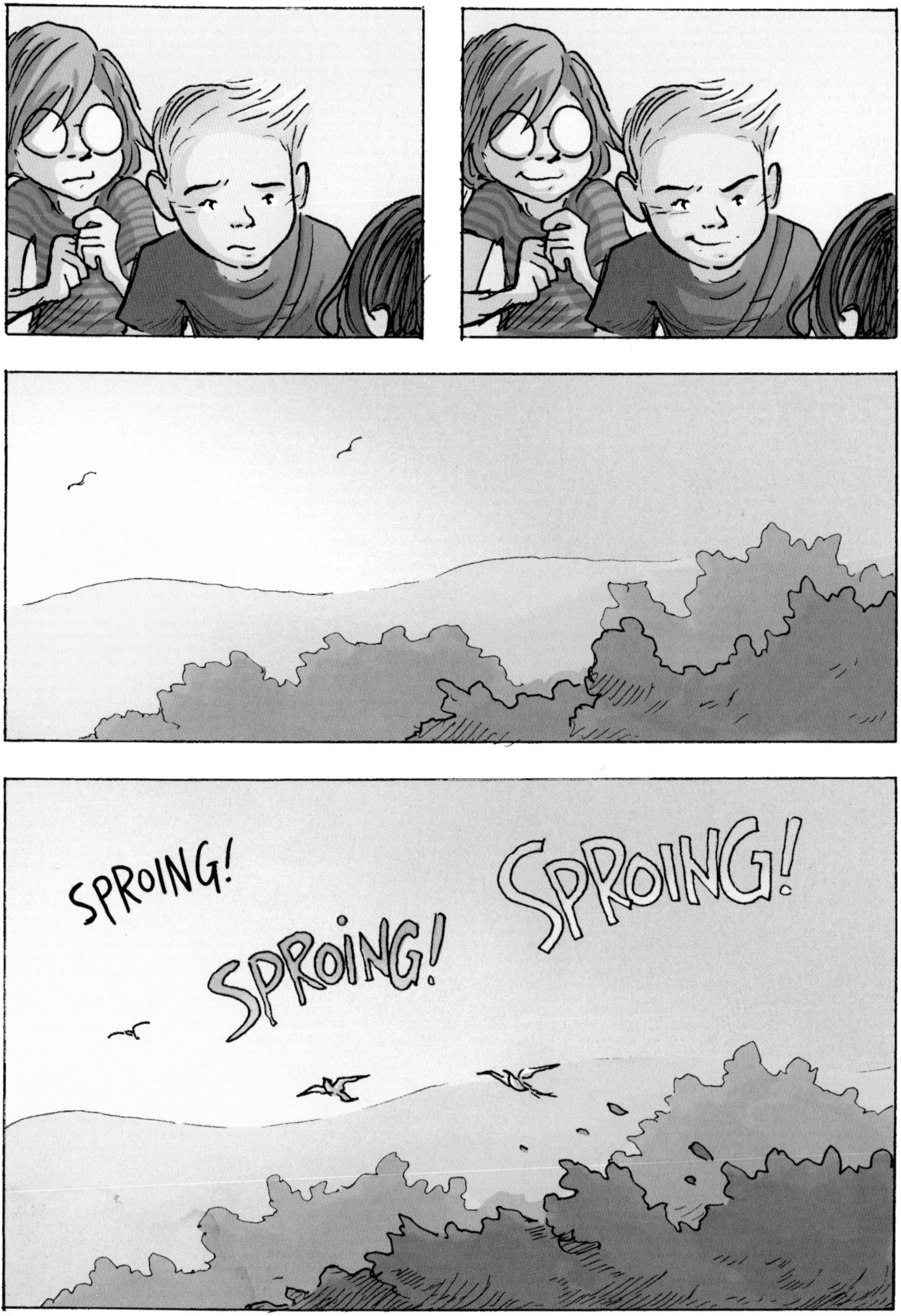
SPROING!
SPROING!
SPROING!

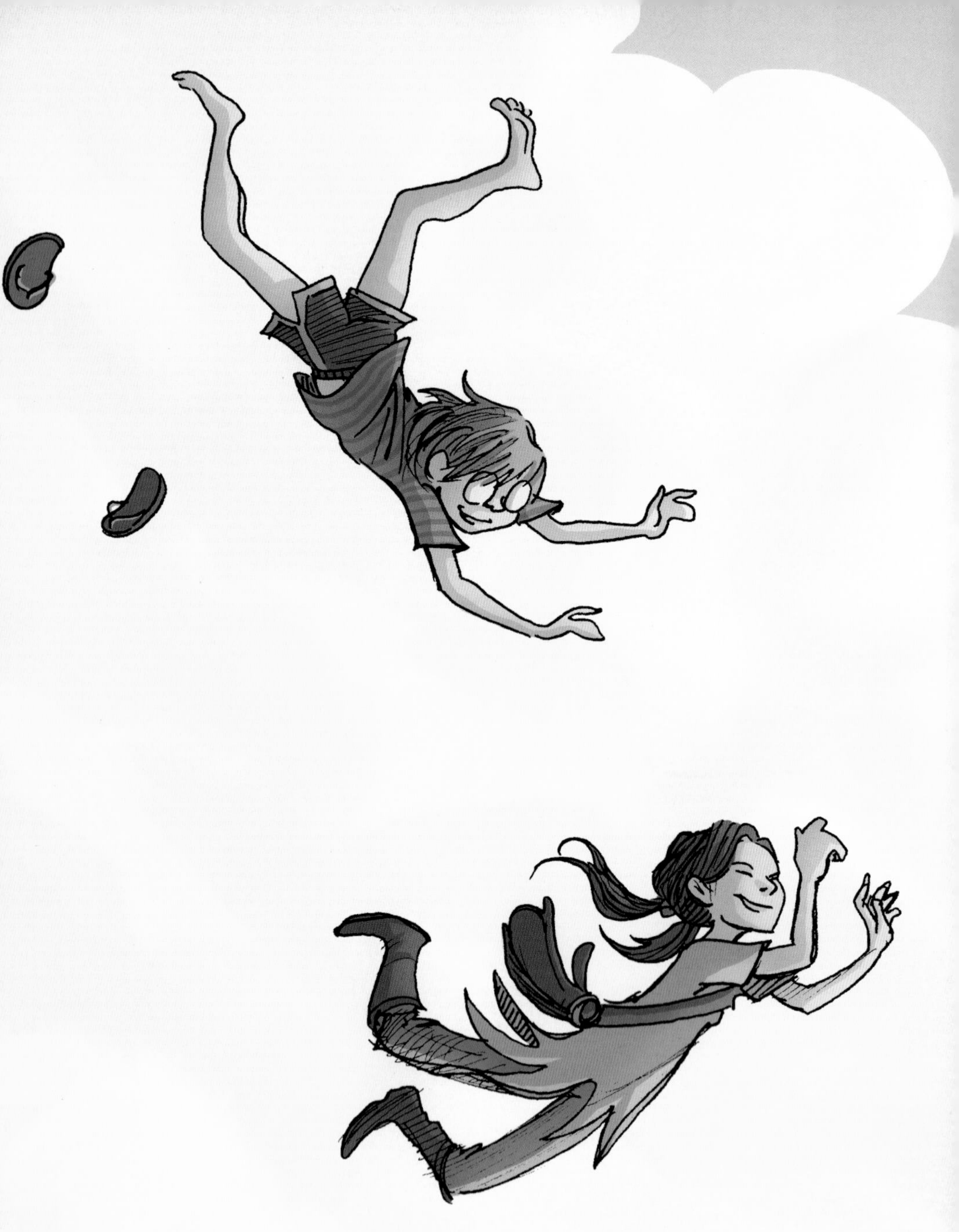

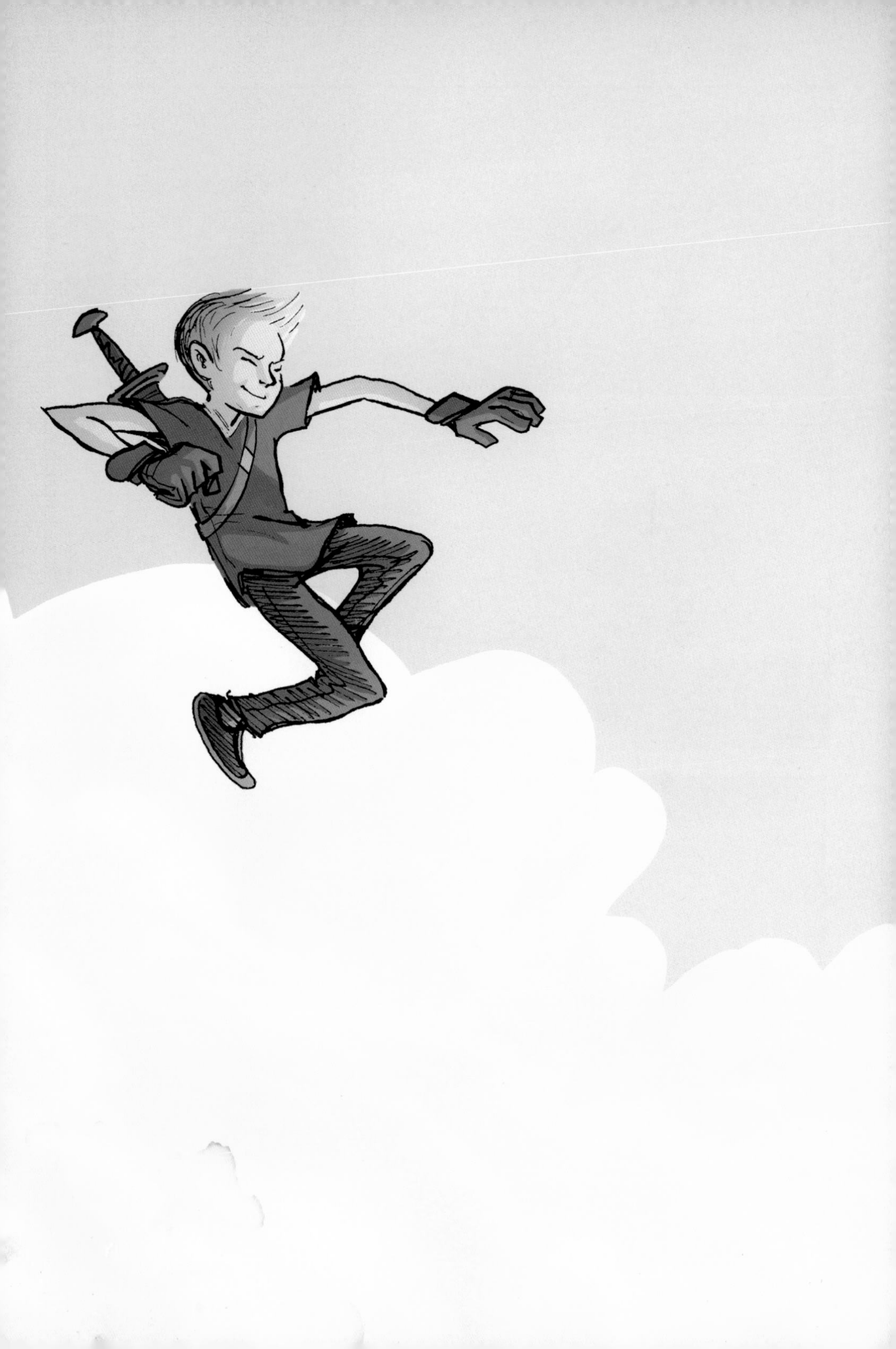

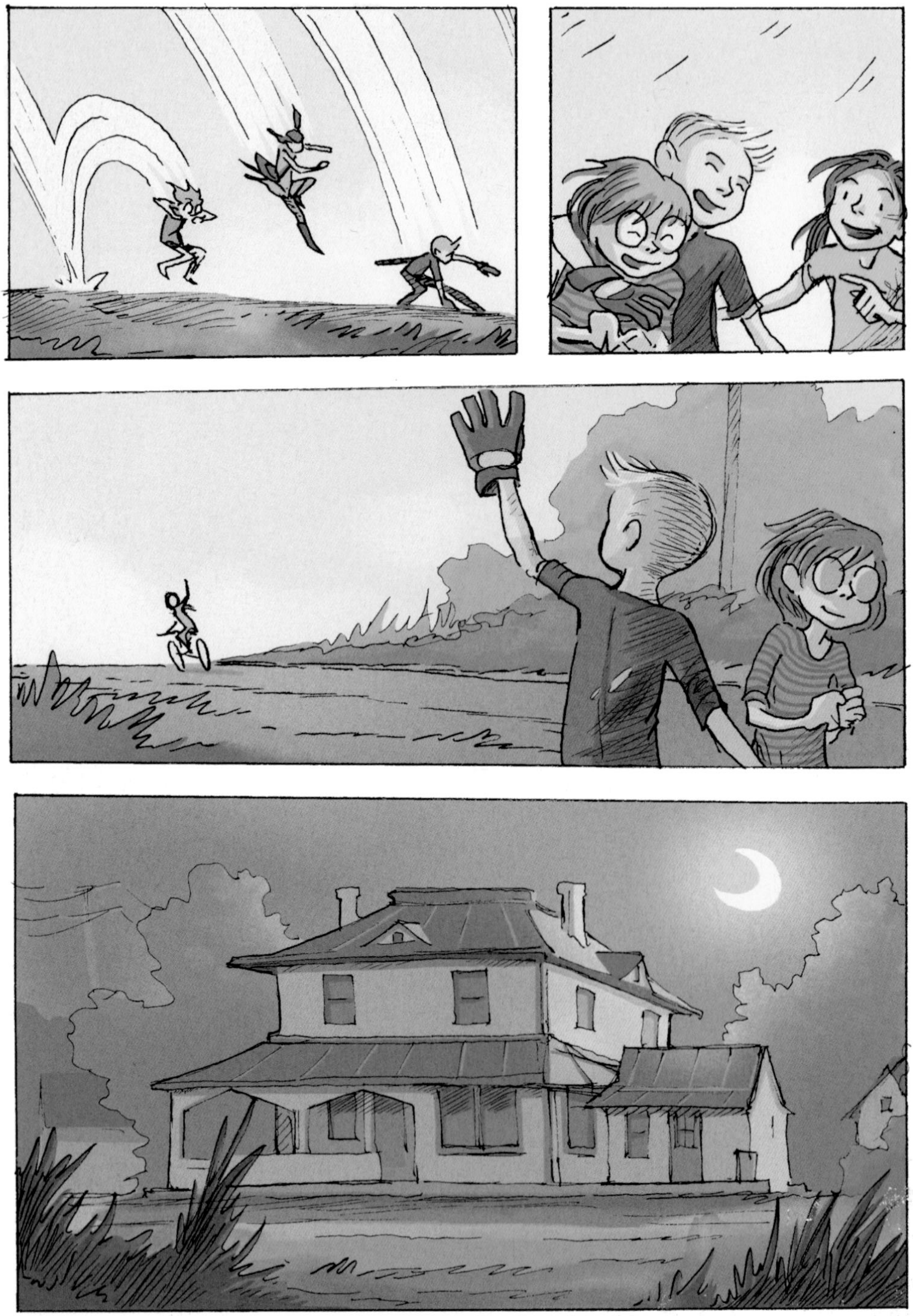

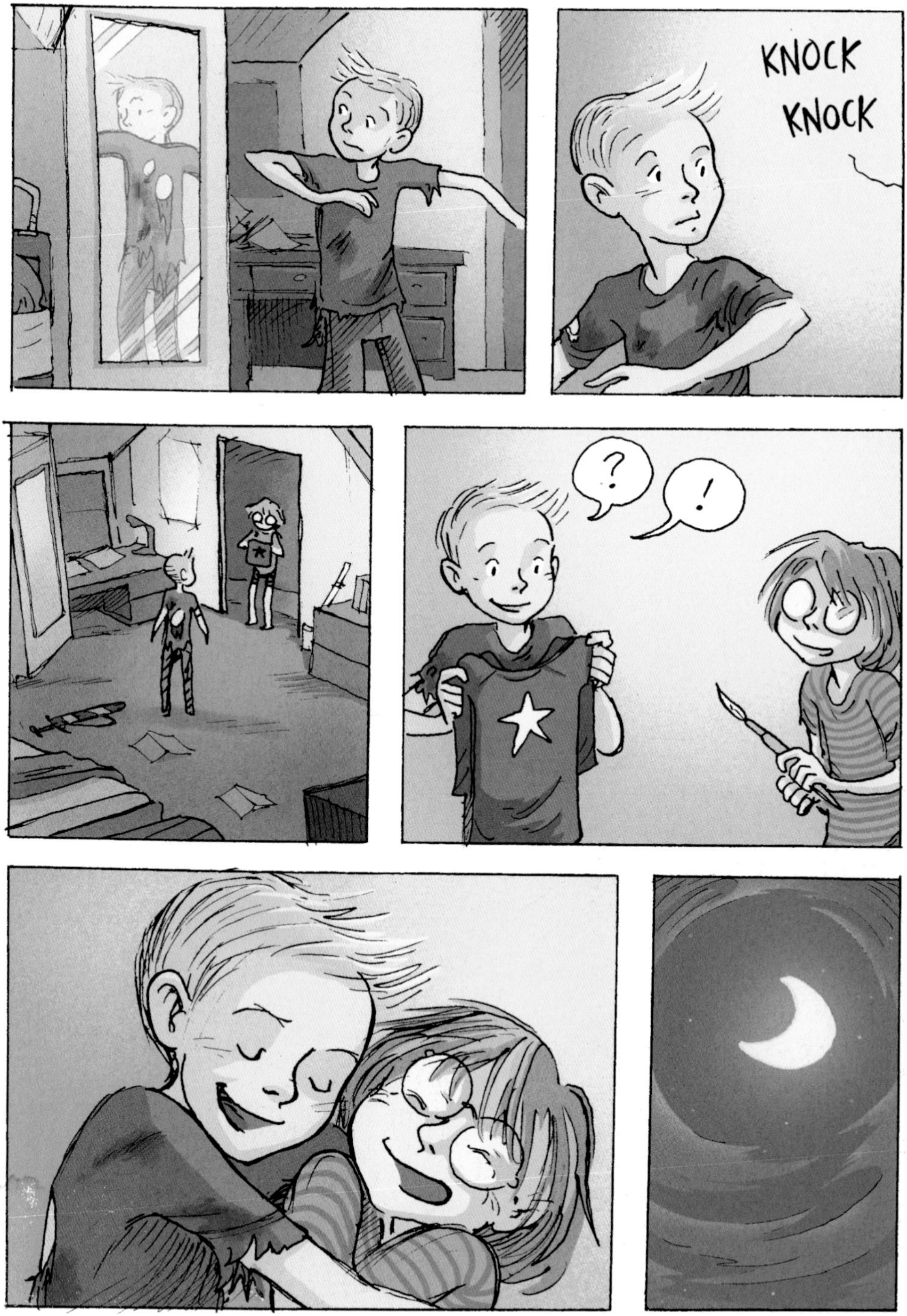
KNOCK
KNOCK
?
!

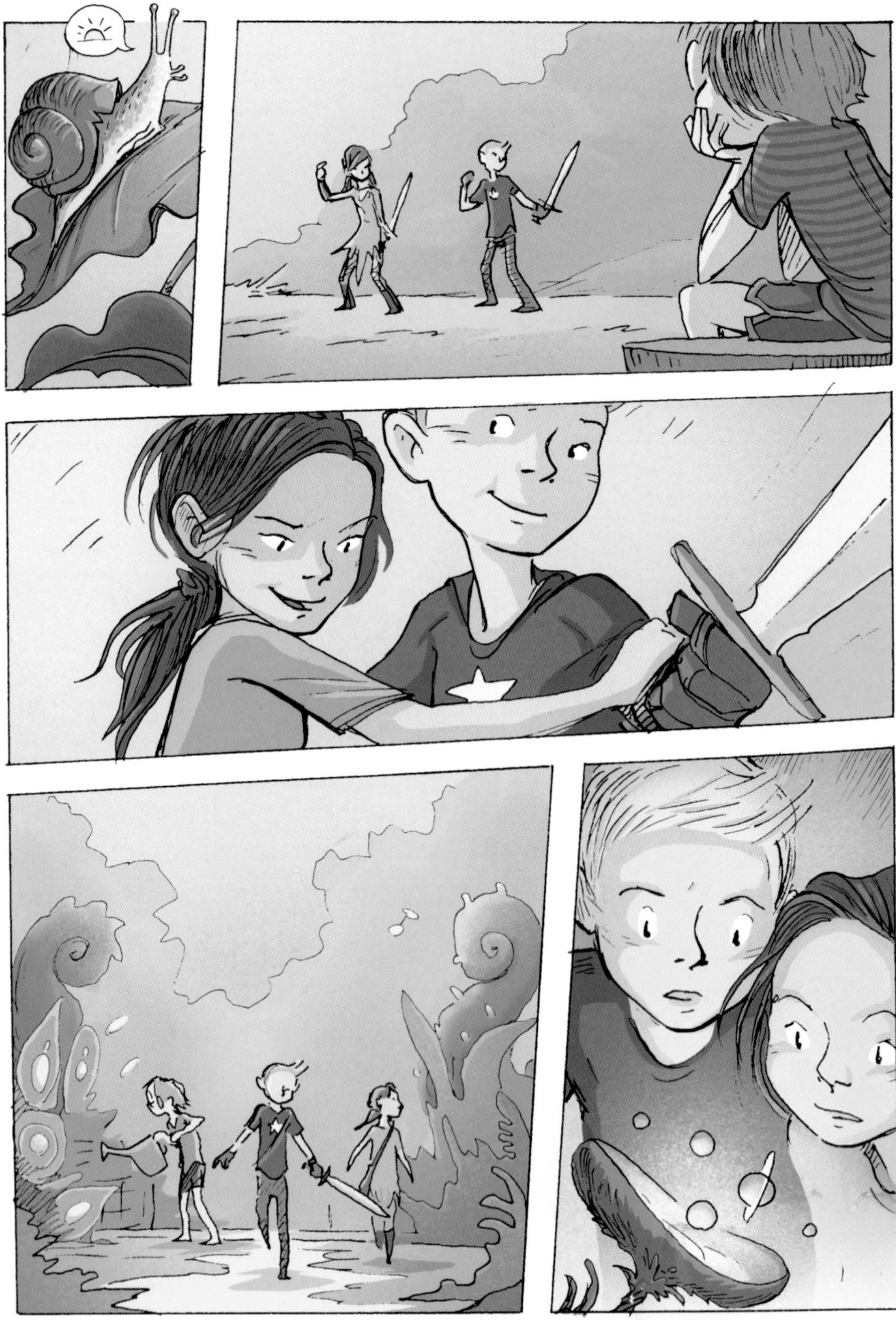

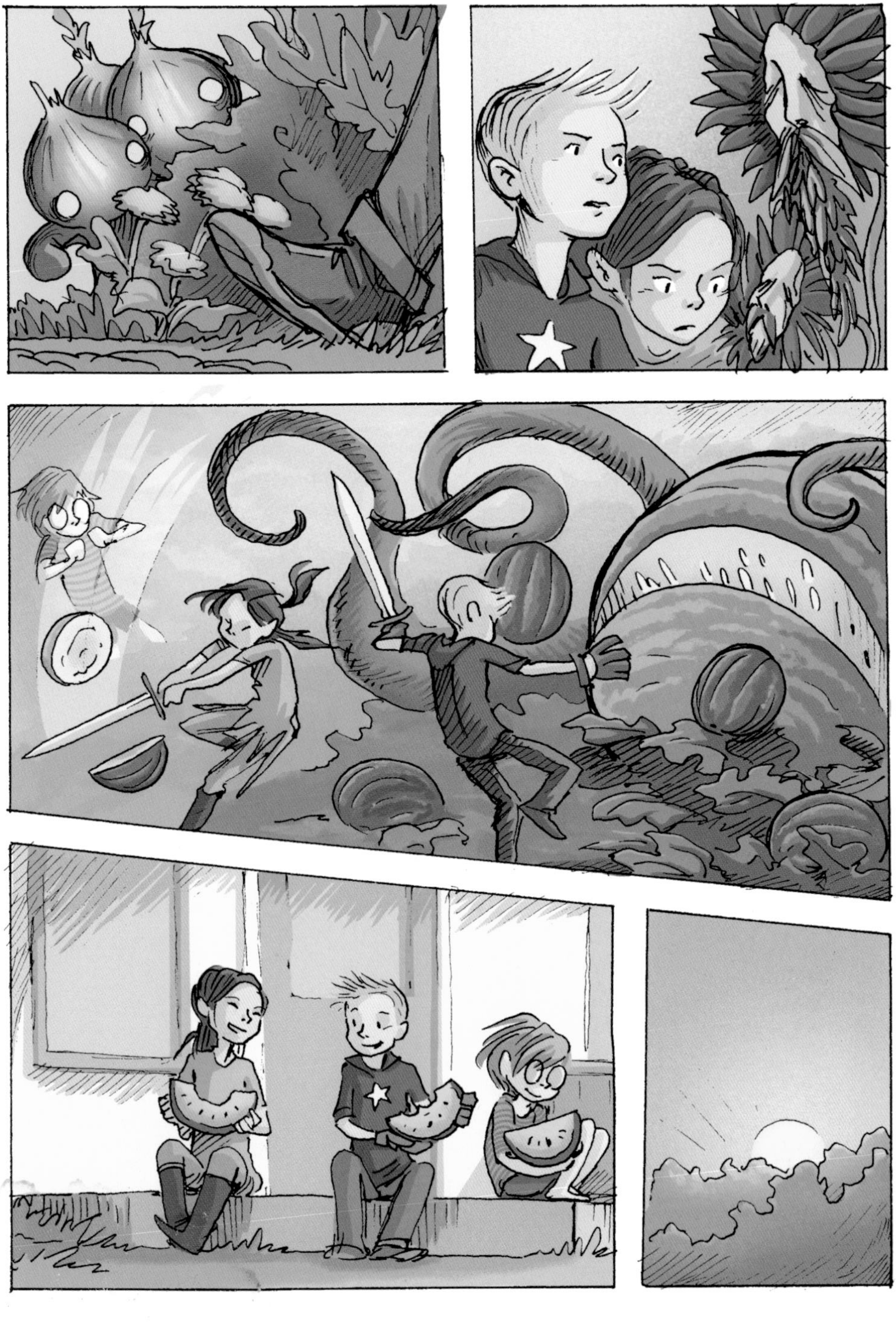

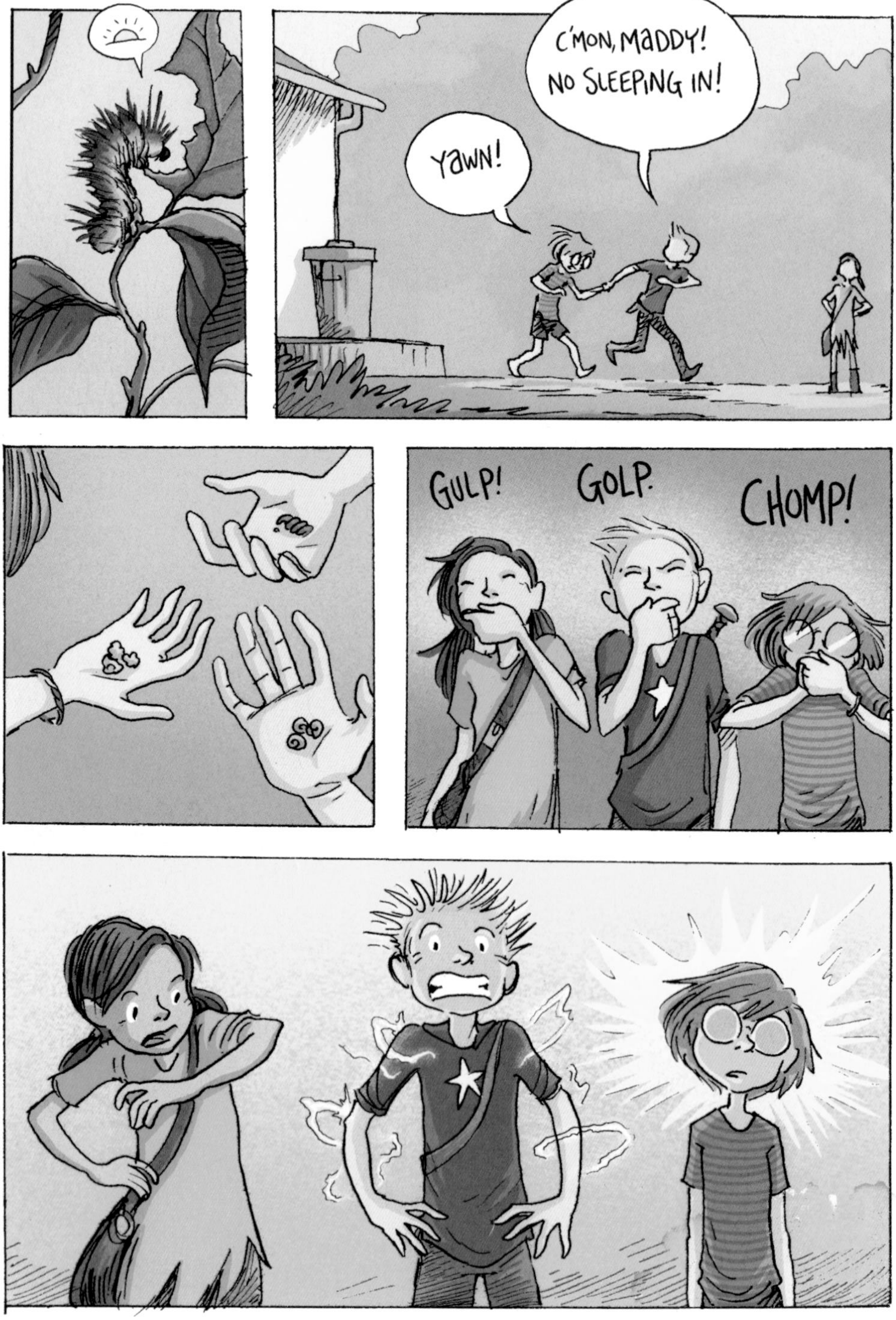
C'MON, MADDY!
NO SLEEPING IN!
YAWN!
GULP!
GOLP.
CHOMP!

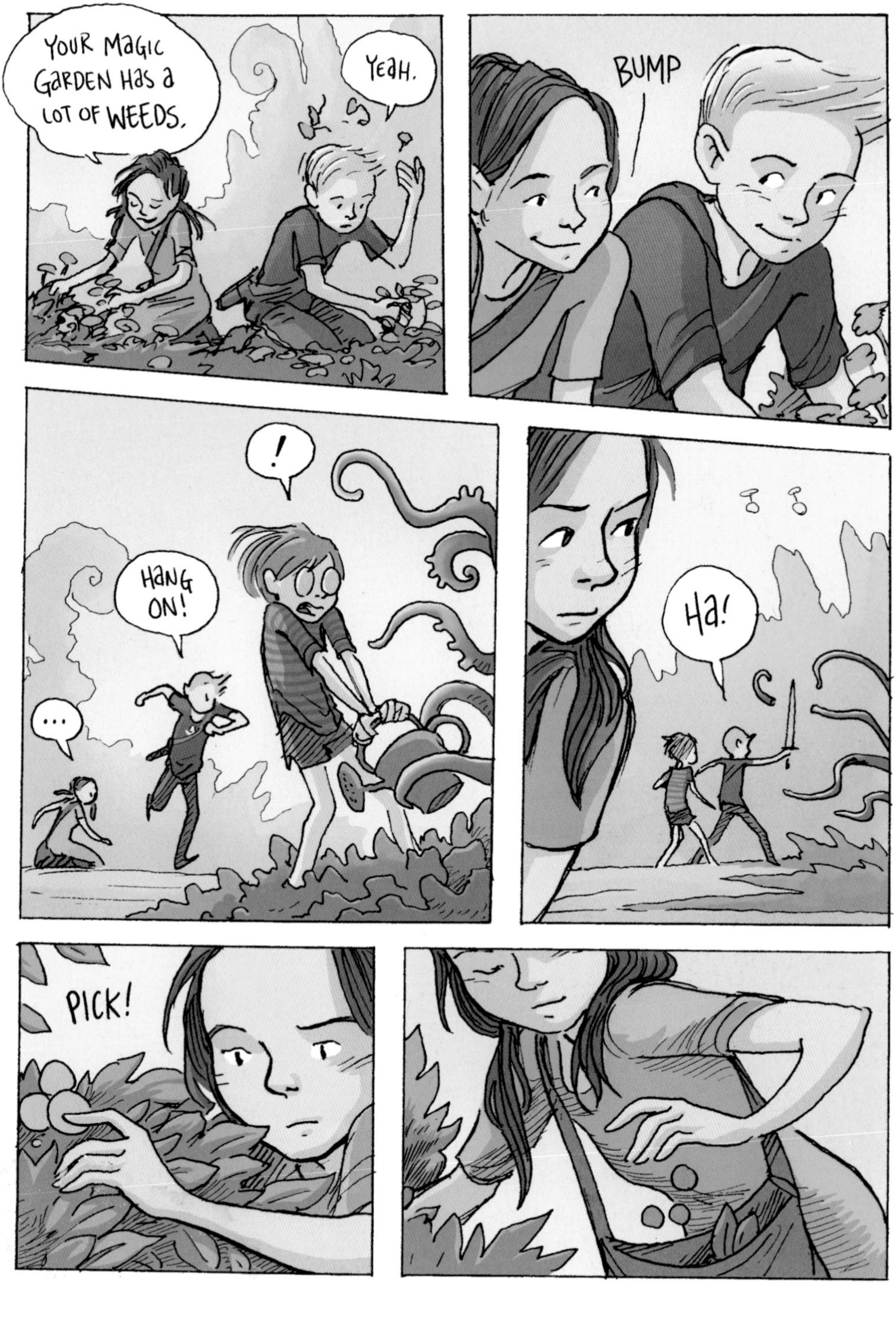
YOUR MAGIC GARDEN HAS A LOT OF WEEDS.
YEAH.
BUMP
!
HANG ON!
...
HA!
PICK!

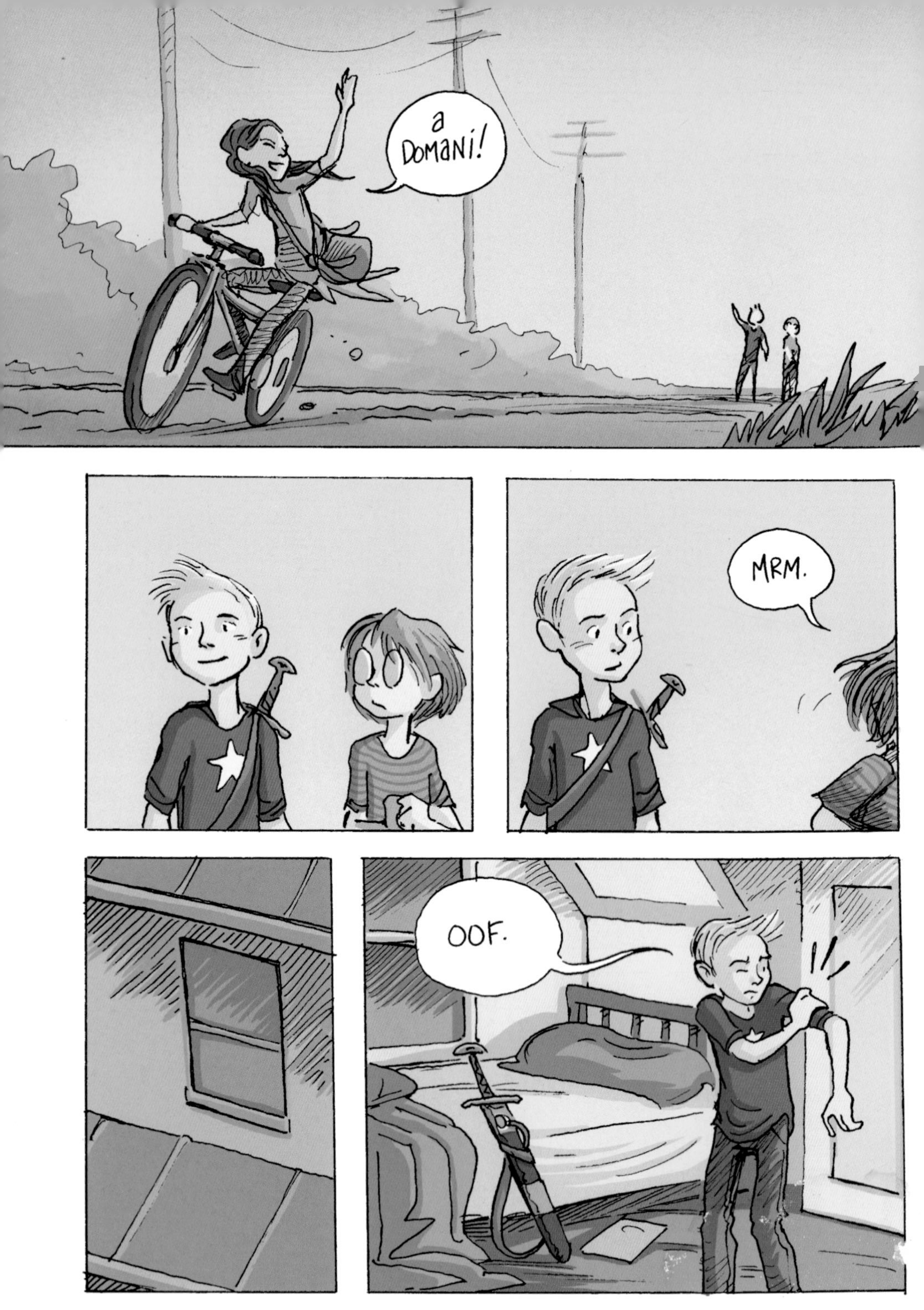
a DOMANI!
MRM.
OOF.

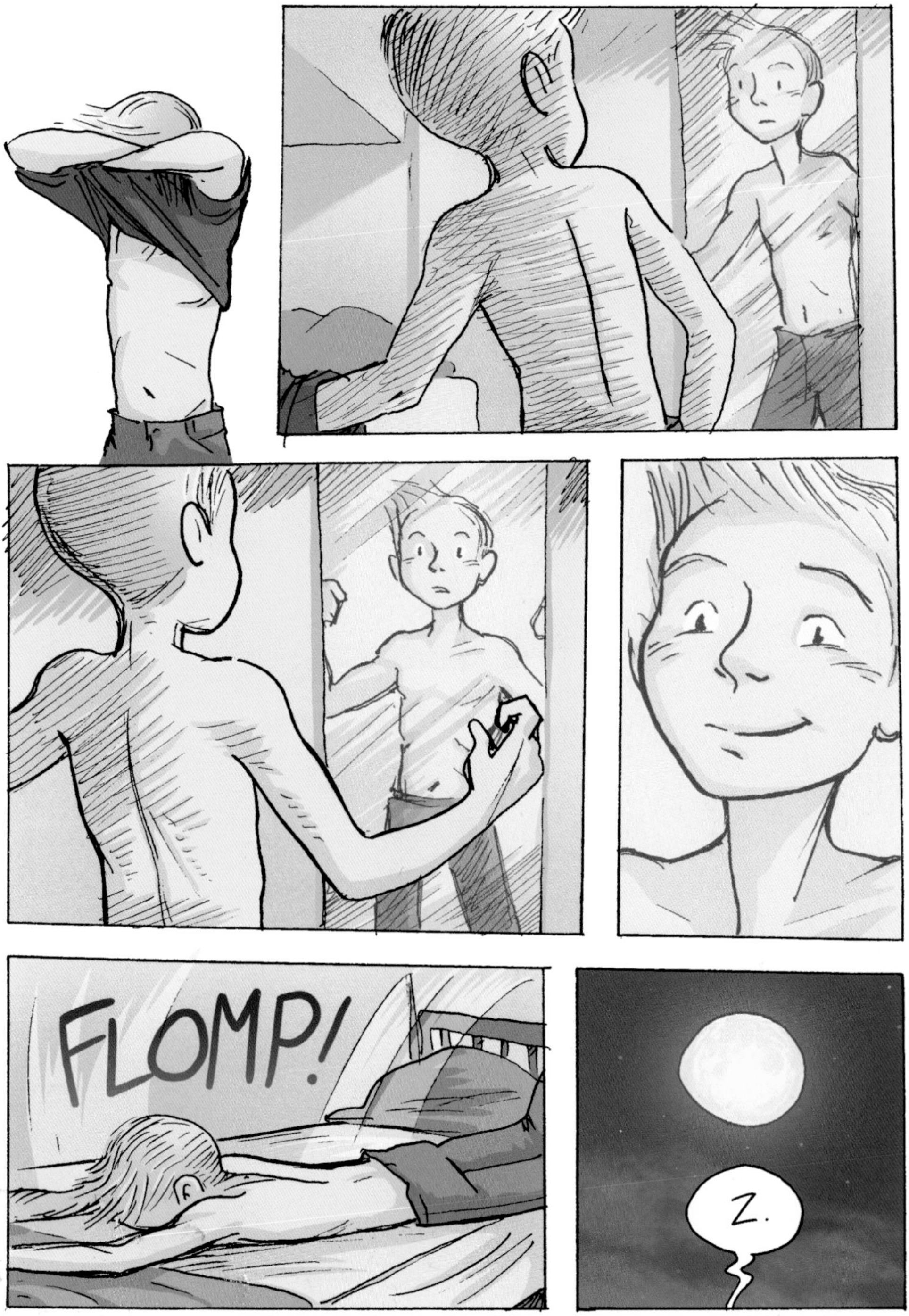
FLOMP!
Z.

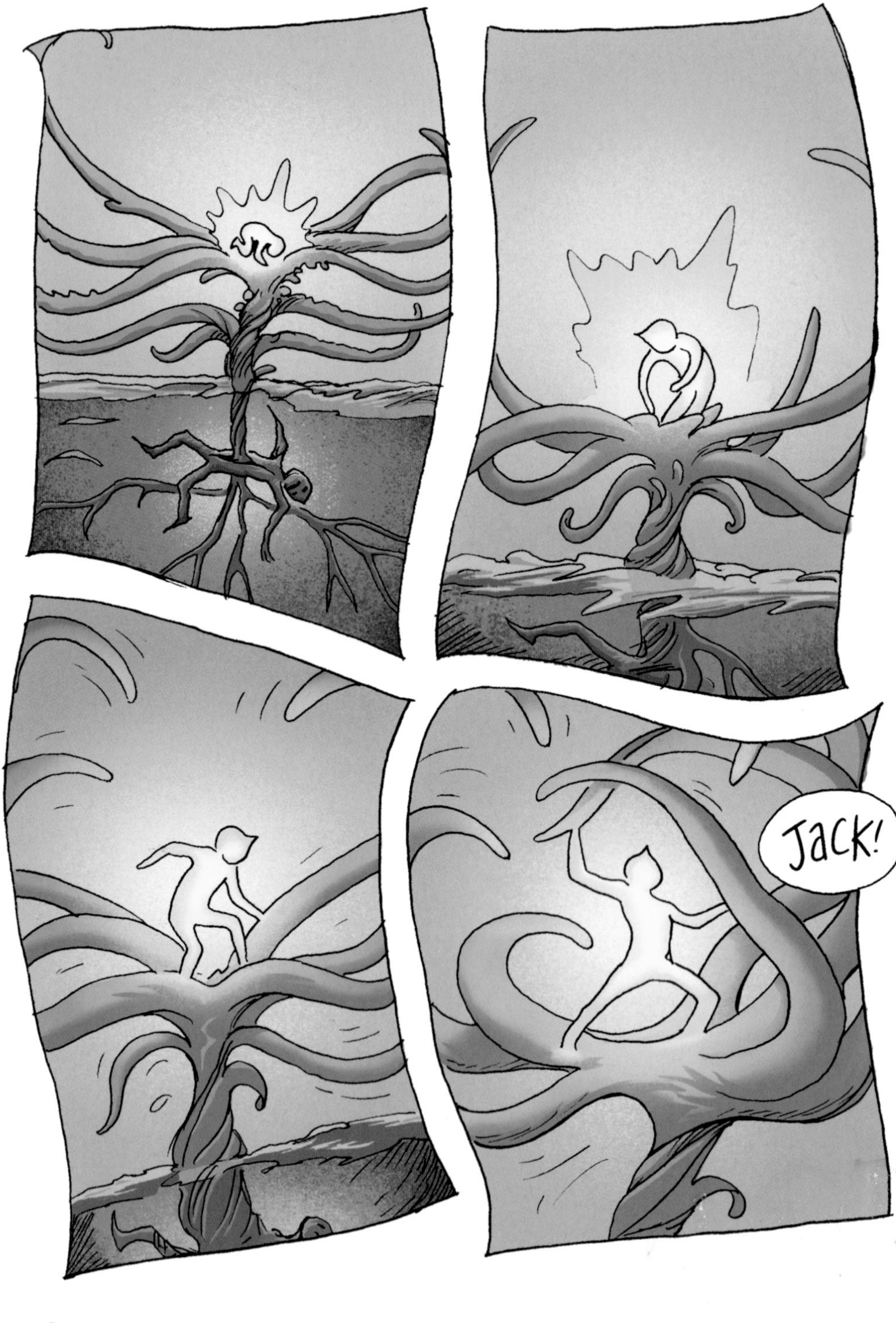
JACK!

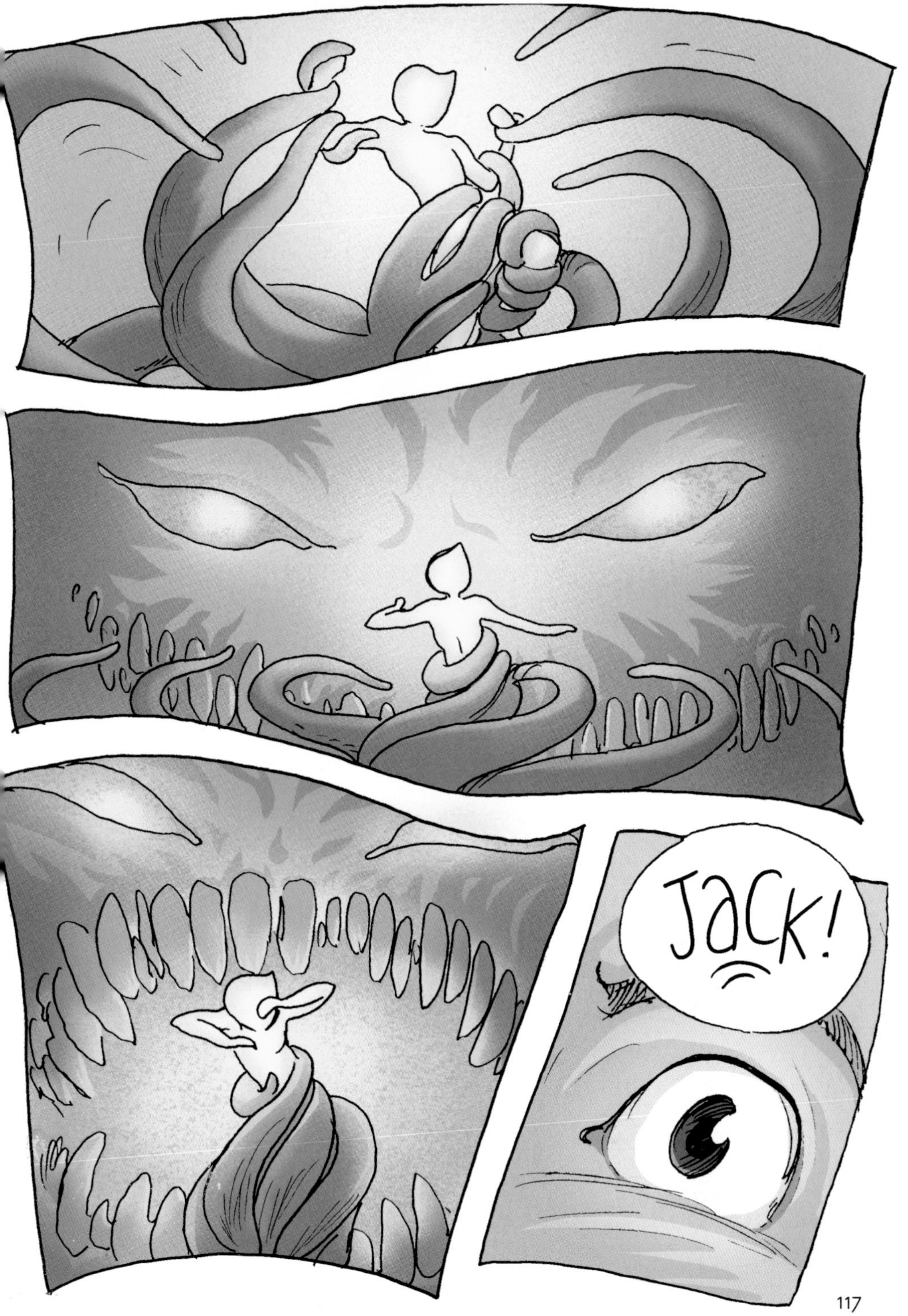
JACK!

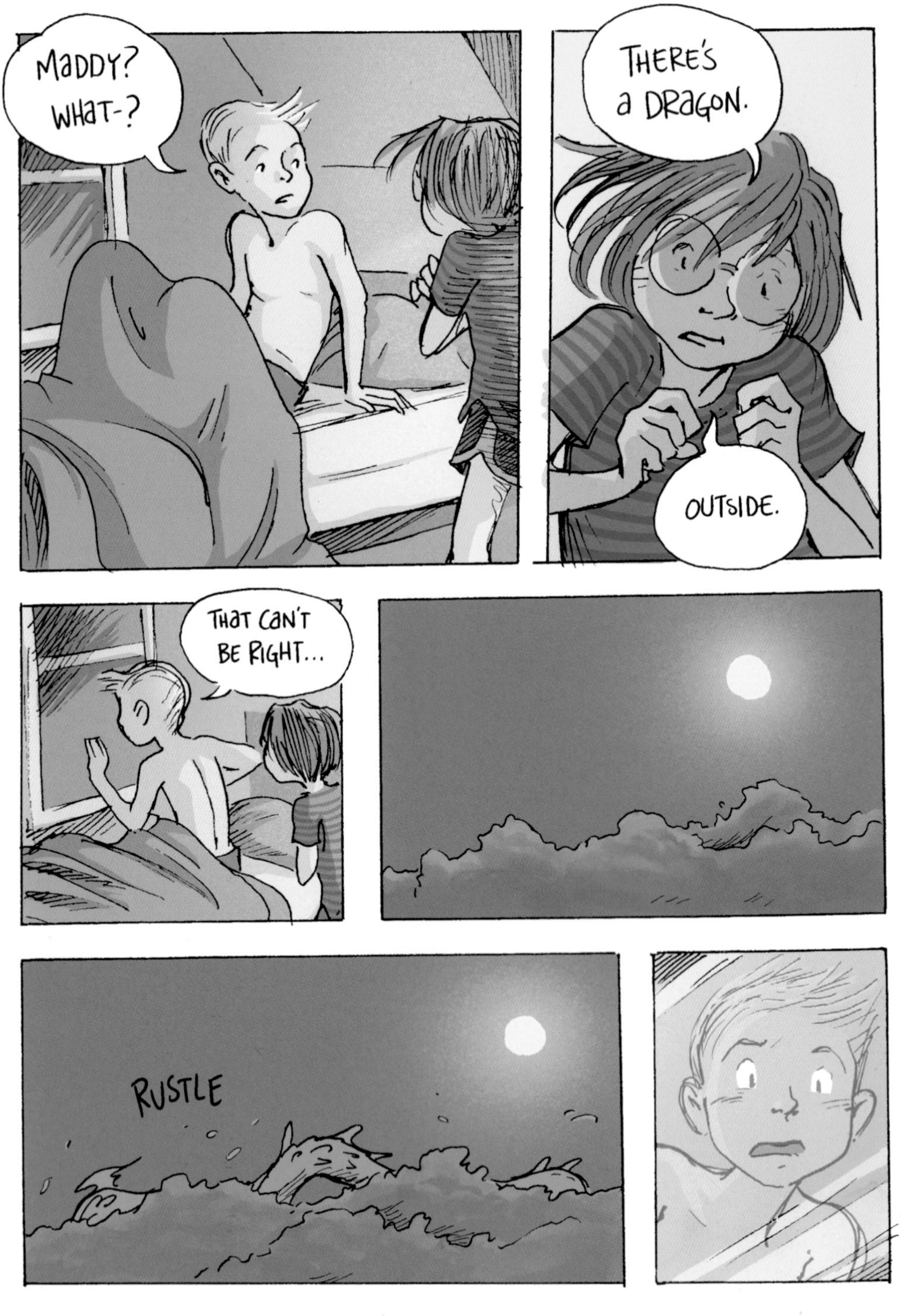
MADDY? WHAT-?
THERE'S A DRAGON.
OUTSIDE.
THAT CAN'T BE RIGHT...
RUSTLE

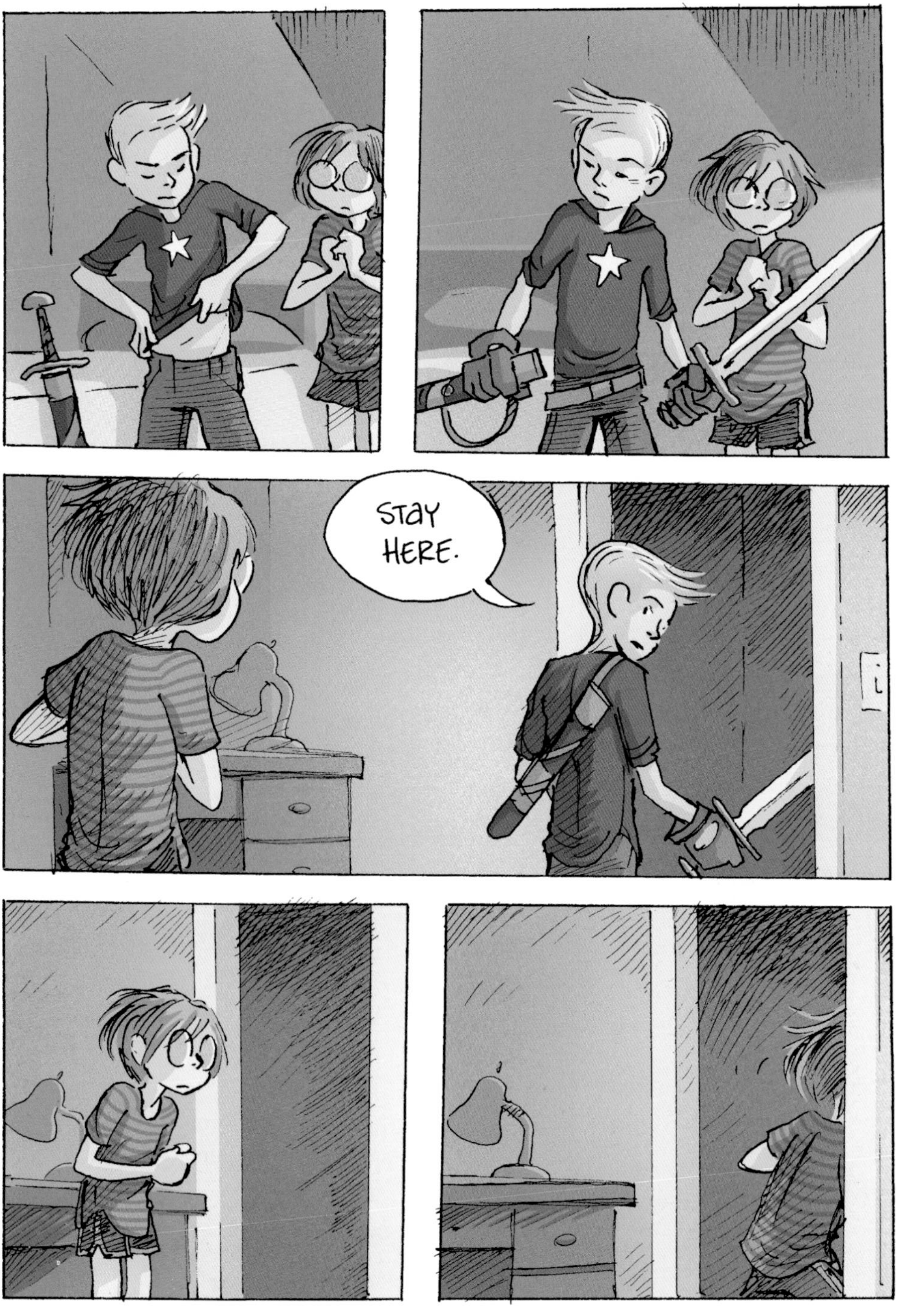
STAY HERE.

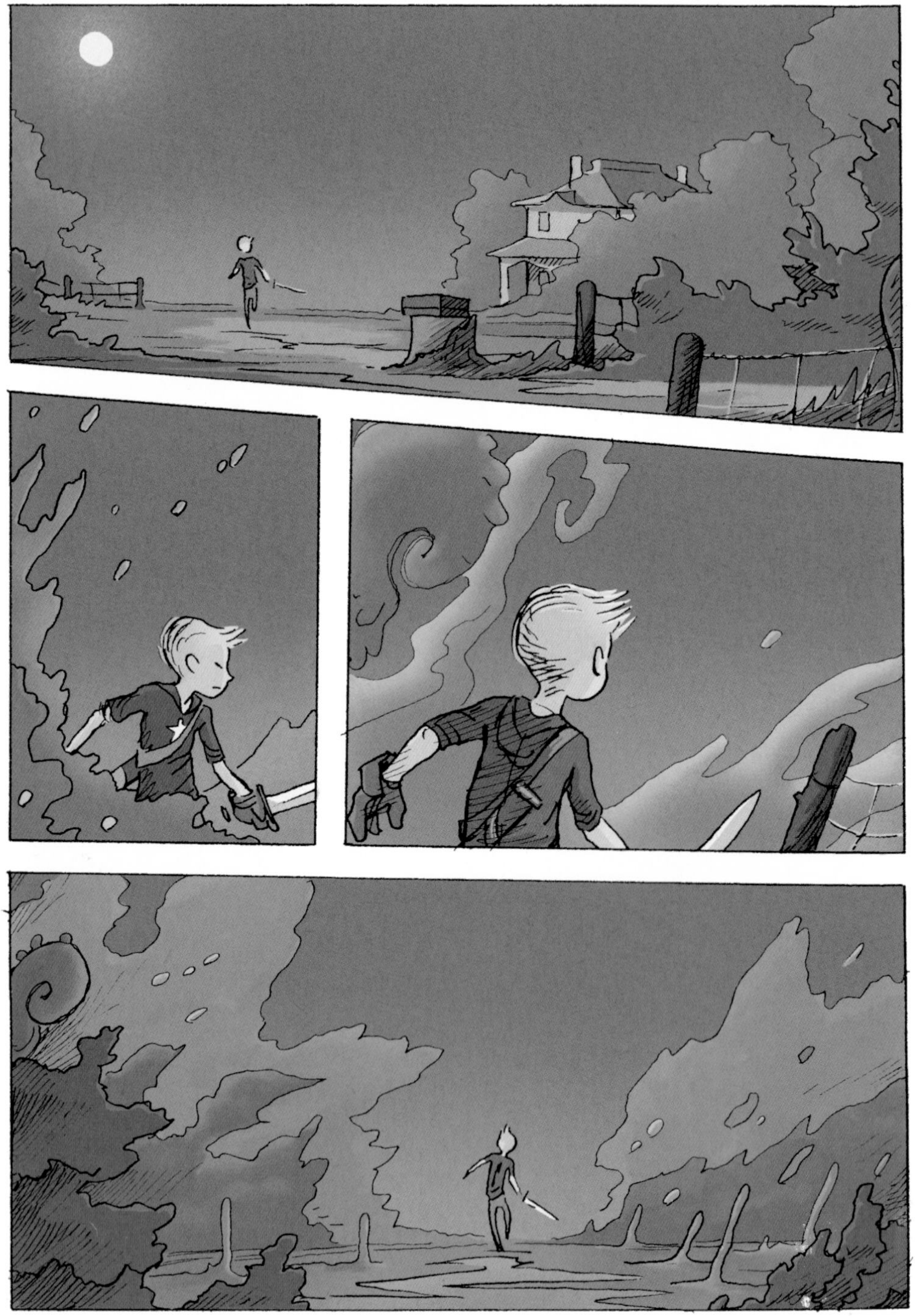

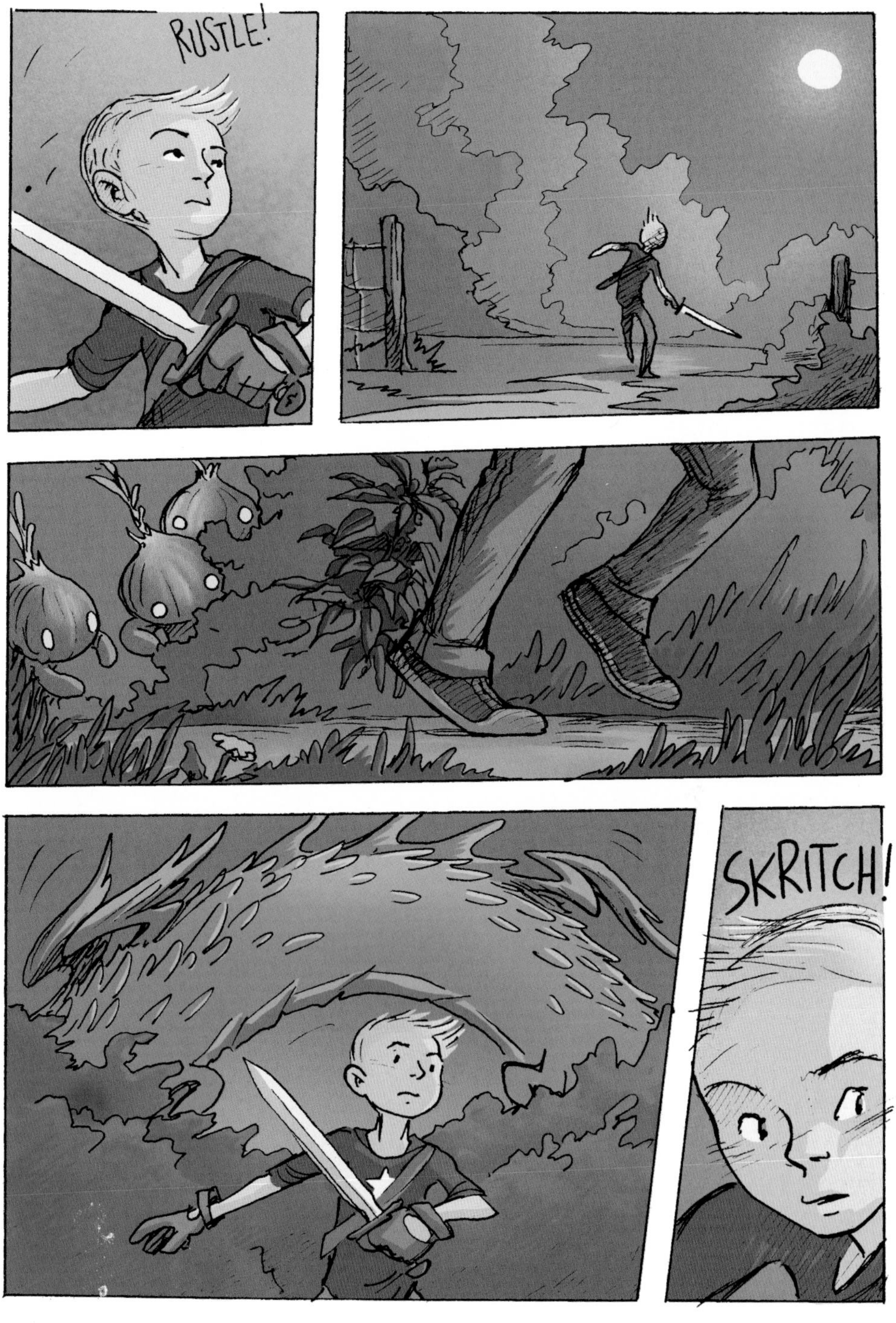
RUSTLE!
SKRITCH!

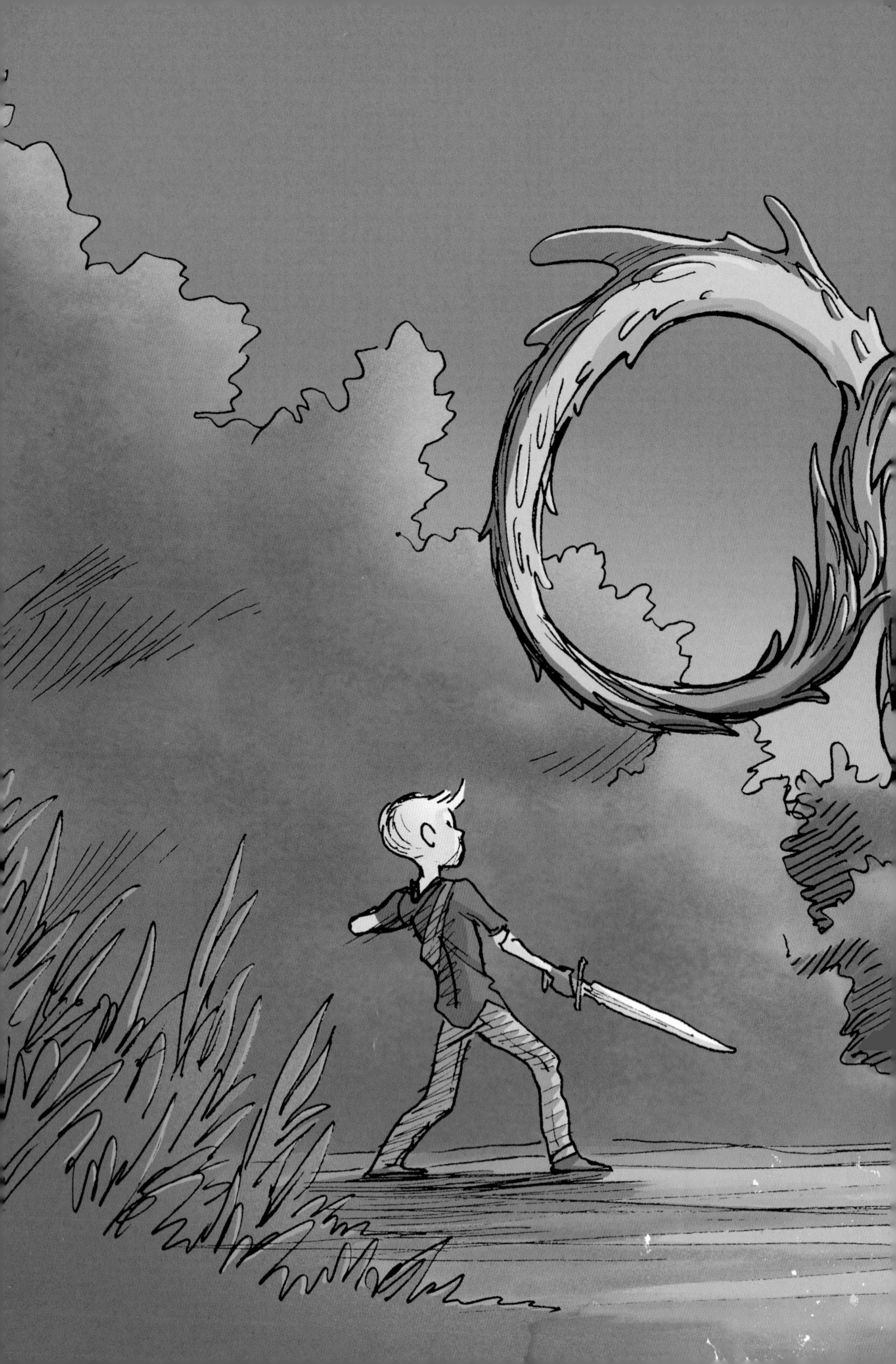

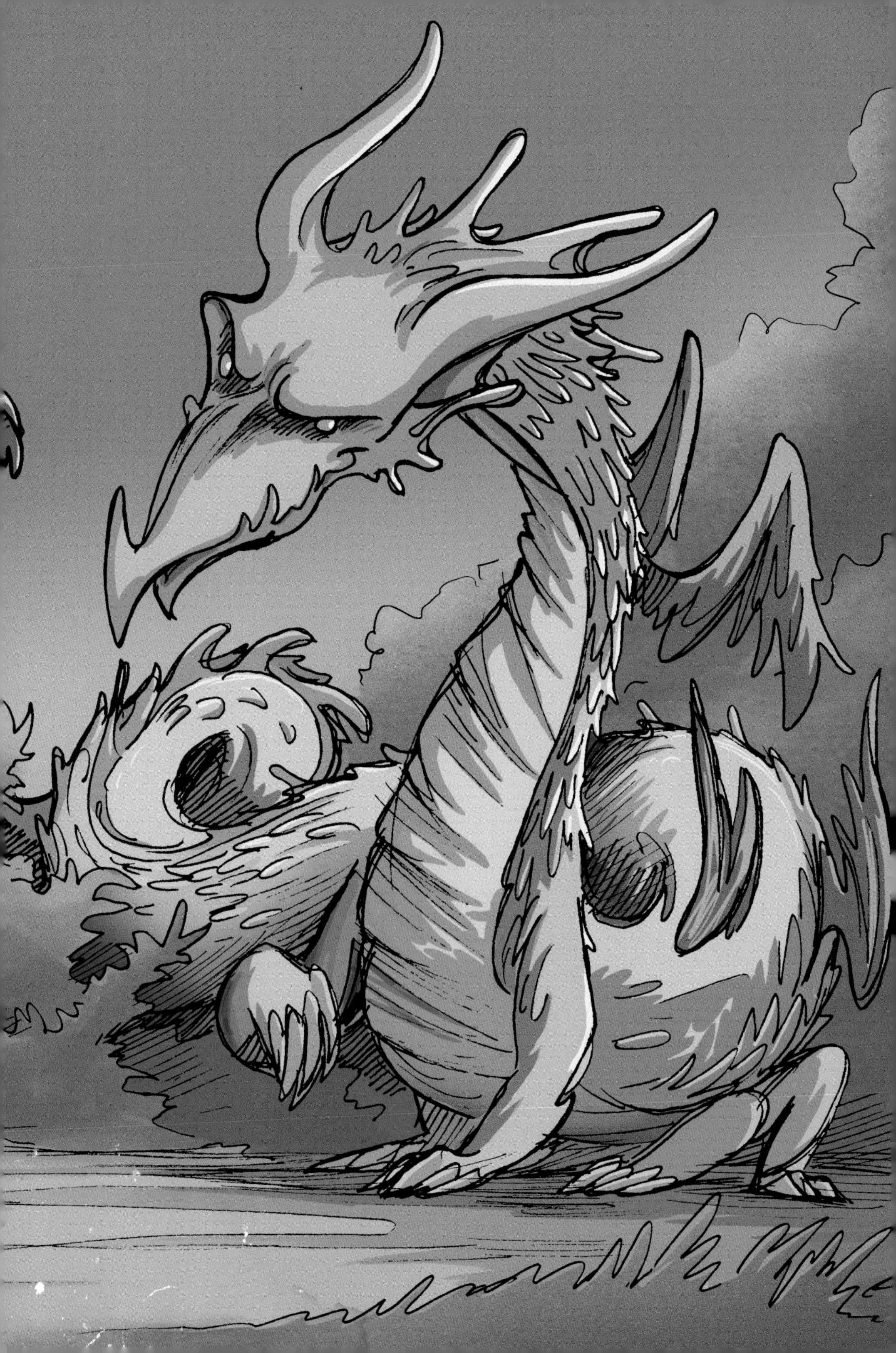

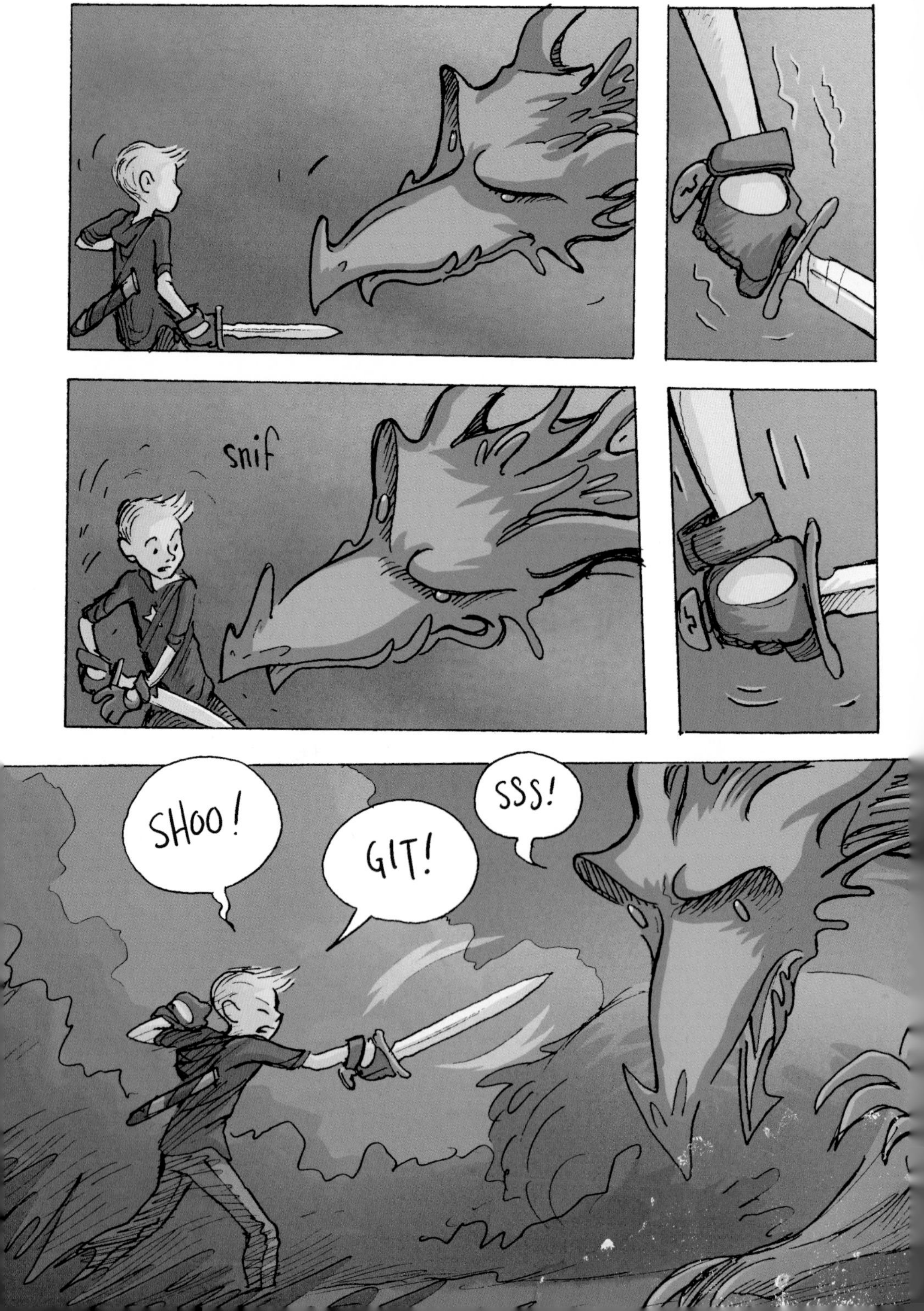
snif
SHOO!
GIT!
SSS!

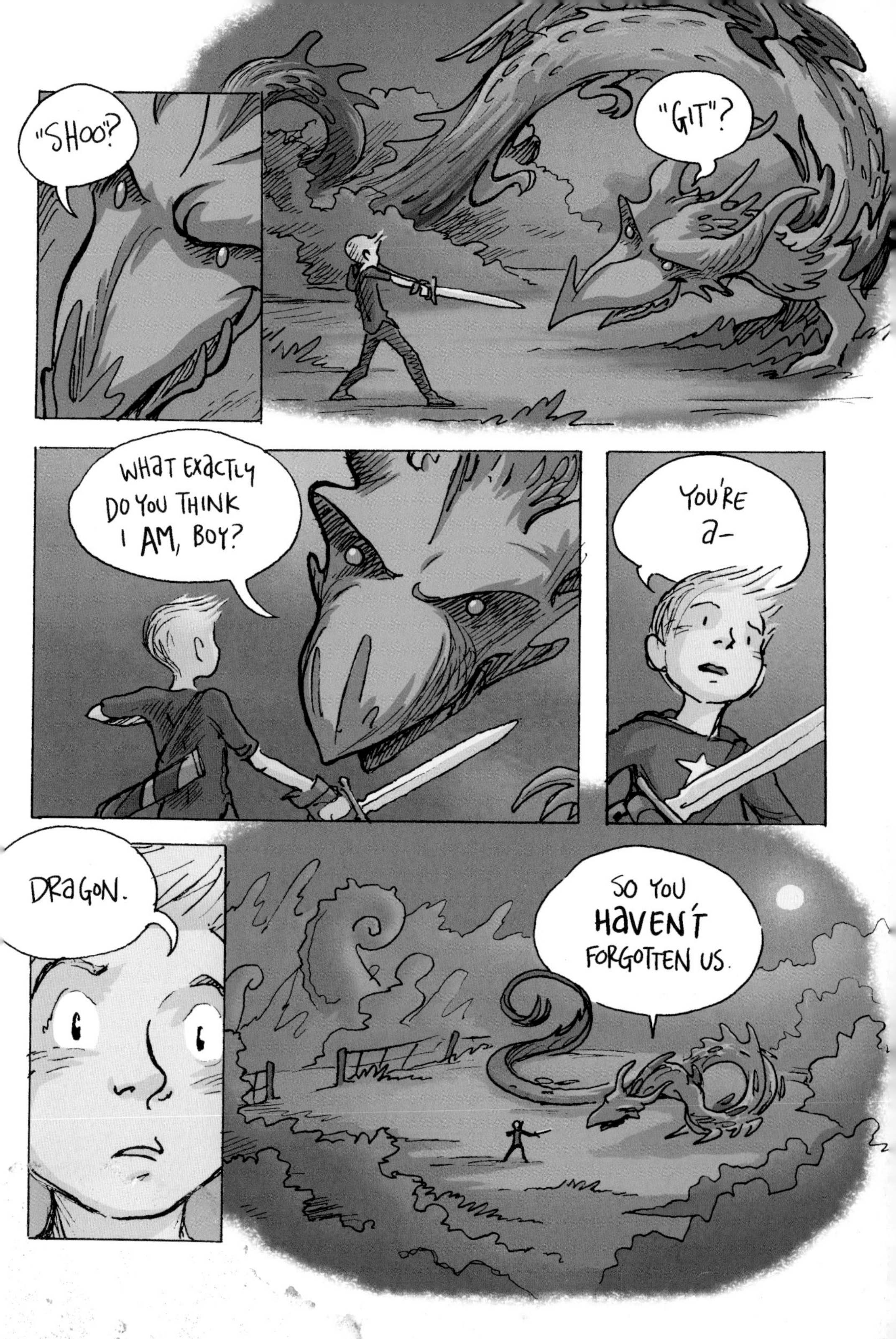
"SHOO"?
"GIT"?
WHAT EXACTLY DO YOU THINK I AM, BOY?
YOU'RE A-
DRAGON.
SO YOU HAVEN'T FORGOTTEN US.

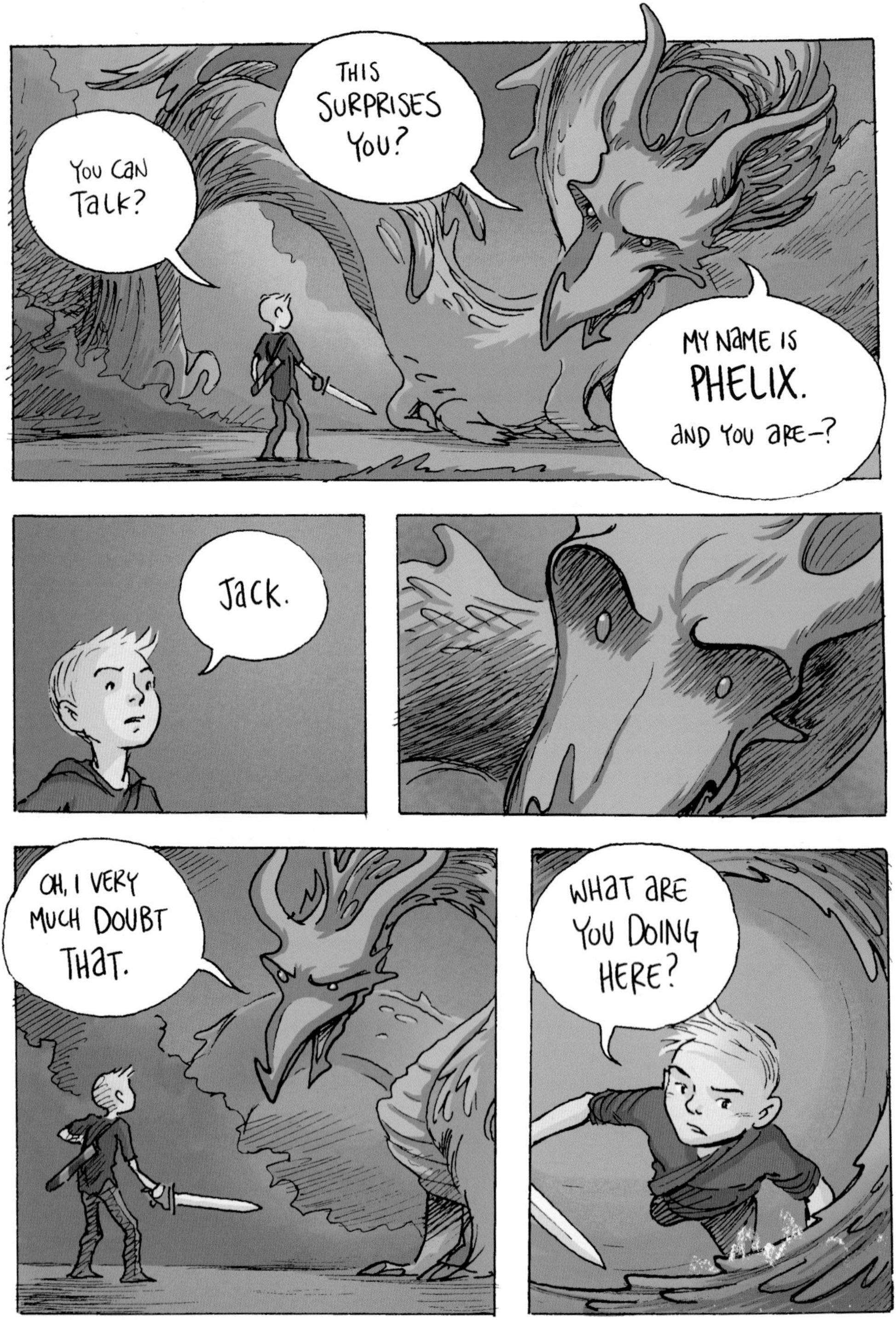
YOU CAN TALK?
THIS SURPRISES YOU?
MY NAME IS PHELIX. AND YOU ARE—?
JACK.
OH, I VERY MUCH DOUBT THAT.
WHAT ARE YOU DOING HERE?

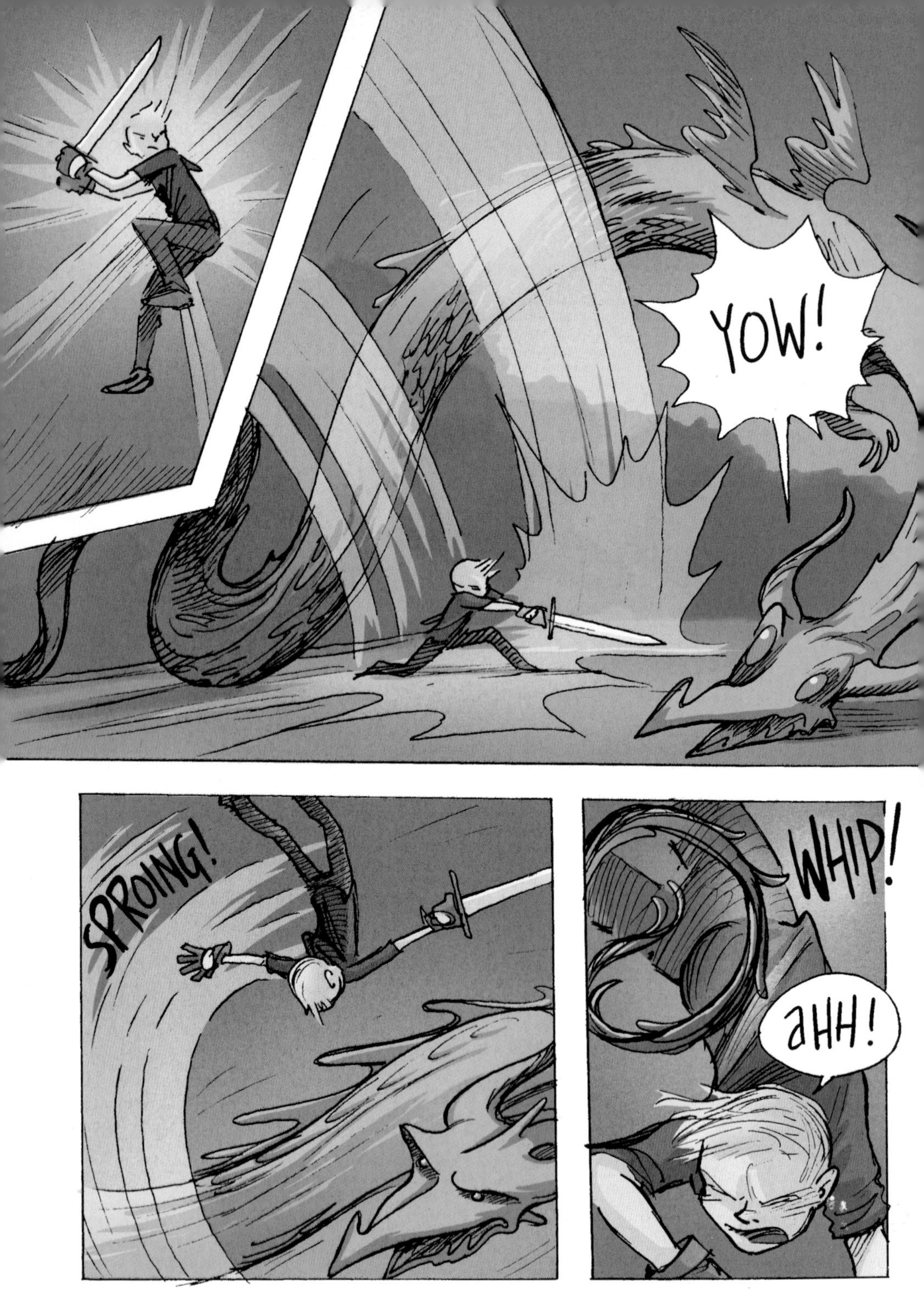
YOW!
SPROING!
WHIP!
aHH!

131

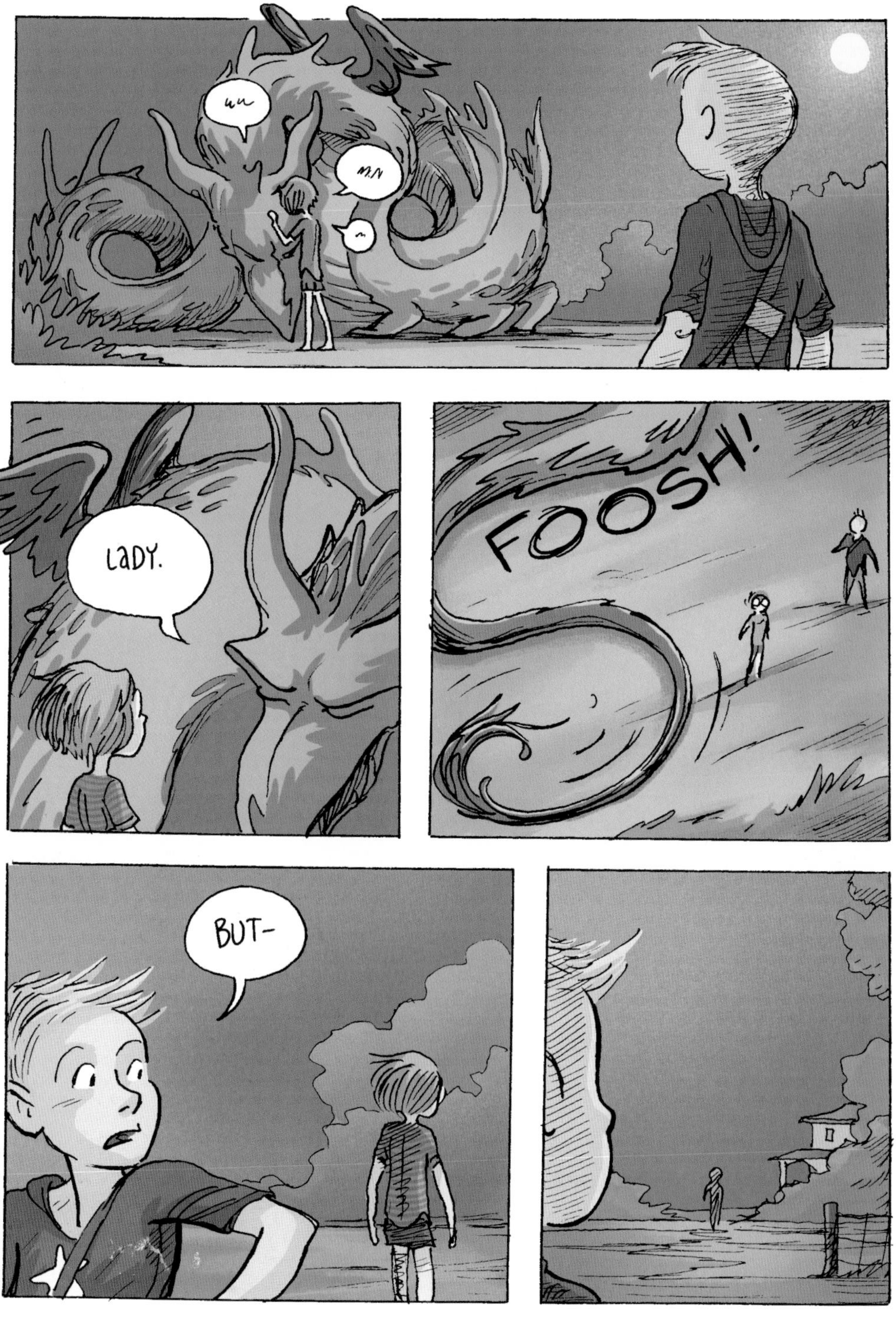
LADY.
FOOSH!
BUT-

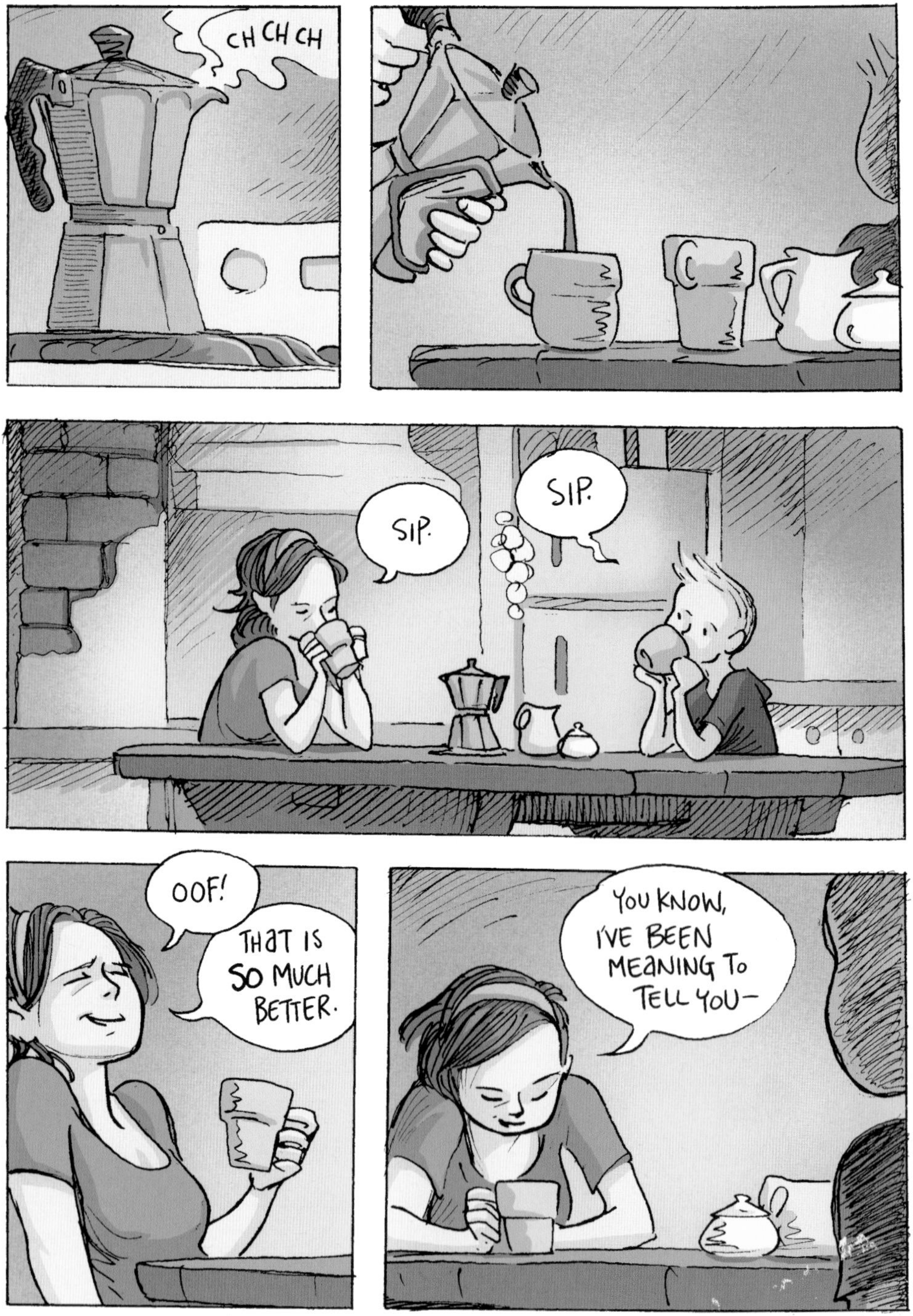
CH CH CH
SIP.
SIP.
OOF!
THAT IS SO MUCH BETTER.
YOU KNOW, I'VE BEEN MEANING TO TELL YOU—

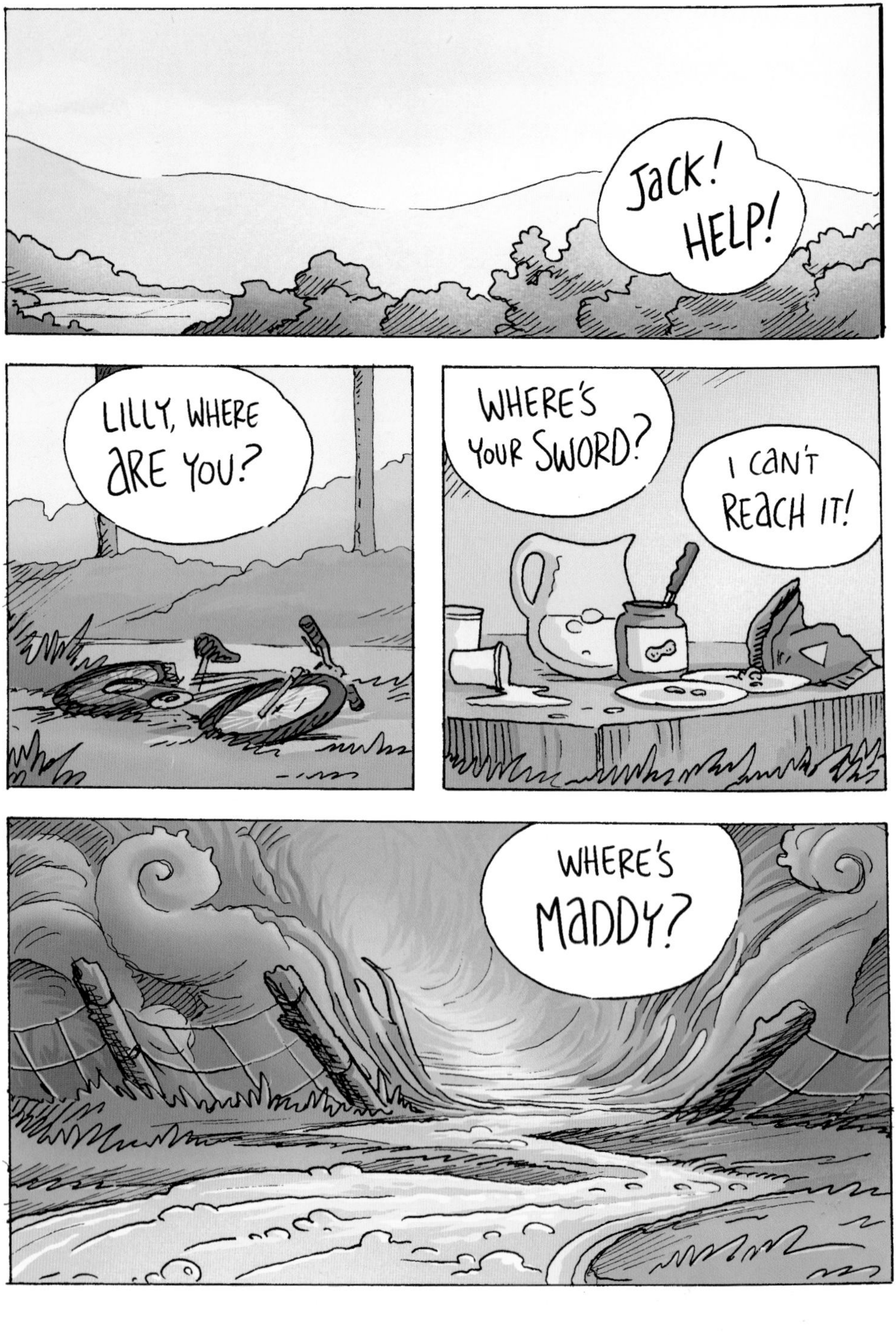
JACK! HELP!
LILLY, WHERE ARE YOU?
WHERE'S YOUR SWORD?
I CAN'T REACH IT!
WHERE'S MADDY?

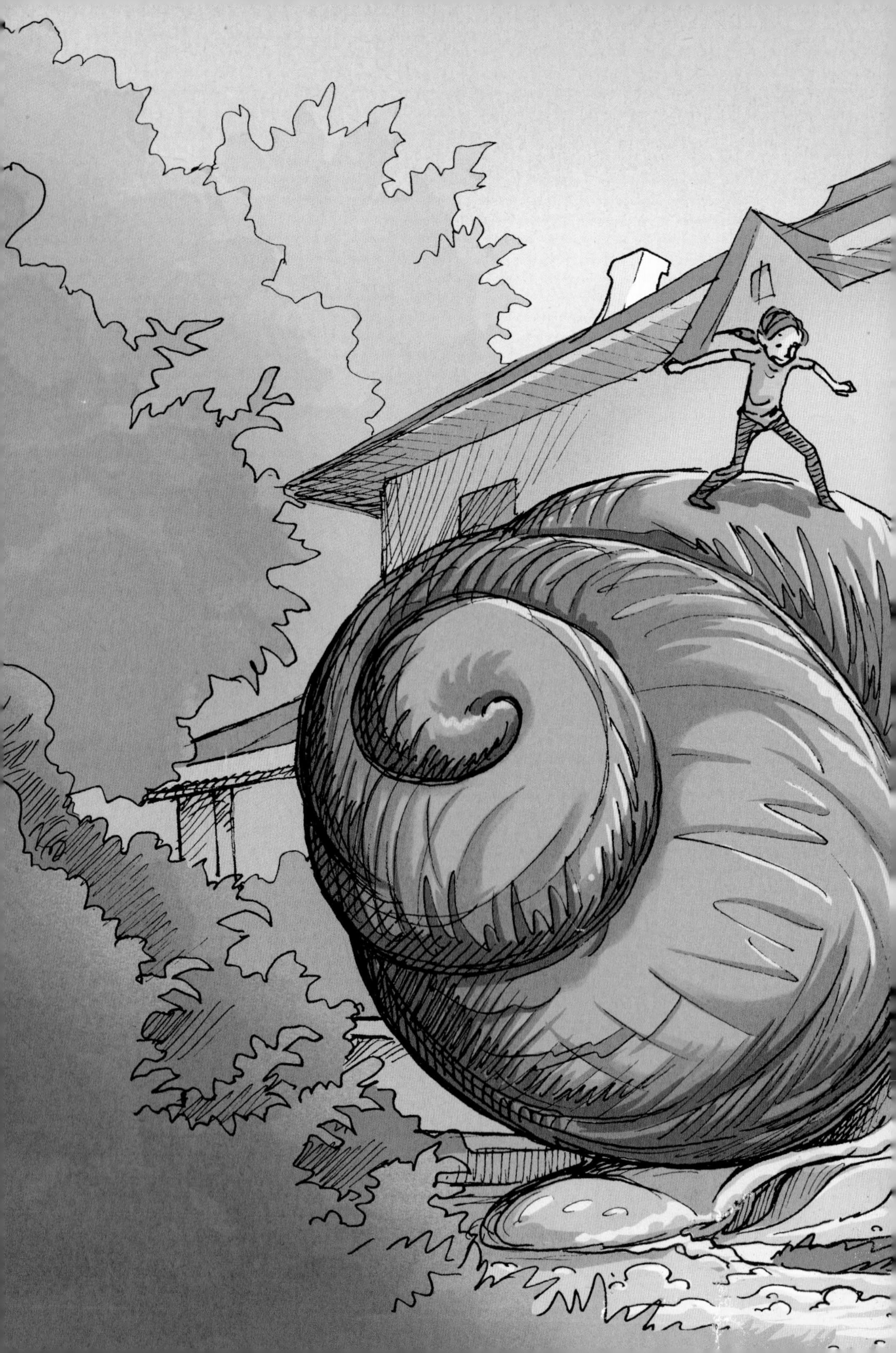

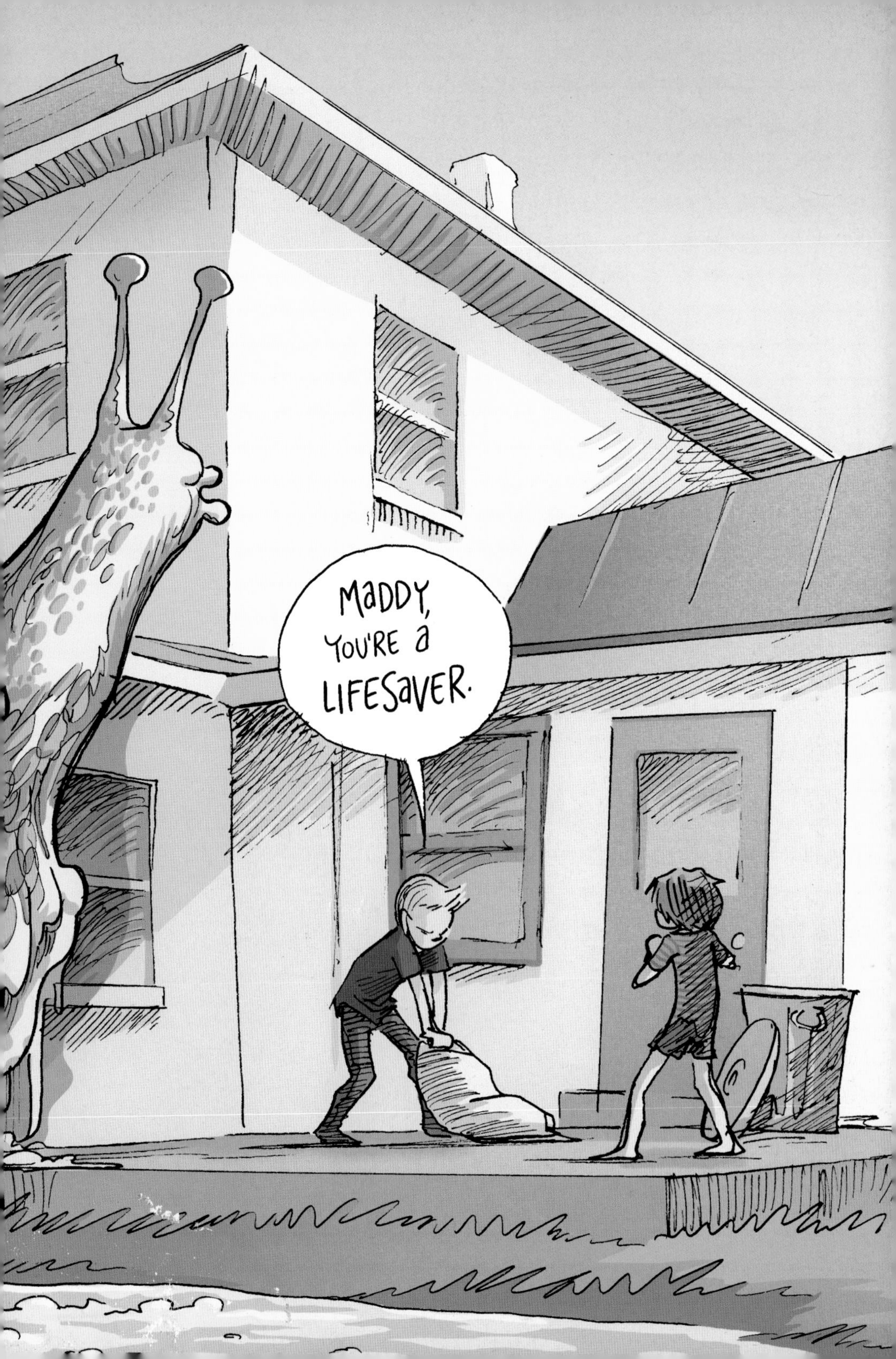
MADDY, YOU'RE A LIFESAVER.

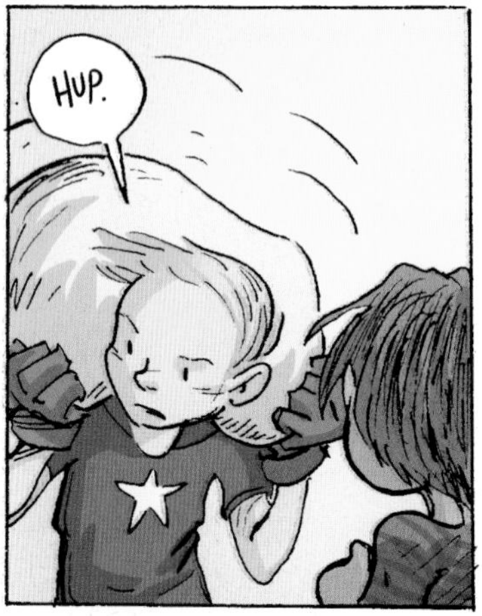
HUP.

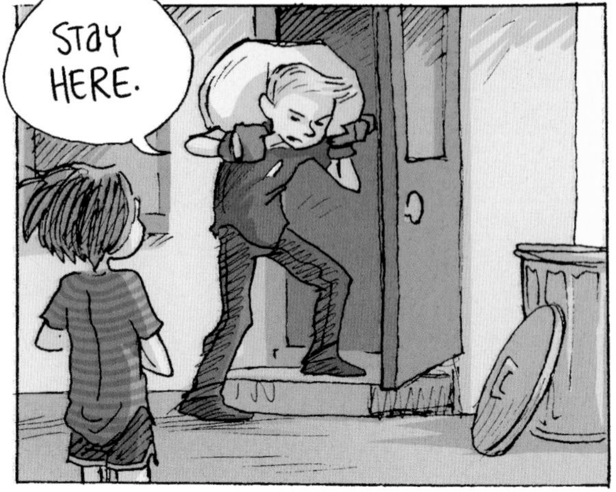
STAY HERE.

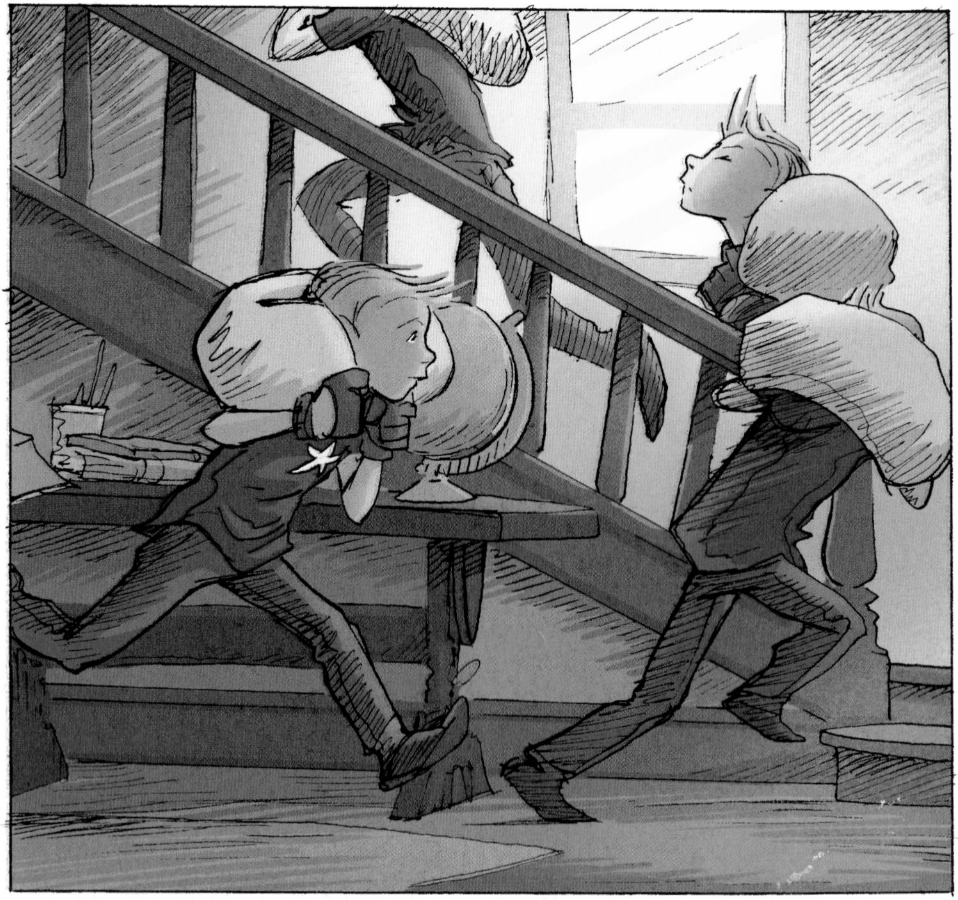

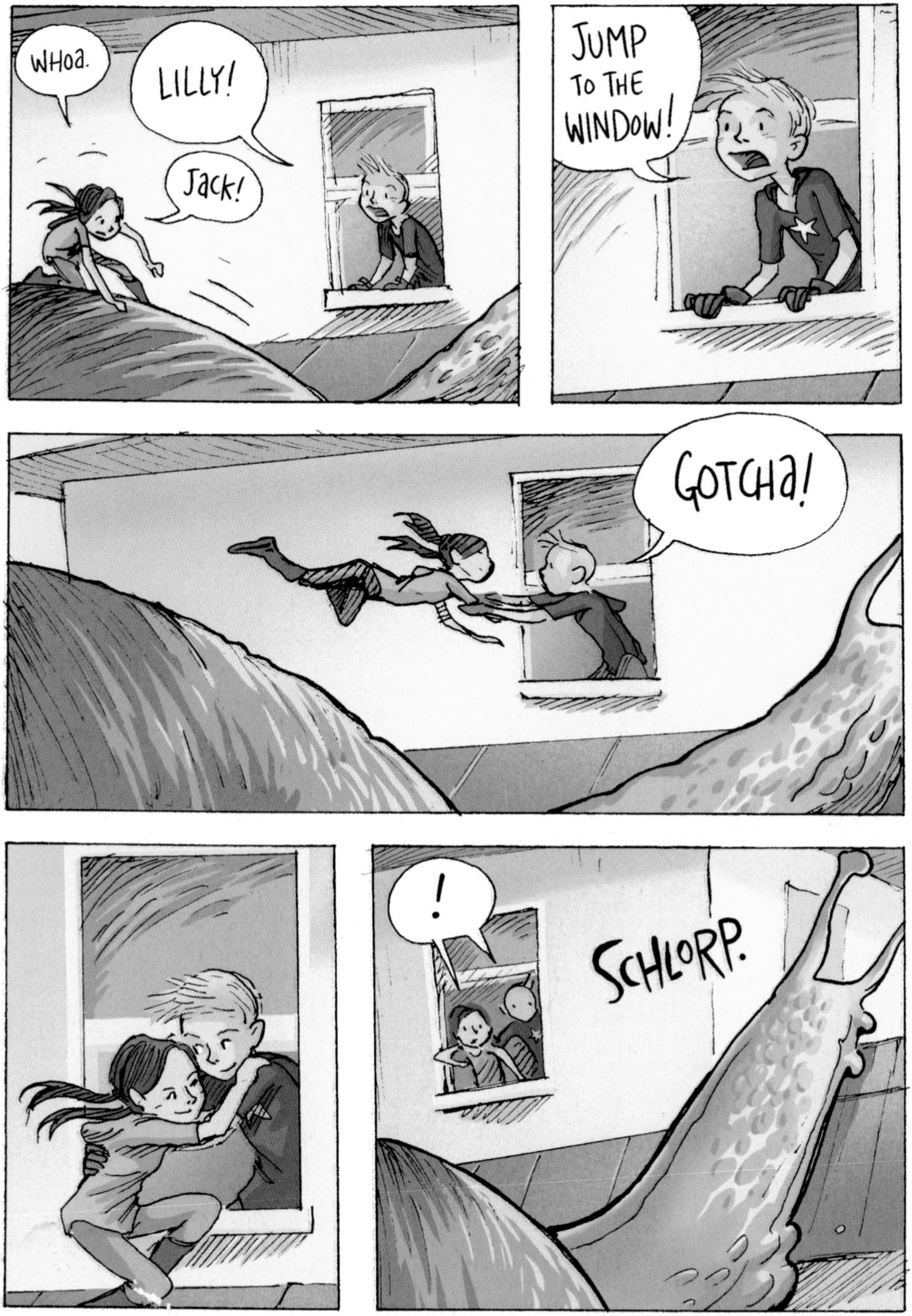

WHOA.
LILLY!
JACK!
JUMP TO THE WINDOW!
GOTCHA!
!
SCHLORP.

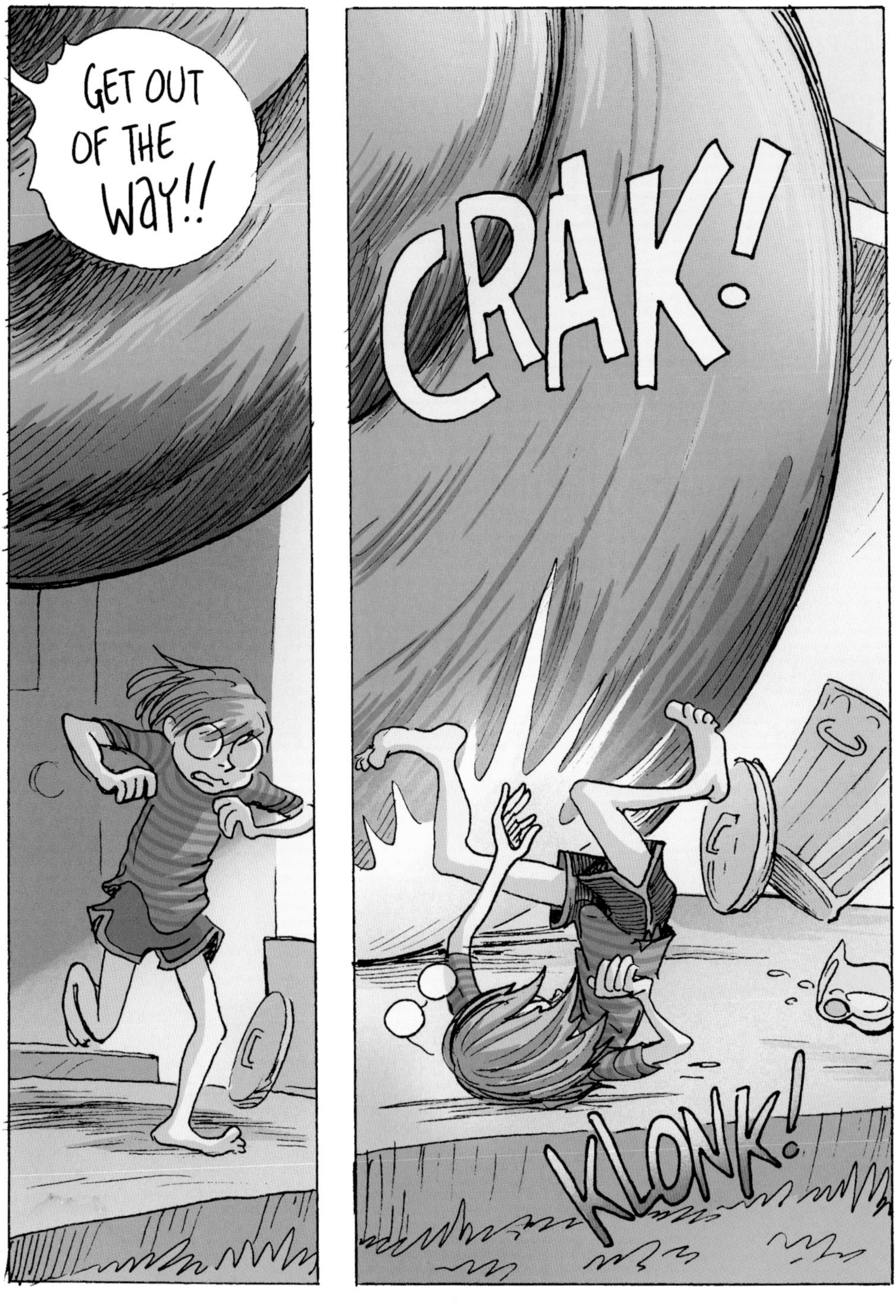
GET OUT OF THE WAY!!
CRAK!
KLONK!

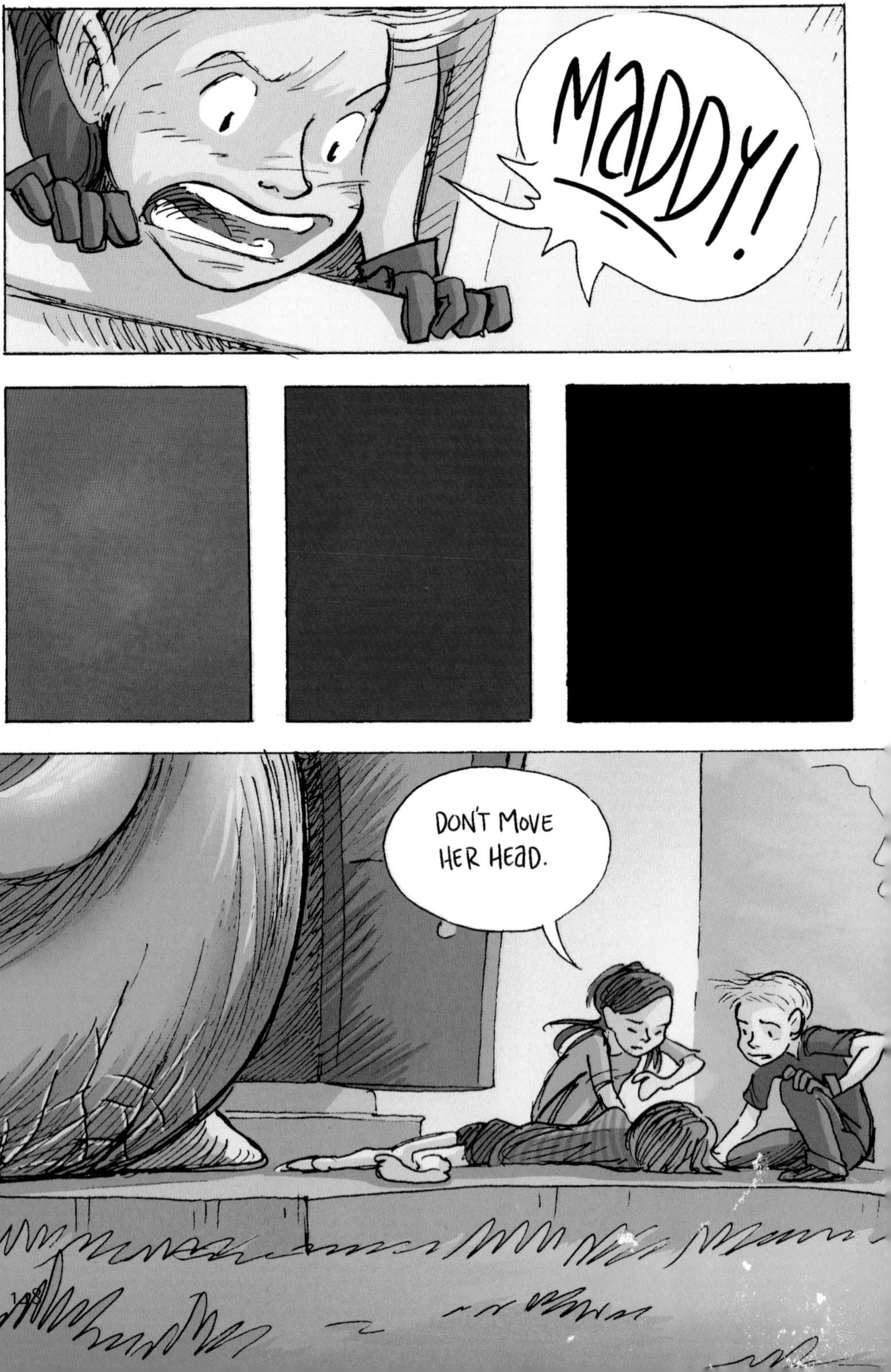
MADDY!
DON'T MOVE HER HEAD.

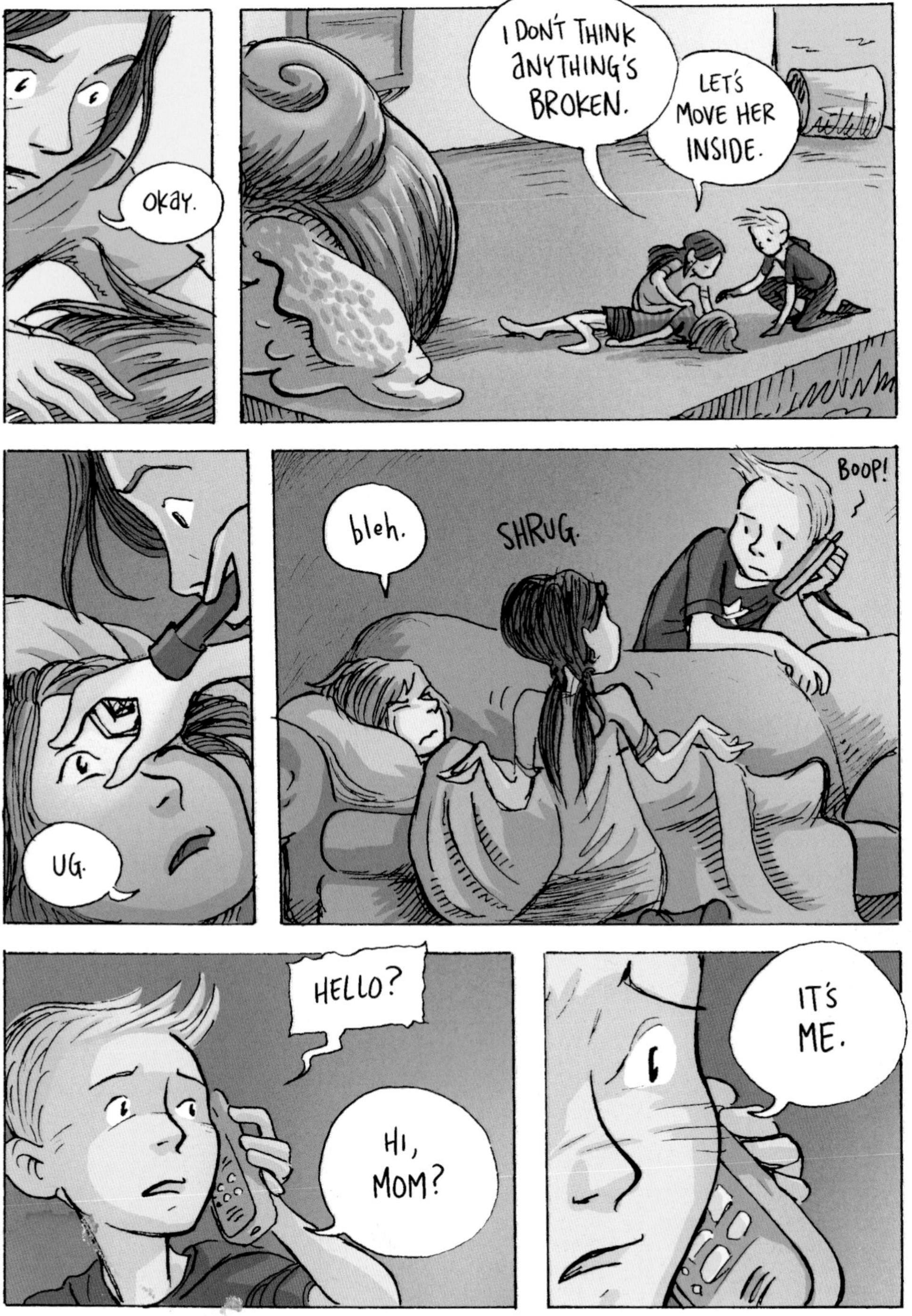
OKay.
I DON'T THINK anything's BROKEN.
LET'S MOVE HER INSIDE.
UG.
bleh.
SHRUG.
BOOP!
HELLO?
HI, MOM?
IT'S ME.

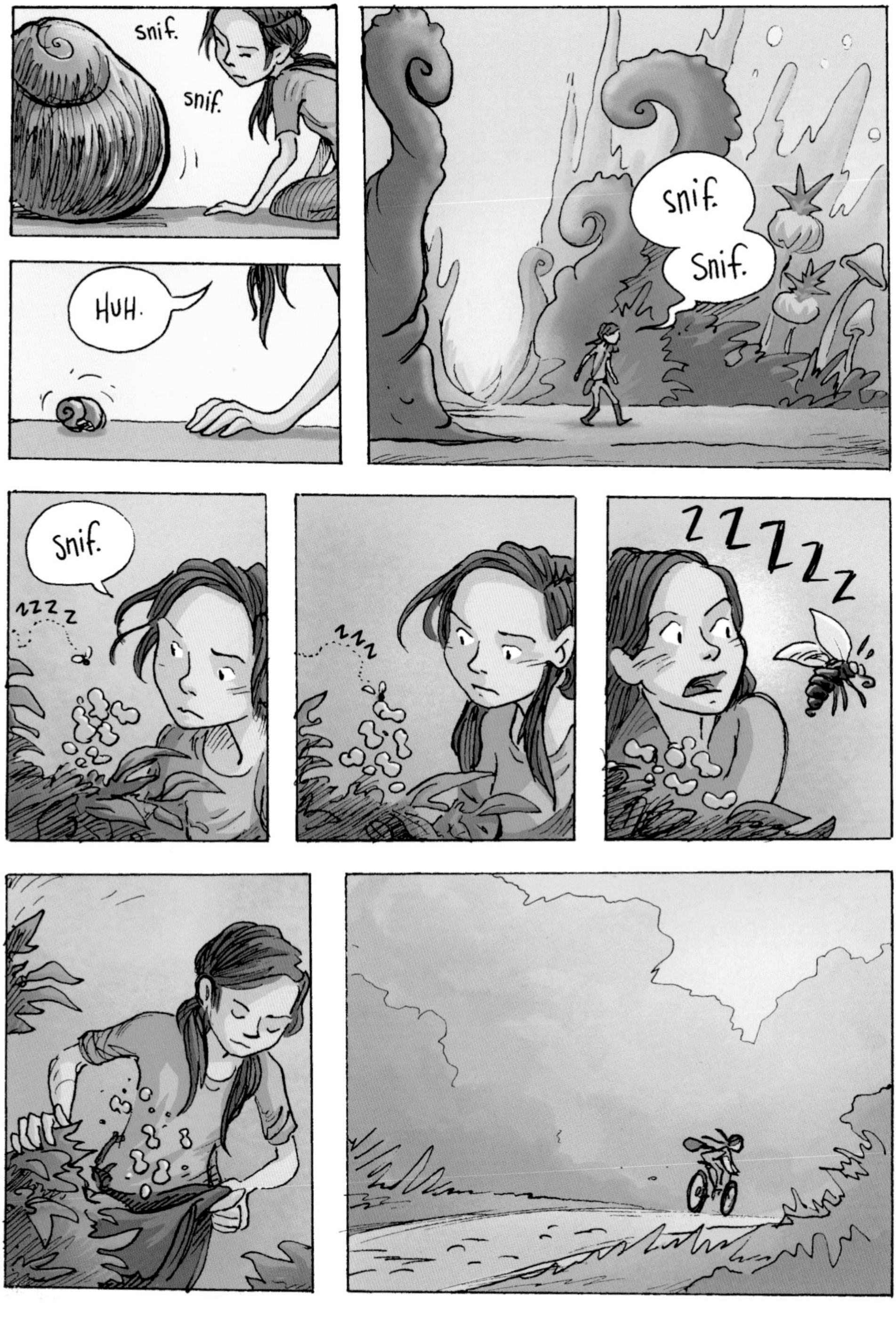
snif.
snif.
HUH.
snif.
Snif.
snif.
ZZZZ
ZZZ
ZZZZZ

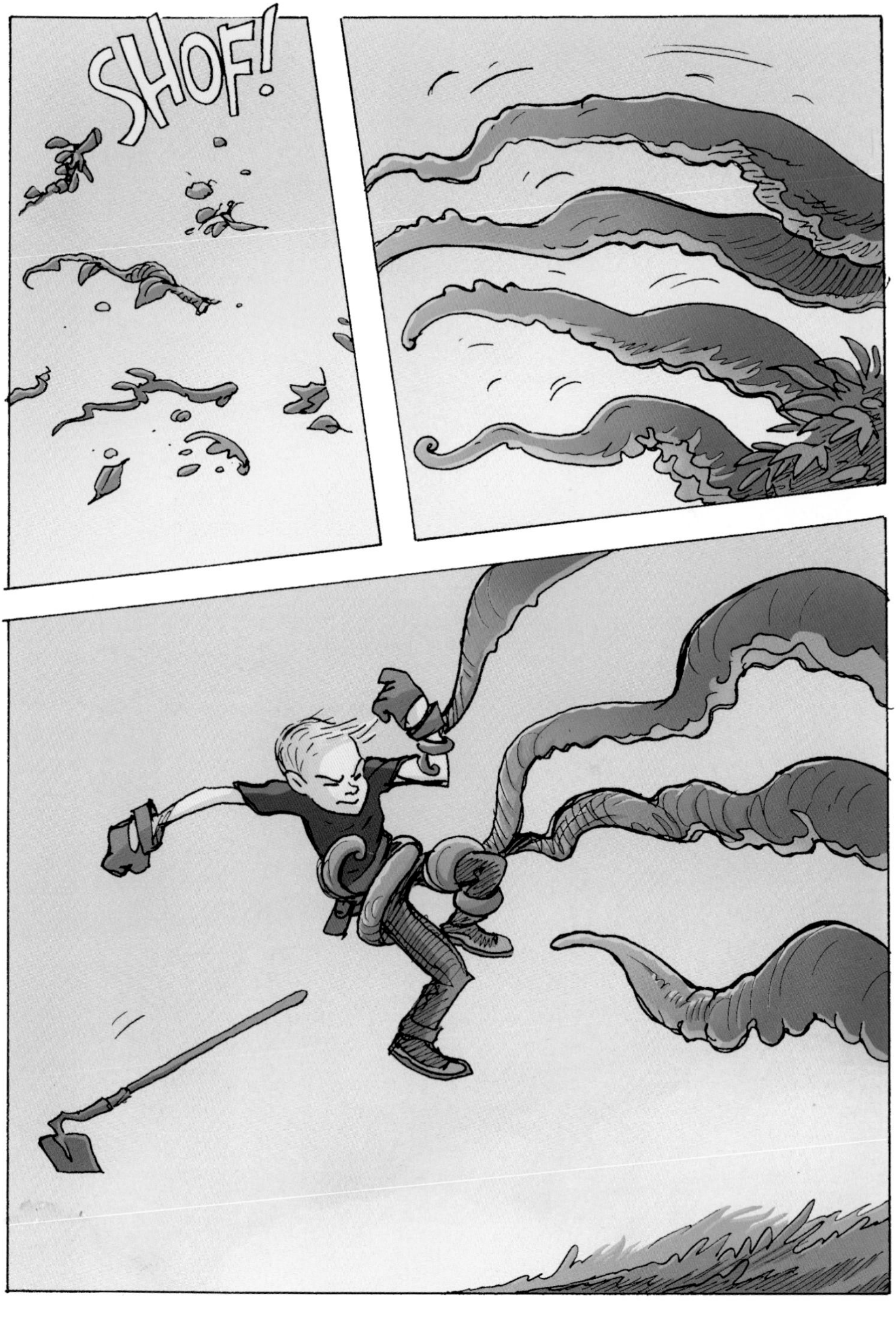
SHOF!

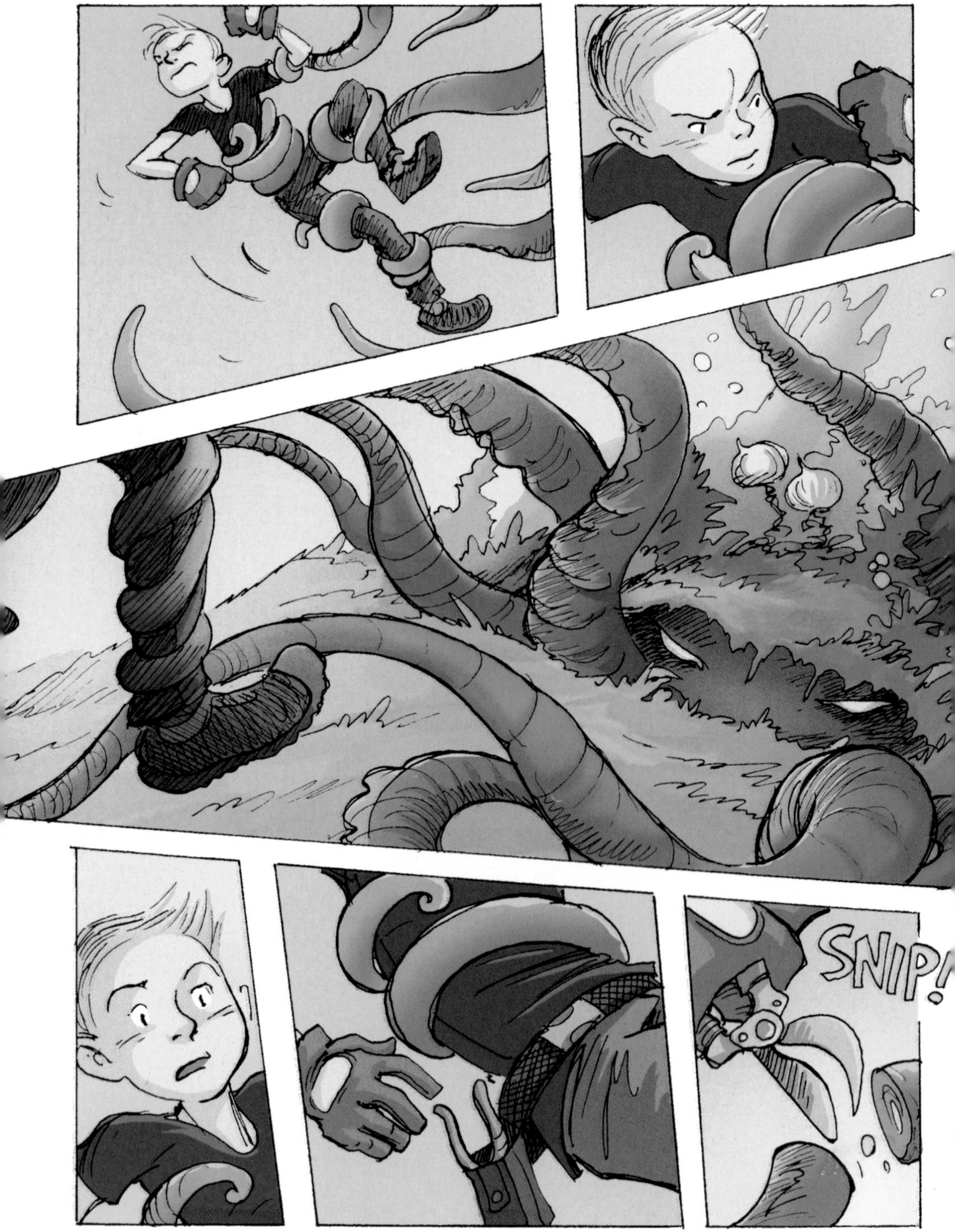
SNIP!

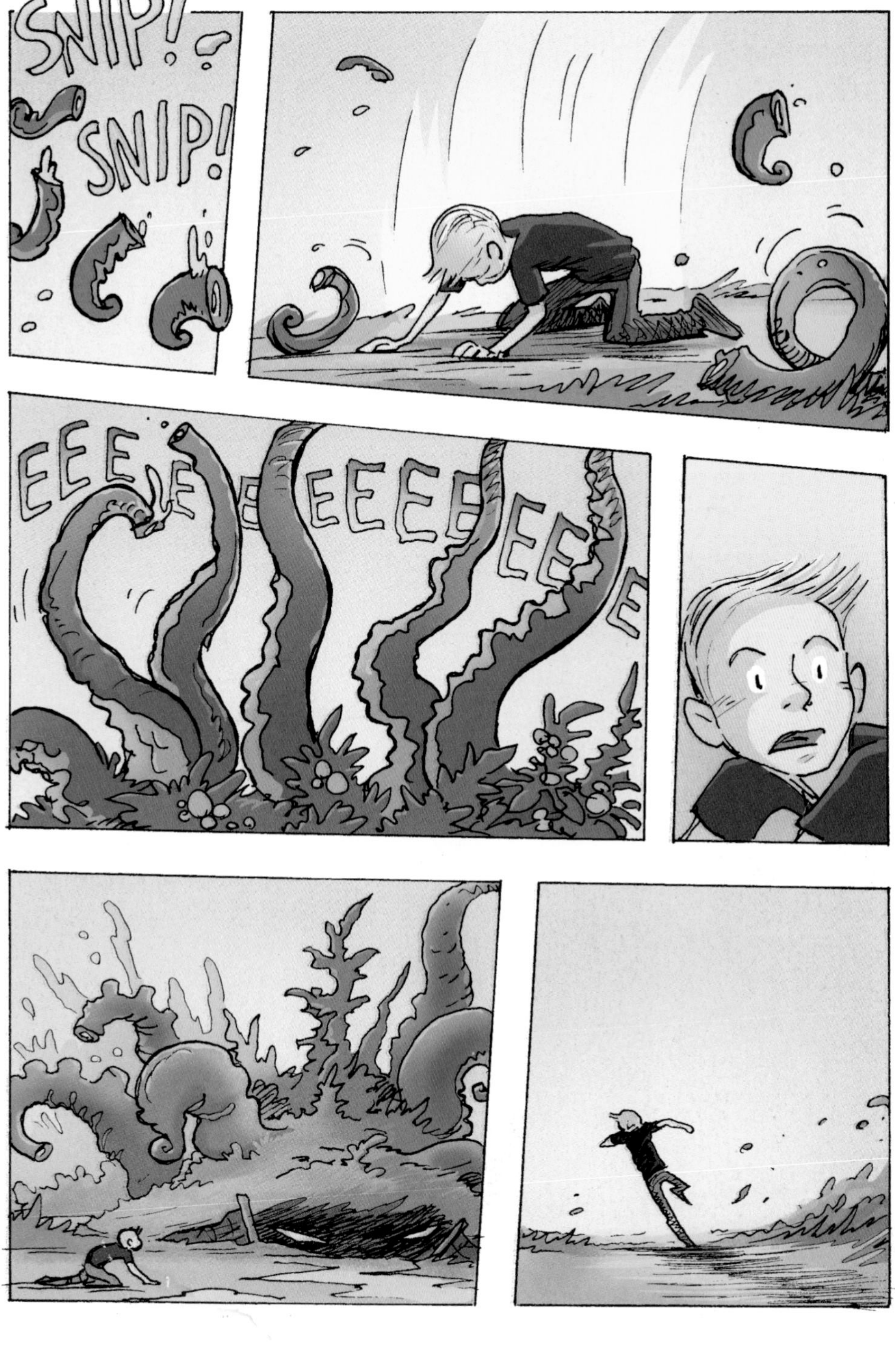
SNIP!
SNIP!
EEEEEEEEEEEEE

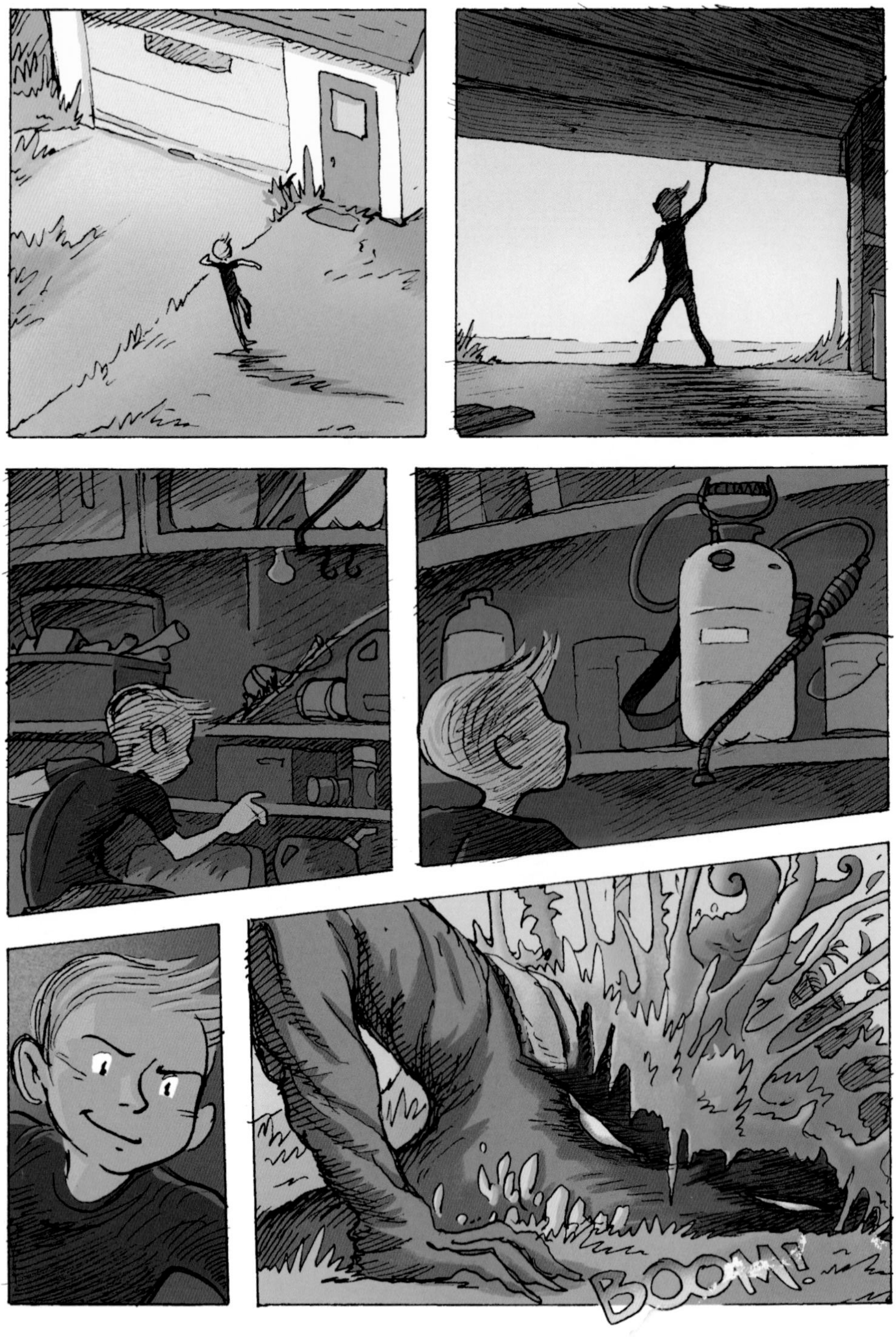
BOOM!

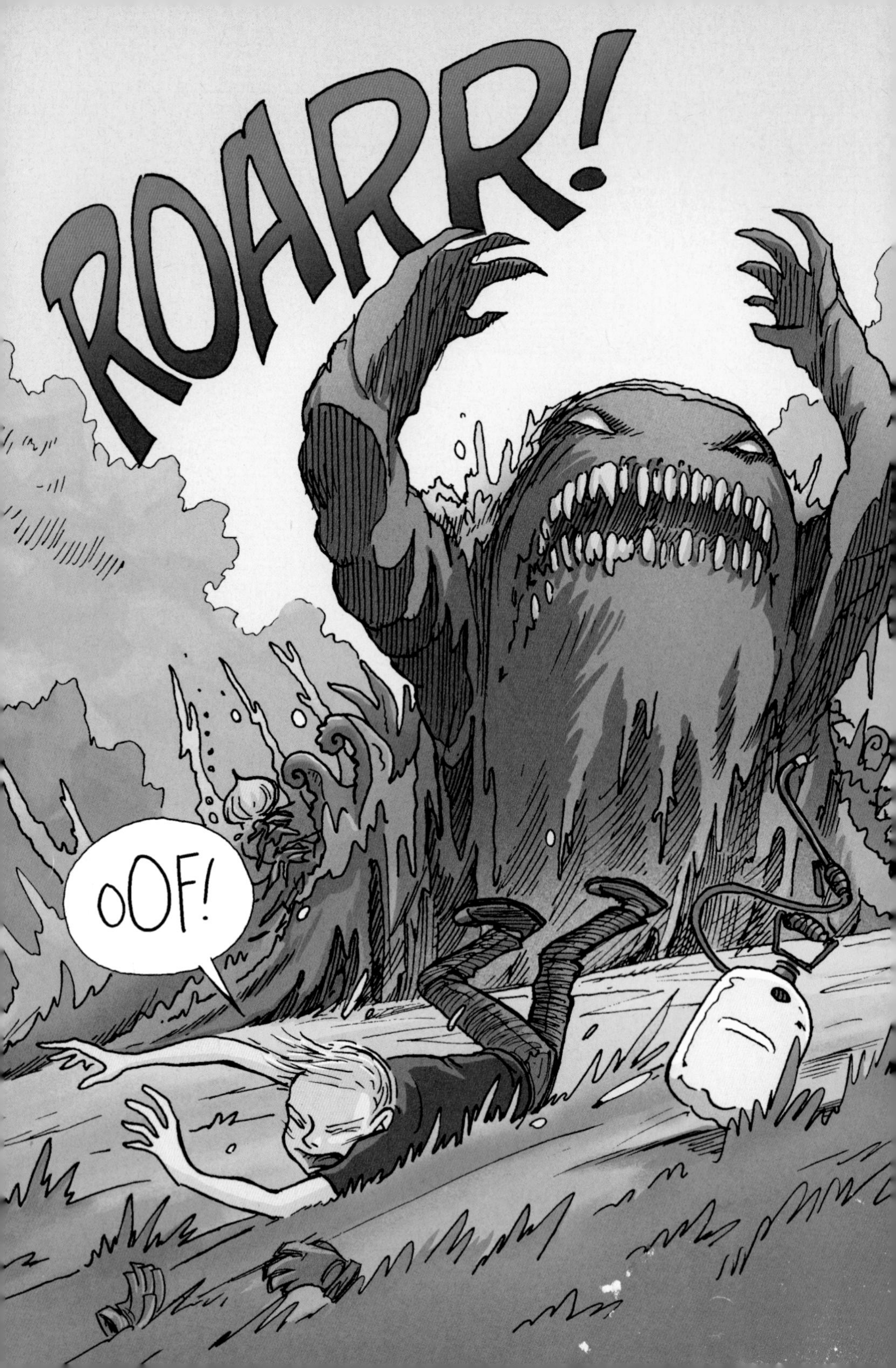
ROARR!
OOF!

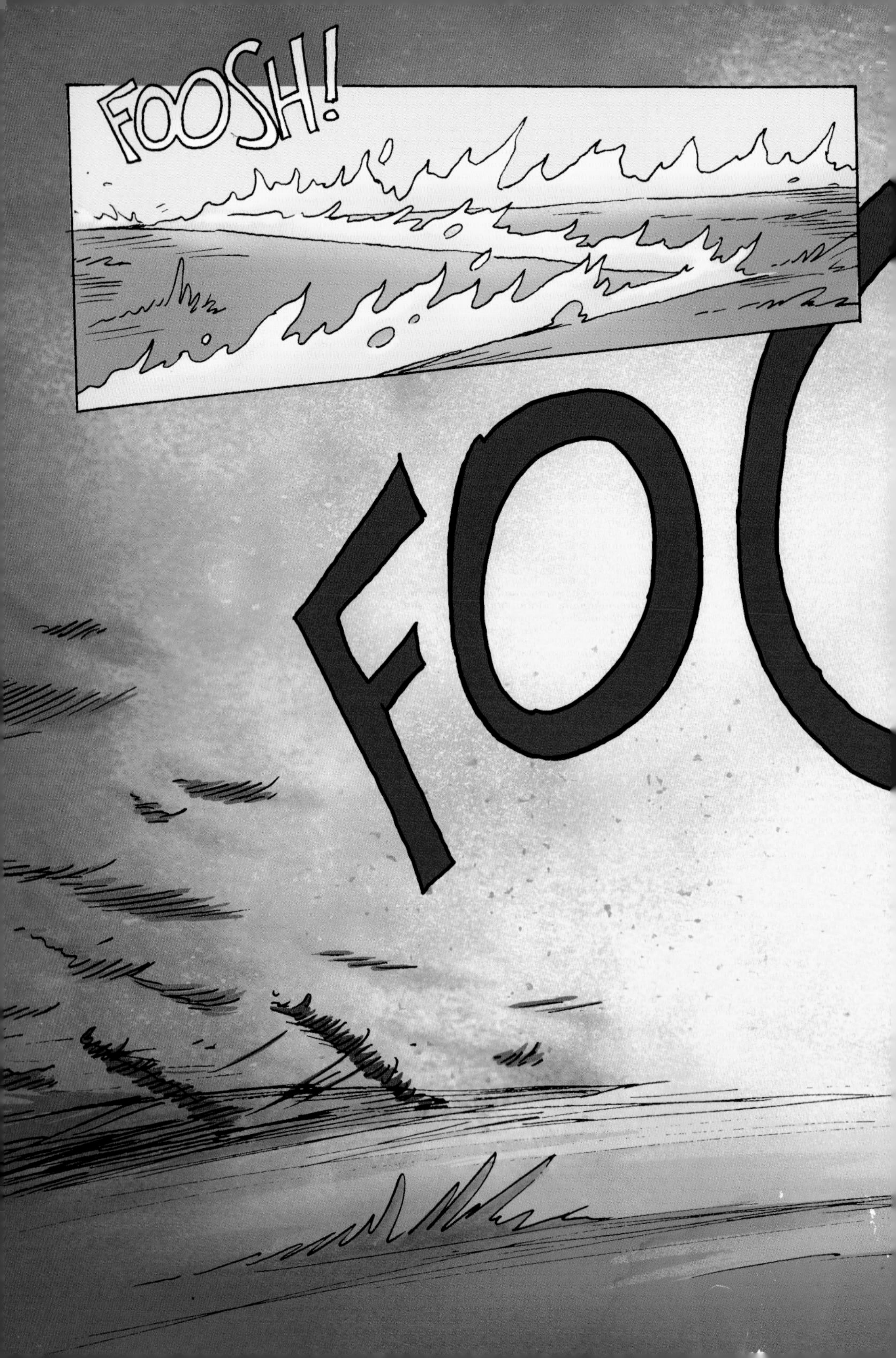
FOOSH!

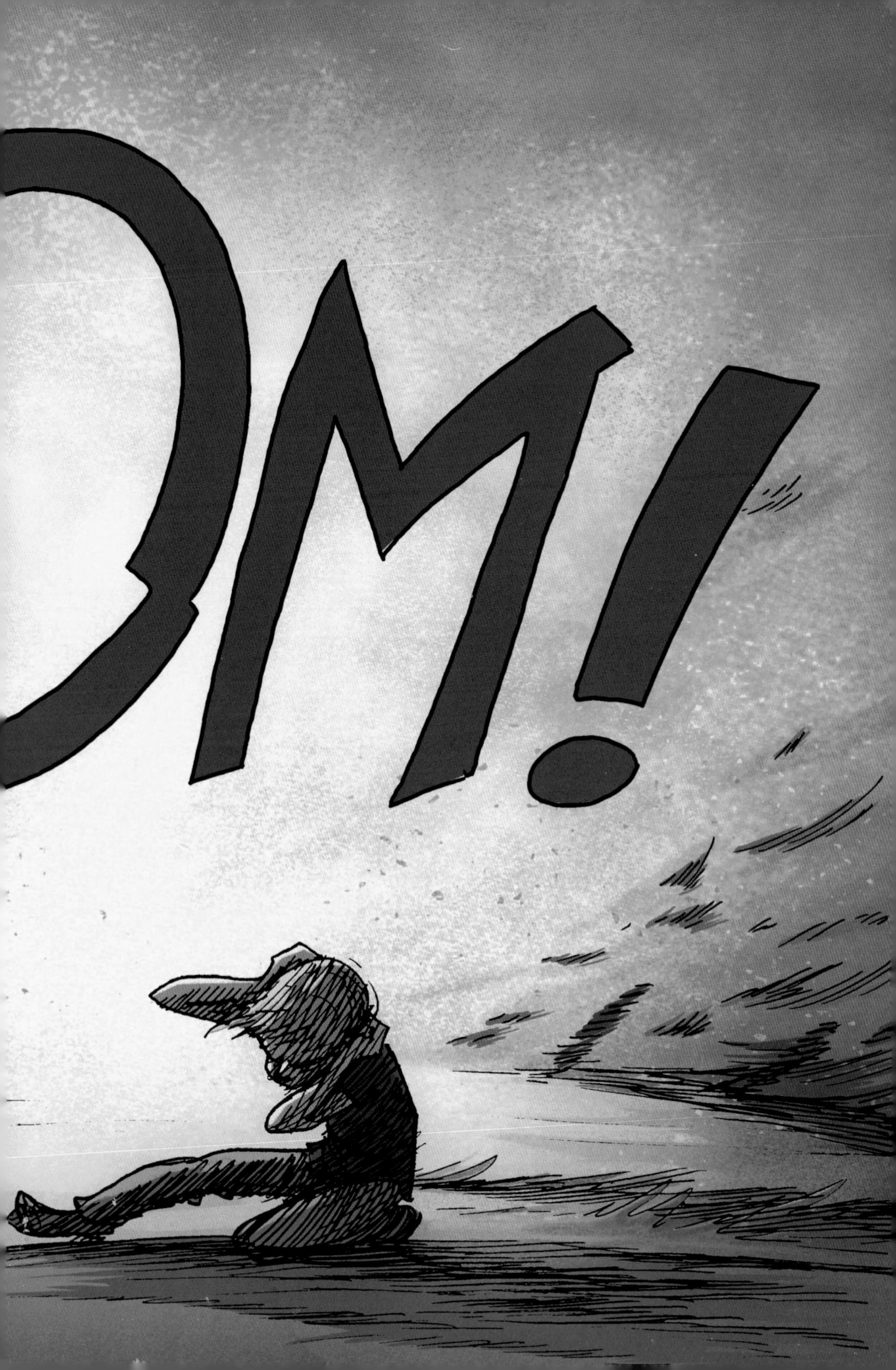
OM!

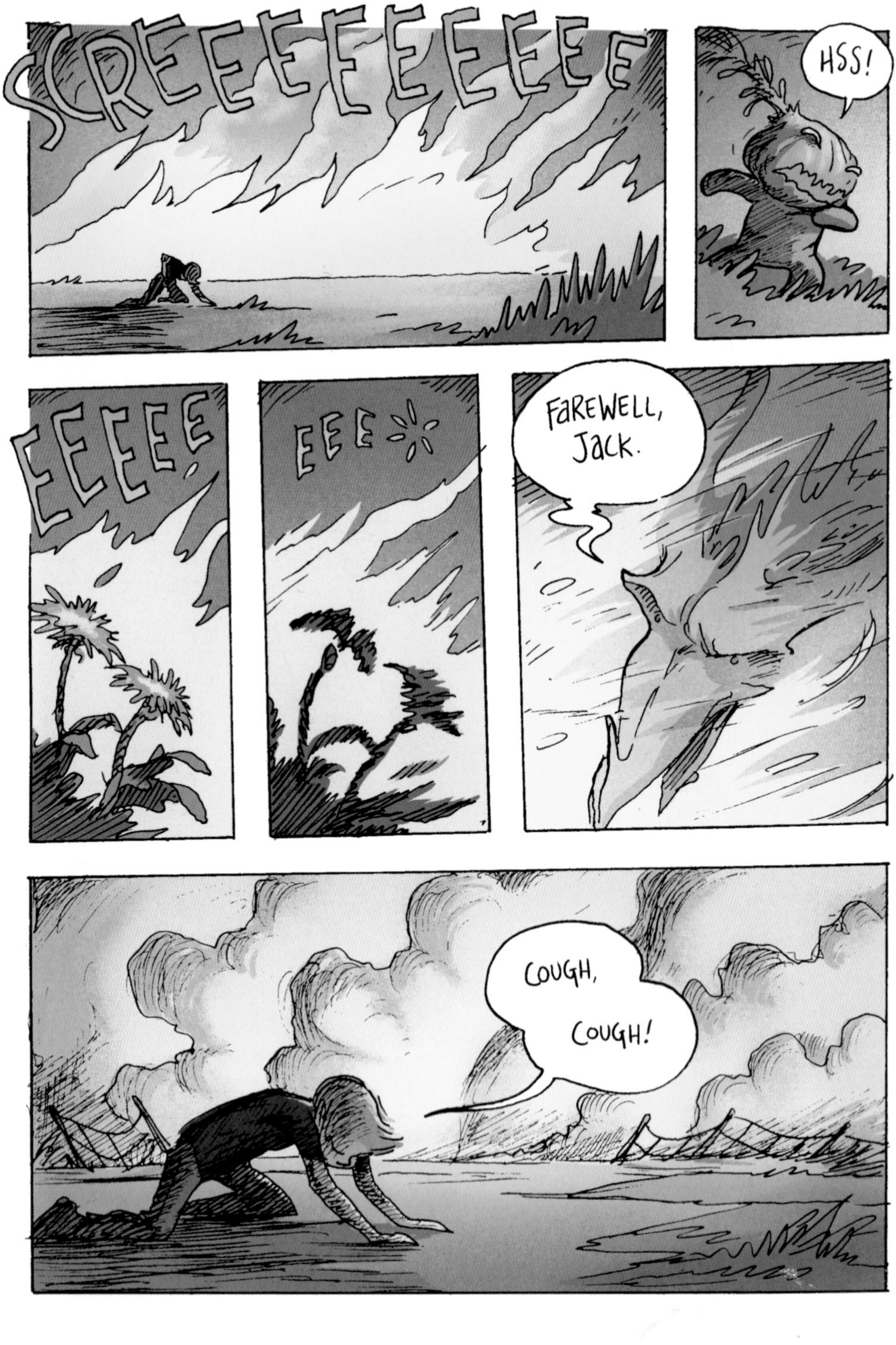
SCREEEEEEEEEE
HSS!
EEEEE!
EEE
FAREWELL, JACK.
COUGH,
COUGH!

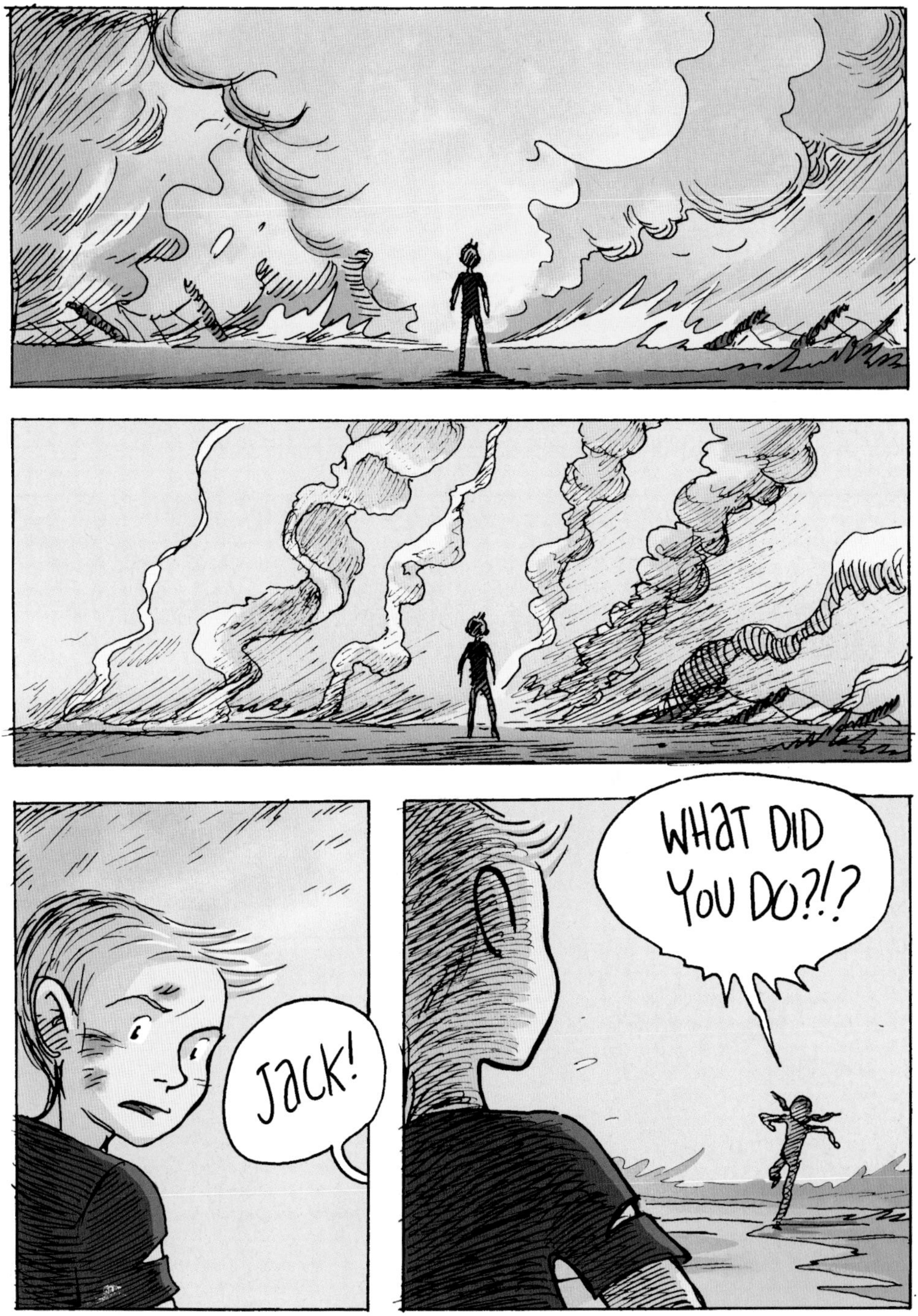
Jack!
WHAT DID YOU DO?!?

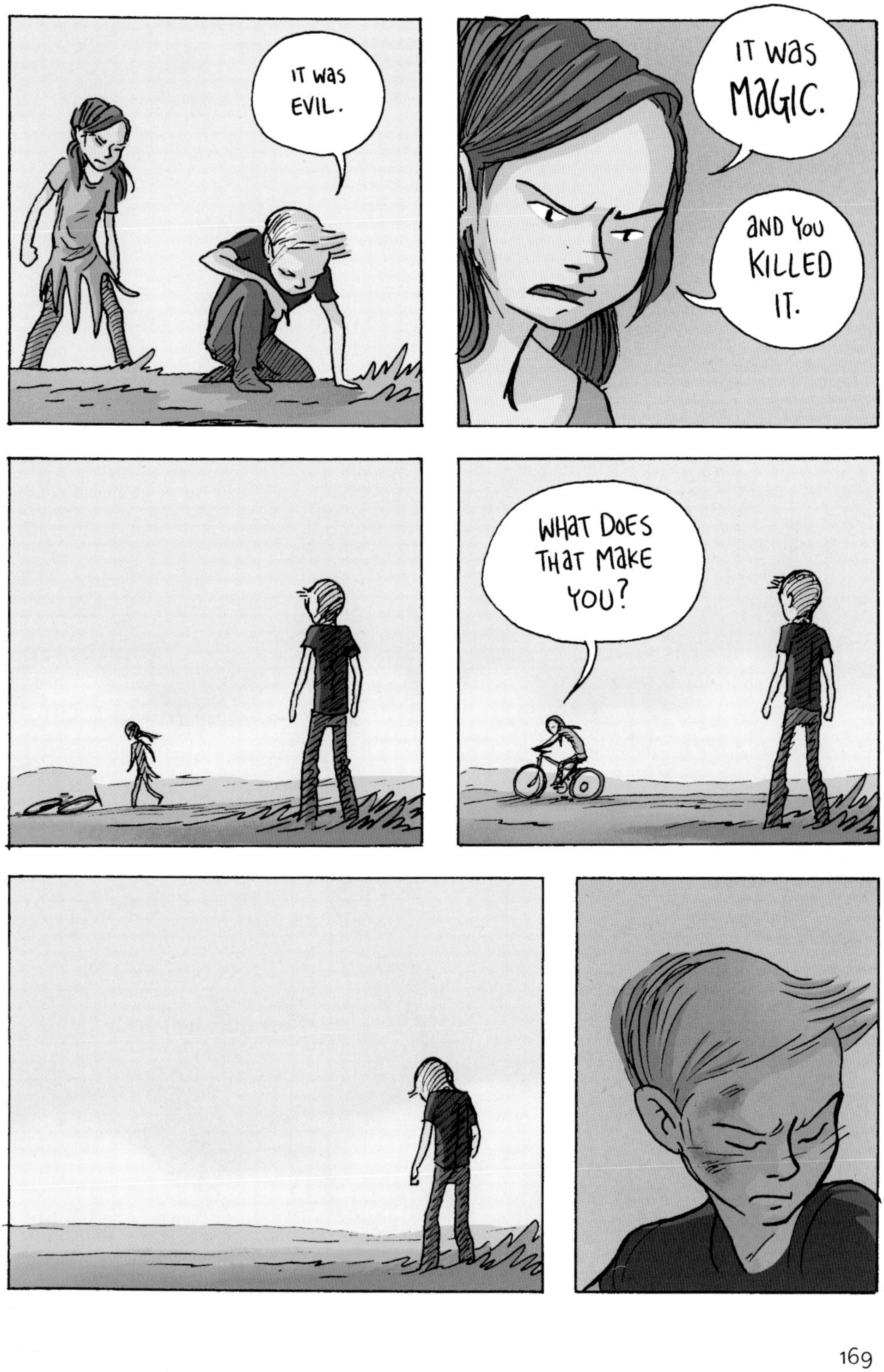
IT WAS EVIL.
IT WAS MAGIC.
AND YOU KILLED IT.
WHAT DOES THAT MAKE YOU?

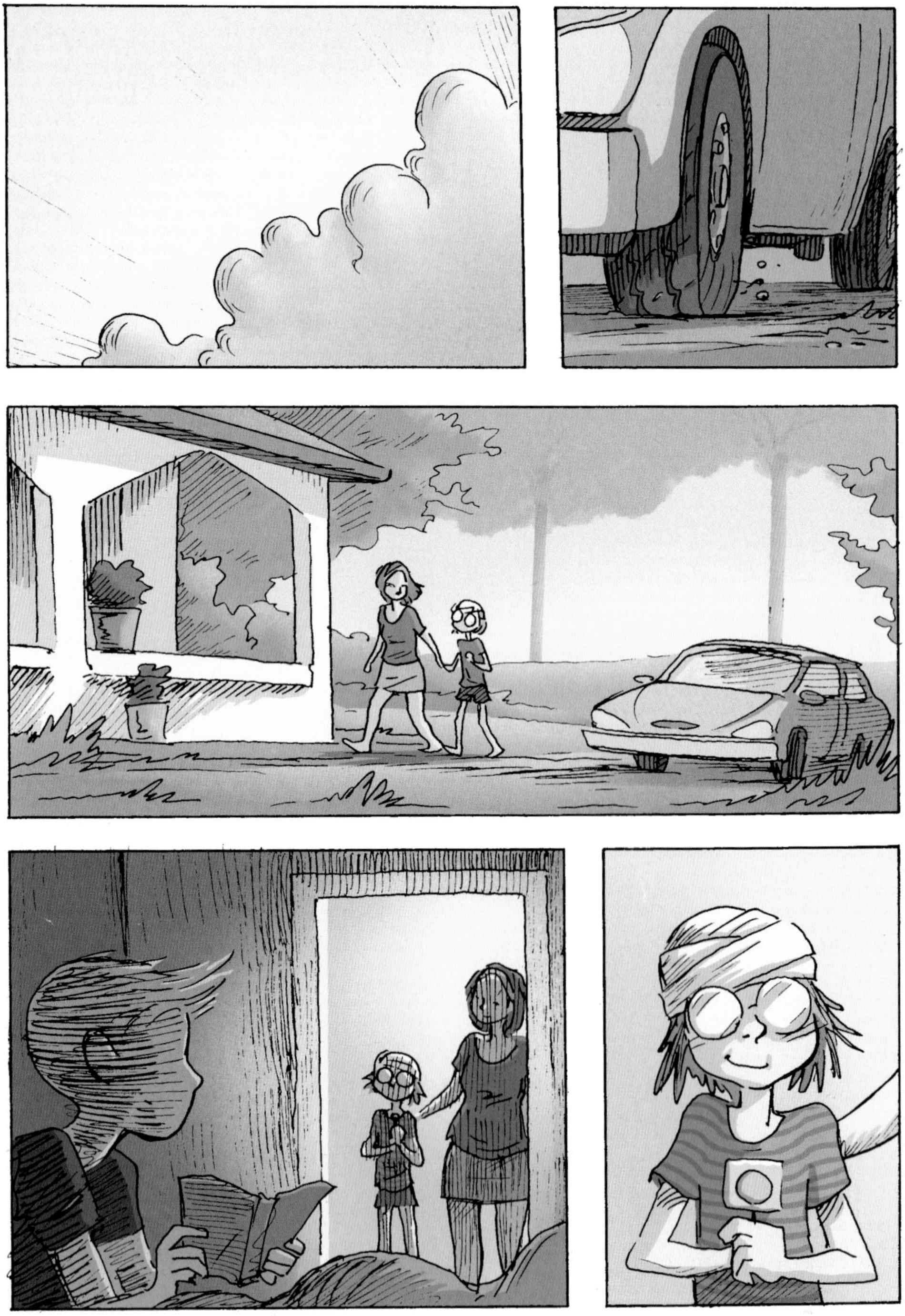

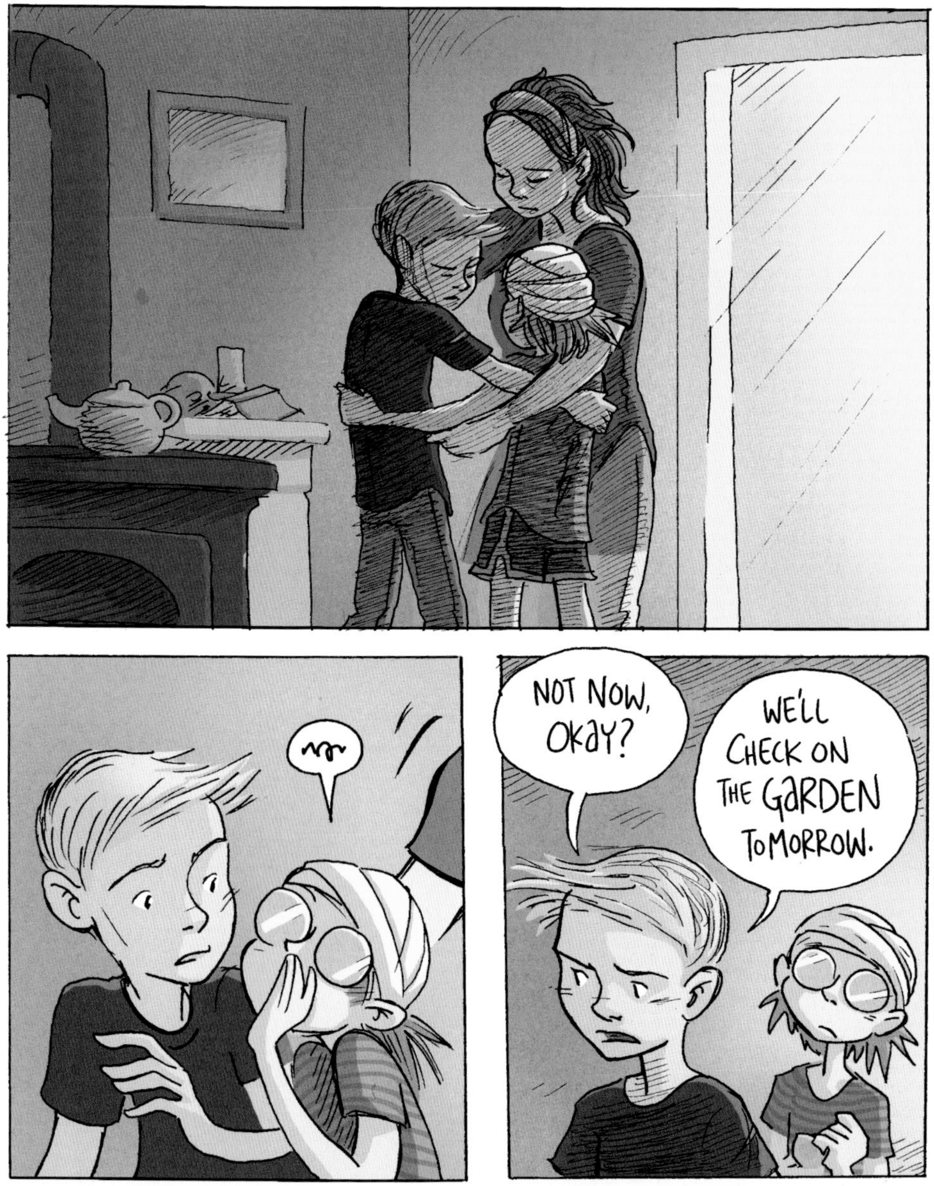
NOT NOW, OKAY?
WE'LL CHECK ON THE GARDEN TOMORROW.

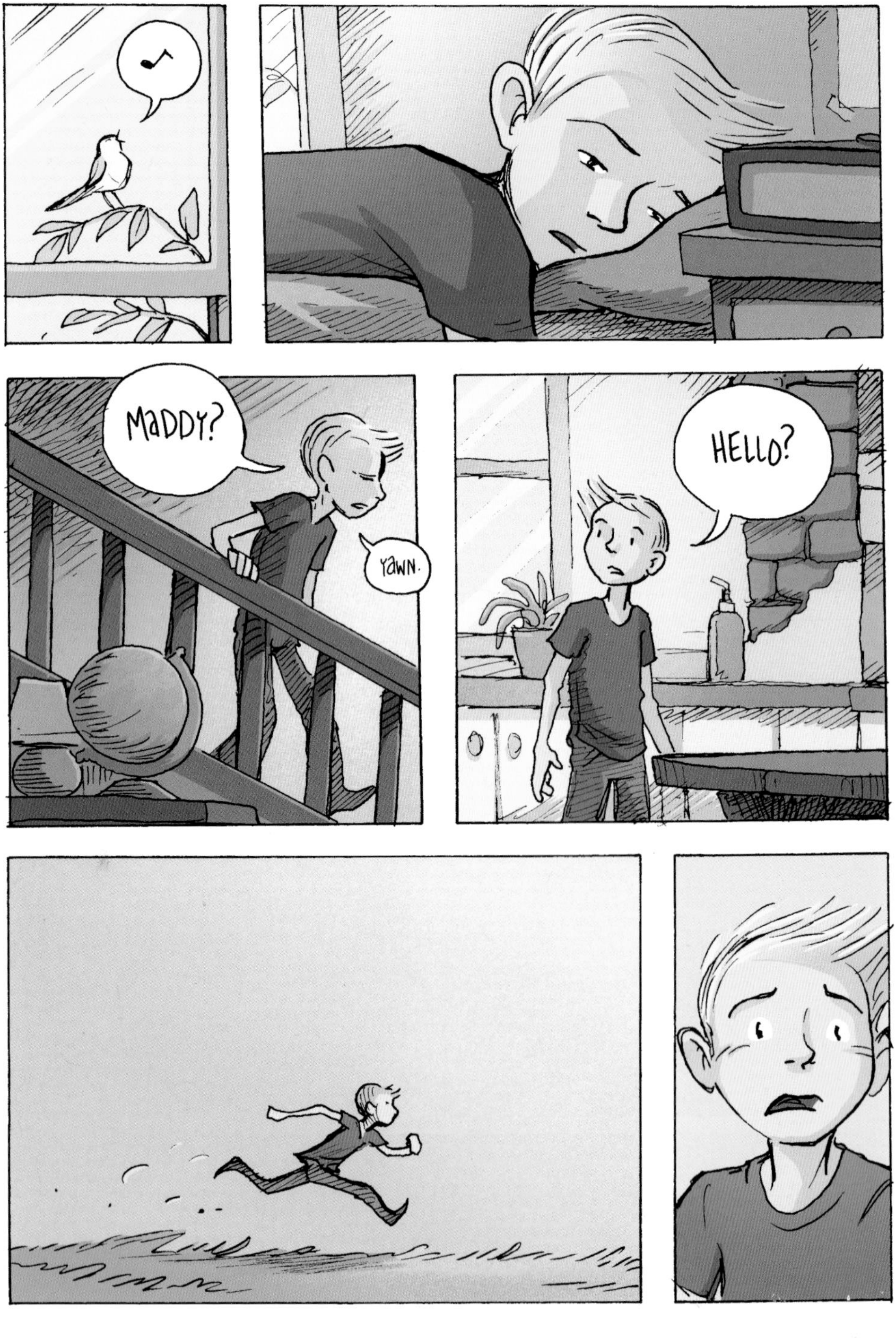
MADDY?
YAWN.
HELLO?

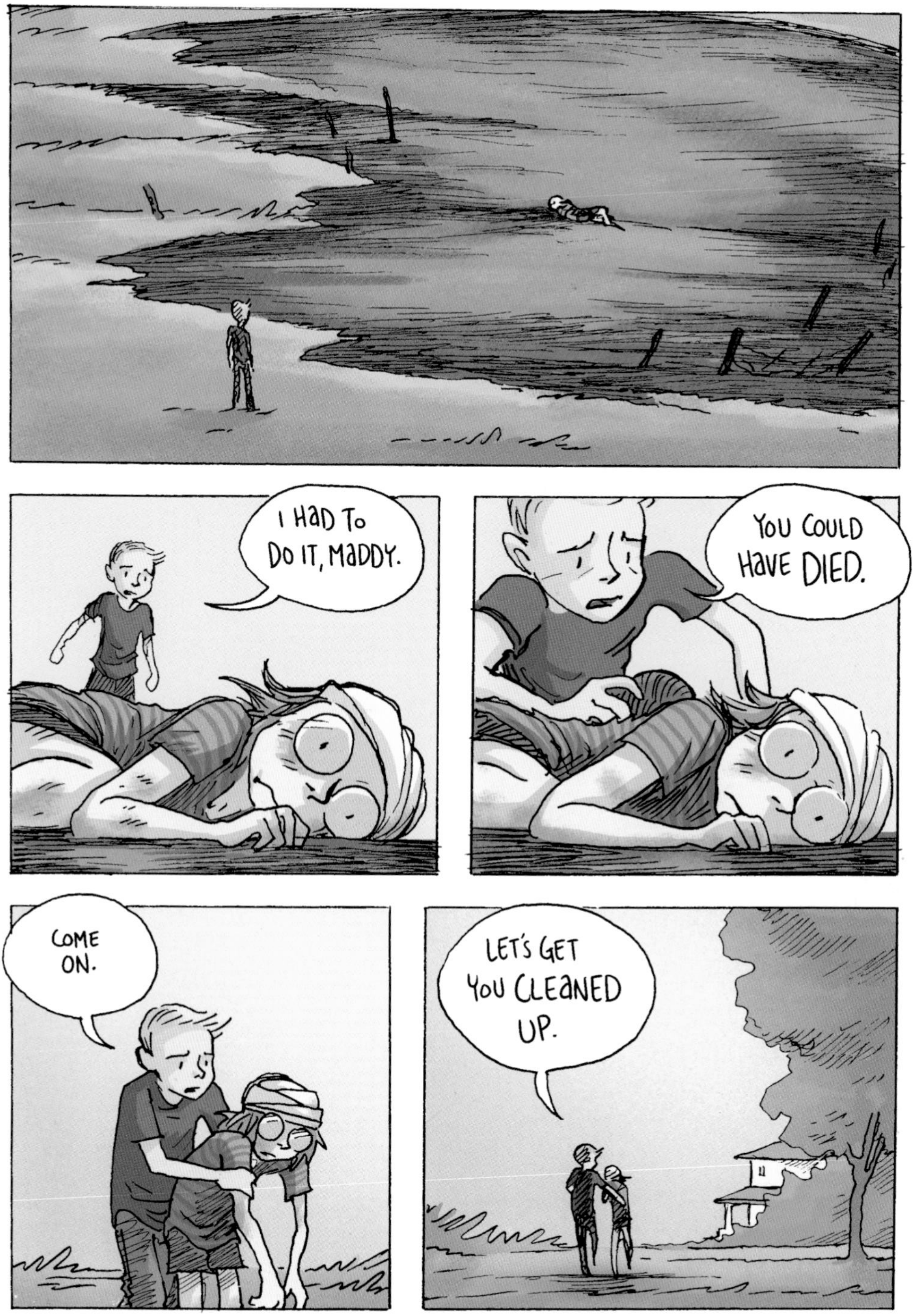
I HAD TO DO IT, MADDY.
YOU COULD HAVE DIED.
COME ON.
LET'S GET YOU CLEANED UP.

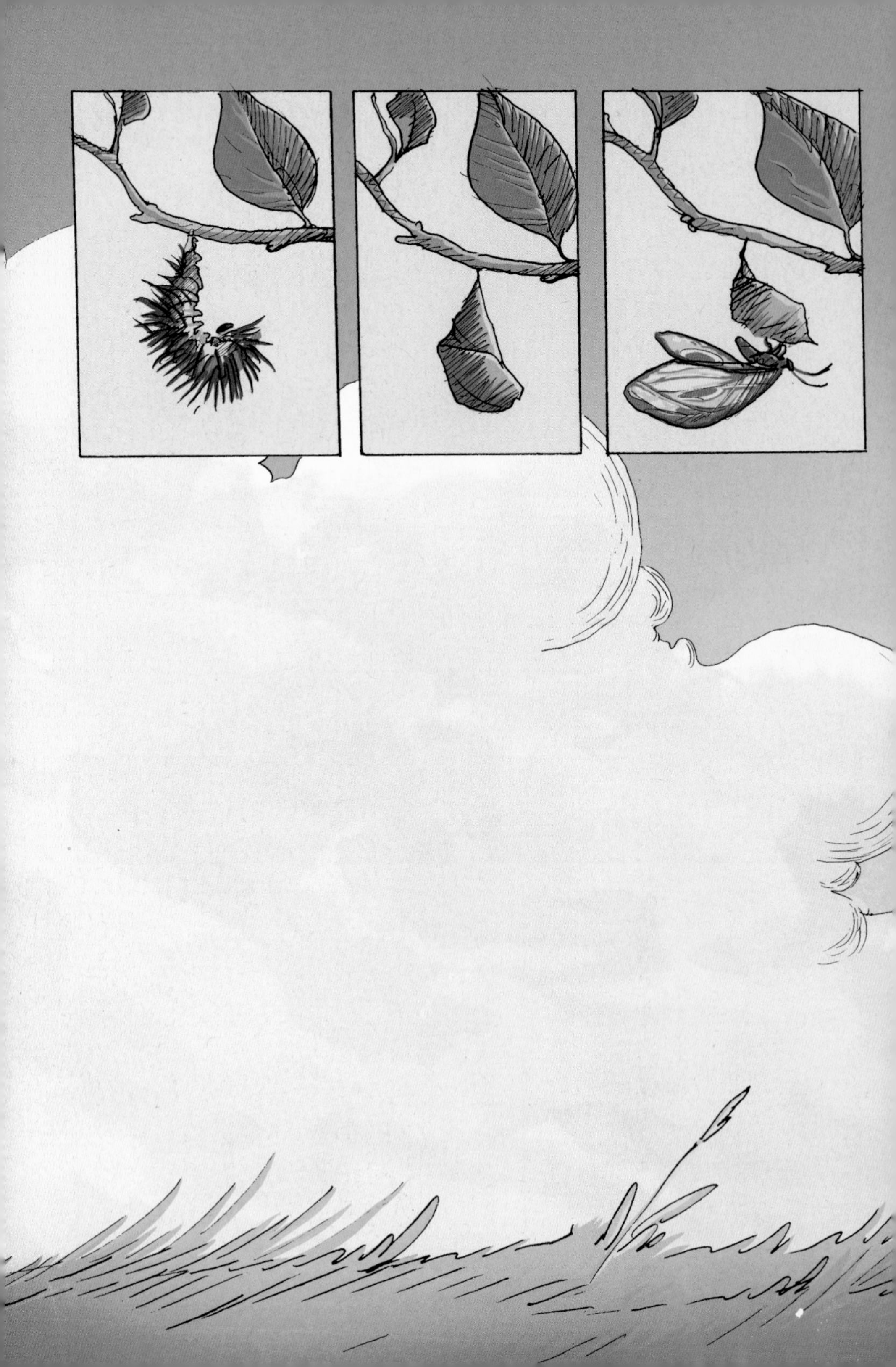

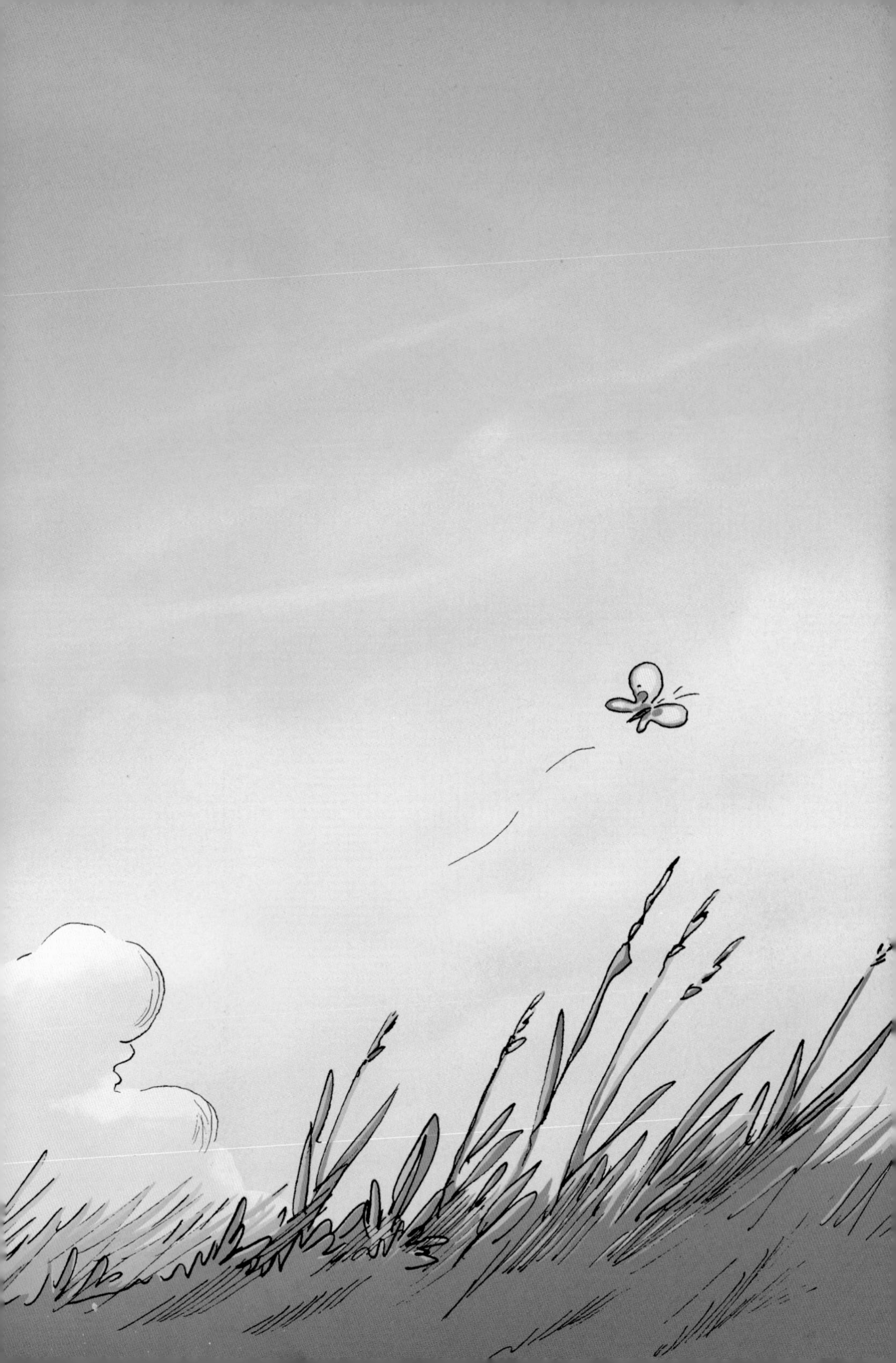

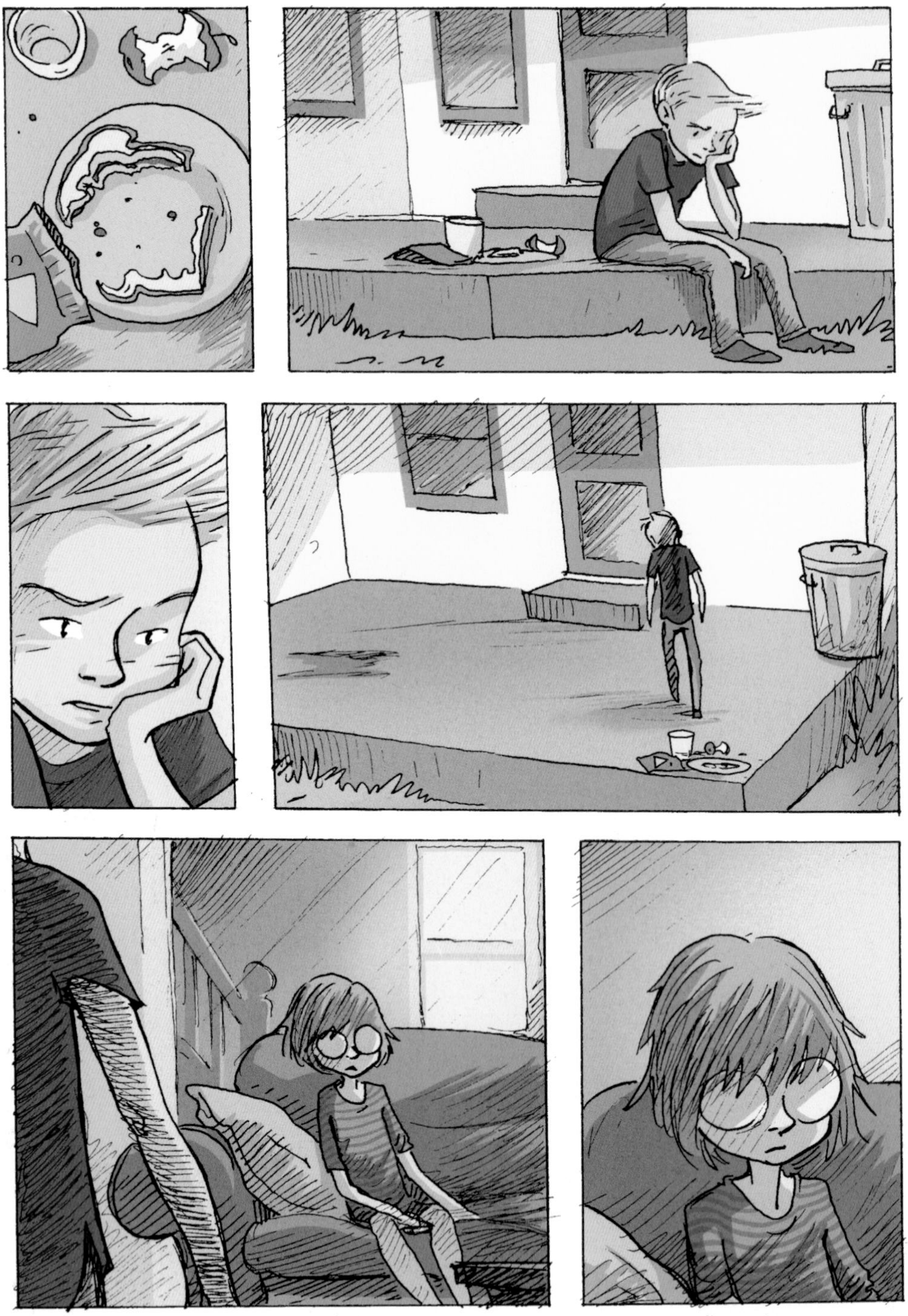

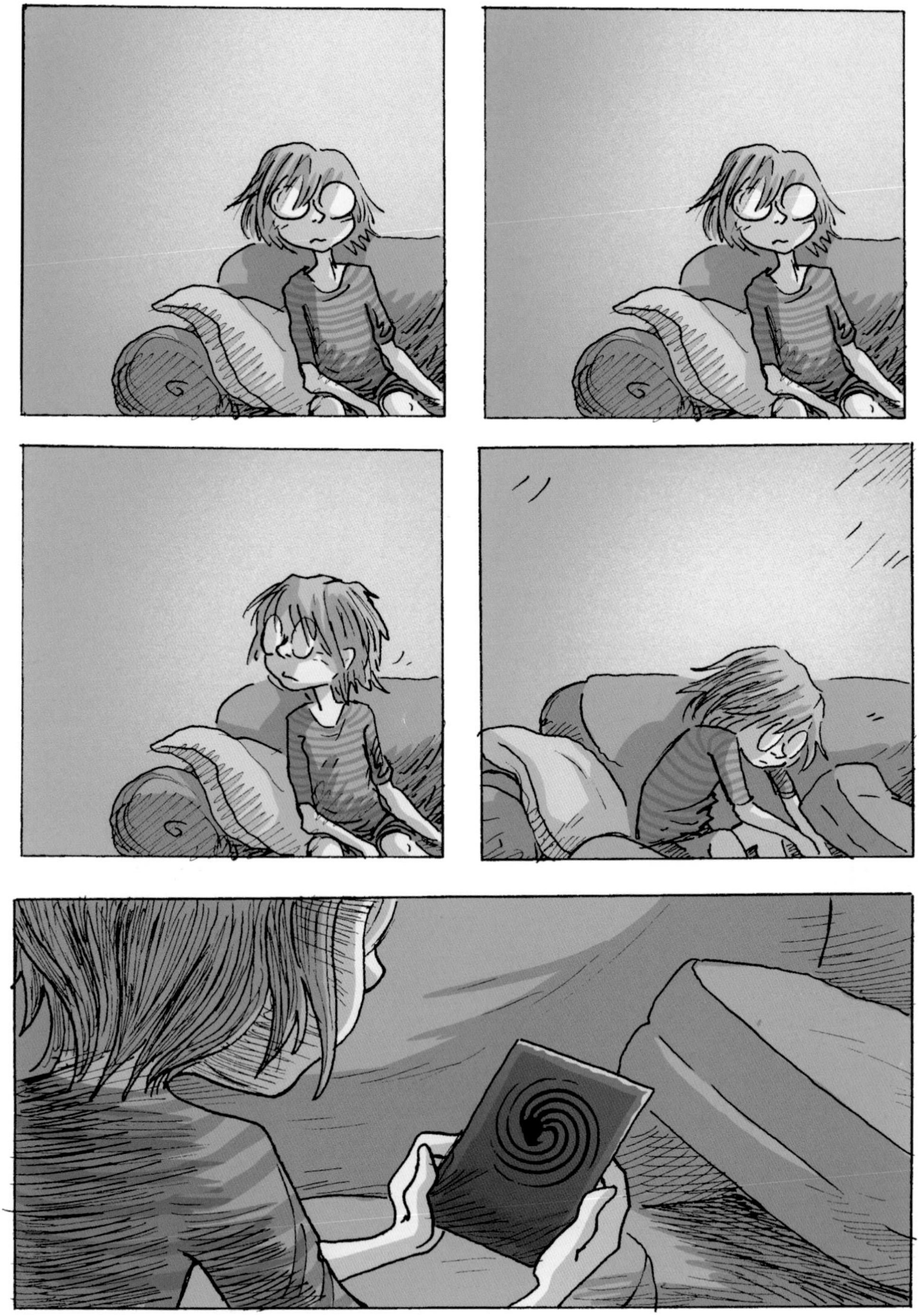

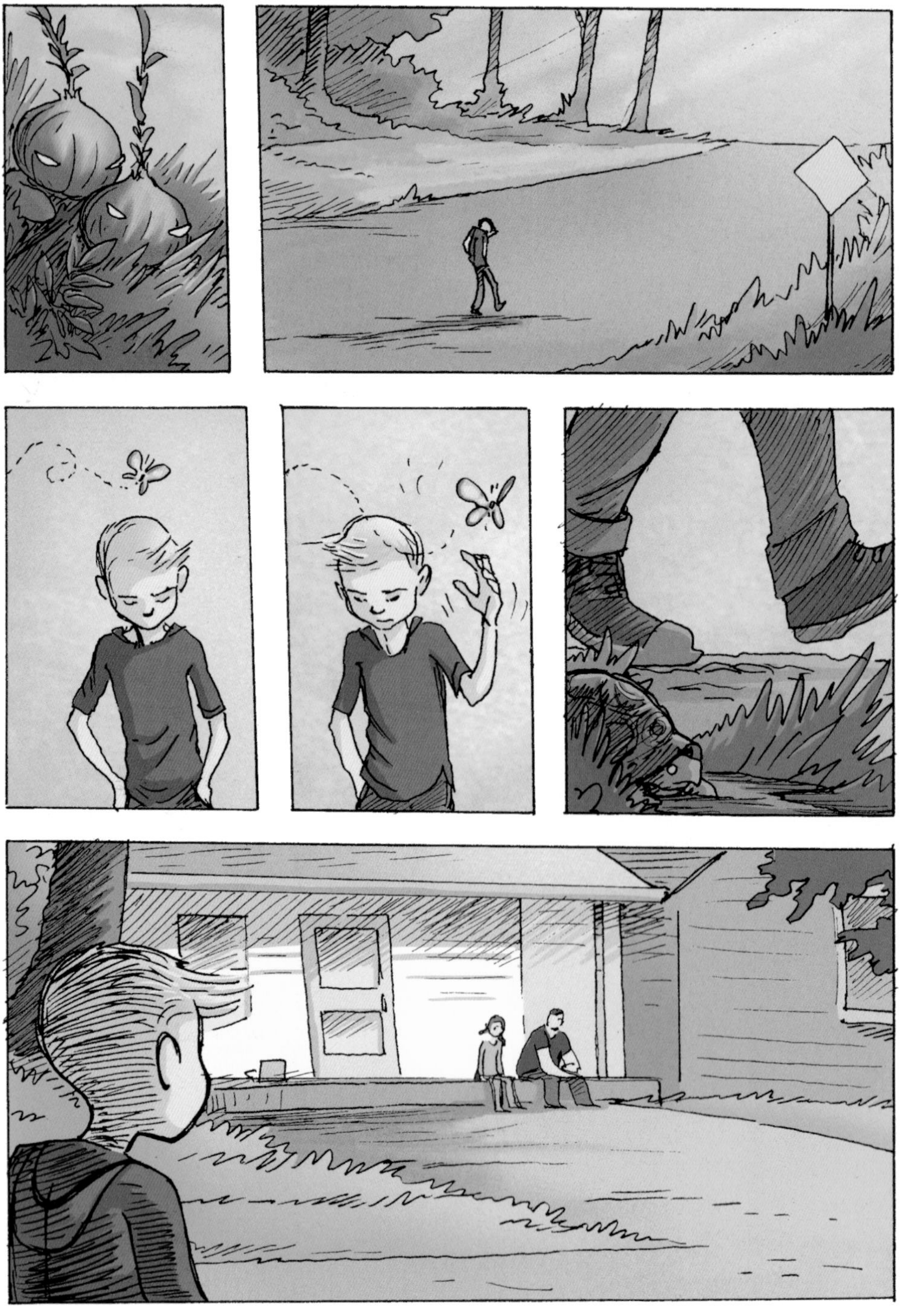

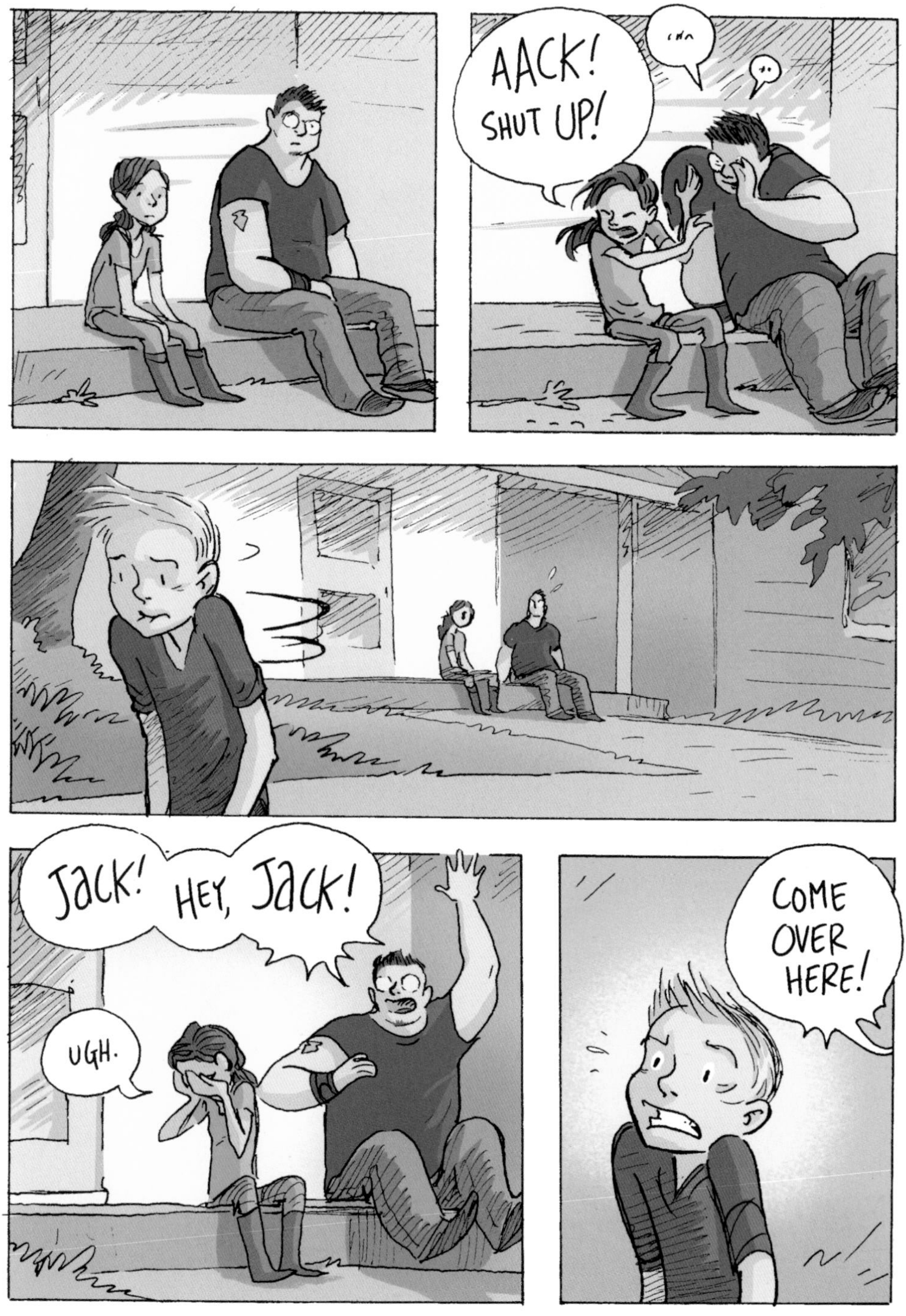
AACK! SHUT UP!
JACK!
HEY, JACK!
UGH.
COME OVER HERE!

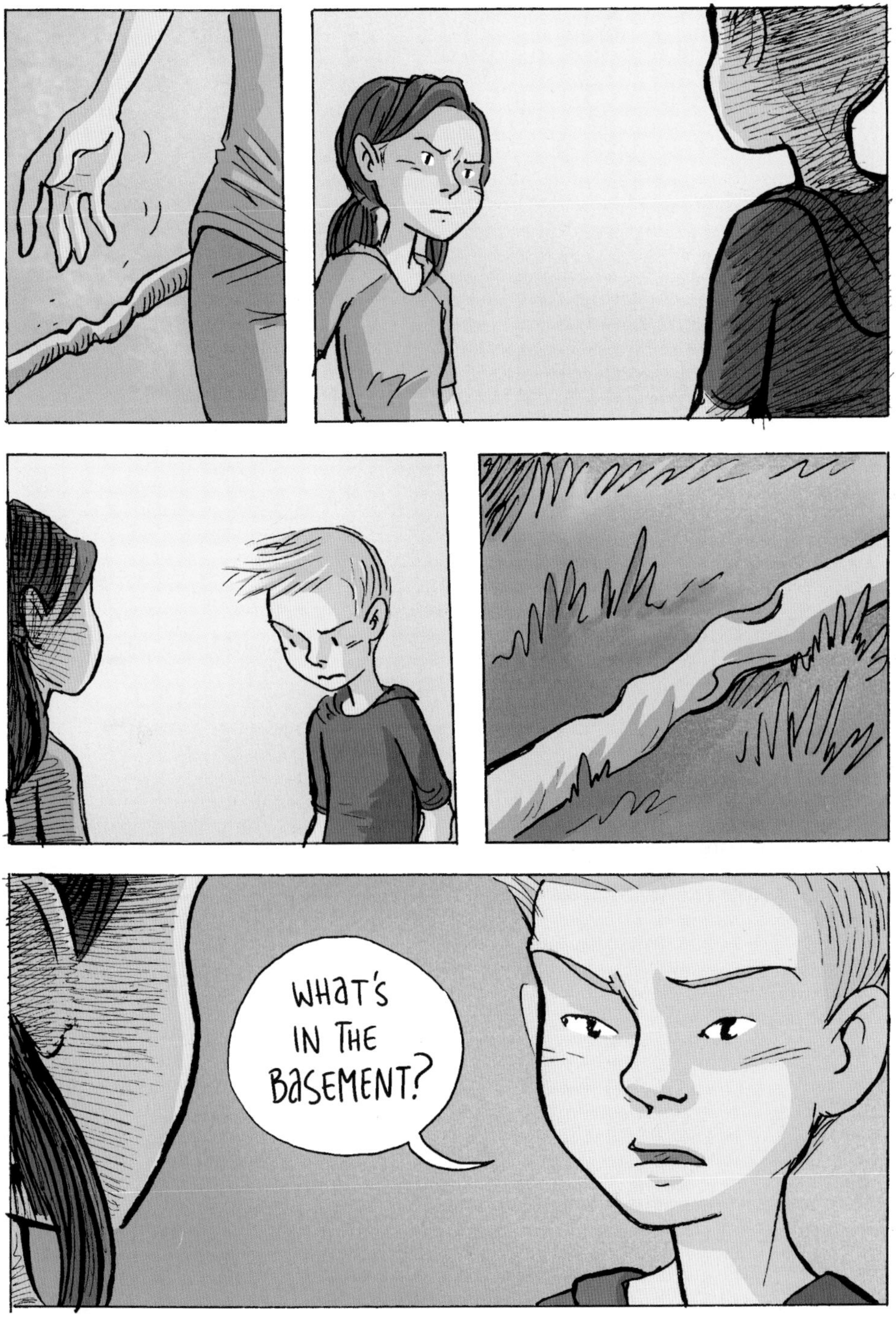
WHAT'S IN THE BASEMENT?

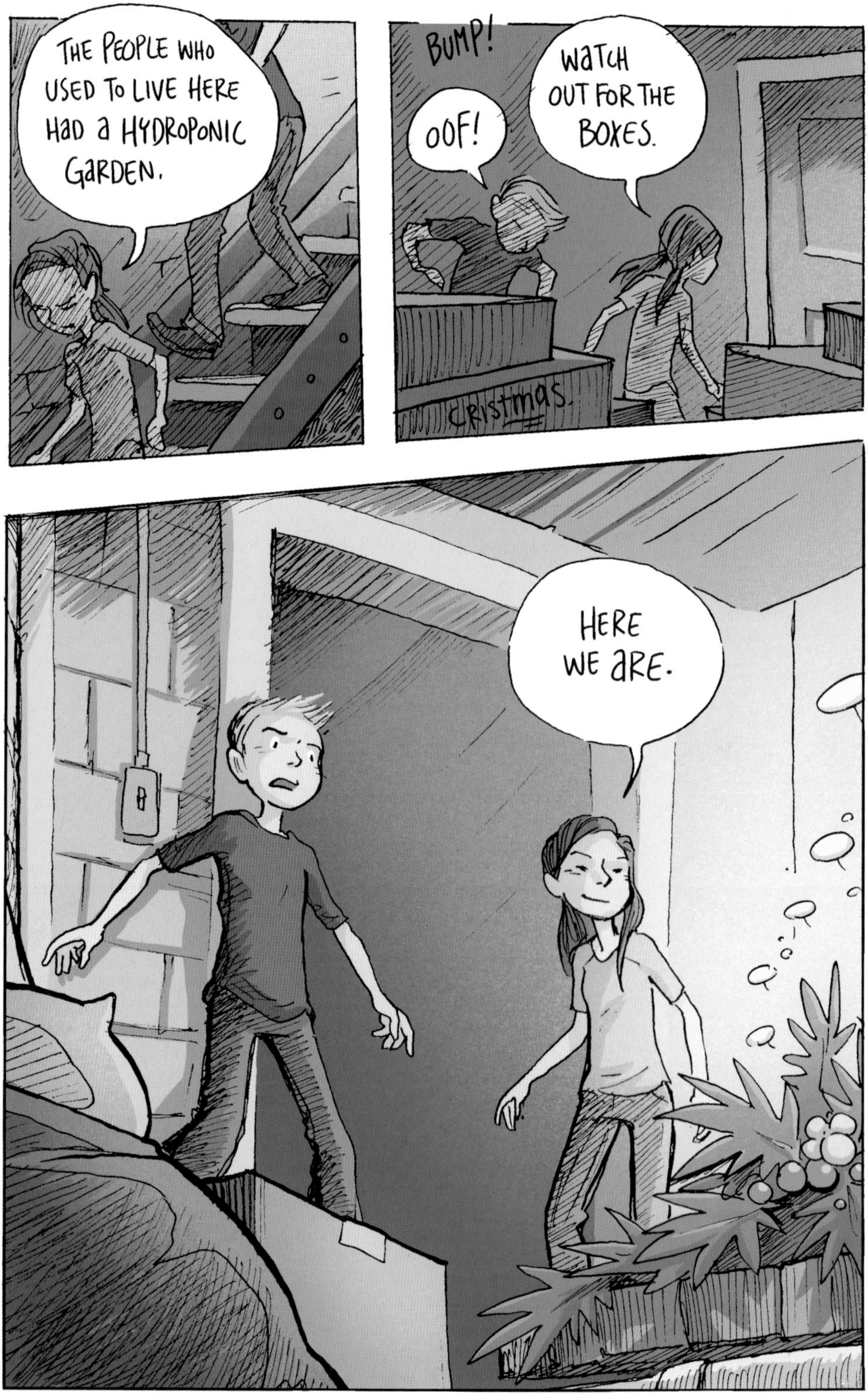
THE PEOPLE WHO USED TO LIVE HERE HAD A HYDROPONIC GARDEN.
BUMP!
OOF!
WATCH OUT FOR THE BOXES.
CRISTMAS
HERE WE ARE.

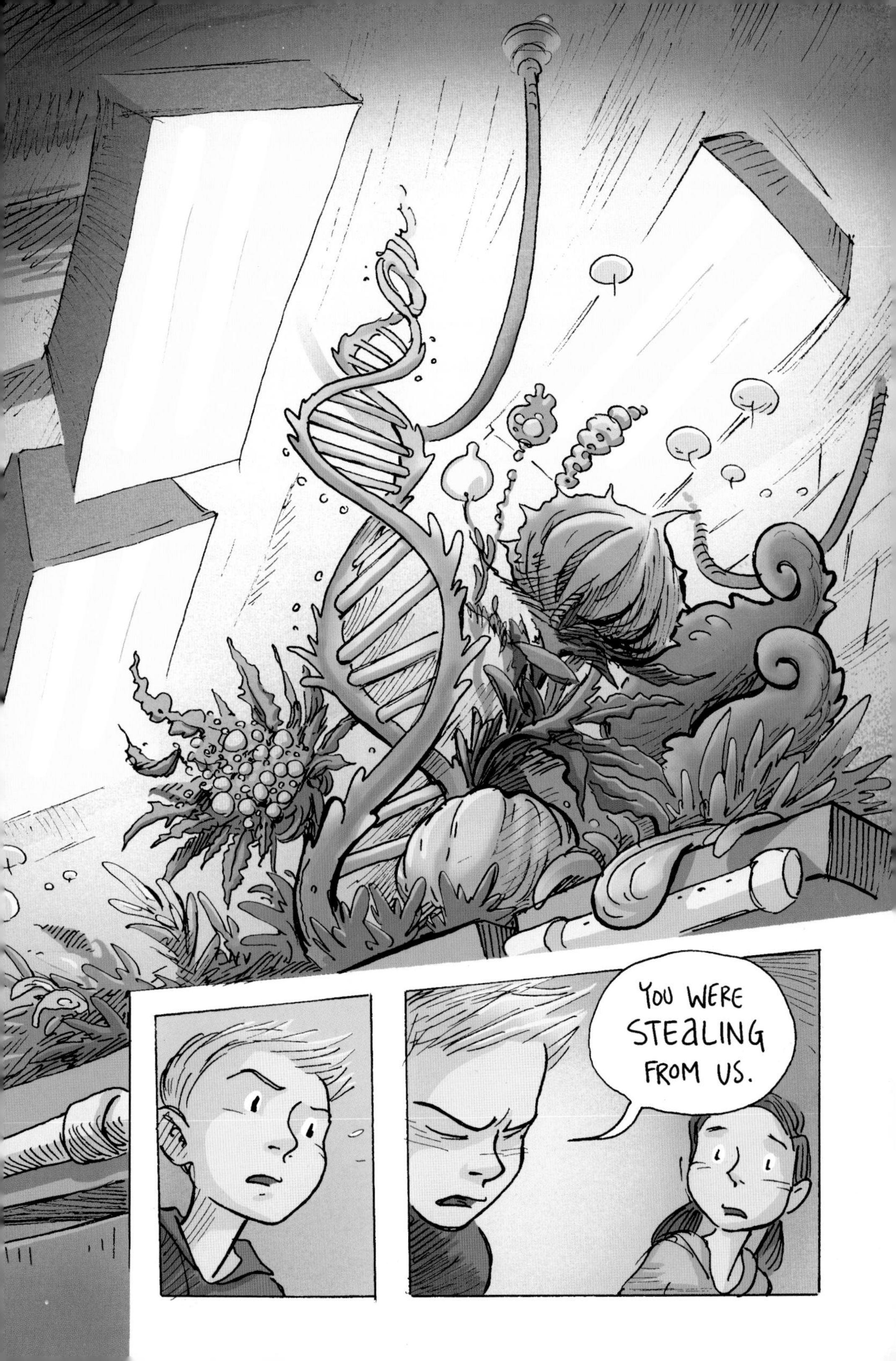
YOU WERE STEALING FROM US.

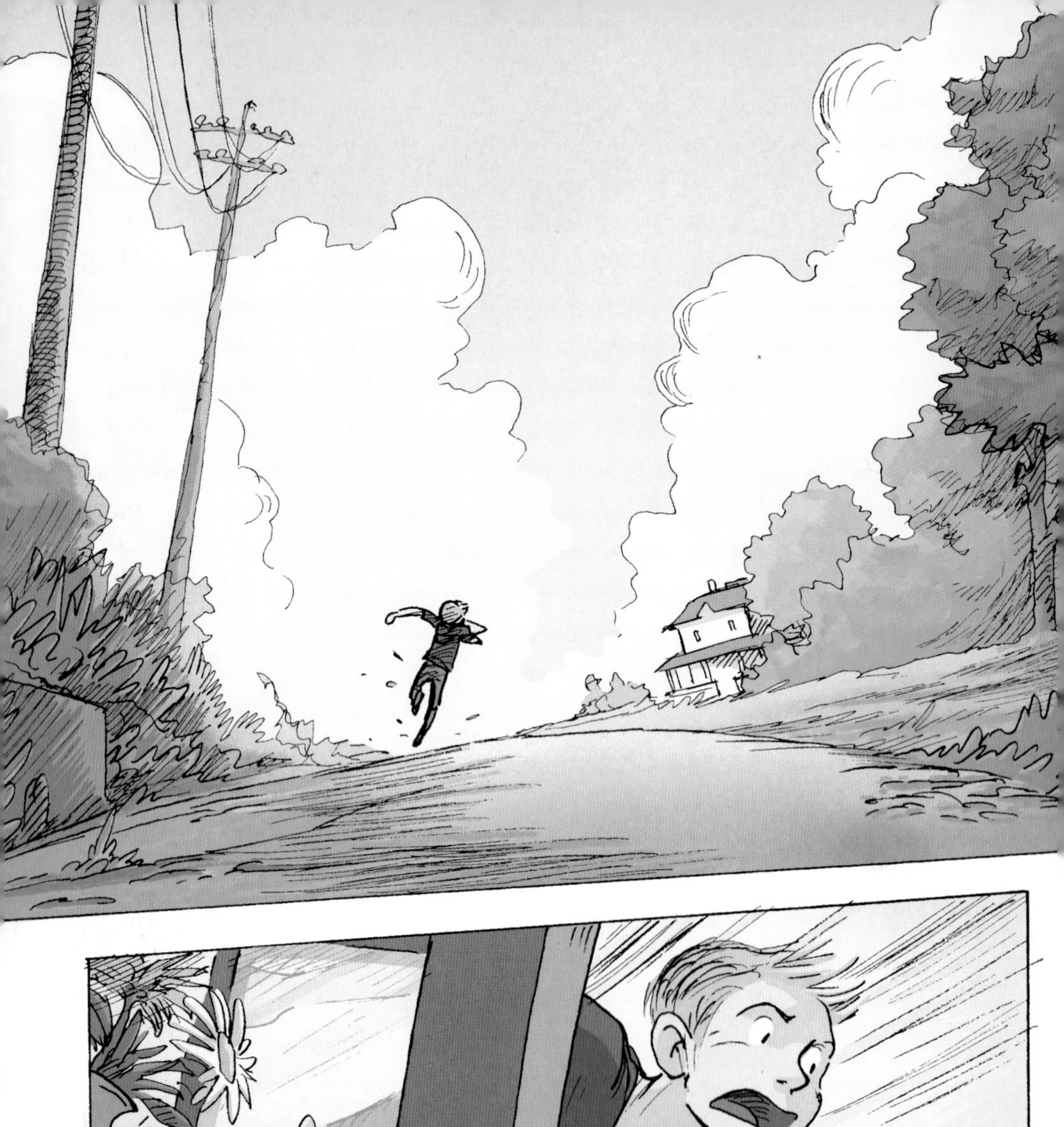

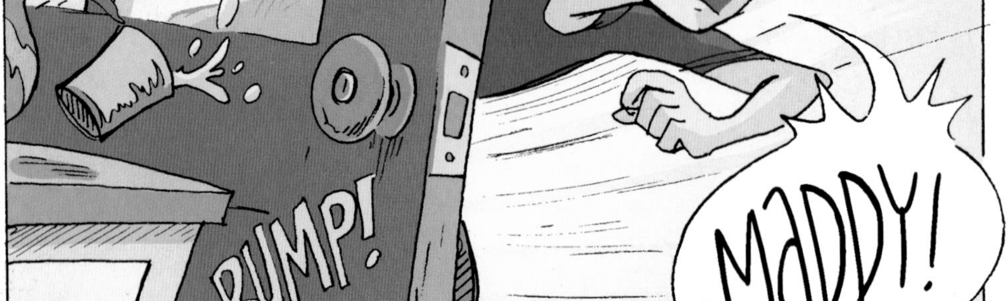
BUMP!
MADDY!

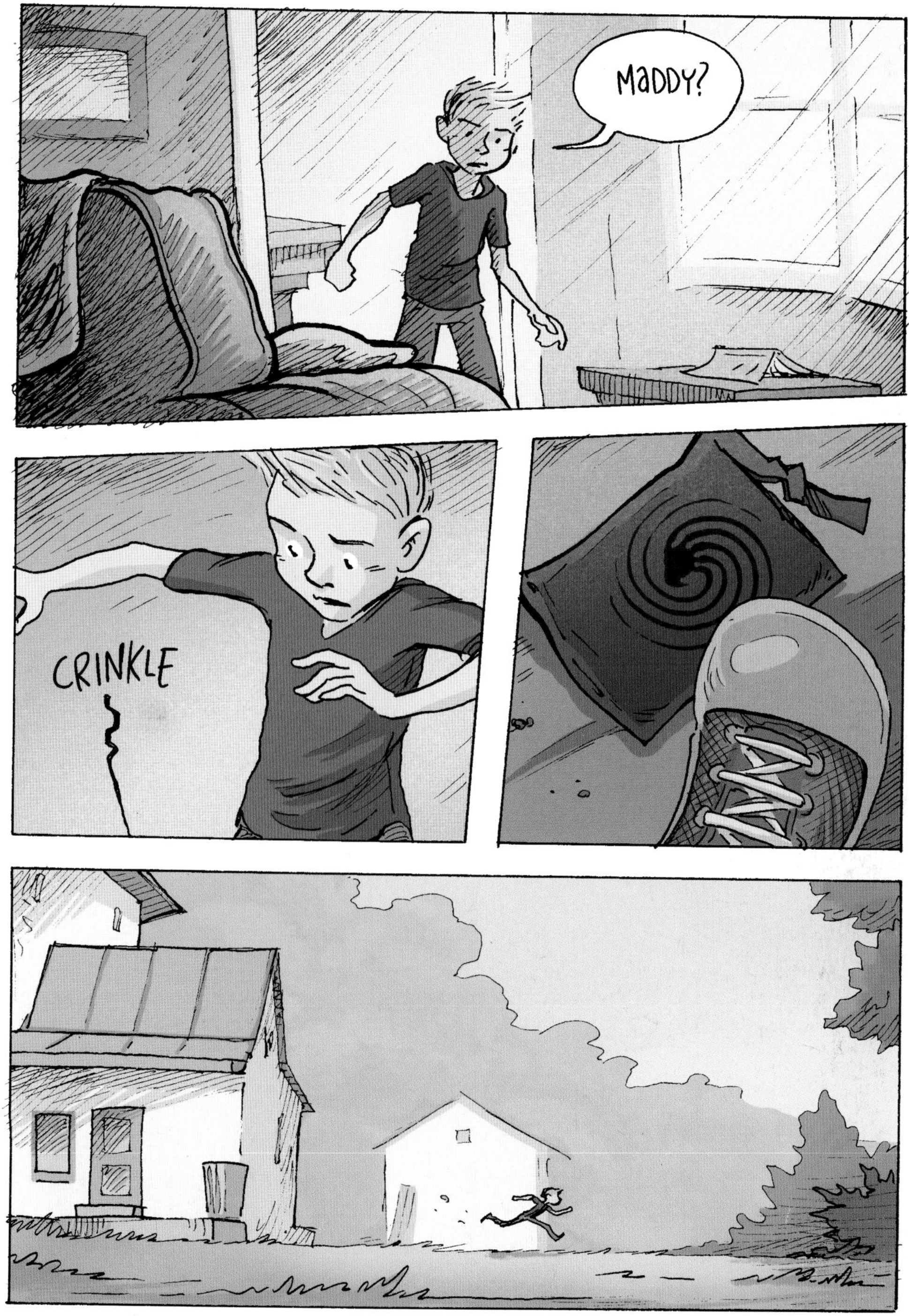
MADDY?
CRINKLE

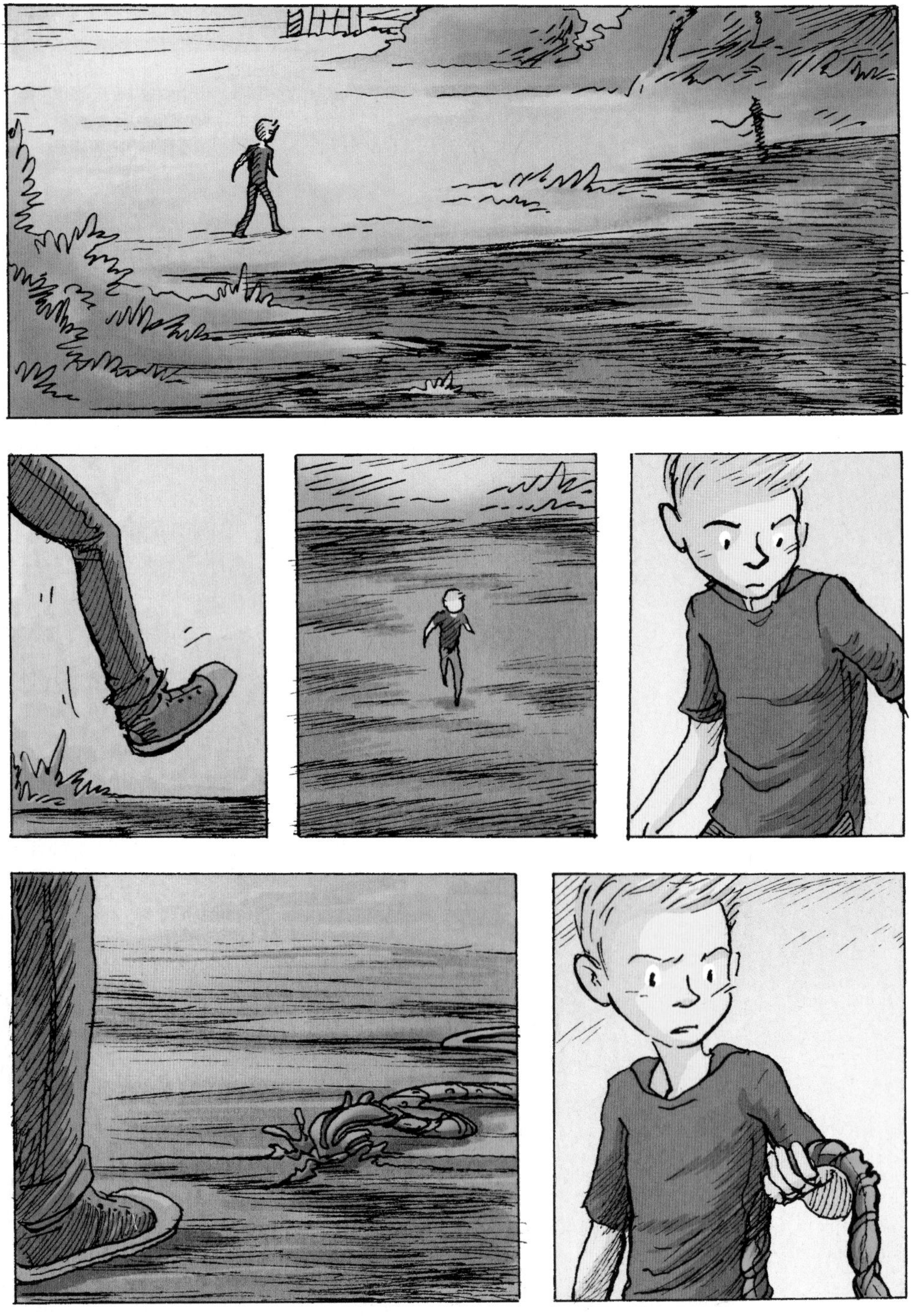

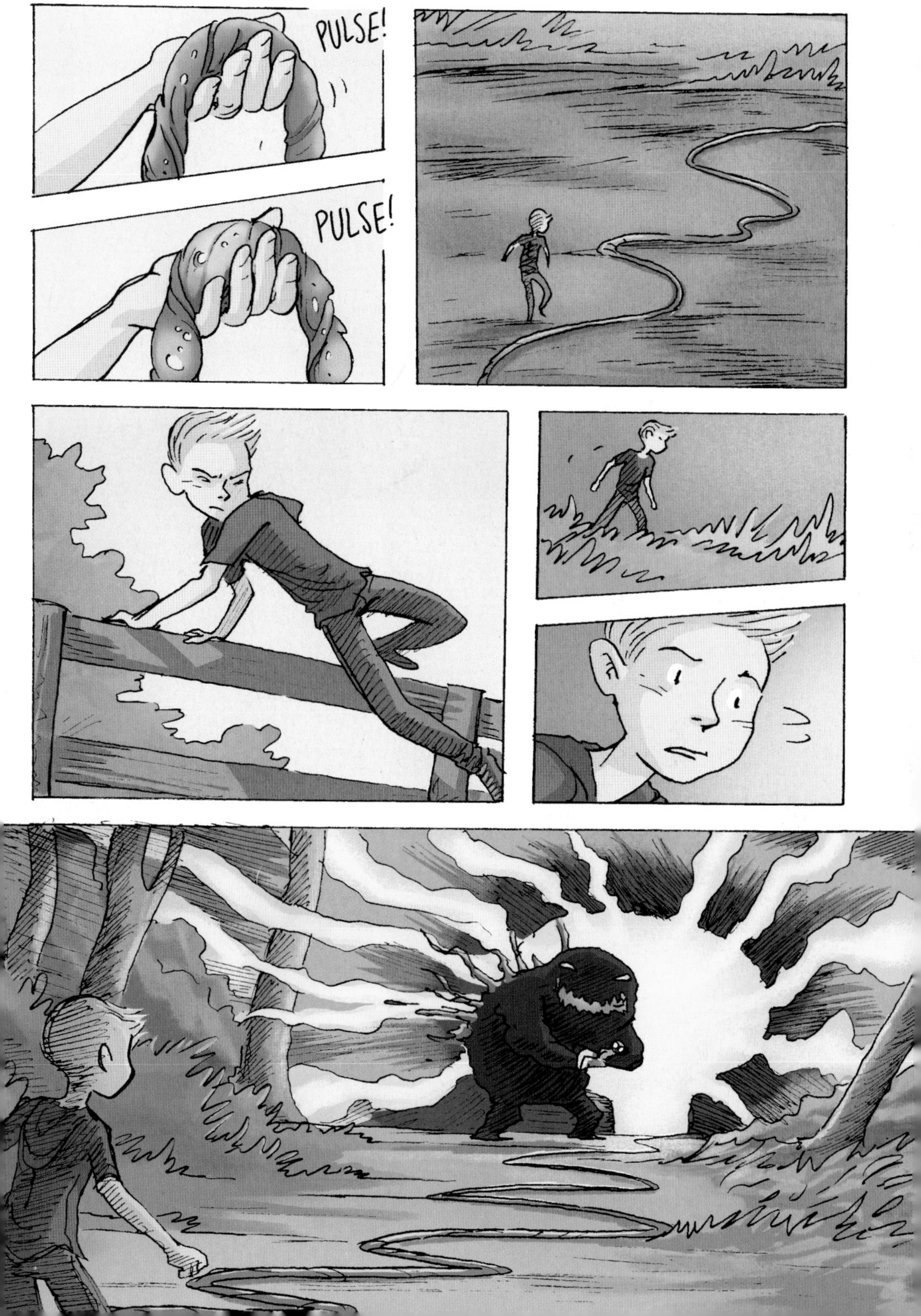
PULSE!
PULSE!

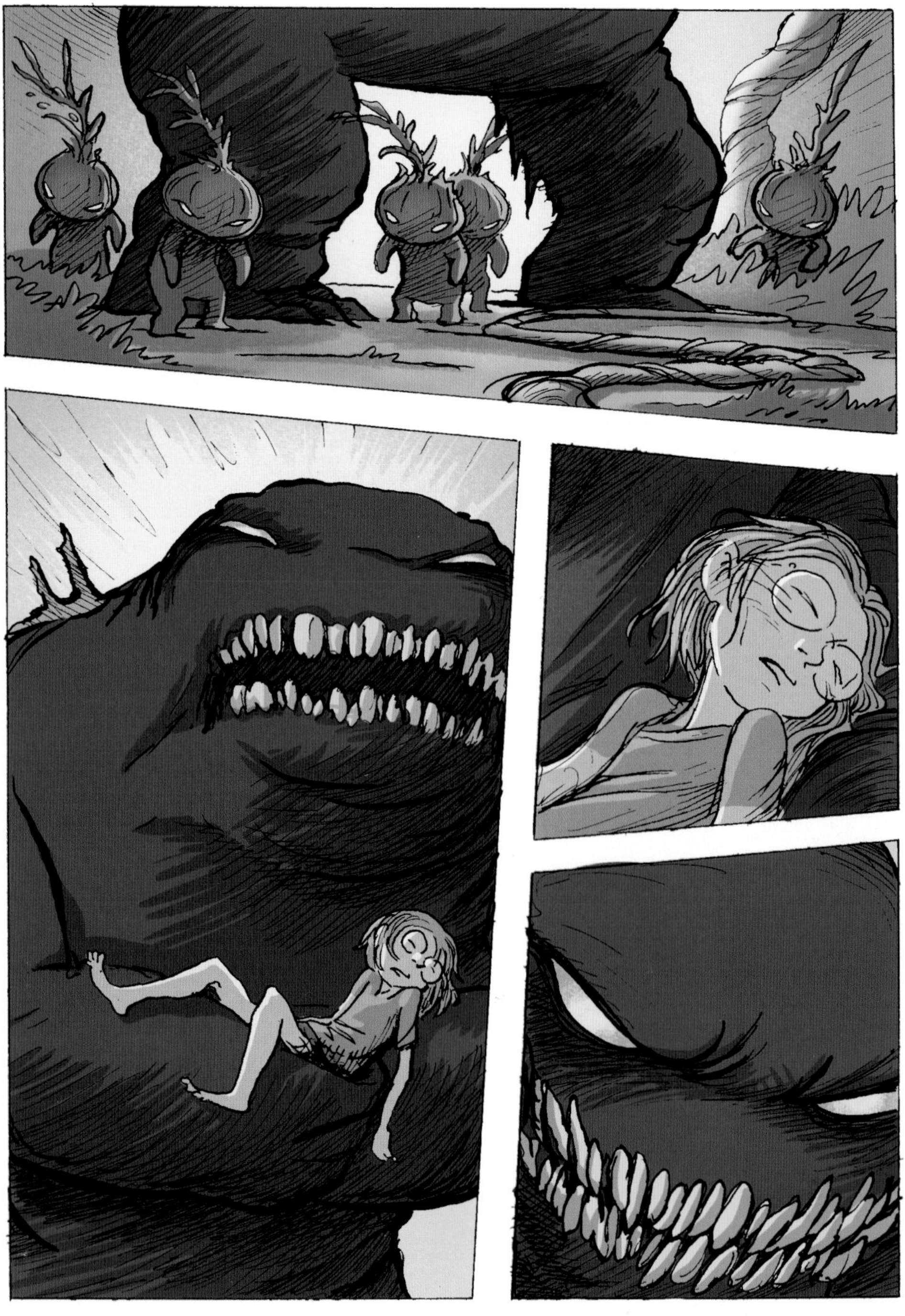

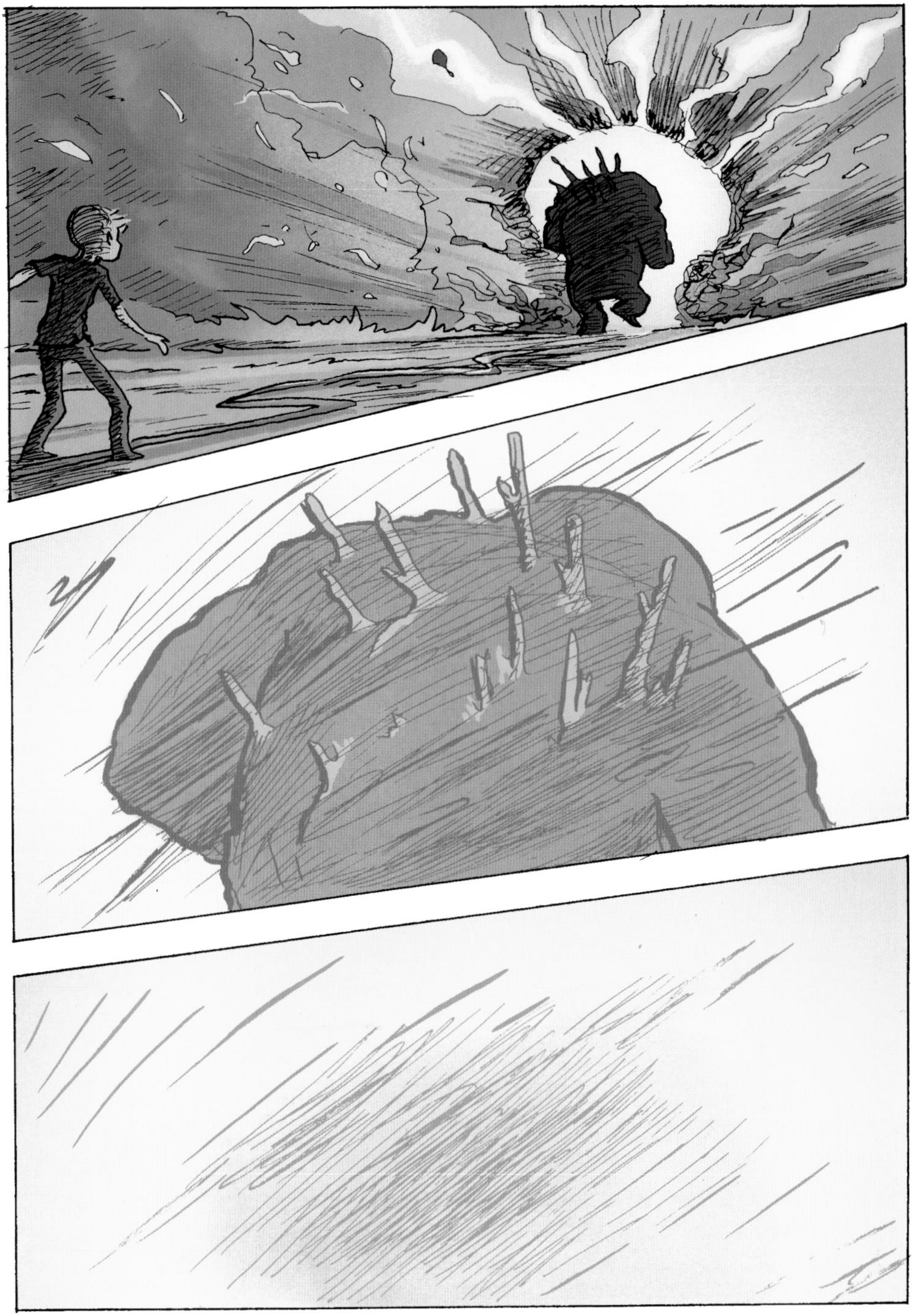

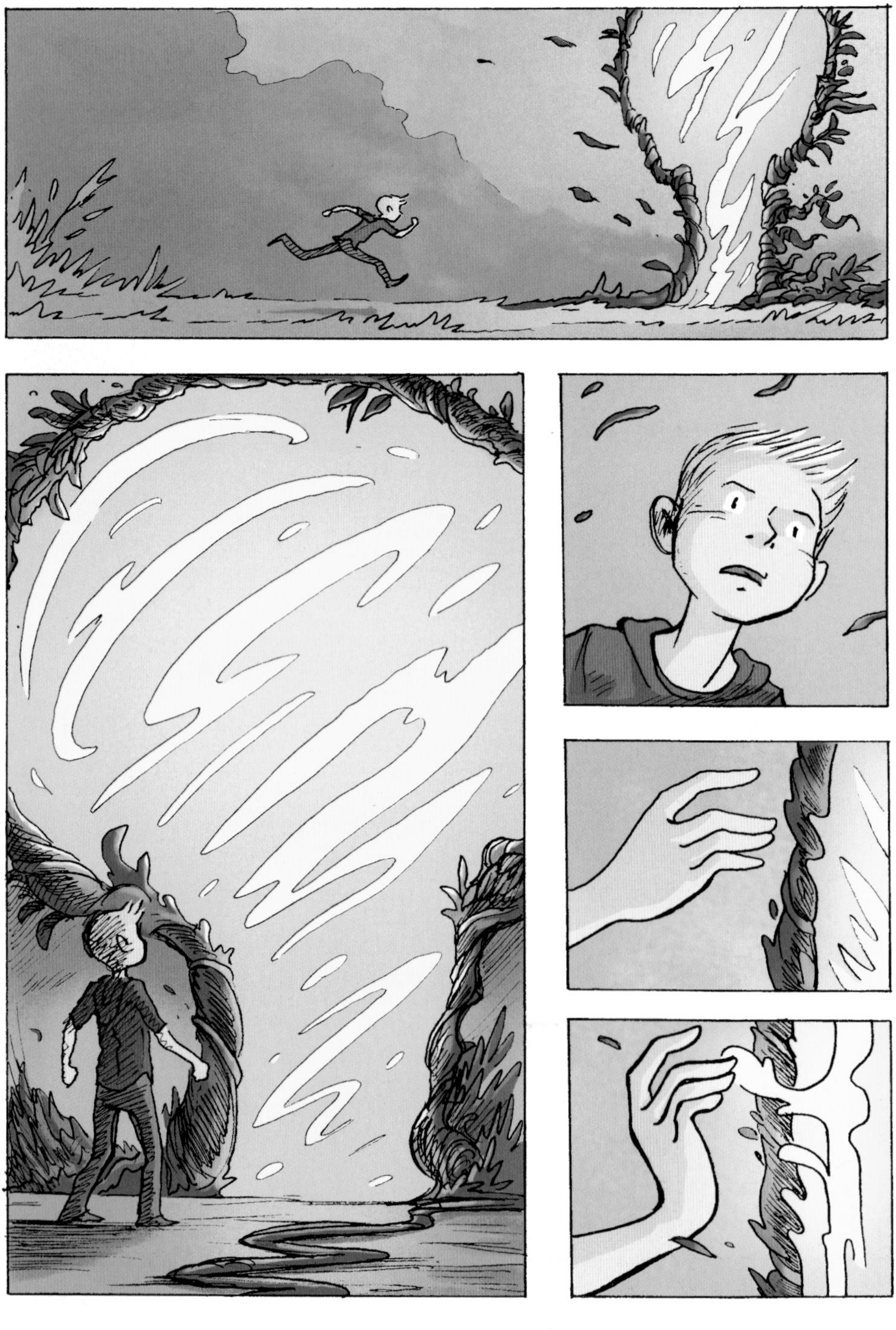

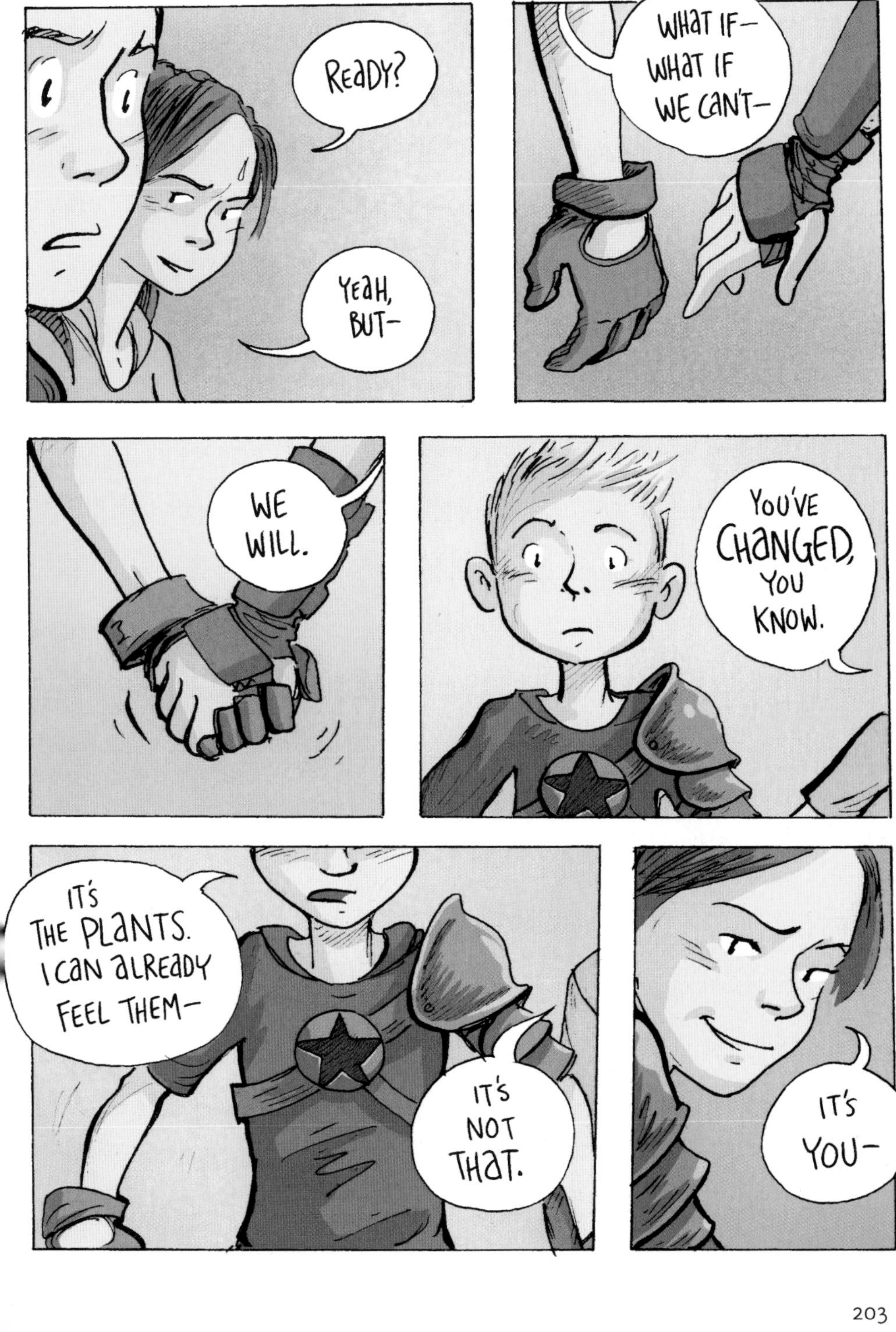
Ready?
Yeah, but-
What if- what if we can't-
We will.
You've CHANGED, you know.
It's the PLANTS. I can already feel them-
It's not that.
It's you-

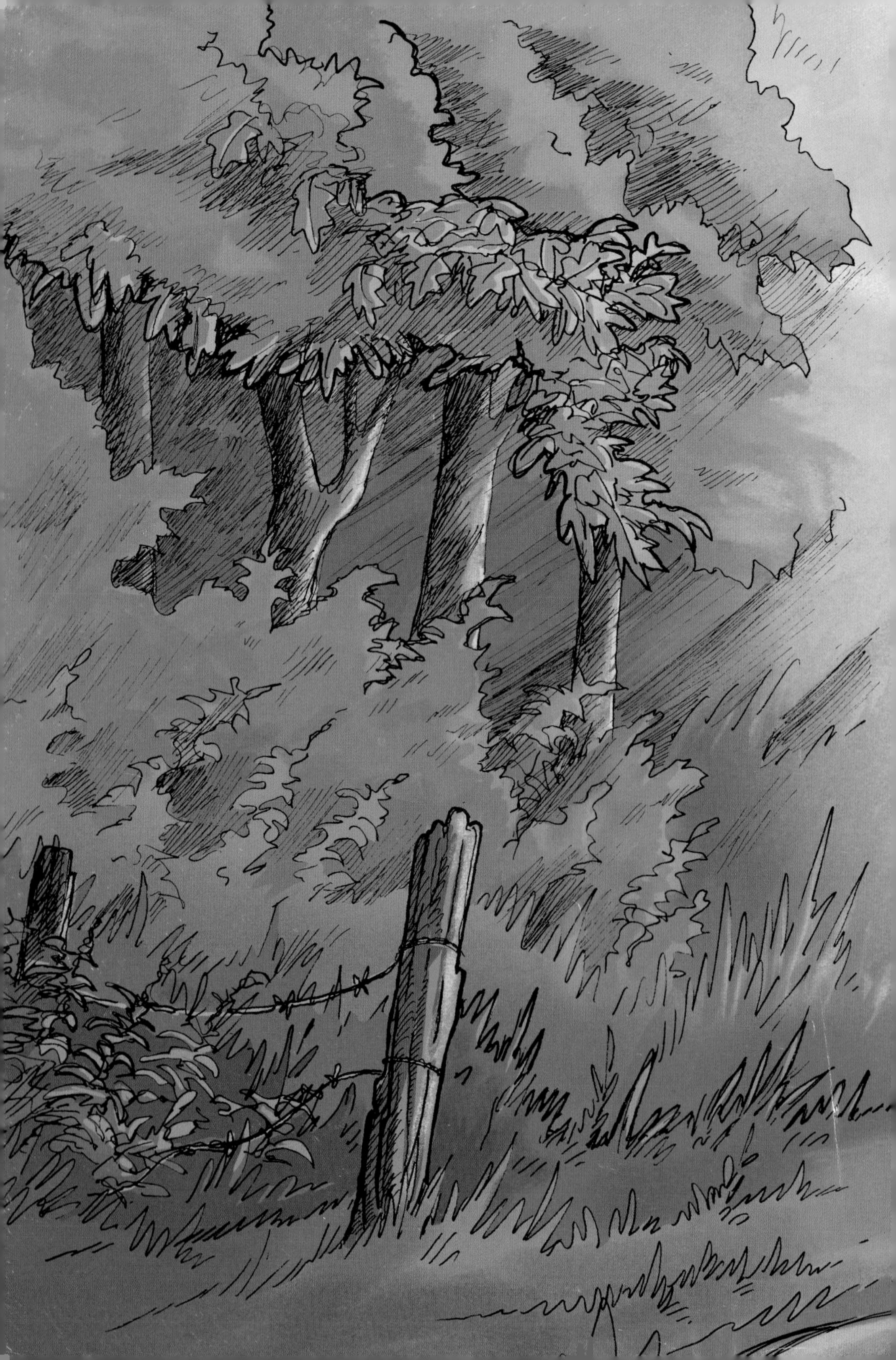

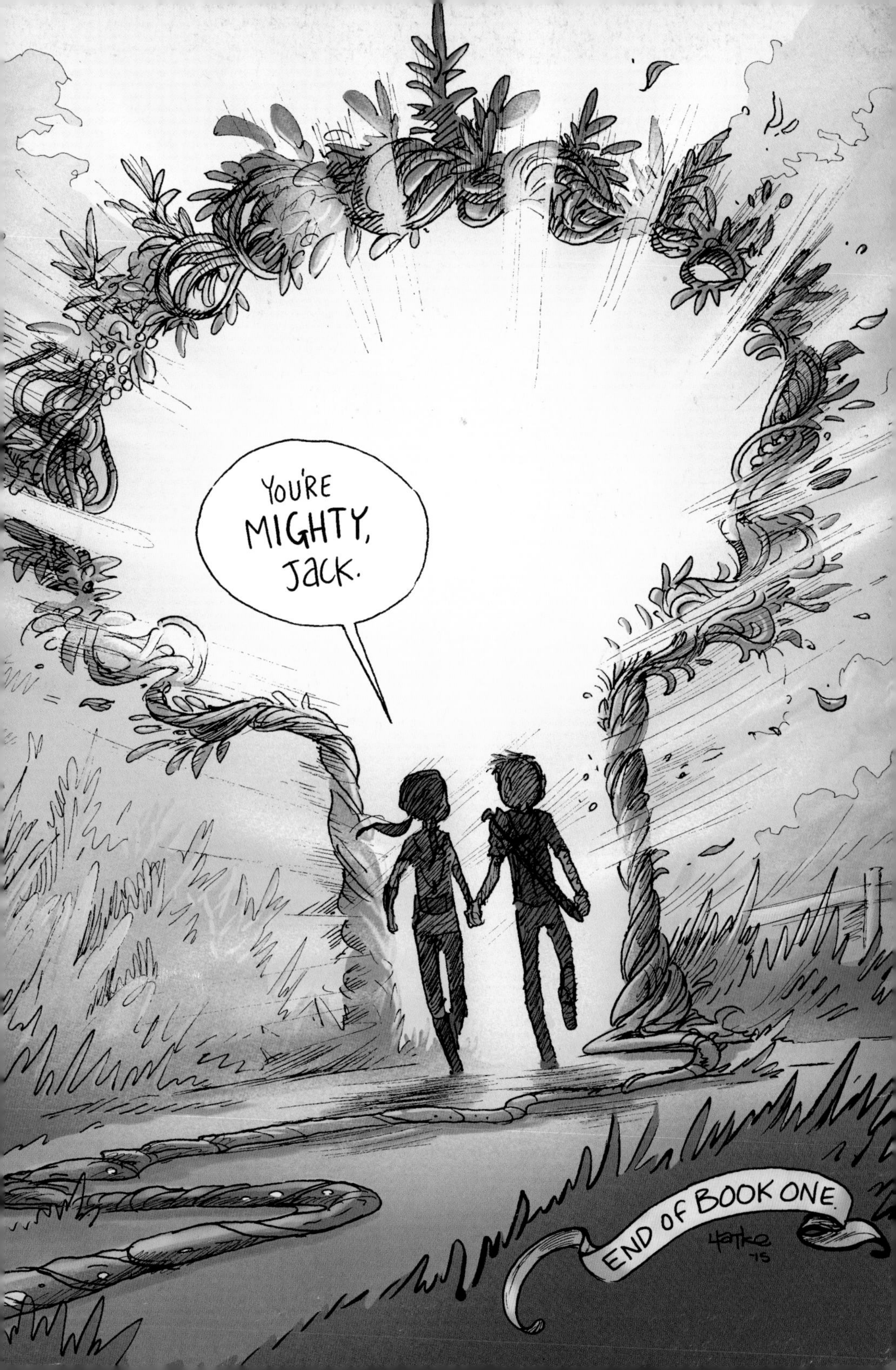
YOU'RE MIGHTY, JACK.
END OF BOOK ONE.

Copyright © 2016 by Ben Hatke
Published by First Second
First Second is an imprint of Roaring Brook Press, a division of Holtzbrinck
Publishing Holdings Limited Partnership
175 Fifth Avenue, New York, New York 10010
All rights reserved

Library of Congress Control Number: 2015951861

Hardcover ISBN: 978-1-62672-265-1
Paperback ISBN: 978-1-62672-264-4

Our books may be purchased in bulk for promotional, educational, or
business use. Please contact your local bookseller or the Macmillan Corporate
and Premium Sales Department at (800) 221-7945 ext. 5442 or by e-mail
at MacmillanSpecialMarkets@macmillan.com.

The art for this book was drawn on laser printer paper with Sakura Pigma
Micron pens (sizes 005, 01, 05 and 08) over light colored pencil. Colors were
accomplished digitally using Photoshop.

First edition 2016
Book design by Joyana McDiarmid
Colors by Alex Campbell and Hilary Sycamore of Sky Blue Ink
Printed in China by Toppan Leefung Printing Ltd., Dongguan City, Guangdong Province

Hardcover: 10 9 8 7 6 5 4 3 2 1
Paperback: 10 9 8 7 6 5 4 3 2 1

ALSO BY BEN HATKE

ZITA SPACEGIRL
BEN HATKE

LEGENDS
ZITA
SPACEGIRL
WANTED
ZITA!
WANTE
BEN HATKE

RETURN
ZITA
SPACEGIRL
BEN HATKE

Little
ROBOT
Ben
Hatke

Ben Hatke
Julia's House for Lost Creatures

Nobody Likes a GOBLIN
Ben Hatke

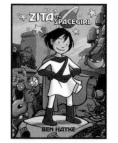

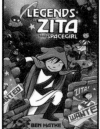

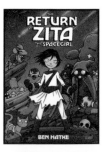

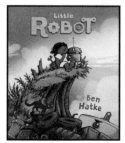

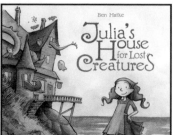

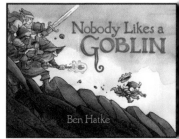